Everyone knew the earl of Penhollow needed a wife, so one thunderous night the villagers gathered together to ask the ocean to deliver a bride to the bachelor lord . . .

THE SEA BROUGHT HIM A WIFE

When Pierce Kirrier, the handsome earl of Penhollow, rescued a mysterious beauty from the billowing ocean waves, he had no idea who she was—or where she came from. But at the first sight of this enchanting maiden, he had to claim her for his own. Taking her back to Penhollow Hall, he pampered her like a princess, determined to win her trust and her heart.

BUT HER PAST COULD TAKE HER AWAY

Nothing had prepared Eden to awaken in an elegant bedchamber in a remote corner of Cornwall. It was like living in a perfect dreamworld, where every wish came true. In Pierce's arms she found a love—and bliss—she never knew existed. But once her secret past caught up with her, those dreams could be shattered—forever.

Avon Romantic Treasures by
Cathy Maxwell

FALLING IN LOVE AGAIN
YOU AND NO OTHER

If You've Enjoyed This Book,
Be Sure to Read These Other
AVON ROMANTIC TREASURES

DEVIL'S BRIDE *by Stephanie Laurens*
THE LAST HELLION *by Loretta Chase*
PERFECT IN MY SIGHT *by Tanya Anne Crosby*
SLEEPING BEAUTY *by Judith Ivory*
TO CATCH AN HEIRESS *by Julia Quinn*

Coming Soon

TO TAME A RENEGADE *by Connie Mason*

CATHY MAXWELL

When Dreams Come True

An Avon Romantic Treasure

AVON BOOKS NEW YORK

AVON BOOKS, INC.
1350 Avenue of the Americas
New York, New York 10019

Inside cover author photo by Glamour Shots
Published by arrangement with the author
Visit our website at **http://www.AvonBooks.com**
Library of Congress Catalog Card Number: 97-94935
ISBN: 0-380-79709-7

First Avon Books Printing: August 1998

Printed in the U.S.A.

WCD 10 9 8 7 6 5 4 3 2 1

To Damaris Rowland
who keeps me on my feet and in the ring

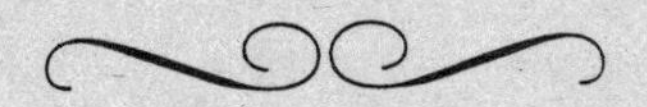

Prologue

Cornwall, 1815

Oblivious to the brewing storm, the Widow Haskell stood on a ledge of rocks jutting out into the sea. Her aged body swathed in a gray misshapen cape from neck to toe, she held the small charm bag up to the night sky. The wind caught and tugged at the strands of her silver hair and molded the cape to her fragile figure. Angry waves tumbled over the rocks, washing her feet, but she wouldn't bend to the howling wind. She needed the force of the elements to make the charm work.

Behind her stood thirty silent villagers from Hobbles Moor. Their grave faces looked like pale moons in the darkness. They had gathered because the Widow said she needed their energy, their combined power. They believed in her and in the magic in her small bags with every inch of their souls in spite of what the vicar said.

Among them was Betsy, a village girl who

worked as a maid for Lord Penhollow. Beside her stood Lucy and Mrs. Meeks, the Penhollow cook and housekeeper respectively. Then there was Seth, the village cooper, who stood close to the mighty Dane, whose hammer rang out all day from the smithy. Also included in the number of villagers were Marten, the fisherman, and Kyle, the poacher who knew his way around the moors in the dark of night. Even Mr. Galesbrook, the tin mine manager, was there.

"It is not a simple task we undertake this night," the Widow said. "For this charm to work, we must all believe. Let the doubters leave!"

No one moved, not even to blink an eye. An occasional drop of rain could be felt now, mixed in with the sea spray.

The Widow Haskell turned three times with the charm bag held high over her head. Even though she had to be close to eighty-five years of age, her footing on the slippery rock was sure. She mumbled an incantation, the words more ancient than herself.

Betsy strained to hear what words the Widow spoke. She'd been raised to have more faith in the Widow's charms and cures than in Dr. Hargrave's entire collection of medicines. Over her eighteen years, she'd seen the Widow cure warts, bring a dead calf back to life, and heal a child of smallpox by hanging a chicken upside down from a cottage beam and plucking its feathers.

But then, tonight they were after more serious business.

The Widow Haskell clasped the bag in one hand and clapped the other against it three times before lowering her arms. She raised her face to the sky and stood a moment, listening.

They all listened, their bodies tense in the silence.

The Widow spoke, her thin, reedy voice now strong with authority. "Lucy Wright, step forward."

Lucy shot a nervous glance in Betsy's direction. "Go on," Betsy mouthed.

"I'm here, Widow," the plump cook said with unaccustomed timidity.

The Widow stared out over the turbulent water as if in a trance. "We cannot trespass where we are not wanted. Tell me again, Lucy Wright. Did you hear the Lady Penhollow, Lord Penhollow's mother, ask for this love charm?"

"Aye, I did. She said she was at her wit's end. She and her son had just quarreled. She demanded that he make an offer of marriage to Mr. Willis's daughter, but he refused, saying she was too young. Then our lady threw a terrible tantrum and insisted he go to London to seek a bride. She said he was rich enough now to tempt the daughter of a duke. He said he'd not have a London bride. You should have heard her, Widow. Her shouts vibrated through my kitchen."

Betsy and the other villagers listened intently. Pierce Kirrier, the earl of Penhollow, was more important to the people of Hobbles Moor than the Prince Regent and Parliament combined. The family lines of the earl could be traced back to the days of King Arthur. The villagers knew this because their own Cornish roots ran just as deep.

Now the Penhollow line was in jeopardy. Lord Penhollow needed to marry and sire an heir—and no one wanted another London bride.

"Aye, our Lord Pierce is a wise one for refusing to go to London. His father made that mistake," Dane said. "London brides lack the proper mettle a Cornishman needs in a bride."

Several heads nodded their agreement. They might sympathize with Lady Penhollow's anxiousness to see her son wed, but they didn't trust her. In spite of having lived in their midst for thirty-four years, the beautiful London heiress Pierce's father had brought to Penhollow Hall as a bride was considered an outsider, and a sorry mother to boot.

"He's lucky he had us to take care of him," Mrs. Meeks said. "After he was born and his father returned to London—"

"And his drinking, gambling," Seth grumbled.

"My lady practically drove him to that," Mrs. Meeks said, bristling with deep-seated loyalty to the old earl. "Furthermore, there isn't much good you can say about a woman who didn't have the strength to raise her son the way she should have. She was a pampered city miss when she first came to us, always putting on airs when everyone knows her wealthy father was really nothing more than a butcher before he made his fortune selling meat to the army. The only thing she's ever worried about is being accepted by the gentry." She said the word "gentry" as if it left a bad taste in her mouth—and Betsy knew exactly what she meant, as did the others. They had no use for the area gentry like Mr. Willis and his friends, Lord Danbury and Lord Baines, with their uppity ways.

"I say it was a blessing we raised him," Dane countered. "Otherwise, he'd have grown into as sorry an excuse for a man as his father. Now he knows how to wield a blacksmith's hammer with the best of them."

"And there isn't a ship on the sea he can't sail," Marten added. "I took him onto my boat when he was half the size of a minnow, and I taught him to swim too. Threw him right into the ocean, I did, and he came up a-swimmin'."

"He rode on my shoulders when I hunted rabbit and squirrels," Kyle announced proudly. "I taught him to respect the land and the wild beauty of the moors."

"And from me, he learned how to mine that same land and grow rich," Mr. Galesbrook said, his deep voice as proud as that of the others.

Betsy nodded. The villagers had raised Pierce Kirrier and molded him into the sort of man they thought the lord of Penhollow Hall should be—and he had not disappointed them.

To Betsy's thinking, there was no finer man walking the face of the earth than her Lord Pierce. He was built like one of Arthur's legendary knights, tall, broad-shouldered, and with the strength of seven men. And he was as handsome as the fabled Lancelot. No one in Hobbles Moor had been surprised that once Lord Pierce had rebuilt the family fortune, young lasses from good families all over Cornwall, and Devon too, were lining up to marry him.

The villagers also agreed with his mother that at one and thirty, the time had come for him to take a wife.

They just didn't agree with Lady Penhollow that there was any woman among the gentry good enough for him—or at least, not that they'd met.

The Widow Haskell interrupted their bragging. She questioned Lucy. "But did his mother ask for a love charm? The charm is only powerful when requested by one who is linked by blood."

"Aye, she did. After he left the room, she shouted after him, 'I'm tempted to use one of those superstitious love charms you Cornish are always brewing.' Those were her exact words and they're enough, aren't they?"

The Widow Haskell drew herself up until she appeared almost twice as tall to Betsy as she had a moment before. Her eyes burned with fury. "She mocks us?"

In one swift movement, she spread her arms out wide, the fingers of her left hand holding the charm bag. "Betsy, where is the lock of Lord Pierce's hair you promised me?"

Betsy fumbled in the pocket of her skirt and pulled out several strands of hair she'd sneaked from the hairbrush in his room. "This is the best I could do, Widow Haskell."

The Widow's bony fingers closed over the silky black hairs before they blew away in the wind. "It is enough," she said. She pushed the hairs through the drawstring opening of the charm and then looked up at the sky.

"Listen, Winds and Force of Night! We ask you for a special blessing, for a charm more powerful than *all* others. We seek a wife, a woman worthy to be a countess, a woman above all others. Listen to what we ask of you."

The villagers now spoke as she'd prepared them to earlier.

"Her beauty must rival that of the roses in a garden," Betsy said.

"But she must be practical," Mrs. Meeks added.

"And intelligent," Samuel Cobbler said. After the Widow Haskell, he was the oldest person in Hobbles Moor and had been Lord Pierce's unofficial tutor of sorts when the family's fortunes had fallen so low they could not afford to hire a tutor. "She must share our lord's love of books."

"She must be gentle, soft, and caring," Dane said, "the way only a woman can and should be."

One by one the other villagers added their requests.

"She must be handy with a needle."

"Kind. Our new mistress needs to be kind."

"And generous too."

"She must be able to laugh."

"Courage," Kyle said bluntly. "May she have a stout heart."

"It would be nice if she had a talent for music," Lucy said wistfully.

When all were done, the Widow Haskell added one final wish. "May the new lady of Penhollow Hall be fertile. May she give our lord many, many sons who will grow to be tall, proud Cornishmen!"

"No daughters?" Betsy was bold enough to ask.

The Widow looked down on her and smiled. "She will have a daughter," she replied with that uncanny certainty that put a chill up Betsy's spine.

The Widow turned back to the sea and held the charm up in the air. "Winds of Love, search the corners of the world, and bring us a bride worthy of our Cornish earl!"

To Betsy's astonishment, the swirling storm clouds parted to reveal a full, shimmering moon as white as silver. Then lightning flashed, its jagged length cutting across the sky to the ocean.

Behind Betsy, a woman screamed. Lucy threw her shawl over her head and huddled to the ground. Betsy ducked down beside her.

Only the Widow Haskell stood tall and proud against the forces of nature.

Slowly, the crone lowered her arms and whispered, "It is done."

She threw the charm bag into the sea.

Chapter 1

London

Theirs was a forbidden friendship. The vicar's wife and the whore. Two lives as boldly different as the sun from the moon, and yet, friendship thrived.

Now it was about to end.

From the safety of a clump of overgrown boxwoods that hid the secret door in the garden wall between the vicarage and the brothel, Eden watched her friend Mary Westchester, the vicar's wife, who sat on a bench in the dappled shade of her garden waiting for Eden to appear. Today, Mary had brought her eleven-month-old daughter Dorothy, knowing the presence of the child would be a rare and welcome treat. She leaned back and held her babe high above her head. Dorothy giggled with delight and, laughing, her mother dropped her down and hugged her close.

Eden stood riveted by the sight and sound of the child's laughter.

The door that separated the modest vicarage

from the house where Eden lived was a reminder of the days when both houses had been part of the same abbey. Eden's home, a four-story Gothic structure built of stone and mortar located not far from the financial center of London, was now an infamous, but expensively discreet brothel ironically called the Abbey.

A wave of jealousy shot through Eden. She ruthlessly pushed the ugly emotion aside. It was not Mary's fault that their lots in life were so different, or that Eden's life was about to be turned upside down . . .

"Hello," Eden said, stepping from her hiding place.

Mary turned with surprise, and then smiled, holding up the baby. "I brought Dorothy. My mother-in-law wasn't feeling well and I was able to sneak the baby out of the house. She hardly ever lets me take Dorothy anywhere. She insists fresh air is bad for children, but I know she is wrong."

Eden came forward. "She's beautiful." Reverently, she dared to reach out and lightly touch one of the baby's silver-blonde curls. She couldn't help herself. The baby's small, shell-shaped ears and perfect fingers fascinated her. Dorothy examined her seriously with wide blue eyes. "She looks exactly like you, Mary."

Mary laughed, obviously pleased with the compliment. "My mother-in-law insists that Dorothy takes after the Westchesters, but I think she is part and parcel of me," she said, nuzzling the baby proudly. "Here, do you want to hold her?"

Eden stepped back. "No, I couldn't."

"Of course you could! She's not going to bite you." Mary held the baby up. "But be careful. She weighs more than you can imagine."

Eden shook her head, shying away. "I can't." She wasn't fit to touch such perfection. She'd seen things and done things that made her feel soiled inside. None of that should ever touch a baby as sweetly loved as Dorothy.

Mary lowered the baby to her lap, her eyes filled with concern. "Eden, what is the matter? You wouldn't hold her the last time I brought her either."

"You wouldn't understand."

"Of course I would. I'm your friend. There isn't anything you should be afraid to confide in me."

Her words caught Eden off guard.

Immediately, Mary came to her feet and crossed to Eden's side, holding the baby on one hip. "Eden, what is the matter? You've gone suddenly pale. Did I say something wrong?"

Dorothy reached for the green silk bow on Eden's bodice. Eden watched the baby's chubby hands pull on the bow, untying it, before answering in a low voice, "I've been sold."

Mary stared at her blankly and then repeated, "Sold?"

Eden ached to kiss the top of the baby's head. She could smell the scent of milk on Dorothy's breath. "Yes. Madame Indrani has finally heard from the Sultan Ibn Sibah. He's agreed to pay the price she has asked for me." Madame Indrani owned the Abbey. Eden reached out with one finger and stroked one of Dorothy's soft curls. She'd imagined it would feel like silk. It didn't. It felt of something finer and more ethereal. She raised her gaze to meet Mary's. "I will be leaving the Abbey in two weeks' time."

Mary's mouth dropped open in surprise. "She can't sell you. People don't *sell* people, not anymore."

Dorothy tried to stuff the end of the ribbon into her mouth. "They do where I come from," Eden said briskly. "Madame Indrani took me in off the street with the intent of selling me. It has always been my destiny." She echoed the words Madame Indrani had used on her only an hour earlier.

"How can you be so accepting of this?" Mary demanded.

"Because I knew it would happen sooner or later."

Mary pulled the bodice ribbon out of Dorothy's hands. "But I didn't know!" She turned her back on Eden, hugging the baby close. Dorothy peeked over her mother's shoulder, intent on the green ribbon.

Eden took a moment to retie the ribbon before answering soberly, "No, I didn't think you would understand."

Mary turned then, tears welling in her eyes. The tears surprised Eden.

"Mary, you're crying."

"What did you expect me to do? I've never had a friend that I've felt as close to as I do you."

Her words deeply touched Eden. "We are such a contrast, you and I. You are all porcelain and lace whereas I . . ." She finished with a small shrug of her shoulders.

"Whereas you are vibrant, alive, bold," Mary declared loyally. "Do you know I'm jealous of you? I'm jealous of your intelligence and calm good sense about practical matters. But I'm also jealous of your looks too. Many times I wish I'd had your dark hair or green eyes." She gave Eden a critical once-over before adding, "Or your perfect figure."

"Mary, your figure is excellent."

"No, it's not. I'm straight and narrow while you are round and full where a woman should be. Of course, now I wish you were ugly, ugly, ugly. Then Madame Indrani wouldn't be able to sell you and you'd stay here. I'd make you escape her clutches and come live with me. I'd introduce you to one of Nate's friends and you'd marry and we could stay as we are. Of course, you wouldn't be wearing silk like you are now. There's not a one of Nate's friends who isn't as poor as we are."

Eden shook her head with a sad little laugh. "I would give up silk for what you picture. But the truth is, Mary, if I didn't look the way I do, Madame wouldn't have taken me in all those years ago and I would have starved to death on the street, or worse. Much worse," she added, dark memories still clear in her mind.

"Worse than being sold?"

Eden knew Mary could never understand. She focused on the sweet loveliness of the child. Dorothy's little fingers clutched her mother's dress like tree roots gripping the ground for water. For a moment, the loneliness of her life almost overwhelmed her. "You don't know how lucky you are."

"We can't let this happen," Mary said authoritatively, "not without a fight. You don't have to do what Madame Indrani tells you to do. This is England! I will go to Nate and tell him of your plight. I know that once he hears of this foul injustice, he will champion your cause. We will rescue you!"

Mary's eyes sparkled with fiery righteousness and Eden realized that she would truly attempt to do as she said. She would risk her reputation, and the living of her husband, for a friend.

Her willingness to perform such a sacrifice melted something hard and distrusting inside of Eden. It allowed her to drop her guard and let Mary see just how distressed she truly was over the news she'd received this morning.

"Mary, you are the only friend I've ever had."

Mary placed her hand over Eden's and drew her to the bench to sit down. "We're as close as sisters, aren't we? Your friendship changed my life, Eden. That day you overheard me crying in the garden, I suffered such a fit of black despair I thought of killing myself. Then suddenly, you were there. Do you remember? You talked and talked to me and wouldn't give up until I was finally able to draw on your strength and grow stronger myself." She hugged Dorothy to her. "If it wasn't for you, I wouldn't have my baby."

Tears burned in Eden's eyes, but she quickly blinked them back. She'd learned long ago that tears never served a purpose. "You would have found your way."

"No, I wouldn't have. My marriage was a shambles, my husband bitter and angry, myself lost, and in the middle of it was my mother-in-law telling everyone how worthless I was. I consider our meeting to be a turning point in my life. I *value* this friendship. Remember when you had to explain to me the—" She waved her hand, still too embarrassed to speak certain words aloud, whereas Eden knew every graphic word for what a man and a woman could do to each other.

"Intimacies?" Eden suggested helpfully, using one of Madame's favorite descriptions.

Mary gave a small sigh of relief. "Yes, intimacies. Poor Nate, his orphanage-raised wife didn't have any knowledge of such things and every time he came near me after our first night, I'd break down in tears. I believed he was quite mad to want to do those things." The color in her cheeks brightened a bit as she added, "But he is very happy now. And I am too. I feel cherished, loved . . . and all because I learned to not fear those moments between us. In fact, I like them a great deal," she confided.

Eden raised a skeptical eyebrow. "You *like* it?"

Mary nodded shyly. "Quite a bit, actually."

Eden found herself curious. Sex was work, not something to be enjoyed.

As if reading her mind, Mary said, "I don't know if I could be like you. I'd have to care about the person before I'd let them do . . . *you know.*" She waved her hand, unable to say the word "sex." "Otherwise, it would be rather disgusting."

Eden shifted uncomfortably and came to her feet. This was not a conversation she wanted.

But Mary was relentless. "How can you do it, Eden? How can you live the life you do?"

"Madame Indrani says that, to men, there are two types of women, the ones you marry and the whores. A whore is a woman who is paid for what a wife does for free."

Mary stared at her, and then answered fiercely, "It's not like that, Eden. There must be more between a man and his wife than just . . . the *intimacies* to make a marriage. I understand that now."

This was a new maturity to Mary that Eden hadn't seen before . . . and her words rang true. Eden looked around at the roses, lilies, and beds of poppies. "One night, I dreamed that I planted a garden like this, only it had more roses and fewer poppies." She slid a self-conscious smile at Mary. "In my dream, there were babies. Little, tiny babies folded into the leaves of each and every rose. They had perfect little fingers and even smaller toes—" She broke off, suddenly afraid to reveal so much.

Mary rose, hoisting Dorothy up in her arms. "Leave Madame Indrani. Right now, this minute. We shall walk in the house and tell Nate your story. He will save you."

For a second, Eden wanted to believe her, that it could be that easy. A sparrow hopped from branch to branch in the pear tree over their heads. It eyed them a moment before flying toward freedom.

Eden spoke. "I can't."

"Yes, you can."

"No, Mary, I can't. I've been trained to be a rich man's mistress. It is the only life I've known."

"It can't be. Surely you came from somewhere. You must have family. You speak too well."

"I have no one." She looked at the stone walls of the Abbey rising up over the garden wall. "I was raised on the streets of London in places you can't even imagine, Mary. I never knew my mother much less my father."

"So? I'm an orphan too."

"Yes, but I've probably done things you would never do just to survive. Mary, it was a blessing when Madame Indrani found me and brought me to the Abbey."

"Where she trained you for a whore's life!"

Eden heard the contempt in her voice. She lifted her chin. "She *saved* my life. And yes, she's trained me for the whore's life. But she also taught me to speak well, and to read because she believes a woman should know such a thing. A woman trained by Madame Indrani is groomed to have more class and distinction than a princess of the blood."

"So that she could someday sell you!"

"No! So that I can find a better life!"

Mary sat Dorothy down on a quilt spread over the soft grass at her feet. "Eden, yours is not a better life. Nor do you have to keep living this life. You helped me once, now let me help you. Madame Indrani cannot force you into slavery."

Eden stiffened at the word "slavery." If only Mary knew . . . "I have no choice. The deed is done. Money has been exchanged."

"You are being so obstinate! Do you want this? Is that why you refuse to accept my offer to help?"

"You don't understand—"

"I'm trying to! But I'm beginning to think you don't want to leave. That you like your life *servicing* men."

"It's the only life I know!"

"Then find another!"

They stood only a foot apart from each other, their stance that of adversaries instead of friends.

The truth of Mary's words sank in slowly. Never before had Eden dared to question Madame Indrani's wisdom . . . or her own desires.

Mary held out her hand. "Come in the house, now, with me, and we shall talk to Nate."

Eden stared at Mary's hand and discovered another difference between them. Mary believed in what she was saying. Eden had lived too hard a life and knew that such opportunities did not exist for a girl born in the deepest dives of London, a girl who had witnessed murder and had feared for her own life.

Mary's words were the stuff of dreams and fancy tales, not reality.

"I can't. I'm sold. My only way out would be to buy myself back. Only then would I be free to leave."

"And if you don't?" Mary demanded scornfully.

"Then she would have me killed."

Mary's hand wavered. "You're joking?"

"I'm not. It is the way of our business."

It took a moment for Mary to understand the very real threat. But she was not dissuaded. "Then we will raise the funds. We will free you."

Eden gave a small, bitter laugh. "You have twenty-five thousand pounds?"

The breath seemed to leave Mary in a rush. She sat down abruptly on the bench. "Twenty-five thousand pounds? For a woman?"

"You're surprised to discover I am worth that much?" Eden said with a lift of one eyebrow. "Only moments ago, you were telling me how unique I am."

"Yes—I mean, no. Oh, I don't know what I mean." Dorothy had started to crawl away and Mary absently bent down to pick her up. "But then, I shouldn't be surprised, should I? You are uncommonly beautiful." She mulled over the matter, her curiosity active now. "Is twenty-five thousand pounds the usual price? I mean, I can see why some women turn to the prostitute's life for that sort of money."

"Not every woman can command that price, but Madame thought she could for me and she has done so. I've actually been for sale since I turned fourteen."

"And how old are you now?"

"Twenty-one."

"Have many men offered for you?"

"In the beginning, when Madame first brought me out, I had numerous offers. But once they learned she wouldn't negotiate her price, most gentlemen lost interest."

"How did they know about you?"

"Men gossip. I think the high price was all part of Madame's scheme. She understands that men want what they can't have. She coined a name for me, 'the Siren.' She has a name for each of us and says it adds to our mystique. About every other week, she hosts soirées to introduce the girls up for sale. She'd have me there sometimes. I'd play pianoforte for the gentlemen's entertainment and occasionally she'd ask for bids."

"They bid on you? Like you are a horse for sale?" Mary's mouth flattened. "This is revolting. I can't believe men could be so base and callous. But I can believe Madame would ask a high price for you. You aren't like the other girls who live in the Abbey."

"How do you know that?"

"I'm not completely blind. I've seen the girls coming and going. They are jaded and hard, whereas you have a certain vulnerability that sets you apart from them. A freshness. It's part of your beauty."

Eden didn't know whether to be happy or sad at Mary's observation. It was true. She wasn't completely comfortable with her life.

"But twenty-five thousand pounds!" Mary repeated, bouncing Dorothy on her hip. "It's a fortune."

"It's the price of virginity."

Mary almost dropped the baby. "You're a virgin?"

"Well, of course," Eden said, surprised by the question. "Madame Indrani could never demand such a price if I wasn't."

"But I thought—I mean . . . well, you've always been so knowledgeable when we talked about . . ." Her face turned beet-red.

"Yes?" Eden prompted.

"Well, I assumed you were . . . *experienced.*"

"I am in many things." Dorothy was laughing up at Eden and again, Eden dared to lightly stroke one of the baby's curls. She let the tip of her finger brush the baby's cheek, and something deep inside of her ached to hold the child. She leaned back.

"But how can you know so much without actually . . . *you know?*" Mary persisted.

"I was trained," Eden answered matter-of-factly.

"Trained?"

"Yes. I was given lessons. I was taught what to do."

The color drained from Mary's face. "Lessons? Like taking lessons in French or mathematics? Or learning from someone how to cook by watching them?"

Eden couldn't help but smile at the analogy. "Yes. Very much like learning to cook."

Mary appeared ready to swoon. "I never imagined such a thing. I mean, did you—

With many men? Wait, no, don't tell me. I'm not certain I want to know!"

With the differences between Mary and herself suddenly emphasized, Eden didn't know whether to laugh or cry. She sat on the bench. "The man who has paid my price wants a virgin, but he doesn't want a woman who is stupid in bed."

"You are not a dog to be purchased, used, and then dismissed with a pat on the head!"

Eden looked into her friend's angry features and suddenly felt an overpowering sadness. "I have no choice, Mary, and I must try to make the best of it. I haven't told you all. The man who purchased me is a Kurdufan prince."

"Kurdufan? I've never heard of such a place."

"It's a long way from England. Madame Indrani was once one of Ibn Sibah's concubines in his harem. She saved his life and he set her free. She then came to London and opened the Abbey. She knew he could afford my price. When I was fourteen, she sent him a miniature of me. However, because of Napoleon and a war on Kurdufan, he was unable to send for me until yesterday. His emissaries have arrived. The transaction is complete. I leave at the end of next week for Kurdufan."

"What?" Mary's voice came out in a whisper of disbelief. "You're leaving England? To live in a harem? Eden, do you know what a harem is? I've heard missionaries talk about the wicked ways of the heathens. It's a godforsaken place where women are not allowed to leave. It truly is slavery."

Eden felt her brave front in danger of collapsing. A hard lump formed in her throat. "Madame assures me that if I please the Ibn Sibah, I may also be set free."

Mary sat down on the bench and stared hard into Eden's eyes. *"But you are already free."*

"I was never free, Mary. Not from the moment Madame took me into her coach."

"Then you should never have climbed into it."

Eden lowered her voice. "You don't understand. I'd seen a man murdered and the one that had done it wanted to silence me completely."

Mary's eyes widened, but then she frowned. "That was years ago, Eden. You do not have anything to fear. Tell Madame to give the money back. Tell her you do not want to go to a harem."

"I can't."

"What you can't do is leave England."

"I must."

On Mary's lap, Dorothy was sucking her fist contentedly. The garden smelled of good earth and sunlight. It was a place of beauty, a place of refuge.

"I'm afraid," Eden confessed.

"I'm afraid for you." Mary's arm came around Eden's shoulders and she pulled her close. "I will say prayers for you every single hour of every day. God will save you."

Eden didn't answer. This God, in whom Mary had such great faith, had done very little for Eden in her life.

"Here." Mary pulled the gold chain around her neck up over her head. "I want you to have this. It's a medallion I was given in the orphanage." She held it out to Eden. Sunlight glinted off the bas-relief sign of the cross on the small circle of gold as it twirled slowly on the end of the chain. Dorothy reached for it, but her mother pulled her arm back. "Come now, take it."

Eden had never received such a gift. "I can't. It's yours."

"I am happy and married. It has served me well. Now you are the one in need of protection." She pressed the medallion into Eden's hand. "I will pray that God gives you the courage to free yourself if the occasion arises, my friend."

Her words broke through Eden's carefully constructed defenses. At last, she allowed the tears to come and she made no attempt to stop them as she wept in her friend's arms.

From Eden's bedroom window in the Abbey, Madame Indrani looked down over the garden wall and saw her Eden crying in the vicar's wife's arms.

Her Eden had never cried, not once in the years that Madame had known her, and yet, there she was.

A tall woman of regal bearing, Madame was the half-breed love child of an Egyptian woman of good family and a ne'er-do-well Englishman. When her mother had died, the family had sold Madame into slavery where she had become Ibn Sibah's favorite.

She knew Eden wasn't happy with her fate and felt a twinge of remorse—which was pacified by the knowledge that Eden's sale had made Madame a very rich woman. It could also be profitable for Eden. Ibn Sibah was a generous man. Since he found Western dress exotic, he'd already gifted Eden with an expensive new wardrobe.

At one time, the growing friendship between the mousy vicar's wife and her star pupil had amused Madame, but not any longer. Now that same friendship threatened a very lucrative business understanding.

Coming to a sudden decision, Madame turned on her heel and went downstairs where she found Firth, her bodyguard and manservant.

"I want that hidden door in the garden wall locked. And watch Eden. See that she doesn't go anywhere unchaperoned until we have her on that ship for Kurdufan."

Two weeks later, flanked by the two turbanned emissaries from the sultan, Eden was put aboard the English vessel *Wind Lark.* She had in her possession the finest wardrobe money could buy, but a gold chain and medallion around her neck meant more to her than the fine clothes and the Sultan's twenty-five thousand pounds combined.

There had been no opportunity to say goodbye to Mary.

Now, walking up the ship's gangway, she clutched the medallion and prayed as Mary had once urged her.

Once aboard ship, Eden had her first taste of harem life. Nasim, the sultan's emissary, ordered her locked in her cabin. She wasn't even allowed to see the ship leave the London dock. Neither the captain nor the crew were permitted to speak to her.

After hours in her hot, stuffy cabin she complained to Nasim that she needed air and sunlight. Nasim agreed that she could take two turns around the deck each day for her health. He expected her to wear a dark, heavy veil that covered her from head to toe whenever she left her cabin. Furthermore, the great, hulking Gadi followed Eden like her shadow. No one was allowed to speak to her but Nasim.

She was taking her late afternoon walk on their second day out of London harbor when Eden heard Captain Sullivan tell his crew, "Say good-bye to England for another year, lads. You won't be seeing her sooner than that."

The crew didn't pay attention, but Eden did. She crossed to the rail and stared hard at the horizon and the gray-green line of land, watching it grow smaller and more distant.

Was Mary still saying prayers?

"Looks like a storm is brewing too," Captain Sullivan observed to Nasim, their conversation drifting toward Eden. "May be a rough night."

"What will you do?" Nasim asked in his accented English. He'd abandoned Western dress for the flowing robes of a desert tribesman that both he and Gadi preferred.

Eden found him easy to distrust. He was a slim man with overbearing ways and eyes so dark they didn't seem to reflect light but peered out at the world with reptilian interest.

He was also not a good sailor. Eden had overheard him complain to Madame about the seasickness both he and Gadi had suffered on their way to London.

"I'll try and bypass it," Captain Sullivan answered. "If she blows, she'll be a mean one. I don't like a wind blowing from the west. I'll go off course if I must to avoid it."

Nasim seemed to feel this was a wise idea.

However, in less than two hours' time, the Channel seas were more turbulent than normal. Locked in her tiny cabin, Eden sat on her bed to keep from tumbling around the room, thrown by the motion of the ship.

She was fortunate. A good sailor, she even enjoyed the wild movement and took no small satisfaction in the fact that Gadi's face was already sickly green by the time he delivered her dinner.

He was so ill, he forgot to lock Eden's door when he left.

She stared at the door, uncertain . . . and then realized that escape was impossible. Where could she run and hide on a boat?

I will pray that God gives you the courage to free yourself.

Mary's words woke Eden in the middle of the night. The ship bucked back and forth now like a child's hobbyhorse. Through the heavy, creaking timbers, Eden could hear the sound of rolling thunder. The storm was upon them.

A heartbeat later, something crashed down upon the deck, sending a mighty shudder through the *Wind Lark*. The ship lurched and rolled precariously.

She strained to hear the sailors' shouts. Feet pounded across the deck over her head. But the ship appeared to be staying afloat.

The courage to free yourself . . .

An idea for escape rose crystal-clear in her mind. It was bold, daring lunacy.

At first, she rejected it, but the idea would not go away.

In the darkness of her cabin, she couldn't even see her own hand. Gadi had forgotten to return to pick up the dinner dishes and the teacup rolled around on the floor. The door must still be unlocked.

And Eden knew this was her only chance.

She lifted the lid of her trunk. Feeling her way in the dark, she took the beautiful dresses made from the finest silks and laces and wadded them into a ball in the center of a velvet cape. They were her only possessions and could be sold for good money. On top of them she threw in several pairs of slippers, drew up the edges of the cape, and knotted the ends into a sack. She felt along the floor until she discovered the knife from her dinner tray.

Then, swathing her nightdress in her veil so that it hooded her face, she slipped out the door, the sack of dresses over her back, the knife firmly in her hand. She made her way up the passageway toward the ladder.

Outside Nasim and Gadi's door, she paused

to listen. No sound came from within the cabin. She tiptoed her way past and climbed the ladder.

Above deck, all was chaos. The mainmast had cracked and fallen to the deck. Sailors who had battled the storm for hours now struggled to roll up the battered mainsail. Without the main mast and sails, *Wind Lark* was at the mercy of the storm.

Eden slipped and skidded her way on bare feet to the aft of the ship where the dinghy was tied to the side by a series of pulleys that could lower it to the water. Lifelines crisscrossing the deck had been covered or knocked down by the mainsail. She hugged the bulwark and worked her way toward the dinghy. By the time she reached it, the veil had fallen down around her shoulders and rain plastered her hair to her head. It rolled in rivulets down her back.

Eden slit a hole in the tarp covering of the boat and stuffed the bundle of clothes inside. Her hands now free, she worked to loosen the knots tying the dinghy to the side of the ship and connecting it with the pulleys. Hurry, she had to hurry. But her fingers couldn't seem to untie the wet hemp rope. Behind her, Captain Sullivan shouted orders at his crew. A seaman cried out as a wave swept him overboard.

Eden kept working at the lines, too afraid to stop. Finally, the knots came loose. The boat banged against the *Wind Lark* and swung out again before Eden could catch it. The next time it came in toward the ship, she grabbed it and without hesitation crawled unceremoniously through the slit in the tarp, holding on to the pulley rope.

She'd just started lowering the boat into the water when she heard a man's voice above the roar of the storm shouting for her to stop. She didn't.

May you have the courage to free yourself.

Instead, she let go of the rope. The dinghy fell to the ocean with a splash. She screamed as the boat shook and rocked on impact.

Looking up at the ship through the slit in the tarp, she was surprised to see Captain Sullivan's face, white and ghoulish in the night, staring down at her. He was shouting but the wind carried his words away from her.

The ocean raised the small craft up on the next swell and sent it crashing against the side of the ship. The dinghy quivered with the force, but was then carried away by the same foaming waves.

She held the edges of the tarp together the best she could in a vain attempt to keep the rain from coming in through the slit. The velvet cape beneath her soaked up the rainwater gathering on the bottom of the boat.

After what seemed like hours on the ocean, she was ready to admit defeat. Her arms ached from holding the tarp.

By dawn, the rain finally stopped. She did her best to wring out the water from the clothes to lighten the boat.

And by the end of that first day, Eden was no longer able to worry about the dinghy's almost constant rocking in the waves or the direction of her craft. She no longer held the tarp closed, but curled up on the bottom of the boat, her knees against her chest. She was thirsty, tired, hungry—and she knew she was going to die.

Courage. The word rang true in her soul. She no longer worried about what she'd done or her fate if she was captured by Madame Indrani or the sultan's emissaries. The idea of death no longer frightened her.

She forced herself to visualize a garden. It was full of roses this time of year. Lush, full-headed roses in every shade of red known to man. If she concentrated very hard, she could even recall their heady fragrance that sometimes drifted on the evening air.

For the space of a few seconds, she was transported to another place and time. The scent of roses replaced the brackish smell of wet tarp and seawater. Wonderful, wonderful roses with a hint of mystery folded and wrapped in their velvety petals.

She drifted on an endless sea dreaming of gardens—full of columbines, bleeding hearts, lilies. Her lips tasted of salt. She wiped them with the rainwater on her velvet cape. She ignored the ache of hunger in her stomach.

Instead, she planned a garden. A garden where she would be safe, secure . . . and cherished.

Chapter 2

Pierce Kirrier, the earl of Penhollow, felt a tug on his fishing line. With a rush of triumph, he yanked on the pole, setting the hook. The fish fought back and Pierce, bootless, strode into the surf, letting the line play out.

He loved the ocean and the clean smell of salt air. It was as much a part of his soul as the hills, rocks, and moors of his beloved Cornwall.

As a lad, he'd spent every moment of every day outside exploring. He'd been happy when he'd not been sent away to school and took inordinate pride in the fact that he was a self-made man. Not for all the money in the world would he exchange what he'd learned through living life to its fullest for an education at Eton and Cambridge.

Of course, he'd learned that lesson the hard way. There had been a time when he'd keenly felt the scorn of other members of his class. When he'd inherited the title, he'd been labeled the "beggared" earl because of his family's bare coffers and his mother's roots in trade.

Now, no one laughed at him.

The success of his horse breeding farm and his decision to reopen the family tin mine operation had restored his fortune. The neighboring gentry now curried his favor, hoping the Midas touch Pierce seemed to enjoy would rub off on them.

However there was a price to pay for his success. Today was the first time in close to a year that he had taken even a moment of free time for himself. Now as he pitted his wits against that of a wily fish, he was thankful to his friend Captain Harry Dutton for literally dragging him away from his desk.

The two men fished at a place called Hermit's Cove. Tucked in the coast not far from Penhollow Hall, the secluded beach was surrounded by high rocky walls with a stage of rocks jutting out over the ocean. It was a place separate and remote from the world beyond it, a place for confidences.

But Pierce wasn't thinking of anything but bringing in the fish hooked on the other end of his line. The day was bright and sunny. A rare and unusual day for Cornwall, but the sort that often followed a major storm. He laughed with the sheer joy of living.

"Harry, this one has plenty of fight in him. Hand me the net, will you?" He caught a glint of silver in the waves crashing against a rock. "This bugger's a smart one. He's trying to break my line." Pierce began walking backward toward shore, the rough, rocky sand giving beneath his bare feet. His boots, jacket, and waistcoat lay on the beach beside the picnic lunch Lucy, the Penhollow cook, had prepared.

Pierce held out his hand, his eyes on the taut line leading into the water. "The net, Harry. I need the net!"

Still no response.

Pierce shot an irritated glance over his shoulder. Harry sat on a rock, a wine bottle in his hand, lost in deep thought. Unlike Pierce who was in billowing shirtsleeves, Harry still wore his coat, boots, and neckcloth. "Harry!"

His friend looked up with a start. "Did you want something, Penhollow?"

"I want the damn net!"

At that moment, Pierce's line snapped clean in two, cut by a cunning fish and sharp Cornish rocks.

"Damn." Pierce stared at the spot where his line had entered only a second ago. "I had him. He's taken my hook with him." Slowly, he turned to confront his friend. "Where the devil were you? Didn't you hear me shout for a net?"

Harry hunched his shoulders guiltily. "Did you call for me more than once?"

Pierce swore under his breath and sloshed his way to shore. He buried the end of his fishing pole in the sand and walked to the picnic basket. Another uncorked bottle of wine sat in the sand. He lifted it to his lips and took a long drink before saying, "Harry, what the deuce is the matter with you? I thought we came here to fish, and yet you haven't thrown out your line once. You were so anxious to come earlier, I would have thought you'd have been the first in the water."

Instead of answering, Harry dropped his empty wine bottle, stood, and, with the air of a child reciting verse for his tutor, announced, "You can't expect to remain a bachelor forever, Penhollow."

The bottle of wine halfway to his lips, Pierce stared at him. "I beg your pardon?"

"It's bloody time you settled down and began behaving like the rest of us!" Harry answered with surprising vehemence. "After all, you are past the time when most men face their responsibilities. Oh—I don't mean to say you aren't responsible, Pierce. Devil the bit, I'd never say that . . . but, ah, marriage is your duty and—" He paused, searching for words, then finished in a rush, "And you'll be much happier once you do—I mean are."

"Are what?"

"Married."

Fascinated by such a startling testimony, Pierce lowered the wine bottle. "Are you saying this based upon *your* experience as a married man?"

Harry shifted uneasily. "I suppose." Eight years ago, Pierce had been a witness to Harry's wedding to Helen Dudridge, the daughter of a prosperous dairyman. Now, four children later, Harry had added at least two stone to his short frame and found himself in charge of more black and white Jersey cows than he cared to count. He'd also grown increasingly henpecked. Pierce had been surprised that Helen had let Harry go fishing.

In fact, it was rather suspicious. "Harry, has my mother been talking to you?"

"No," Harry denied quickly, and then admitted, "But she has been talking to Helen and you know I can't gainsay Helen."

Pierce walked over to the rock and sat. "Here, sit." He scooted to make room on the same rock and offered Harry the bottle. "And take off that silly neckcloth, will you? You look like you should be sitting in church rather than on the beach."

Dutifully, Harry practically clawed the knot in his neckcloth loose before plopping down on the rock beside Pierce. He took a healthy swig from the bottle.

Squinting into the sun, Pierce stared out over the ocean. A small fishing boat floated far past the rocks. Perhaps that fisherman would catch the fish he'd failed to bring in.

He took the bottle from Harry and had a drink. "Now, what is all this marriage nonsense?"

Harry had the good grace to look penitent. "Your mother, Pierce. She's relentless."

Pierce made an impatient sound. "Don't I know. She's paraded so many women in front of me, and in such an obvious manner, I'm beginning to feel like Cornish King," he said, referring to the top stud in his stables and his pride and joy. Horsemen from all over England and Europe came to use him as a stud.

"You really can't blame her," Harry said, taking the bottle back. "It is your responsibility to beget an heir and all that. You're not getting any younger." He cast a critical glance at Pierce's flat stomach and then his own bulging paunch. "Although you don't seem to be aging."

Pierce laughed and pushed his hair back from its perpetual place over his forehead. He came to his feet. "Well, neither you nor Mother need have any fears. I understand my responsibilities. I'm just not ready to marry yet." He turned his back on his friend and looked out over the ocean. The boat was still there; there was a small flicker of movement from within. For a brief moment he wondered what it would be like to be a simple fisherman with no one hounding him to marry.

"It's the way women are," Harry said. "The sight of an eligible, unmarried male gets their hunting instincts up. It's the same sort of feeling we have when we flush out a nest of grouse."

"They want to shoot us dead?" Pierce asked dryly.

Harry heaved a weary sigh. "Not quite . . . but close. Helen and your mother think you should make an offer for the Willis chit. They want me to convince you to do so. They thought you would listen to another man's opinion."

Pierce rolled his eyes. "Have you been in the sun too long? Victoria Willis is barely out of the schoolroom. I'd spend the rest of my life bored to death."

"But you need someone young and she looks like a good breeder."

"Harry, we're talking about a woman."

"Yes, thoughtless of me, but you understand. After all, we're both in the breeding business—you with the horses and me with those damn cows. What's really important," he said, warming to his topic, "is that her great uncle is a duke and she'll bring you three thousand a year which is the best you can do in Cornwall. To do better than three thousand, you'll have to go to London."

Pierce shook his head. "I'll not go to London for a bride. My father did that and my mother has always resented living so far out in the country." He walked back to the water's edge, feeling the cold waves lap against his feet.

"What your mother resented was being left behind in Cornwall while your father went to London and had a fine time," Harry answered with the candor of long-standing friendship and the effects of good wine.

"Aye, you're right. But I'll not follow in his path. Besides, Harry, there has to be more to marriage than dowries and family ties. Look at you and Helen. She isn't related to a duke."

"No, but she had an income of one thousand pounds and High Road Dairy."

"A man doesn't marry for a mere one thousand pounds."

"Perhaps you don't, but I did. Look at me, Pierce." Harry got up to his feet with a slight hiccup."I'm not tall and handsome like you. I don't have those sharp blue eyes that drive the women crazy and I'm not even as smart as you are. I graduated from Oxford, but I haven't opened a book in years."

"You had a successful military career."

"My father purchased my commission to get me out of his house, and I hated it. People shoot at you and the Iberians are completely uncivilized. No, one thousand pounds a year and command over a regiment of cows sounded like a fortune to me at the time and I was happy to marry for it."

"And now? Was the price worth it?"

Harry swayed a moment, mulling his question. "Sometimes I'm happy."

Pierce snorted and walked over to the hamper to pull out a fat roasted capon wrapped in a towel. He pulled off a leg and tossed it to Harry before ripping off the other for himself. "I should think you are happy all the time. Helen is a lovely woman and you've got your children. Married life is good to you."

Harry dropped back down on the rock and stretched his booted feet out on the sand in front of him. "Sometimes it's good and other times, well, marriage can try a man's patience." He paused. "I say, did Lucy pack another bottle of wine?"

Pierce finished his chicken leg and wiped his greasy hands on his breeches before pulling out the third bottle. He also took out bread and cheese. He offered all three to Harry who reached for the wine.

"I'm just as happy to get drunk."

"Well, it's a good day for that," Pierce observed. It had been too long since he felt the sun warm his face, and had such an open conversation with Harry. He tore off a piece of bread and a hunk of cheese, put the rest of the food back in the hamper, and sat cross-legged on the grainy sand beside his friend.

Harry continued his original train of thought. "There are many times I wish I'd stayed a bachelor like you. Of course, I would have been a *poor* bachelor with nothing to my name but my military pension."

"Harry, I'm not a bachelor because I want to be." Pierce took the bottle and washed down the bread before admitting, "It's just that I haven't found the woman I want to spend my life with." He gazed back out at the sea, noticing that the little boat drifted closer and closer. It was halfway covered by a tarp that flapped in the breeze. So, it wasn't a fisherman, he mused idly.

"And you won't ever," Harry said with authority. "I mean, you think you will—I thought I had with Helen. They are all so cute and sweet and lovely—but something happens to women once they tie the parson's knot."

"What do you mean?" Pierce asked, truly curious. He turned his attention back to Harry who was trying to remove his jacket with a good deal of grunting exertion.

"So how do women change?" Pierce prompted.

"They change, they change!" Harry reiterated. "For example, they think you are clever and witty before the ceremony but the minute the 'I do's' are spoken, the first thing your new wife wants to do is remake you into something better of her own design. Suddenly everything you say is subject to debate and you can't do anything right anymore. One time Helen had a fit of tears because I slurped my soup at one of her dinner parties. I've always slurped soup! You know that, Penhollow. Have you ever seen me not slurp soup?"

"I hadn't noticed."

"Oh, but Helen did and once we'd married, it was no longer acceptable. And this idea that a man's home is his castle . . . what rubbish! The only room a man controls in his own home is his privy and that's because it is the only place he can hide from his wife and her incessant demands."

"Oh, come now, Harry. It isn't as bad as all that."

Harry took another healthy drink from the wine bottle. "Yes, it is. When I married Helen, I thought she was the most biddable of young women. Now the only words I'm allowed to say are 'Yes, dear.' 'You are right, dear.' 'Of course, dear.' *I'm* the biddable one!"

Pierce, who had always thought Helen to be too strong-minded for his taste, was more shocked to learn that Harry had at one time thought the woman "biddable." "But you are happy," he insisted.

"I'm happy as long as Helen is happy." He leaned forward. "Trust me, Pierce, that's our family motto and could be emblazoned under a coat of arms. All the statements vicars and priests make about marriage and women obeying their husbands is a good deal of rot. It wouldn't be so brutal if a man could at least plan on a little *warmth* from his wife now and then—if you know what I mean—but there is no assurance to that fact either. You, a single man, probably have the opportunity to enjoy yourself under the covers more than I ever do lying beside my wife every night. I tell you, something happens to women when they marry. By the way," he said, boozily. "Are you still seeing that widow in Exter?"

"Occasionally." He didn't want to change the subject to his personal life. Not right now. Harry was telling him things he'd never heard before. "I would think that would be one of the advantages to matrimony: that a man could be with his mate every night. I assumed that since you and Helen were having children . . . ?" He let his voice drift off and pitched another stone into the ocean.

"Women don't like *it* as much as men."

"Truly?" Pierce hadn't found that to be true in his experience.

Harry snorted and lowered his voice. "I'm not proud to tell you I can count on one hand the number of times Helen and I have—well, *you know*—over the past year. She's either been pregnant or too tired. My life is going to the damn dogs. I think often of taking on a mistress, but I'd pay a terrible price if Helen found out—and she would find out."

"Then why are you encouraging me to get married?"

"Because Helen promised a bit of—well, *you know*—if I had this talk with you. 'Course, as you can see, I'm making a muddle of it." He reached for the wine bottle. "But I'm a desperate man." He drained the bottle.

Pierce leaned back against the rock, staring up at the blue sky. Huge, puffy white clouds sailed across it. "I'm just sorry you're not happier."

"Married men weren't meant to be happy," Harry said philosophically. "At the pub, all of us married ones are more than a bit jealous of you." He came down to sit on the sand beside Pierce. "But you know, you've got to join the ranks with the rest of us sooner or later. There are no Cornish dukes and few earls. To most of the common folk in Cornwall, the Penhollows are royalty. You have to sire an heir, Pierce. Your title demands it." He snorted. "Even the villagers in Hobbles Moor are anxious for you to marry."

"I know that," Pierce answered, his gaze still on the sky. "And I plan on marrying. That is, once I meet the right woman."

"A woman with an income of three thousand a year sounds like the right woman to me," Harry said with conviction.

Pierce shook his head. "Money isn't enough. My father married my mother for her fortune and then proceeded to make her life miserable. There has to be something more."

"More than money? What else is there?" Harry asked. He blew across the top of the wine bottle, making a tooting sound.

"I don't know . . ." Pierce began and then paused. He turned to Harry. "What about love?"

"Love?" Harry stared at him as if there was a third eye growing in the middle of his head. "Have you gone daft?"

"I don't think so. Don't you love Helen?"

Harry drew away. "I liked her a great deal at first."

"But do you love her?" Pierce insisted.

"It's hard to love someone who is constantly criticizing you." Harry crossed his arms, cuddling the empty bottle. "Besides, love is a bunch of romantic claptrap," he said at last. "Don't tell me you believe in such a thing?"

"No, I don't—at least, not yet." He contemplated the waves rolling up onto the small stretch of beach. "But I want to believe. I know I have to sire an heir, and I know time is running out, but deep inside something whispers to me to wait." He could feel it even now, that inner sense that someday he would find what he was searching for.

He shot a rueful grin at Harry. "I imagine I sound foolish to you."

His friend didn't laugh. Instead he admitted softly, "It's not like I don't have certain feelings for Helen. It's more that we seem to have lost track of each other. Of course, if she were less irritable . . . ?" His voice trailed off.

A movement from the boat caught Pierce's attention. He jumped to his feet and stared intently out at the water, not certain of what he'd seen.

"What is the matter?" Harry asked, also coming to his feet.

"That dinghy. I could have sworn I saw someone in it."

"And what if you did? Do we have another bottle of wine?"

"Look how close the boat is to the rocks, Harry. It'll be smashed in a moment or two."

Harry scrunched his eyes to look in the direction of the boat. "I don't see anything."

At that moment, a rolling wave lifted the boat and tilted it, and Pierce saw a flash of human flesh. Someone was lying in the bottom of that boat! And it was about to be splintered apart on the rocks.

He took off running. With a skill and experience honed since childhood, he made his way over the slick rocks guarding the entrance to Hermit's Cove.

The rocks the boat was in danger of crashing against jutted out of the ocean several yards from shore. Pierce went as far by land as he could and then dove into the seawater.

He was a good swimmer. His strokes were sure, but with respect for the currents that ran their way along the coast. Harry was shouting at him from shore, too tipsy to be of much help.

He reached the boat. A hank rope, one end tied to an iron ring on the bow, hung in the water. Pierce grabbed it, scraping his toes on a jut of rock below the water's surface, and then used that same rock to push off and away.

It was slow going. The boat and ebbing tide impeded his progress. His arms grew heavy, his legs tired. Through sheer force of will, he kept going, heading for the smoother water in the cove.

At last, his feet brushed against land. A few more strokes and he could stand.

He heaved the boat to shore until its bow was safely buried in the sand. Then he fell to the earth and lay there willing his labored breath back to normal.

"You could have drowned, Pierce," Harry was saying.

Pierce fobbed him off with a wave of his hand and closed his eyes.

A second later his eyes popped open when Harry exclaimed, "God in heaven, it's a woman. A naked one!"

Pierce rolled over onto his feet. "A what?"

Harry was leaning over the boat, his eyes practically bulging with his excitement. He drew out the syllables. "A wo-man. Naked."

Pierce came up beside him. Harry was right. There was a woman on the bottom of the boat.

A beautiful woman.

She was unconscious, her lips pale, her skin tinged slightly red from sunburn. One arm crossed her body modestly. Thick, spiked lashes rested on high cheekbones and her full lips were slightly parted. The sun glinted off a gold chain around her neck.

She was not naked, but very close to being so. The thin white cotton of her nightdress was soaked by the sea and clung to every lush curve of her body like a second skin. Long tendrils of dark hair covered the high tips of her breasts, but nothing else was left to the imagination. Her feet were bare, her legs long and shapely up to the dark triangle of hair between her thighs. For one wild moment all Pierce could do was stand beside Harry and gape with sheer masculine appreciation.

The cry of a gull brought him to his senses. He closed his mouth and pressed his fingers against the pulse point at her neck. Her skin was as smooth as satin and as hot as one of the irons Dane, the blacksmith, heated in his forge. To his relief, her pulse beat steadily. He leaned over and felt her breath against his cheek.

"It's a mermaid," Harry rasped out.

"Oh, no, she's very human." He lifted her out of the boat. "Spread my coat out," he ordered Harry who hurried to comply.

"Who is she?" he asked.

"I don't know," Pierce said, laying the girl on his jacket.

"Is she alive?"

"Yes, but she's not well. She's obviously been floating out there for some time." He took a water flask from the hamper and poured some between her lips. No reaction. "We must get help for her, and quickly."

"Where will we take her?" Harry asked, staring down at her.

Curiously proprietorial, Pierce took off his wet shirt and laid it over the woman to cover her from Harry's prying eyes. "Hand me your jacket. She's had enough of sun and wind."

The corners of Harry's mouth turned down as if he were disappointed he could no longer feast upon her nakedness, but he did as he was asked.

"This seems odd," Harry said. "You don't always find people floating around in boats unconscious off this coast. Quite dangerous."

"No," Pierce agreed absently, ignoring Harry's wine-induced speculation. He attempted to wet her lips with water again. The woman shifted and frowned.

Pierce pulled back, watching.

He was rewarded for his patience when she opened her eyes. They were the deep, vivid green of bottled glass.

For a second their gazes met and held. Pierce felt a tremble, a sense of anticipation, flow through him.

He wasn't a superstitious man, but in that moment, he had the eerie feeling that this woman and he had been destined to meet. Perhaps they'd met before?

He didn't think so. He would have remembered her. Even wet and beaten by the sea, she was an uncommon beauty . . . but there was something else. Something about her that pulled him to her.

Her lips curved into a small half smile and then she closed her eyes, sinking back into the bliss of unconsciousness.

He pulled on his boots, shrugged into his jacket, and picked her up in his arms. She weighed next to nothing. He strode toward the narrow passageway leading out of Hermit's Cove.

Harry had bent over to retrieve the sopping material out of the bottom of the boat. "What have we here?" he asked, and then noticed that Pierce was leaving. "Wait, Pierce, where are you going? What are you going to do with her?"

"I'm taking her to Penhollow Hall," he answered without looking back.

Chapter 3

The sound of roaring waves in Eden's ears subsided and turned softer, gentler.

She didn't want to wake up. She wanted to keep her eyes closed and drift in a state of half-consciousness forever.

Even as wakefulness pulled at her, she snuggled deeper into the fresh, starchy sheets. The air smelled of beeswax and the sound of water splashing was so restful—

Sudden, terrifying visions of the storm rushed into her head, tumbling with memories of what she'd done. She'd escaped, but in doing so, she had gone against Madame Indrani and a powerful sultan. Fear ran cold inside her.

Then she heard a woman's voice say, "She's been like this all night, poor thing. She'll be all calm and restful-like, then the next moment very agitated. She mutters a bit but I can't make out a word she is saying."

Eden went still, her eyes clamped shut. Where was she? Who had found her? The woman leaned over her—Eden could feel her body heat—and fluffed the pillow beneath her head.

"Here now, Betsy," the woman said. "We must clean up around this bed." The woman lowered her voice confidentially. "You know what a stickler Lady Penhollow is and she's already a bit put out, with his lordship marching into the house with this poor lass."

"What would she have had him do, Mrs. Meeks?" Betsy asked. She had the sweet, eager voice of a young girl. "He couldn't leave her on the shore, could he?"

"I don't think she knew what to make of the matter. Lord Pierce swept through the front door half dressed, shouting orders, and with this girl in his arms. Rescued her from a boat, he did, and felt responsible for her. He even stayed half the night in that chair right there in the corner until Dr. Hargrave announced that she'd taken a turn for the better. Wouldn't leave her, he wouldn't. Not until his mother claimed it was unseemly to have him hovering over her that way. 'Watch her for me, Mrs. Meeks,' he said, and I did exactly that. Watched her the rest of the night as if she was my own, I did."

Eden's heart beat with alarm. *Who was this Lord Pierce?*

"You must be exhausted," Betsy said.

"That I am."

Eden slitted open her eyes. Mrs. Meeks was a roly-poly woman with a huge bosom and salt-and-pepper hair. Betsy was close to Eden's own age and wore a very large mobcap from which squiggles of unruly red hair peeked out beneath. Both women appeared as if they had never known a day of hunger in their lives.

"Lord Pierce has left word he is to be notified the very second she wakes," Mrs. Meeks said. "I must go attend to a few matters and I want you to stay here at the lass's side."

Betsy dropped her voice. "Do you believe she's the one? The whole village is talking about it. The Widow won't say yea or nay."

"I don't know. Certainly she is beautiful. I've never seen a lovelier woman."

Eden could feel them both looking at her now, staring. *The one what?* She could barely breathe.

"She looks a bit like what you'd imagine a sea sprite would," Betsy said. "You know, with long curling hair and fine, black, spiky eyelashes."

"Or she could be some poor unfortunate soul whose ship was wrecked in that terrible storm," Mrs. Meeks answered in a practical tone. "Lord Pierce sent out riders last night to search for information. He'll have the right of her story soon enough."

Betsy shook her head. "He'll find nothing. Trust me, I have a sense about these things, even my ma says so. It's no simple accident that the sea threw this lass into Lord Pierce's arms."

"Well, if she *is* the one, it's too bad we didn't think to ask for her to be rich. This poor child arrived to us practically naked, wearing little more than that gold chain around her neck. Indecent she was. I had to dress her in one of my old night rails. It's far too large for her but it's more substantial than that shift she was wearing."

"Oh, but she *is* rich," Betsy said.

Rich? Eden wondered.

"Rich?" Mrs. Meeks repeated. "How so?"

"You haven't seen the clothes then?" Betsy asked.

"What clothes?"

"The clothes Captain Dutton found in the bottom of her boat."

"No one told me about them," Mrs. Meeks said, genuinely vexed.

"Perhaps because you were so busy in here," Betsy suggested helpfully. "Mrs. Ivy had Lucy hang them in the laundry. You should see them, Mrs. Meeks. One dress looks as if it has been spun from gold."

A cramp formed in Eden's foot from lying so still. She slid her other foot over to press against the cramp, easing the pain slightly, while praying the two women didn't notice. She needed them to leave her alone so she could escape this house. Nasim and Gadi could be out searching for her already.

Betsy sighed. "Mrs. Meeks, you've never seen the likes of these dresses. They are the sort of clothes only a princess would wear. One gown has real pearls—*jewels of the sea*—sewn across the bodice. And they're all the finest silks. Lucy told me so. She and Mrs. Ivy spent a good part of the night trying to salvage them. Mrs. Ivy doesn't think the seawater did too much damage since they were wrapped in a heavy velvet cape."

"What does Mrs. Ivy know about seawater

damage?" Mrs. Meeks asked indignantly. "I'm the expert on laundry in this house. I've told her time and time again to keep her uppity nose out of my business, but does she listen to me? No! She just up and goes wherever she pleases, believing being Lady Penhollow's dresser gives her special privileges!"

She turned and looked down at Eden who closed her eyes and feigned sleep just in time. Eden could feel her scrutiny. *Forget me. Think about Mrs. Ivy.*

"Why wasn't I told of these dresses immediately?" Mrs. Meeks demanded.

"Because Mrs. Ivy told Lucy you were too busy nursing this poor lady and she would take care of them."

"She *would*," Mrs. Meeks snapped. "Well, she's not going to get away with it this time. I will see those dresses for myself and decide what shall be done. Here, you stay with the lass while I go to the laundry."

"Please take me with you, Mrs. Meeks. I only saw the dresses for a moment and Lucy wouldn't let me touch 'em. I'd so like to feel the pearls on that dress. I've never felt real pearls before. Even Mrs. Ivy said she'd never seen such large pearls in her life. Lucy said Mrs. Ivy rubbed one of them against her teeth and then practically keeled over in a faint. She kept saying, 'They're real, they're real.' "

"You can't come with me. Someone must stay here."

"Please," Betsy beseeched. "Look at her, Mrs. Meeks. She's still dead to the world. I'll run right back the minute I feel that pearl."

Take her, Eden silently urged.

The housekeeper relented with a short sigh. "Very well, one minute, and no more! But let's hurry. If Lord Pierce discovers the lass alone, we're apt to have a rare taste of his temper."

Eden waited until she heard footsteps moving down the hallway. She opened her eyes. She lay in the middle of a canopied bed centered in a huge, handsomely furnished room. The furniture was polished to a high sheen. Along the wall beside an ornate wardrobe was a set of French doors. One was slightly open and the drapes covering it shifted gracefully in the breeze. Lord Pierce was a man of means.

She threw back the sheets. Her first impulse was to flee. Immediately. They could keep her dresses. She wanted her freedom.

However, her first attempt to stand was not successful. The world spun dizzily and she sat back down on the edge of the bed. On the second try, she succeeded in maintaining her balance and carefully made her way across the thick carpet over to the ornate wardrobe.

Clothes, she needed clothes. The oversized cotton and lace nightdress she had on kept slipping down over her shoulder. She needed a serviceable dress that wouldn't call too much attention to herself.

She threw open the wardrobe door. It was empty.

Alarmed, she started to hurry over to the dresser on the opposite wall, but swerved abruptly when she heard footsteps in the hallway. Betsy giggled and a deep male voice answered.

Eden panicked. She didn't want to be trapped here in the room until she knew if she was in danger or not. Without pausing to think, she slipped out the French doors—and stopped.

Before her lay the most magnificent garden she'd ever seen. It was as if the garden she'd conjured in her dreams had come to life. Her fears faded, replaced with awe.

Blue delphinium, yellow coreopsis, and purplish-red bee balm mingled with daisies, violet-blue flax, evergreen germander, and the silver, fleecy leaves of the herb lamb's ear. The blooms all crowded and tumbled over each other in profusion, creating a visual feast in the morning sunshine.

Roses were everywhere. They climbed the gray stone walls of the house that hemmed the garden in on three sides. Rosebushes formed a border around a charming stone pond with a single fountain sprouting water upwards into a cloudless blue sky. This was the sound of water that she'd heard.

The house itself was a hodgepodge of styles as if each succeeding generation had added its own mark, but it wasn't unattractive. Instead, the house looked lived in, and loved. A person who belonged here would be most fortunate.

She followed the flagstone path, drawn to the music of splashing water. Dew still clung to the leaves of white sweet alyssum, pinks, and daisies lining the walk. Not a soul stirred from the windows overlooking the garden and she could almost believe herself alone in the world.

Filled with wonder and a sense of contentment, she flipped her hair out of the way over one shoulder and bent down to smell the fragrance of a single, red rose. The petals felt velvety cool against her skin. *Oh, that everything in life could be this perfect . . .*

A prickling sensation along her neck warned her she was being watched. The garden's spell was broken. She whirled to look back at the doors she'd just exited. No one was there. She turned—and then froze.

A man stood by the corner of the house.

He was darkly handsome with hair as black as coal. His thick brows gave his face character, preventing him from being too physically perfect while adding to his masculinity.

For the space of several heartbeats, they stared at each other, unmoving. Eden could feel his presence even with the distance between them.

He began striding toward her. She watched him, mesmerized.

This was no mere mortal—he couldn't be! As he came toward her, the morning sun seemed to form a halo around him.

The plain white shirt he wore open at the neck emphasized the strength and breadth of his broad shoulders. His buff-colored breeches clung to powerful thighs and sunlight glinted off the shine of his black top boots. A slight breeze ruffled his hair and he impatiently flicked it back with his fingers.

He stopped, the red rosebush between them.

His eyes mirrored the same vivid blue of the sky above them. Eden stared at him, taking in the shadow of his beard, the laugh lines at the corner of his wide, generous mouth.

"You're awake." His voice was a deep, rich baritone. She could feel its timbre all the way down to her toes.

She pulled back, suddenly remembering herself. She might have turned to run, except that he'd anticipated her move and caught hold of her hand.

His hands were rough, a sign he was accustomed to hard work, but the fingers were long and tapered.

"Don't be afraid," he said. "I won't harm you. I want to help." He paused, and then raised her hand to his lips, his gaze locking with hers.

Something distinctly feminine rose and unfurled inside Eden. The garden, the sky, even the firm feel of the earth beneath her feet faded into oblivion and there was only this man, and the brush of his lips against the back of her hand. Her skin tingled at his touch, and then warmed.

"Let me be bold enough to introduce myself. I'm Pierce Kirrier, the earl of Penhollow."

Lord Pierce. And he was everything she'd ever imagined a lord should be.

Eden gave her head a small shake, struggling to clear her befuddled senses. The oversized gown slipped off one shoulder. His eyes followed the movement of the material, and then rested on her bare shoulder. His hold tightened and she could feel his body tense.

Eden recognized the flash of lust in his eyes. Numerous men had stared at her in such a way . . . but this time, she seemed to be equally affected.

He released his hold on her hand and it took a second before she realized she was free. She demurely pulled the gown up over her shoulder. "It is a pleasure to meet you, my lord." She almost didn't recognize the huskiness in her voice.

"As I am you," he answered with a cavalier's courtliness before prodding, "Miss . . . ?"

"Eden—" she started without thinking and then stopped. *What was she doing?* What sorcery did this man wield to make her forget how dangerous her situation was?

"Eden," he said, testing her name, and then smiled as if he liked it. "Like the garden."

"Yes."

"And your last name?"

Eden shook her head. She wasn't about to divulge any more information. Images of Nasim and Gadi flashed through her mind. She shied away, backing toward the French doors.

He followed. "Wait, I've upset you and that wasn't my intention. I need to know where you're from and how you came to be adrift in that boat so that I can help you."

Eden hurried toward the French doors. She wasn't going to give him information that would lead anyone to her.

He grabbed her elbow and turned her around, gently forcing her to face him. "Miss Eden, you have suffered a horrible ordeal. You do not need to tell me any more than you wish. I will not pry. I think only of seeing you safely returned home."

"Home?" she repeated bitterly. "I don't think I know the meaning of the word." For the first time, she realized exactly how alone she was, how hopeless her situation. The colorful flowers of the garden started spinning, and to her horror she discovered she was about to swoon.

"Miss Eden, are you all right?" She heard his voice as if it came from the end of a very long tunnel. She reached out, searching for something to hold—and found him.

Strong arms captured her before she fell to the ground and she was vaguely conscious of being carried over to the bench beside the fountain.

Pierce carefully lowered the young woman to the bench, very conscious of the fact she was naked beneath the oversized nightgown. He knelt on the ground beside her, an arm around her shoulders. Her hair felt silky smooth. He could see the shadow of her nipples beneath the material.

No woman had been more aptly named. *Eden*.

Lush. Exotic. Mysterious Eden.

The heady, demanding rush of sexual desire pounded through his veins, mingling with common sense. She'd been running away from him before she swooned.

Her lashes fluttered.

"Are you all right?"

She blushed. The color was becoming in

spite of the sunburn she'd suffered. Several pale freckles dotted her nose. "Yes, I think so." She sat up on her own, pulling away from him, her gaze lowered. "Thank you. I've never done that before."

Pierce rose to his feet. "You shouldn't feel embarrassed. You're lucky to be alive."

"I am, aren't I?" She raised magnificent green eyes up to meet his, pinning him with her gaze. "And I have you to thank for rescuing me."

For the first time in his life, Pierce felt tongue-tied. He dared not speak for fear he'd babble. His throat had grown dry and the air around them seemed to have suddenly turned unusually warm . . . especially when he noticed that her nipples had hardened, tempting him to throw civilization aside and make love to her on the garden bench in the bright, full light of day.

Mrs. Meeks's voice snapped him back to reality. "Lord Penhollow, we're blessed that you found her!"

She charged across the garden to them while Betsy stood anxiously in the doorway.

"We only turned our backs on her for one moment, my lord, and the lass disappeared. Lucky we are you found her." The housekeeper skidded to a halt and bobbed a quick curtsy. "I'll take her in now. Dr. Hargrave has just arrived and is anxious to see her."

Pierce stepped protectively in front of Eden. "Mrs. Meeks, I thought I ordered you to stay by her side."

The housekeeper winced. "That you did, my lord."

Pierce shook his head. "You heard about the dresses in the laundry, didn't you?"

"Oh, they are beautiful, my lord," she said on a sigh.

"I suspected you would have to take a peek. Let's see if we can't take better care of our guest, shall we?"

"That we shall, my lord. Come, dear, let's take you inside," Mrs. Meeks said, motioning Eden to step forward, but the young woman turned to Pierce.

"You aren't going to punish her, are you?" she asked, her eyes wide with alarm.

He gave a sharp laugh. "If I thought it would do any good, I might try. No, Miss Eden, I wouldn't dare punish Mrs. Meeks or any of these rascals from Hobbles Moor who claim to be *my* servants. Mrs. Meeks has been with the family since before I was born and I know her better than I know my own mother."

"And listens to me better, too," Mrs. Meeks added cheekily. She didn't wait for Pierce's retort but reached for Eden and started shepherding her toward the bedroom door. "You poor lass," she crooned. "You must be in a terrible state to be wandering the garden half dressed. And barefooted too! We shall change all that, and I'll send Betsy for a pot of tea and some toast. You'd like that, wouldn't you, miss?"

Eden nodded but sent a cautious look over her shoulder toward Pierce. He nodded his encouragement but she didn't seem to relax. In fact, Mrs. Meeks was almost having to prod her toward the house.

Very curious . . . Pierce found himself wondering just exactly why Eden had been in the garden when she obviously should have stayed in bed and rested. The dark circles under her eyes attested to her need for more rest.

His mind mulling over Eden's contradictory behavior, he followed the women. He was not so lost in thought that he didn't enjoy the glimpse of very trim ankles from beneath her oversized nightdress. *Eden.*

The pert Betsy noticed his interest and, as he entered the door, she gave him a knowing wink of approval, but they both sobered immediately when they stepped into the bedroom and discovered his mother waiting impatiently. Beside her stood a short, balding man with a bulbous nose, Dr. Hargrave.

At one time, Lady Penhollow had not only been a great heiress but one of the reigning beauties of London. Pierce favored her in looks. They both had dark eyebrows, strong jaws, and blue eyes that could slice a person open with their displeasure if they wished to do so.

But life had been hard for her. After her marriage, she'd thought to settle down to the life of devoted, and beloved, wife. Such was not the case. Pierce's father had not only been vain and selfish but also a dedicated gambler. He'd left his London bride in Cornwall and had gone on to enjoy the high life in the city without the encumbrances of family.

He'd heaped on further humiliation when he'd died leaving his small family destitute. Pierce had been fifteen at the time but he'd grown up fast.

"Why was our guest wandering around the garden?" Lady Penhollow demanded, her voice imperious.

Eden took a step back and almost walked into Pierce. He placed a reassuring hand on her shoulder. Her tension eased slightly. "Miss Eden, this is my mother, Lady Penhollow, and Dr. Hargrave," he said before answering his mother. "She woke and must have become disoriented."

"Disoriented?" Lady Penhollow asked. Her gaze slid from his face down to where his hand rested on Eden's shoulder. She lifted an eyebrow. "Then it is a very good thing Dr. Hargrave is here," she replied succinctly.

Crossing over to Eden, she stepped between the girl and Pierce. Placing her own Norwich wool shawl around Eden's shoulders, she steered her toward the good doctor. Eden looked back at him, anxiety widening her eyes.

Pierce knew his mother well. She wasn't motivated by a sense of protectiveness. No, her actions were her not-so-subtle way of letting him know she considered Miss Eden unsuitable.

He stepped forward, refusing to be ruled by his mother. "It is good of you to drop by, Horace," he said. "This is Miss Eden. I'm afraid she doesn't seem to remember her last name," he said.

"Doesn't remember?" Dr. Hargrave said, a sparkle of interest appearing in his eyes.

"How odd." Lady Penhollow droned the words out with just the right suspicious inflection.

Pierce felt a flash of anger, especially when Miss Eden looked ready to stammer out some sort of explanation. He smoothly took command. "Miss Eden, Dr. Hargrave is the best physic in Cornwall. Trust him . . . and don't feel you owe any of us an apology of any sort," he said in a low voice.

She glanced up at him, and then rewarded him with a shy smile. *It's impossible,* he thought. *She's even more beautiful when she smiles.* Lost in that smile, he almost forgot where he was—that is, until Dr. Hargrave spoke.

"Explain to me again what happened when she woke, Lord Penhollow," he ordered. He set his black doctor's bag which carried his leeches and the like by the side of the bed, giving Pierce a moment to regain his bearings before repeating the events from when he found Eden in the garden.

"This isn't a good sign. Not good at all," the doctor said. "I shall have to examine her."

"Examine?" Eden asked, turning to Pierce.

"It's all right," he assured her. "Dr. Hargrave won't harm you."

"Of course, I won't harm her," Dr. Hargrave said. He lifted her chin and looked into her eyes. For a moment, Pierce sensed the doctor was not immune to Eden's beauty either and he felt a second of jealousy.

But then Dr. Hargrave blustered, "That nonsense about fearing physicians is old-fashioned. There are few of us who are quacks anymore. It's all science now." He began feeling her head with his fingertips as if searching for bumps. "For privacy's sake, I'm going to ask you and your mother to please step from the room, my lord. It should only take a few minutes. I would also like you to leave one of the maids, if you would."

Pierce nodded for Mrs. Meeks to stay and then gestured for his mother to precede him in the direction of the door, but Eden's voice stopped them.

"Please, is it possible that I may have one of my dresses?" she asked diffidently.

Pierce looked to Mrs. Meeks who answered, "They are still far too wet, miss, but Betsy can find you something suitable from . . ." Her voice trailed off as, uncertain how far she could go, she looked toward his mother.

"I'm sure something can be found," his mother said briskly and left the room.

"I'll have Betsy give a look," Mrs. Meeks assured Eden. "We'll find something nice and bring you tea and toast too. She can have that, can't she Dr. Hargrave?"

"Tea and toast? Of course!" he replied absently, as digging in his black bag he pulled out a small, corked bottle and a large spoon. "And while you're at it, I'll give her a dose of castor oil. Good for the system," he assured Eden.

"Castor oil?" Eden blurted out.

"Aye, it's the best medicine there is," Dr.

Hargrave answered, pouring the oil into the spoon. Betsy bobbed a curtsy and quickly left the room.

Eden turned to Pierce with pleading eyes. "I'm not going to swallow castor oil."

"Just a wee bit," Dr. Hargrave promised.

"I don't—" Eden started to protest but whatever else she was going to say was cut off when the good doctor slipped the spoon in her mouth.

For a second, she sat wide-eyed, her mouth full of castor oil. She looked up at Pierce in distress.

"Best medicine there is," he reminded her, his tone deliberately light.

She shot him a fierce frown in response.

"Swallow it up," Mrs. Meeks advised. "It won't go away any other way."

With a grimace, Eden did just that. Her expression was almost comical except that Pierce sensed real upset in her. Dr. Hargrave's castor oil cure was probably the worst way to top her day. "I'll tell Betsy to add some jam to your order of toast." He left the room, closing the door behind him.

His mother waited for him in the hallway. "This girl doesn't remember what happened to her?" she demanded with patent disbelief.

"That's what Miss Eden said." Pierce shifted his attention from his mother to study the portrait of one of his ancestors hanging on the wall.

"Perhaps we should send her to the vicar. Let the parish take care of her."

Her words grabbed his attention. He faced

her. "Absolutely not. She stays here." Where he could protect her.

"I don't think it is wise. We don't know who she is. It's unreasonable for her to stay here."

"Mother, she's in need of our charity."

She drew back, the lines of her face tightening with suspicion. "Is she?"

Pierce made an impatient sound. "You aren't going to suggest that she shipwrecked herself, are you? I find that idea ludicrous."

"No! But I am suggesting that perhaps she would be better in the hands of the parish." She raised a hand to stop him from protesting. "I understand why you brought her here, and I'm glad you did. However, I would be remiss if I didn't express concern."

"Concern over what?"

His mother clasped her hands in front of her. "Pierce, you must understand, women are intuitive. We perceive things about each other that men don't often see. My intuition is telling me that Miss Eden is not what we think she is."

"And upon what basis do you make such a judgment?"

"Not any one thing in particular. It's just a feeling I have. For example, she's too beautiful and too well-spoken to be found adrift alone in a boat."

And it is obvious that your son is too attracted to her, Pierce thought cynically. His mother was a manipulator. Sometimes he wondered if that wasn't why his father had left.

"She's a soul in need of our help," he said quietly.

"True," she hurried to agree. "However, what respectable young woman would be walking in our garden with nothing on but her nightdress?"

Pierce clenched his fist. "A disoriented one. A woman who woke without knowing where she was or why."

"Yes, yes, you're right, but . . ." She hesitated dramatically and then shrugged. "I can't help my worries. I'm your mother after all. I'm just questioning whether *we* are doing the right thing."

Pierce stared through her. "She stays." With those words, he crossed his arms, signaling that their discussion was ended, and waited for Dr. Hargrave to finish his examination.

Around the corner of a hallway leading to the kitchen, Betsy eavesdropped on the exchange between mother and son. When she heard Lord Pierce put his mother in her place, she did a small victory jig and set off to tell the others in the kitchen what she'd just seen and heard.

Chapter 4

Eden heard the sharp voices outside the door but she wasn't able to make out the muffled words. She knew with certainty the argument between Lord Penhollow and his mother concerned her.

Lady Penhollow didn't like her. Eden had sensed it immediately . . . and she knew why. It had to do with the almost magnetic attraction between herself and Lord Penhollow.

Eden had never felt such an awareness for a man before—and that didn't bode well for her own plans which were to escape this house and be on her way as quickly as possible. Especially if Dr. Hargrave insisted on another dose of castor oil!

The doctor and Mrs. Meeks both pretended they hadn't heard the arguing although she'd caught them exchanging glances. Eden decided she could pretend too.

"Does this hurt?" Dr. Hargrave asked, interrupting her thoughts. His fingers pressed into her scalp. Eden winced.

"You feel that bump there, don't you?"

"A bump?" Eden raised her hand up to where his fingers were. She'd cracked her head on the side of the dinghy when it had fallen into the ocean. The bump was the size of a robin's egg.

"Does it hurt?" he asked.

Eden shook her head. "I barely noticed it."

"Good," he said in his abrupt way. He sat on the chair in front of her. "Everything seems to be fine, Miss Eden. I can detect no ill effects from your mishap other than a bit of sunburn. Perhaps it was good that Lord Penhollow refused to let me bleed you last night. He sensed you would come around on your own and so you have. But I need to ask you a few questions, if you would be so patient?"

Aware of Mrs. Meeks's presence, and the woman's penchant for gossip, Eden forced a smile. "I'll answer whatever I can."

"That's all I ask," the doctor said. He leaned forward, pushing his spectacles up on his nose. "Lord Penhollow said you don't remember your last name. Is there anything else you don't remember?"

"Would I know what to remember if I didn't remember it?" Eden hedged, shifting uncomfortably on the edge of the bed.

Dr. Hargrave blinked, then gave a sharp bark of laughter. "Very good, yes, very good. Well, we shall see now. Tell me, do you have any family?"

"I don't know," Eden answered truthfully.

"Think, Miss Eden. Search your memory for any clue. There must be people who care for you. Someone who would miss your presence?"

Eden pretended to do as he asked, while her mind scrambled frantically, trying to decide what to do. After several minutes, she shook her head. "No, Doctor, I remember nothing." He was such a kind man, she had trouble meeting his gaze, but better to say nothing than to give herself away.

The corners of Dr. Hargrave's mouth curved down thoughtfully. "This is not good. Not good at all." He proceeded to ask her many questions about her past.

To each she answered, "I don't know." She felt foolish, sure that at any moment Dr. Hargrave would denounce her as a liar, but it was the course she'd started and the only way to not divulge personal information about herself.

Surprisingly, he grew more excited with each "I don't know" answer.

A knock on the door interrupted them. Betsy entered with a tray. "Ah, the toast and tea we ordered," Dr. Hargrave said heartily. "And exactly when we needed it."

Betsy set the tray upon the bedside table and unfolded a dress she held over one arm. It was a simple dress of plain burgundy cotton. "This is the best I could find," she told Mrs. Meeks.

"It's last year's uniforms for the staff," Mrs. Meeks said apologetically to Eden. "The dress is a bit worn, but it is clean and serviceable."

"It will be fine," Eden assured her, taking the dress from Betsy. In fact, it would be a better disguise for hiding from Nasim than the rich dresses she'd brought with her.

As Betsy poured out a cup of tea, Eden's stomach growled loudly at the smell of fresh bread. She wished she'd thought to ask for an egg too.

"Ah, she's hungry," Mrs. Meeks said with a motherly smile.

"And it is a good sign too," Dr. Hargrave said, rising. "I shall leave you to your breakfast, my dear, while I consult a moment with Lord Penhollow and Lady Penhollow." He motioned for the servants to leave with him, shutting the door behind them.

At last, Eden was alone.

Taking a huge bite of buttered toast, she counted to twenty-five before she put the bread back on the tray. Tiptoeing to the door, she cracked it open. She could see the back of the doctor's head and a portion of Lady Penhollow's face. Lord Penhollow was out of her view. She slid down to the floor to listen, praying that Dr. Hargrave wasn't suspicious.

Dr. Hargrave was having an earnest discussion with Lady Penhollow and her son.

". . . suffered a bump on the head which has led to a loss of memory."

Lady Penhollow's eyes narrowed. "Did you *feel* a bump on her head when you examined her?"

"I did, my lady. It's located on the right side, twenty centimeters above the ear. Furthermore, a trauma of some sort can cause memory loss. It's rare, but there are recorded cases of such a thing happening."

"Humph," Lady Penhollow said, her lips pinched together in disbelief.

Eden leaned her head against the door frame in surprise. Who would have thought there was such a thing as memory loss? And how fortunate the doctor believed she suffered from it.

"I know it sounds freakish," Dr. Hargrave quickly averred. "But it can happen. There are documented cases of people forgetting who they are even down to their very own names."

"But our patient has some memory. Are there recorded cases of such a thing as that?" Lady Penhollow asked, arching one eyebrow.

"Yes," he said, removing his spectacles from his nose and polishing the lenses with a kerchief.

"Will her memory ever return?" Lord Penhollow asked.

"I don't know," the doctor answered. "She may recover her memory in an hour or two or perhaps not for years."

"Years!" Lady Penhollow interjected. She turned to her son. "She can't stay here for years!"

Lord Penhollow ignored her. "Is there a name for this condition?"

"They call it amnesia. When I return home, I intend to consult my medical journals for as much information as I can read on the subject. Until then, I presume she is under your care."

"Yes," Lord Penhollow said.

"But she *can* remember her first name," Lady Penhollow protested.

"Amnesia appears to have that effect on

some victims," Dr. Hargrave answered. "I remember reading a particularly interesting treatise on a patient who could remember everything that had happened five years earlier in detail, but could not remember her husband, whom she'd married during that missing five-year period of time, or the children they'd had together."

Eden listened carefully, so that she could convincingly pretend to have this amnesia.

"Do you believe she is married?" Lord Penhollow asked. "With a husband and children?"

"I don't know," Dr. Hargrave said. "She doesn't wear a ring but you said yourself there wasn't a sign of money or identification with her other than the religious medallion around her neck. Because of her youth, I only made a cursory exam, but from my initial observations, I doubt if she has had children. I could be wrong."

"The medallion and her clothing are our only clues to her identity," Lord Penhollow said thoughtfully. "Her wardrobe could belong to a princess."

"A princess! Now, Pierce, you are being fanciful," his mother said.

Eden rather liked the comparison.

"Am I, Mother? Yes, I do suppose her story sounds a bit like a fairy tale."

"Or a Banbury tale," she shot back.

"Either way, we will know the truth soon," Lord Penhollow said. "The riders I sent out last night are all back. There is no word of a shipwreck or of anyone missing a wife, sister, or daughter in the ports of Plymouth, Weymouth, or Touquay."

"Are you not surprised?" Lady Penhollow said, her voice laced with sarcasm. She leaned toward her son. "Turn her over to the parish. You've done what you can for her."

He sliced his hand through the air, a warning to his mother. "It has already been settled. She will stay with us until we can locate her family."

The hem of Lady Penhollow's skirts swayed as she bristled with irritation, but she didn't argue with him. Instead, she said in a long-suffering voice, "Very well. I cannot prevent you from being a fool. Come, Doctor, let me see you to the door." She turned on her heel and without waiting, marched away.

The good doctor looked from Lord Penhollow to the retreating figure of Lady Penhollow and back. He shifted, closer to the door, blocking Eden's line of sight. "I'm sorry if my diagnosis has created some problems for you."

Lord Penhollow shook his head. "It isn't your fault, Horace. You know how she is."

"Yes." Dr. Hargrave paused thoughtfully. "Still, I'm sorry."

Lord Penhollow made no response.

Having nothing further to say, the doctor hurried after Lady Penhollow.

Eden sat back, turning over in her mind everything she'd just witnessed. Absently, she pressed on the door to close it and was surprised when it didn't shut.

She glanced up. Shining black topboots stood in the doorway . . . Her gaze traveled upward. Lord Penhollow leaned against the door frame, the tips of his fingers pressing the door open.

Eden rose to her feet. She'd been caught. Her flesh heated with embarrassment, but she brazened it out. "I needed a fresh pot of tea."

His eyes gleamed with amusement. He knew exactly what she'd been doing. "I'll see that one is sent to you."

"Thank you." She started to close the door but he reached out and held it open with the flat of his palm.

"I don't blame you for being anxious, or curious, Miss Eden . . . but I hope you don't take anything my mother says seriously. She has the alarming habit of jumping to conclusions and overstating her mind. She means nothing by it."

"I doubt that."

He pushed the door open further and slipped inside. The force of his presence filled the room. Her heart beat heavily as she looked up at him. They stood only a hand's width apart and yet she couldn't move, even to take one step back.

He closed the door but left his hand on the handle. "I don't want you to worry. However long it takes, you're safe here . . . and if you recover your memory and discover there are desperate circumstances that led you to risk your life in that small boat, you have only to turn to me. I will see that no harm comes to you."

Eden stared up into his eyes. She could see tiny reflections of herself in them. "And what do you expect me to do in return?"

Her words caught him off guard. She could tell by the sharp intake of breath and the way his eyes darkened as the meaning of her words struck home. He shifted away, his manner suddenly formal and correct. "Miss Eden, if I've given you the impression that you are expected to *repay* me in any fashion, I am sorry. My offer was made without conditions attached."

The spell between them had been broken and Eden quickly moved back. She groped for words. "I'm sorry. I didn't mean to sound churlish."

He didn't answer immediately but studied her a moment. Eden feared he could almost see down into her soul. She crossed her arms protectively against her chest.

"I also thank you for saving my life," she said stiffly. "You are an extraordinary man to go so far for a stranger."

"I didn't do anything that another Cornishman wouldn't have done. We take care of our own here."

"Still, I shouldn't have jumped to a conclusion, especially after you warned me about your mother's alarming tendency to do so."

For a second, their eyes met . . . and then he did something completely unexpected—he smiled. His smile was slightly crooked, not perfect or polished. Eden stood rooted to the floor, charmed.

"I'd wager, Miss Eden, that your wariness comes from experience. Men must often make fools of themselves in the face of beauty such as yours."

She'd been paid compliments before, but none as openly. If he'd opened his arms at that moment, she would have stepped into them.

Instead, he changed the subject. "I shall see that another pot of tea is sent to you and perhaps, when you are dressed, you will allow me to give you a short tour of Penhollow Hall. Dr. Hargrave warned us not to let you over-exert yourself but he did say a touch of exercise is permissible."

"Perhaps we may take a turn in the garden?"

That smile sprang to his lips again. "It would be a pleasure to show you my garden—after you've had a chance to rest. I'll knock on your door in say an hour or so? Will that be fine?"

Eden nodded her head, all power of speech robbed from her by his lazy smile.

"Very well." He opened the door. "I will see you later." He left.

She sank down onto the chair by the bed, her legs no longer able to hold her. Her pulse raced as if she'd run a long distance. What was it about Lord Penhollow that made her mind turn inside out with little more than a smile?

Oh, but it was something more and she knew it. He offered a gallantry she'd only read about. He was like Lancelot and Gawain rolled into one. A hero, a champion . . . a knight in shining armor when she needed one so desperately. And yet she didn't dare embroil these kind people in her problems.

Nassim and Gadi would search for her. They might even return to Madame Indrani for assistance—and Eden feared Madame's anger. What she needed was to keep her wits about her and find a safe haven where no one would look for her.

She washed down the toast with the last of the tea and dressed. Betsy brought her the promised new pot of tea and something she deeply appreciated, a pair of shoes.

"I'm guessing at your size, miss," the maid said. "They may be a bit big, but they are serviceable. Your other shoes were destroyed beyond repair by the saltwater."

Eden tried the black leather shoes on. They were flat-soled and very plain but fit rather nicely. "They will do. Thank you," she told the maid.

Betsy looked as if she'd like to linger and gossip a bit, but Eden discouraged her by asking her to deliver a message to Lord Penhollow.

"Please tell him I've decided to rest and must forgo the pleasure of a walk in the garden."

"Yes, miss," Betsy said with a curtsy and hurried down the hall with bustling self-importance. Eden shut the door. She didn't have time to waste.

She regretted leaving the rich dresses behind, but didn't see how she could sneak through the house and fetch them from the laundry without someone seeing her. Instead, she considered them payment for Lord Penhollow's saving her life. If anything, the dresses might even encumber her plans of escape since selling them would make it easy to trace her.

It was now past mid-morning. Eden slipped out the garden door and paused. The blossoms appeared even more bright and colorful in the full light of sun.

It was all so beautiful and peaceful here. She touched the medallion Mary had given her. A longing for something she couldn't have tugged at her soul, urging her to linger. But she couldn't. If she was ever going to be free, she must travel as far from the coast as possible.

She turned away from the garden and, head held high, walked across the lawn beyond the garden toward a pine forest, hoping to escape unnoticed. At the edge of the forest, she looked back at the gray walls of Penhollow Hall. No cry went up to stop her.

Again, she felt the longing to stay, to belong. But it wasn't to be. She turned her back and slipped into the shelter of the pine forest unnoticed.

The only evergreens Eden had ever seen had been those trained for a garden. But the trees in this forest had grown wild, their trunks massive, while here and there overgrown branches brushed the ground. The floor was layered deep in orange pine needles, muffling all sound. Not even birds could be heard singing.

Eden hesitated. Sunlight filtered down through the trees in definite rays of light. It was like a separate world from the happy color in the garden.

Cautiously, she walked forward, the ground spongy beneath her feet. She'd not gone more than a dozen steps when a voice, crackled with age, said, "This forest was built two centuries ago to break the wind between Penhollow Hall and the sea."

Eden shrieked in surprise and whirled to face the speaker—and then feared her eyes deceived her.

Beneath the sheltering branches of a pine sat an old woman watching her with filmy blue eyes. She was dressed in brown and gray homespun and the lines on her face had been etched there by age. She had a great head of silver-gray hair she wore gathered at the nape of her neck. A huge brown sack of the same homespun lay on the ground beside her.

For a second, Eden believed she'd conjured the woman from her imagination and fanciful stories of trolls and fairies.

The old woman rose to her feet, leaning heavily on a walking stick. She'd been sitting on a three-legged stool toward which she now nodded. "I have to take it with me everywhere. I don't walk as much as I used to. I need to rest from time to time."

Eden closed her gaping mouth. "Excuse me, are you speaking to me?"

The crone frowned. "Who else would I be speaking to, my dear? There is no one here but you and me . . . except you were leaving. Where were you going?"

"Do you know who I am?" Eden asked.

The woman gave her a toothless grin. "Do you know who *I* am?" she parroted.

Eden took a step back, and then decided this conversation was ludicrous and to keep walking. Her head down, she started to do exactly that when the old woman cried out, "Halt."

Eden stopped.

"You can't run away from your destiny," the woman said. Her words rang in the stillness of the forest.

Eden turned. "Who are you?"

"I'm the Widow Haskell, dear. I've been waiting for you."

The Widow Haskell . . . the woman Betsy had called a charmer. "For me? You don't know me."

"Oh, but you are wrong, Eden."

"How do you know my name?"

"I've seen you coming. I called you from the sea. We've all been waiting for you."

A coldness crept up Eden's spine at her words. "I don't know what you're talking about."

"Of course you don't. But I can't let you run away. Not yet. Your fate is here."

Fear of discovery coursed through Eden. "What do you know about my fate, or about me?"

The Widow leaned heavily on her walking stick. "I know it is not your time to leave. You've only just arrived and must see the play through to the end."

"The play? You're speaking gibberish. I know nothing of a play."

"Of course you don't, child, but you have a

role nonetheless. And you must stay until it's done."

"I can't stay," Eden confessed with brutal honesty.

The Widow picked up the three-legged stool. "I will not argue with you, Eden. Your fate is here. The question is, are you bold enough to meet it?"

"There are people who will be looking for me. I must not let them find me."

"So you plan to run all your life?"

Eden fingered the medallion Mary had given her. "I have no choice."

"We all have choices, Eden. Every one of us. But I will tell you this, there is no finer man than the Lord of Penhollow. You have been sent for him and he will protect you."

"He barely knows me."

The crone smiled benignly. "The choice is yours." She tucked her stool into the sack. Hoisting the sack on her shoulder, she turned and began walking away from Eden through the forest.

Eden took a step after her. "Wait! I want to know more. Why do you say I was sent? *How* can he protect me? What do you see that I don't?"

But the Widow kept walking.

"Please!" Eden called.

"Courage," came the faint response as the old woman continued her way out of the forest without stopping. A few seconds later, she was out of sight.

Courage. *May you have the courage to free yourself.* Mary's words.

Eden clasped the medallion in her hand. Courage.

She stood in indecision, "what if's" crowding her mind . . . but in her heart, she wanted to believe the Widow's words—even as her common sense warned her there was no such thing as fate or destiny. Not for girls born in the gutters of London. Not for slaves running from their captors.

But then, a man offered protection in return for certain favors . . . and a woman would be very fortunate to have Lord Penhollow for a protector.

Eden turned and faced the direction of Penhollow Hall. The sunlight shafting through the pine branches seemed to mark a path back in the direction from which she'd come.

Fate.

Slowly, almost without conscious thought, she began walking back toward the house, the garden, and the Lord of Penhollow Hall because just for once, she wanted to believe.

In a scene that was replayed in the homes of every member of the gentry boasting a marriageable daughter, Mrs. Willis burst into her husband's bedroom without knocking. Her hair was half combed, her toilette half complete, and she still wore her dressing gown. Her husband, who enjoyed late mornings, slept soundly.

"Mr. Willis, you must wake this very second! Something dreadful has happened!" She gave his shoulder a rough shove.

Mr. Willis came awake with a groggy start. "Are the stables on fire?"

"No, it's something worse!"

His eyes opened wide at her statement. "Something worse?" he repeated in disbelief. He pushed back the bedclothes and squinted at his wife from under his night cap. "What is it, my dove? Has the King died and we are forced to crown that fool Regent? Or has Napoleon escaped again and is now threatening Cornwall?"

Mrs. Willis sat down on his bed with a flounce. "Lord Penhollow has chosen a bride."

She had Mr. Willis's full attention now. "A bride! Penhollow? This is a bit sudden, isn't it? And what of our Victoria?"

"What *of* our dear daughter?" his wife cried. "She shall be heartbroken . . . and just when I was beginning to have hopes. He's always been unfailingly polite to her. Very proper. In time she would have sparked his interest. Now, I feel betrayed. Betrayed, I tell you!" She broke out into noisy tears.

Mr. Willis climbed from his bed. He wore a nightshirt that hung down past his bony knees. He slid his feet into his slippers. "That's preposterous! I saw Penhollow the day before yesterday. If the man had contracted a marriage, he would have told me so himself. What proof have you that he has made an offer?"

Mrs. Willis loudly blew her nose into her delicate lace handkerchief. "I had the information from my dresser, who heard it from the cook, who received word of it last night from her cousin whom she went to visit in the village *and*—" She emphasized the last word lest her husband think she were trading in rumor. "—to be certain . . . I questioned the downstairs parlor maid, who claims the story is true. The maid said that everyone in Hobbles Moor knows that Lord Penhollow's bride has arrived. She said the bride is at Penhollow Hall at this very moment."

Mr. Willis sank down on the bed beside his wife. "Well, this is unusually fast action for Penhollow. I'd always thought him a singularly prudent and circumspect young man. Are you certain, my dove?"

"Would the servants be gossiping about it if it wasn't true?"

"No, of course not." He sat in silence a moment, before conceding with a sigh, "I see nothing we can do but to wish him well then."

"Nothing we can do?" Mrs. Willis jumped to her feet. "I'm not going to give up. Not yet! He's too good a match."

"But what can you do, Dovie?"

Mrs. Willis marched to the door before announcing grandly, "I will see this woman for myself! You are right, Mr. Willis. This is all too quick. Furthermore, Annabelle Penhollow would have told *me* if her son was planning to become betrothed. I want to see this 'bride' for myself!"

On those words, she sailed out the door to finish her morning toilette.

Chapter 5

Lady Penhollow sat on one of the cushioned chairs in her favorite room in the house, the Garden Room. The bank of windows overlooking the garden was open and she could hear the splashing water in the fountain, a usually soothing sound. But not today.

She stared in front of her with unseeing eyes, her mind reeling from the implications of Pierce's infatuation with this stranger.

No, warned a small voice inside her, *this is more than mere infatuation. She's the one.*

The one.

Her future daughter-in-law . . .

Her every mother's instinct warned her that this could be so. There was an air of interest about Pierce that was a touch more intense and marked than he'd ever demonstrated for a woman before.

Then there was his almost proprietary behavior toward the girl, as if in saving her life she'd become his personal responsibility. He'd been genuinely disappointed when Betsy had delivered the message that Miss Eden wished to rest and would not be able to go for a walk. And instead of returning to his study or going about his business as he normally would, he'd actually lingered around the hallway leading to her room, his expression concerned.

If Lady Penhollow hadn't known better, she would have said this Miss Eden had cast a spell upon her normally sane and sensible son—

She broke off such silly thoughts, chiding herself for thinking nonsense! He was interested in Miss Eden because she was uncommonly beautiful. Her looks would interest any male . . . although beauty alone had never turned Pierce's head before, she realized with dismay. After all, she'd already paraded a host of girls as beautiful as Miss Eden before him without any desired effect.

So why was he so taken with this one?

Lady Penhollow loved her son and wanted to see him dutifully married. He had a responsibility to produce an heir and the time had come for him to get on with it.

But a suitable bride for Pierce would have to have a sweet, amenable disposition—the kind of young woman who would not insist Pierce move his mother out of the house.

She did not want to spend the last years of her life lonely and unwanted. She was all too aware that in spite of her title, she was still Annabelle Longstead, the daughter of a very wealthy butcher. Her marriage settlement was long gone and she had no family left other than her son. She wanted to stay at Penhollow Hall and feared being sent away even as far as the dowager cottage. She longed to hold her grandchildren in her arms and hear the sound of childish laughter again in the hallways and corridors of this heartless Cornish estate.

What would happen to her if Pierce formed an attachment for this Miss Eden?

Last night, he'd refused to leave her side until after the doctor had seen her and even then, he and Dr. Hargrave had argued over her treatment. Of course, one rarely argued with Pierce. His was an iron will and few people opposed him.

She also knew that one of the reasons he hadn't married yet was because of her relationship with his father. His view of marriage was not a happy one—but marrying a complete stranger of unknown social class was not the answer!

At that moment, Rawlins, the butler, interrupted her thoughts. "Lady Penhollow, Mrs. Willis, Lady Baines, and Lady Danbury have come to call. Shall I send them in?"

"Yes, please, and have Lucy prepare a tray for us. Cakes and Ratafia, if we have any. Oh, yes, and a pot of tea for Mrs. Willis. She is very fond of tea."

"Yes, ma'am." He bowed out.

Lady Penhollow was thankful for her friends' timely arrival. They were new friends actually. It had taken years before Cornish society, such as it was, had accepted Annabelle, the countess of Penhollow, and even now she was aware that their acceptance hinged on the goodwill of her son whom all seemed to like and respect.

They would not visit her if she was reduced to living in the dowager's cottage.

A moment later, Millie Willis sailed through the doorway. "Annabelle! What a lovely morning. Can you believe our good fortune to have two perfect days in a row? It feels almost as if we were in London." Mrs. Willis detested country life and enjoyed rattling on and on and on about the sights in the city. Lady Penhollow had often wondered, based upon what the woman said, if Mrs. Willis had ever been there—but she didn't dare question her.

"How good to see you all," Lady Penhollow said. "I've asked for a pot of tea and some Ratafia. I hope you have time to share a glass."

"Oh, we do, we do," Mrs. Willis responded, pulling off her gloves. She smiled at Betsy who was carrying the tray loaded with tea items into the room. "I've always liked this room, Annabelle."

"Yes, it's my favorite too," Lady Baines chimed in. She perched herself on the edge of the chintz settee. The heavier Lady Danbury sank down beside her.

For a moment, they discussed banalities like Lady Penhollow's needlework while Betsy finished setting up the tray on a table in front of the settee. "Please shut the door behind you, Betsy," Lady Penhollow said when the maid was done.

"Yes, ma'am." She closed the door.

The lock no sooner clicked into place than Mrs. Willis whirled around to confront her, her face a mask of fury. "And this room is where we've spent *hours* discussing ways to get our two children together in marriage. Annabelle! I can't believe you would be so unfeeling as to let us learn from the servants instead of informing us yourself."

"Learn what?" Lady Penhollow asked. She looked at Lady Baines and Lady Danbury who also frowned at her with disapproval. "I'm sorry, is something the matter?"

"Oh, no, nothing is the matter," Mrs. Willis said with false sweetness before adding through clenched teeth, "Only that your son has contracted to be married!"

"What?" Lady Penhollow exclaimed, but Mrs. Willis wasn't listening.

"You know Victoria has been besotted with him ever since she left the schoolroom last year."

"It's true, it's true," Lady Baines said, helping herself to a tea cake. She offered one to Lady Danbury.

"Wait. Please," Lady Penhollow said, holding up her hands for attention. "What are you talking about?" She glanced over her shoulder before adding, "And please, let us keep our voices down. You know how the servants like to eavesdrop."

"I know all too well," Mrs. Willis said stiffly. "However, I'm afraid I won't be able to stay. Neither will Letitia or Emily." Both Lady Baines and Lady Danbury, upon hearing their names, guiltily put the cakes back on the plate.

Mrs. Willis moved to the door. "I only came here to confront you with the truth and to let you know I think it shabby beyond repair that one of your closest friends must learn secondhand of your son's betrothal."

"Betrothal—?" Lady Penhollow almost choked on the word.

Mrs. Willis would have marched out the door, followed by Lady Danbury and Lady Baines, except that Lady Penhollow hurried to block her way. "Millie, there is no betrothal," she said.

"No betrothal?" Mrs. Willis said, lifting a skeptical eyebrow.

"No," Lady Penhollow said. "My son is not contracted to be married. He is still an eligible party."

Mrs. Willis reeled back. "Still eligible?" She glanced over her shoulder at Lady Danbury and Lady Baines who listened round-eyed. She turned back to Lady Penhollow. "Perhaps I have been hasty. We obviously need to discuss this matter."

"You are so right, my dear," Lady Penhollow agreed. She waited for the volatile Mrs. Willis to take a seat before collapsing on the settee next to Lady Baines. Lady Danbury took the seat nearest the cake plate.

"This has already been a trying day," Lady Penhollow said. "You have no idea what my life has suddenly become. But where did you hear such a thing?"

A line formed between Mrs. Willis's brows and she looked sheepish. "I'm not certain."

"But you must have heard it from somewhere," Lady Penhollow prodded.

Finally, Lady Danbury admitted, "*I* heard the news from the downstairs maid."

"And I from the dairyman who told our cook," Lady Baines said.

"Never mind where I heard it," Mrs. Willis grumbled. "But it was the same avenue."

Lady Penhollow rubbed her temples with her fingertips, a headache beginning to form. "I swear, the villagers of Hobbles Moor are going to drive me to madness."

"What do you mean, Annabelle?" Mrs. Willis asked.

Lady Penhollow dropped her hand. "They are on *her* side. I could read it in Mrs. Meeks and Betsy's faces. Even the cook acted strangely when I said something about that woman. They are such a superstitious lot, they've probably decided she's the queen of Cornwall or some such nonsense."

"What woman?" Lady Baines asked, moving to the edge of her seat.

"The woman my son rescued from drowning yesterday."

"Tell us about it," Mrs. Willis said.

Lady Penhollow quickly went over the details.

"Lost her memory?" Mrs. Willis asked.

"Yes. Dr. Hargrave calls it amnesia. The only thing she has remembered so far is her first name, Eden. Isn't that a ridiculous name?"

"Almost sacrilegious," Lady Baines agreed.

"Heathen," Lady Penhollow answered. "But apt. I fear this woman has the ability to wrap my son around her fingers."

"Penhollow?" Mrs. Willis asked in disbelief.

"I'd always thought him the steadiest of men."

"There is something about this woman, something vulnerable that seems to bring out the protective instincts in my son," her hostess answered.

Lady Danbury and Mrs. Willis had been listening to Lady Penhollow's story intently, but Lady Baines's attention appeared to have drifted. Since this was not uncommon for her, it didn't concern Lady Penhollow until Lady Baines asked, "Does she have a perfect figure, flawless skin, and thick, curling sable hair?"

"Why, yes, she does. And green almond-shaped eyes. Cat's eyes. Have you met her, Letitia?" Lady Penhollow said.

"No, but I believe she's strolling in the garden at this very minute."

The three other women turned as one to look in the direction of the garden. Even Lady Penhollow was astonished by the change in Miss Eden. When she'd last seen her, the girl was lovely, yes, but still had the air of a wounded sparrow, shy, diffident.

The woman in the garden was a glorious creature. Somehow, she'd gotten one of her dresses from the laundry. The high-waisted dress was of jade-green silk with a lace overdress and a very low-cut bodice. Little more than a scant piece of expensive lace covered Miss Eden's impressive cleavage while the dress's color drew the viewer's gaze up from the perfection of Miss Eden's figure to her smooth complexion and magnificent eyes.

Her glossy hair was curled and piled high

on her head, captured there by a length of ribbon. The impression was that if a person pulled on the ribbon in just the right manner, her hair would tumble down past her shoulders in wanton disarray.

"She's very . . . pretty." Lady Danbury was the first to break the silence.

All four women stared out the window at the intruder who could destroy Mrs. Willis's and Lady Penhollow's plans for their children. Very deliberately, as if she knew her way, Miss Eden walked across the garden, taking a path that went around the side of the house.

"I can't imagine where she is going with such purpose," Mrs. Willis observed.

"Yes," Lady Danbury echoed. "It's almost as if she is searching for someone."

There was a heartbeat of silence and then Lady Penhollow said, "My son."

"What?" Mrs. Willis asked.

"That path leads to the stables . . . She's looking for Pierce," she concluded with dawning horror. "She's dressed herself up to go meet my son!"

Lady Penhollow turned and would have charged from the room to go in the direction of the stables if not for Mrs. Willis placing her hand on Lady Penhollow's arm.

"Annabelle, don't be foolish."

"Foolish? Did you not see the girl?" Lady Penhollow demanded. "He will take one look at her and be smitten. All will be lost!"

"Yes, and you won't change anything if you run down to the stables at this moment other than to throw him into her arms."

"I want to protect him—"

"But he's a man, Annabelle, and he won't feel he needs protecting. He will not thank you, I can assure you."

"But what do I do? I can't just let her have him."

"Perhaps she is a great heiress," Lady Baines said, "and a wonderful match. Then your fears would be all for naught."

Her friends turned on her, aghast at her disloyalty.

Lady Baines swallowed. "I was attempting to make Annabelle fell better."

Mrs. Willis glared at her.

"But won't Miss Eden be leaving soon? I mean, you can't keep her forever," Lady Danbury offered hopefully.

Lady Penhollow shook her head. "Pierce sent messengers out last night searching for word of a shipwreck or someone missing a sister or daughter. They returned this morning with no word at all. He'll send the messengers out again, but I fear she will be with us for a very, *very* long time. He's insisting she stay until she recovers her memory."

"Wait! I have an idea," Mrs. Willis declared.

"What is it?" Lady Baines asked.

"We shut her out," Mrs. Willis said ruthlessly. "We make him realize she is unsuitable. Even better, we make her miserable until she steps back from Penhollow."

"But how do we do that?" Lady Danbury asked.

The four of them stared at each other. No one spoke until Mrs. Willis piped up again. "I have it! We shall throw a dinner party. We'll say we are welcoming her." He will discover that she doesn't fit in, and see for himself she is not suitable. Nor will he suspect we are anything but gracious."

Lady Baines cast a doubtful eye in the direction of the garden. "I'm not so certain. She is remarkably beautiful."

"Oh, Letitia, don't be so downhearted," Mrs. Willis said. "A man wants more in a wife than looks. If that were the case, opera dancers would be duchesses! This woman has no family, no fortune." Mrs. Willis laughed. "And no memory! Pierce is far too proud and practical to waste his title on a nobody."

"I only pray that you are right," Lady Penhollow said.

"Of course I am," Mrs. Willis answered. "Now draw closer. We have a dinner party to plan."

Her ear to the keyhole of the Garden Room door, Betsy gasped in disbelief. She looked up at Mrs. Meeks and Rawlins standing behind her. "You won't believe what they are planning to do!" she whispered.

"What?" Mrs. Meeks asked.

"They don't believe Miss Eden is good enough for Lord Pierce." Betsy put her ear back to the keyhole and listened again. "They are going to hold a dinner party so that he can see how out of place Miss Eden is and they are going to have their husbands talk to him. Make him understand he can't marry a nobody."

She stood. "Silly aristocrats. Don't they understand? Lord Penhollow is already in love."

"How can he be?" Rawlins asked.

"He's under the spell of the charm," Betsy said confidently. "He's destined to marry Miss Eden. He can't help himself."

Mrs. Meeks wrung her hands. "Charm or not, those women are going to do everything in their power to make sure he *doesn't* marry her."

"Then we'll have to make sure their plans are all for naught, won't we?" Rawlins said.

Both Betsy and Mrs. Meeks turned to the usually dour butler. "What do you have in mind, Mr. Rawlins?" Betsy asked.

"Where is Miss Eden now?"

"I sent her in the direction of the stables, where Lord Penhollow is," Betsy said with a knowing wink.

"Well, if they can get together and make plans, it seems we should be able to do the same," he answered. "What say you to our adjourning the discussion to the kitchen?"

Betsy's face split into a big grin. "I think it is a capital idea."

Chapter 6

The stable yard was quiet after a busy morning. Dane the blacksmith had finished the shoeing and was picking up his tools to walk the mile back to Hobbles Moor. He was a large man with a bald head that matched his size. Few men picked a fight with Dane Smith.

Most of the grooms were busy repairing tack in the shade of the stable or performing other chores assigned to them by Jim, the head groom. Jim was as short as Dane was tall and the two of them, both good friends, made a rather odd couple. Dane rarely spoke whereas Jim never kept his opinions to himself. They enjoyed sharing a pint almost every night in the local public house, and woe to the man who thought to interfere in their discussions for the two of them were fiercely protective of each other.

Fortunately for Pierce, their loyalty extended to include him. He admired both men greatly. They'd taught him everything he knew about horses and had served as surrogate fathers on an occasion or two.

Right now, Pierce was putting that expertise to use as he inspected the most recent addition to his stable, a bay mare that had belonged to one of the Penhollow Hall neighbors. "She's a beauty," he said to Jim.

Jim snorted. "You paid too much."

"Aye, but Royster Blackburn knows I've coveted this animal since I first laid eyes on her. Besides, I'll make back twice her price on each colt I sire off of her and Cornish King."

"But think what you could have made if you'd paid half the price," the Cornishman countered as Pierce leaned over and ran his hand over the mare's glossy coat.

"She's worth the money," Pierce answered. "Plus I like her height and her strength." Leaning over, he admired the broadness of her chest, exactly the way he liked his horses. "But I don't want to turn her over to King right away. Let's give her six months or so. There's no hurry. And what do you think about this cut here?" He motioned to a small surface cut on the animal's knee. "Looks as if she rubbed against something. We'd better apply that salve your wife cooks up. I like it the best of any. I wish she'd share the recipe," he hinted, as he always did when the subject came up.

Jim didn't answer, but Pierce didn't think a thing about that. He rubbed the animal's nose. "She carries the right name—Velvet. You're a beauty, aren't you, girl?" he crooned softly to the mare and received a nudge of appreciation from Velvet.

Pierce laughed and looked over his shoulder

at Jim. "We'll put her in the far—" He broke off, realizing that Jim was not attending him. Instead, the man stared off in the distance—and he wasn't the only one. Dane stood stock-still while the grooms had come to their feet, the tack on the ground around them. All of the men silently watched some point behind Pierce.

Curious, he turned, and then his own mouth dropped open.

In the afternoon sunlight, Eden stood on the path leading to the house, a vision of feminine beauty. She wore a dress of green silk and lace that followed the curves of her lush figure. Her eyes seemed to sparkle while her hairstyle emphasized the perfect oval of her face and the graceful line of her neck. Pierce closed his hand into a fist, his fingers aching to pull the ribbon that held her thick glossy hair up in curls and let it come tumbling down around her—

He broke his thoughts off abruptly. "Miss Eden," he said in greeting, thankful that his voice sounded normal, although a touch strained. He regretted he'd not thought to add a jacket and neckcloth since their last meeting, wishing for the first time in his life to look every inch the earl.

Miss Eden did not seem to be offended by his casual dress. "Lord Penhollow," she greeted him in her low, musical voice that sounded as sweet and welcoming as a siren's song.

Aware they had a very curious audience, Pierce was by her side in four strides. He lowered his voice. "This is a pleasure." He took the hand she offered. She didn't wear gloves and her hand was warm to his touch. Bending over it, he couldn't help but admire the way her breasts swelled over the bodice of her dress, although they were discreetly shielded from his complete view by a piece of strategically placed lace.

Her fingers tightened momentary over his, calling his attention back to her. "I hope my visit to the stables isn't an imposition," she said. "I felt the need for a walk and followed this path by chance."

"How fortunate for me," he answered, straightening, and meant every word.

She didn't answer, but he knew she'd heard the heat in his voice because her cheeks blushed becomingly—and her nipples tightened against the green silk bodice of her gown.

Lust shot through him. He wanted to cover the outline of those buds with his lips, to slip her dress down over her shoulders and feel her against him, right here in the bright light of day . . . and he could swear he saw an answering desire in the depths of her clear green eyes.

Velvet whinnied, bringing him to his senses. Conscious that he'd been holding her hand the whole time, he released it, but not before glancing over his shoulder and noticing that both Jim and Dane's eyes were alive with interest. He took a step back.

Eden had caught his glance in the direction of the grooms and moved back a few steps toward the shelter of the tree whose branches dipped over the path, giving the two of them more privacy from prying eyes. "You should be proud of your gardener, my lord," she said primly, as if they hadn't almost set each other on fire only seconds ago. "I have never seen a more beautiful place on earth than your garden."

Her appreciation was so obviously sincere, Pierce admitted something he rarely said to others. "Actually, I planted the garden, although I have gardeners who take care of it now."

"You planted it? The roses? The flower beds?" She shook her head. "I would never have thought a man could plant such a garden. You're an artist, my lord. You love beauty." She touched his arm. It was a light touch, but it burned through him.

"I started the garden when I was thirteen. Several of the villagers at Hobbles Moor helped. I planted it for my father."

"Your father? Did he also enjoy gardening?"

Pierce almost laughed at the thought. "No, he wasn't a gardener. Actually, when I planted it, he was quite ill. He'd lived in London most of my childhood so I was happy when he returned. Of course, by then he wasn't able to ride or fish or do the things I enjoyed. His breathing was so labored, he couldn't even climb up the stairs to the second floor. That's why we prepared a room for him on the first floor. It's the room you're in."

Her lips formed an "oh" of understanding. "He suffered from consumption."

"Yes." Pierce didn't like to remember. When his mother had discovered that his father also suffered from syphilis, the consumption had been a blessing. He could still recall the ugly fight between his parents he'd overheard coming from his father's bedroom. Pierce had been right outside the French doors, weeding one of the flower beds. Weeding . . . because he'd wanted a father's approval and would never have it.

His father had died without ever mentioning the garden.

She touched him again, this time lightly upon the back of his hand. "He was not a good father, was he?"

Pierce paused, reevaluating his opinion of her. There was more depth to Eden than met the eye. She read people well. He forced a smile. "He had his ways."

"But you were a good son, because that is the type of person you are."

"And what type is that?" he couldn't resist asking.

Her smile was sure and quick. "Noble."

The word pleased him.

Her fingertips brushed his arm again. "You should have no regrets. People are selfish. They do what they wish in spite of the consequences."

There was a beat of silence and then he said, "Sometimes the consequences are worth the endeavor."

Their gazes held. "Yes, sometimes," she echoed.

Jim's loud clearing of his throat broke the spell between them. "Do you want to keep this horse standing out here all afternoon, my lord?" he asked.

Pierce moved back on the path and then stopped. Jim and Dane stood next to each other like matchmaking mamas. Even the grooms were all grinning like whip-silly fools.

"We don't want to disturb your little *tête-á-tête,*" Jim said, his broad Cornish accent butchering the French words.

Pierce shot him a frown but the little groom returned his look with one of wily innocence. Dane was good enough to give Jim a poke in his ribs with his fist.

But Eden ignored the good-natured teasing, walking down the path and into the stable yard. "So these are the most famous stables in England," she said and then gifted the hired men with such a radiant smile, even Jim appeared stunned into silence. "Betsy was telling me about them. She said there are no finer horses in England."

Jim puffed his chest out with pride. "Aye, there are not," he declared, and his grooms nodded agreement. "Wait until you meet King, miss."

"King?" Eden said with surprise. "You know the king, my lord?"

Jim didn't wait for a response from Pierce but shouted at one of the grooms to go fetch Cornish King. "And take this mare back to her stall," he ordered another.

"He refers to my stallion, Cornish King," Pierce told her.

"And no finer horse in all England," Jim declared. "Isn't that right, Dane?"

"Aye, no finer," the blacksmith answered perfunctorily although the two had argued that claim for years. And then the usually closemouthed Dane did something completely out of character. He stepped forward and said almost eagerly, "Did you know that Lord Pierce here is descended from kings himself? King Arthur to be a fact. Penhollow Hall is built right on the foundations of Camelot itself." Then, a dull shade of red creeping up from his neckline, he stepped back beside Jim.

Eden tilted her head up to Pierce with interest, a teasing light in her expressive eyes. "I've heard it said that half of England claims to be descended from Arthur, my lord. Are you one of that half?"

"If half of England is Cornish, it's true," Pierce replied, but conceded with a smile, "But then, there are at least three other lords in Cornwall who also claim that distinction. Of course, I'm the true one."

"And how do you know that, my lord?"

"Because Arthur was a Celt and I'm the only one of the four of us handsome enough to have been descended from Celts."

Her eyes twinkled with laughter while the grooms guffawed. "Celts?" she asked. "Weren't they small men who ran around in wolf skins?"

"You can't see me dressed in wolf skin?" he said, pretending to be offended.

"I could never picture you as a *small* man," she said, flattering him immensely, and causing the grooms—and himself—to go round-eyed. "Although I could see you with your face painted blue for battle."

"Blue?" he countered with a mock gasp of outrage.

"However," she continued, "I seem to have read in a book somewhere that the Welsh claimed Arthur."

Pierce pulled her to his side and made a show of looking right and left as if guarding a secret. "Never say that in Hobbles Moor! They are all very proud of our claim and are willing to fight over it."

"But then I have your protection, my lord," she returned stoutly.

He paused, pretending to mull over the matter. "I'm not certain you can count on my protection, Miss Eden. After all, you informed me I wouldn't look good in blue paint."

Her laughter pealed to the sky with unconcealed enjoyment, charming every man in the stable yard. "Then I'll change my opinion," she promised. "I think you would look *best* in blue paint."

Suddenly, her eyes widened and she took a step back as the groom led Cornish King from the padlock. King was an impressive animal, dappled gray, fifteen hands tall and powerfully built. Every inch of him bespoke his proud Arabian bloodlines.

Two huge wolfhounds and a small terrier trailed behind him. Seeing Pierce, the dogs bounded forward to greet him but were quickly diverted to the newcomer.

Eden gave each dog an absent-minded pat while they sniffed at her hem, but her gaze was on Cornish King. "He's magnificent," she whispered.

Pierce walked over to the horse which nuzzled him with obvious affection. He rubbed King's nose and received a nudge, begging for more. "See, for all his great size, he's a kitten. Come give him a pet."

"I like him well enough from right here," she answered, and Pierce could see that she was truly wary of the horse. Another piece of the puzzle to her identity. Eden had not been raised around horses. Nor was she overly familiar with the dogs other than giving them a friendly pat.

"Come here, Miss Eden," he commanded quietly.

"Why, my lord?" she asked, her brows coming together in uncertainty.

And she wasn't one to trust easily, Pierce added to the mental list of clues to her identity. "Because I asked you to," he replied readily. "Please."

Her lips pressed together and for a second, he sensed she was going to reject his request . . . and then she moved forward until she stood before him. "What is it you wish, my lord?"

Pierce held King's halter. "Pet him. He won't harm you."

She glanced doubtfully toward Jim.

"Yes, miss, go on," Jim said. "If you are going to be living here, you'd best get used to horses."

Pierce frowned at his choice of words. Eden wasn't going to be living with them, but he didn't correct the groom. Instead, he concentrated on Eden. He'd never seen a reason for anyone to fear horses.

She glanced up at him, admitting, "I'm not accustomed to being around horses."

"And you don't ride either, do you?" Pierce asked, searching for the truth in her eyes.

Eden gave her head a small shake. "I don't ride."

Pierce felt a stab of disappointment. This beautiful sea waif was flawed. She knew nothing about horses.

At that moment, King decided matters for himself. He reached down and nuzzled the lock of hair curling down over her shoulder.

She jumped at the brush of the horse's nuzzle against her skin, and Pierce reached out to reassure her. "He's being playful. He won't harm you. He wants you to touch him."

Her gaze locked with his and then slowly, she lifted her hand. Her fingers brushed King's nose and her eyes widened. "He likes this."

"Like any man," Jim said baldly. "Headstrong and irritable if he doesn't get his way, but ready to curl up his hooves over a spot of attention." The grooms chuckled at the image and Dane gave him another punch in the ribs.

"Go ahead, pet his neck," Pierce urged Eden, letting go of her arm. It was very important to him that she like King. "He loves to be made much of. Watch his hooves though. They won't curl up like Jim claims, but they will crush your toes if he steps on them."

King shifted position and Eden took a step

back. Then, tentatively, she reached out and stroked the animal's neck. "I can feel the muscles ripple beneath his skin. I've never seen a more beautiful horse. Ever."

"During his heyday, there was no horse faster than him," Pierce said with pride. "Or is there one as intelligent. Here, Jim, let me have the red kerchief from around your neck. We need to show Miss Eden King's tricks." He tucked the kerchief in the waistband of his leather breeches, one tattered end hanging out. Walking a few steps away, he turned his back on King, pretending to ignore him.

King, who understood his role in this little farce, clopped over to Pierce and pulled the kerchief from his waistband as he ambled past.

Then Cornish King did something that astounded even Pierce: he turned and walked back to Eden. With a shake of his head, he offered it to Eden who was dauntless enough to accept it from the horse's teeth.

Impressed, Jim said, "That horse grows smarter every day." He took back his kerchief.

"Yes, soon he'll have your job," Dane answered dryly, and earned a bark of laughter from the grooms.

Eden stroked the horse's forehead. "Thank you," she whispered for the horse alone, and again a strange feeling of harmony with this woman, much as he'd felt the day he'd found her in the boat, rolled though Pierce.

"You've made another conquest," he said, coming up behind her. Actually, she'd made more than one. All the grooms appeared moony-eyed over her, even the tough old rooster Jim and the solemn, quiet Dane.

"Another?" She slid a glance from beneath long, black eyelashes in his direction and only then did he realize what he'd said.

Well, he couldn't deny it. He told himself all he felt toward her was a strong sense of responsibility, but he wasn't sure that was true.

"We shouldn't let you overexert yourself," he said. "Let me walk you back up to the house."

"I'm not ready to go back to my room yet. It's such a beautiful day, I'd prefer to stay out here just for a moment or two longer."

"Aye, the mist rolls in and out of Cornwall and you never know what the weather will be," Jim chimed in. "Tomorrow you may not be able to see your hand in front of your face."

One of the grooms agreed that was so and Pierce decided he'd prefer to spend his time with her alone rather than sharing her attention with the grooms. "Do you feel well enough for a small walk?"

The radiance of her smile was all the answer he needed. "We're taking King back to pasture, Jim."

"Aye, my lord."

Pierce nodded his head and said, "Follow, King." The horse began following him, as well trained as any dog.

Eden walked beside him as they followed a dirt path leading around the stables to a fenced field in the back. Next to the path was a good-sized pond with a number of gray ducks swimming on it. Waddling around the perimeter was a hissing white goose.

"Watch out for that one," he warned Eden. "He's fat and ill-tempered and next Christmas he will be our dinner."

At that moment, the goose stretched out his neck and hissed at them as if confirming Pierce's words. With a laugh of surprise, Eden quickly put Pierce between herself and the goose.

The dogs ran ahead of them, already aware of which pasture Pierce would use. King for his part was far from his best behavior. He kept nudging Pierce in the back, pushing him ahead.

"Is he always this anxious?" she asked.

"When he is heading toward his pasture," Pierce said, giving King a mild rebuke on the nose for his pushiness. "He enjoys the freedom."

"Did Jim help you train Cornish King to do those tricks?" Eden asked.

"No, I did that myself. There was no Jim in those days. This was before my father came home sick." The words had slipped out almost before he'd realized what he was admitting.

He stopped and she stopped with him. "Is something wrong, my lord?"

For a moment, he studied her, the fine lines of her face, the intelligence in her eyes.

He'd never talked about his past with anyone—but now, he felt an urge to be completely honest with Eden. Better she know everything from the beginning and not learn small pieces and bits from others the way his mother had about his father.

"My father enjoyed gambling," he said without preamble. "One day, a messenger from London arrived with Cornish King, only the horse didn't look like this. He was a young colt, half-starved and neglected. Father had won him in a game of chance. He couldn't even remember winning the horse because he was a man given to drink." He stroked King's neck. "From the moment I laid eyes on King, I knew he was a winner. But even more important, at a time I needed a friend, he was there. After Father died, I decided to race him. I rode him bareback over these pastures. There were times I could almost believe we were flying. I told Dane of my plan and he guided me toward Jim who was working for a neighboring stable. I couldn't pay him the wages he was earning but Jim said he'd be honored to work for me." Pierce gave a small smile. "After all, I am the true descendant of Arthur."

"And they really believe that?" she asked, more a confirmation than a question.

"Absolutely, blue paint and all."

She smiled the way he'd hoped she would. He continued, "Between the two of us, we proved I was right about King. There wasn't a horse in England that could beat us," he said, his voice full of fierce pride. "Today, horse owners come from all over Europe to breed off him." He opened the pasture gate. "Go on with you, King."

The great stallion ambled through and then wasted no time in stretching his legs, running the length of the field and back. The dogs barked excitedly after him, unable to keep up with the horse.

Leaning against the fence, Pierce said, "We are no longer allowed to breed thoroughbreds with Arabians anymore and race them. Cornish King is three-quarters Arabian. He has a strength and speed few horses will have years from now, and that is why he is in such demand as a stud."

Eden leaned against the fence, her attention no longer on Cornish King but on him. "So, my lord, you did not have the usual childhood of an earl."

"Why do you say that?" he asked.

"I assume earls would not need to turn to blacksmiths for advice. Am I wrong?"

The woman was damned perceptive. Pierce shifted uncomfortably. After all, he'd opened this Pandora's box. "Father was not a successful gambler. When he died, he left us penniless. And it's true, I hadn't been sent off to school or even university like the other boys. I was tutored at home."

"You're obviously not penniless now."

"I rebuilt the family fortune, and I did it through hard work," he added almost defiantly. "I am no London dandy or even a—" He shrugged his shoulders, uncertain of what terms the *ton* used in London nowadays. "—or would fit in with the Almack's set." He gave a short laugh. "I doubt if I would fit into the coffeehouse set. But in Cornwall, I wield considerable influence. And, of course, having money in the bank has enhanced my prestige," he added with a self-deprecating smile.

Eden laid her hand on his arm, her gaze rising to meet his. "I think you are every inch the gentleman, my lord," she said fervently. "Not every man would do as you have done to help a stranger."

"I only did what any Cornishman would have done."

"You are too humble, sir. There are few men like you."

Her gaze was filled with such hero worship, Pierce could have basked a lifetime in it. He felt the urge to gather her in his arms and promise to slay dragons and keep her safe forevermore . . .

But that would be foolish. He took a step away. He'd never been a fanciful man, and yet Eden seemed to bring out that side of him.

Almost brutally he said, "I'm no paragon, Miss Eden. My mother's father was a butcher. He made his money in trade. He was a very smart man and he wanted a title for his daughter so he bought one. My parents' marriage was one of convenience. I'm the product of that marriage."

She leaned against the fence. "So, not only was your father not a successful gambler, but the marriage was not successful either."

Pierce nodded, and shifted his gaze to where King grazed in the pasture. "My parents hated each other and it grew worse after Father gambled the money away. Even today, the subject of my father is best avoided around my mother. It is also wise not to mention her tradesman roots."

"But it doesn't bother you?"

Did it? He'd never considered that question. "I refuse to think of myself or any man as lower-class. Not when a man knows how to make his own way in the world."

"Do you have any other family?"

A breeze swept through the trees. Large puffs of clouds floated across a blue sky. Pierce answered her. "I was raised by the people of Hobbles Moor. My mother was not a happy woman and shortly after I was born she became ill and took to her rooms. Mrs. Meeks is the one that mothered me and I consider myself fortunate. She nursed me when I was ill, lectured me when I deserved it, and if she wasn't available then Dane or Rawlins or a host of others took the task upon themselves. I didn't need a London tutor because I learned my letters from Samuel Cobbler, a retired vicar in the village. I learned sailing from village fishermen and mining from men who were born with spades in their hands. They taught me what I needed to know to refill the Penhollow coffers. From Cornish King's winnings, I reopened the tin mine that had been closed decades ago. There were those among my neighbors who called me mad to take such a risk." He faced Eden, his lips curving into a smile of satisfaction. "Today the Penhollow Mine is the most productive mine in Cornwall. I'm also not afraid to pay my people the highest wages."

He pushed away from the fence. "You asked if I had family. The people of Hobbles Moor are my family."

He waited for her to laugh or tell him he was ridiculous for caring so much about the villagers as so many others had over the years.

Instead she said quietly, "I've never had a family and very few friends. Madame Indrani would say they aren't practical, but I believe they are." Her hand came up to touch the gold medallion around her neck. "The one I had gave my life new direction."

"Who is Madame Indrani?"

She stared at him blankly.

"You just mentioned Madame Indrani. You're starting to remember. It must be a name from your past. Can you recall anything else?"

Her face drained of all color and Pierce feared she was about to swoon. He started to reach for her but she backed away, shaking her head. "I don't remember. I don't think I know that name."

She was lying. He sensed it. "Miss Eden—"

She cut him off by whirling away and would have bolted for the house, but stopped suddenly with a small cry of alarm.

Pierce grasped her elbow just as she stepped back toward him for protection. He looked in the direction she was staring, and then smiled.

"Good afternoon to you, Widow Haskell," he said.

The crone didn't answer but studied Miss Eden intently. He rested his hands reassuringly on Eden's shoulders. "There is no need to have any fear," he said in her ear. "The Widow Haskell will do you no harm."

As if to confirm his words, the Widow gifted

Eden with one of her rare smiles. Leaning heavily on her walking stick, she raised a gnarled finger. "This is as it should be," she said in her weak, raspy voice. Without waiting for a response, she turned and hobbled her way back up the path to the stables.

As if realizing she practically rested in his arms, Eden straightened her shoulders and pulled away from him. "I think I need to return to the house now."

He dismissed the Widow's words with a wave of his hand. "She's harmless."

Eden brought a hand up to her neck, clasping the gold medallion. "I have the feeling she can see right through me."

"Yes, well, the villagers believe she has that ability. They think her a 'charmer.' Her appearance is somewhat disturbing but she is a good person." He placed her hand in the crook of his arm. "Here, perhaps we've overdone it for the first day. I'll walk you to the house."

She didn't speak but nodded her assent. Nor did they speak again until Lady Penhollow met them at the door.

"I have good news," she said cheerily. "Our neighbors Mr. and Mrs. Willis have insisted on hosting a dinner party tomorrow evening to welcome Miss Eden. Isn't that a splendid idea?"

Pierce looked from his mother to Eden. Eden's brow was still slightly furrowed in worry. "Yes, Mother, provided it doesn't overtax Miss Eden's strength," he answered, his attention more on the silent young woman at his side than his mother's dinner plans.

Without a further word, they left Lady Penhollow at the door. He escorted Eden to her room. "I'll send Betsy to you. I think you should lie down and rest. Don't worry about coming down to dinner. I'll have a tray sent to your room this evening."

She turned the handle. "Yes, that would be nice." She started into the room but paused a moment. She glanced over her shoulder at him. "Thank you. I have rarely spent such a lovely afternoon." Her words were sincere. She entered the room and closed the door.

Pierce stared at the door for a long moment before going to his study.

He rang for Betsy. "Miss Eden needs you, and make sure she stays in her room this evening. I want her to rest."

"Yes, my lord."

The moment Betsy left, Pierce pulled out pen and ink. *Madame Indrani,* he wrote on a piece of paper. Tomorrow, he would send a man out first thing to search for this woman . . . and he would almost wager Cornish King that she lived in a city. He would make certain the man went to London with his inquiries.

Eden closed the drapes to the garden and lay on her bed in the darkened room.

How could she have so carelessly blundered and let Madame Indrani's name slip out? Worse was that woman, the Widow Haskell. Even with clouded eyesight, the Widow seemed to divine all of Eden's secrets—and yet she'd chosen not to give Eden away. She'd even assured Eden that Lord Penhollow would become her protector!

She could be thankful for that. Lord Penhollow was like no other man she'd ever met. There was an honesty about him she hadn't found in other men . . . and a sense of honor.

While listening to him talk, she'd even caught herself wondering what it would be like to lay with him, to touch him as she'd been taught to touch a man. For the first time in Eden's life, the thought of being with a man in that way made her body feel jittery and excited, cold and hot all at the same time.

She sat up abruptly. *Stop it,* she warned herself. *You have other problems to worry about.* She couldn't put her faith in the words of a superstitious "charmer" like the Widow Haskell.

She swung her legs over the side of the bed and began pacing the length of the room. It was too soon for Madame to know she had run away. How many days did she have? Two? No, more like a week. One week was all she had to make plans, to find somewhere to hide, and to decide how she was going to make peace with Madame Indrani. It would involve money, there was no doubt about that.

But then, the Widow had said Lord Penhollow would protect her. He would be her protector.

Eden sat back down on the bed. Offering herself to Lord Penhollow would not be a chore, no chore at all. The image of his body joined with hers, in the way she witnessed countless times as part of her training under Madame's tutelage, almost robbed her of breath. But could he afford the price—?

A knock sounded on the door.

Betsy entered without waiting to be summoned. She balanced a tray of food on one arm.

"Please go away. I'm not hungry," Eden said.

Betsy ignored her. "Yes, you are. You must get your strength up. After all, you're dining with the gentry tomorrow evening and we must have you ready for that." She set the tray down. "By the way, Mrs. Meeks says I'm to be your maid. Your personal lady's maid. Don't that sound grand?" She walked over to the windows as she talked and flung open the drapes, flooding the room with late afternoon sunlight.

Eden squinted with irritation. "I don't know if I will be able to accept an invitation tomorrow night. Or if I need a maid."

"Oh, don't worry, miss. I'll have you ready. After all, I am one of those who knows your secret and it's safe with me."

Now she had Eden's undivided attention. "Secret?"

"I know where you came from," the maid said. She picked up a wineglass from the tray. "I poured you a spot of sherry. Thought you could use some."

Eden was tempted to drain the glass in one gulp. She forced herself to be calm. "How do you know my secret?"

"Everyone in Hobbles Moor knows. Shall I help you undress so you can be comfy?"

Eden shot up from the bed. "No! How could they know?" *It didn't make sense!*

"Well, Hobbles Moor is a small village. There isn't much that goes on that we all don't know. Word travels fast, and bad word even faster." She picked up a hairbrush from the vanity. "Would you like for me to brush your hair out now?"

Eden crossed to her, the blood beating in her ears. "No, I want you to answer my questions. How did you know about me?"

"How?" Betsy blinked at her as if such a question was silly. "Because we conjured you, that's how."

"Conjured?" Eden asked, bewildered.

"My heavens, you don't look as if you're feeling good at all, Miss Eden. Sit on the bench and I'll take the ribbon and pins out of your hair. It will help you relax."

Eden let herself be led around to the front of the vanity bench and sat down before the mirror. "Conjured."

"The Widow Haskell is a charmer and knows a thing or two that the rest of us don't. She's the one that brought you here, although we all helped."

Eden stared at Betsy's reflection in the mirror. "She brought me here?"

Pulling the length of ribbon out from Eden's hair, Betsy nodded. "Aye, during the last full moon, we gathered at a place called Hermit's Cove. Oh, it's a rocky and dangerous place, Miss Eden, but full of magic. Or at least the Widow says it is and now I believe it's true because here you are and you are everything we asked for."

Removing the few pins holding Eden's hair in place, she began brushing Eden's hair. The brushing felt good. Almost against her will Eden began to relax, closing her eyes.

Betsy continued talking. "That night, the Widow made a special charm just for Lord Pierce because we all love him so much. But if you don't mind my saying so, you are much better in person than any of us had hoped for."

Eden smiled dreamily, the tightness in her neck slowly fading. "Betsy, I don't know what you are talking about. If you were looking for a person, then I'm certain I'm not the right one." *She couldn't be!*

"Oh, yes, you are, miss," Betsy said, fervently. "You are *exactly* what we wanted."

"And what is that?" Eden asked, lost in the soothing movement of the brush.

"The perfect bride for Lord Penhollow."

Bride? Eden's eyes popped wide open!

Chapter 7

Brest, France

Nasim shoved open the thin wood door to their room in the inn. Inn! It was nothing more than a waterfront hovel.

Gadi sat at a small table, sharpening the curved blade of his scimitar. The blade gleamed wickedly in the candlelight.

"Did you find passage for us?" Gadi asked. They'd disembarked from the *Wind Lark* at the first port. Nasim was not happy that the English captain had refused to turn back once they'd discovered the girl missing. Instead, the captain had been more concerned about his ship and the storm damage that cost them several days' travel. The crew of the *Wind Lark* had been fortunate that a passing military frigate had caught sight of them and helped tow the ship to harbor.

Nasim crossed to the table where Gadi worked. A bowl containing a melon, grapes, and several oranges from Spain sat beside a jug of sweet cider. Nasim poured himself a glass. "Finally. It took me most of the day. We leave on a fishing boat at first light."

"A fishing boat?"

"It was the best I could do. Now that the war is over, the French and English are happy to do business with each other. There wasn't another boat to be chartered."

Gadi curled his lip. "It will probably stink like fish." After their bouts with seasickness, neither one of them was anxious to board another boat.

"Probably." Nasim helped himself to the grapes.

"Are you going to send a message to Ibn Sibah and tell him *why* we are delayed?"

Nasim paused. "I will tell him we are delayed."

Gadi stroked his beard thoughtfully. "I would tell him we have lost the virgin, and what she has done. Ibn Sibah is a fair man. He will not punish us."

Nasim slammed his hand down on the table. "I have never failed my master and I will not now." He walked over to the pile of charts and maps the two men had pored over that morning and, lifting the top map from the pile, studied it. In the dim light, his gaze followed the English coast and the lines showing the currents. His nose flared with anger. Who would have thought that a mere slip of a girl could escape them?

They had been so ill, they hadn't learned of her escape until late the next morning after the storm. To add insult to injury, the English captain had insisted Nasim pay for the missing dinghy before he would let them go to shore.

Nasim wrinkled the map as his hands clenched in frustration. The virgin had appeared biddable and compliant but he'd been wrong. He would not underestimate her again.

"I was thinking," Gadi said, "the virgin could have floated her boat to France."

Nasim shook his head. "She would be fighting the current. Remember, she has lived her life in a city. She knows nothing about boats or how to sail. The ability to cross the Channel in a small dinghy is beyond her." He walked to the table and placed the map beside the candle. "No, my friend, she is somewhere here." He pointed to the English coast off the Isle of Wight.

"Are you sure?"

"Yes. Inside of me—" He thumped his chest. "—I am sure she is alive and in England. After all, why would she journey to a strange land?"

Gadi leaned forward. "Tell me, my friend, why should we waste our time searching for her? Why do we not say she died in the storm?"

"You are looking for the easy road?"

"No, I'm looking to go home," he answered wearily. Leaning his arm on the table, he urged quietly, "Let us find a virgin here. Many women would be willing to serve Ibn Sibah."

"This virgin is not just any woman," Nasim said. As he'd tramped from wharf to wharf searching for passage, he'd asked these same questions himself. He stretched out in the chair opposite Gadi. "She has been trained in the desires of men by Ibn Sibah's favorite harem slave, Madame Indrani."

"The woman we purchased her from?"

"The same. Ibn Sibah gave the woman known as Madame Indrani her freedom after she saved his life during a palace uprising almost three decades ago. Still, he has mourned her loss and hopes to recapture a part of his youth and the spirit Madame had with this virgin."

"Perhaps it is not Allah's will that he have the virgin," Gadi said carefully.

"Perhaps." Nasim sat back in his chair. "But will you be the one to tell Ibn Sibah this?"

Gadi shook his head, his face under his beard turning pale. "No, I fear being that man."

"Then we have only one thing to do, my friend. We must find the virgin."

Gadi tested the sharpness of his scimitar by running his finger along the blade. A line of blood rose on the tip of his finger. He smiled. "We will find her, my friend. She is only one small woman and we are two men with a purpose."

"Yes, and when we have her, she will not escape again."

Chapter 8

Eden woke the next morning to find the garden shrouded in a thick, misty fog, just as Jim had promised the day before. She hung back the drapes and climbed back into bed, not ready to leave her pillow.

The sheets felt good against her cheek. She'd slept well, even though her sleep had been filled with vivid dreams, erotic dreams. Dreams she'd never had before . . . and Lord Penhollow was in them.

Eden rolled over on her back and stared at the ceiling. She mustn't think of him this way. She had to leave—and yet Betsy's words that she'd been chosen to be his bride repeated over and over in her head.

It had taken Betsy hours to convince Eden to even consider such a possibility. *Countess of Penhollow.* If Eden hadn't felt the force of Widow Haskell's presence herself, she wouldn't have given the matter a second thought. But now she did—*because she wanted to.*

Eden lay in the bed, her arms outstretched,

and let herself believe. The wonder of it all made her tremble with excitement. "Countess of Penhollow," she whispered.

"What are you still doing in bed?" came Betsy's irritated voice from the doorway.

Eden hadn't even heard her open the door. She turned to the maid with a smile. "I just woke." She stretched. "Isn't it a beautiful day?"

"It looks like rain later and you shouldn't be such a slugabed," Betsy informed her briskly, walking into the room and toward the wardrobe. "You should be breakfasting with Lord Penhollow right this very minute. I've been in the kitchen cooling my heels and waiting for you to ring." She threw open the wardrobe door and began riffling through Eden's dresses. "It's a good thing I'm impatient. He's almost done with his breakfast. We're going to miss him completely if we don't hurry."

Eden bounced out of bed, in the best of moods at the thought of seeing Lord Penhollow.

Betsy pulled her head out of the wardrobe. "I wish you had more clothes and more day dresses."

"I'll wear the green lace once again."

"You can't! He's already seen you in that. Wait! I have the perfect idea." She poked her head back into the wardrobe and then came out a moment later, frowning. "You don't have a riding habit. I never realized it until this moment."

"No." It was not an item Madame Indrani

felt Eden would need after she was locked behind harem walls.

Betsy groaned with frustration. "Why didn't you tell me this last night?"

Last night, Betsy had shared with Eden everything she knew about Lord Penhollow. Eden now knew his habits (he always breakfasted after he'd made his morning rounds of the stables, usually between eight and nine), his favorite food (mussels steamed in wine), color (blue, Betsy thought), books, music, wine . . . the list went on and on. The servants had put together the list, reasoning, quite rightly, that such information would help Eden capture his heart.

"What did I tell you over and over again last night that Lord Penhollow values?"

"His reputation and his horses," Eden answered dutifully.

"And don't you think you could have told me at some point during our conversation that you don't own a habit?" Betsy asked, her hands on her hips in exasperation.

"No," Eden replied reasonably. "I don't ride and he already knows that."

"Oh, but he thinks you want to learn to ride."

"Wherever did he gain such an idea?"

"I told him this morning over his breakfast. I said—" She adopted her best "servant's" voice. "—'Lord Penhollow, Miss Eden wondered if you would be able to teach her to ride.' " She grinned. "He jumped at your request like a dog after bacon and says he will meet you out front once you are dressed."

Eden practically stood up in the bed. "But I never made any such request!"

"He doesn't know that," Betsy replied, and returned to the wardrobe. She pulled out a dress of soft periwinkle-blue silk. "Here, this is what you'll have to wear until I can find you a habit. I'll explain the delay to Lord Penhollow."

"I don't want to learn to ride," Eden insisted mutinously. "And I prefer the rose muslin."

"But blue is Lord Penhollow's favorite color."

"And rose brings out the color in my cheeks. But I won't ride."

Betsy switched the blue for the rose. "You can either have a lesson this morning with Lord Penhollow, or—" She paused dramatically. "—be here for your appointment with Dr. Hargrave and receive another dose of castor oil."

Suddenly, the choices before Eden were clearer. "I've always wanted to learn to ride."

Betsy shook the wrinkles out of the dress. "Oh, you mustn't just learn to ride, miss. You must be able to sail over the hedgerows with the finest riders in England."

"Sail?"

"Umm-hmmm," Betsy said, laying the dress on the bed and helping Eden pull her nightdress off over her head. "The countess of Penhollow must know how to ride. It's expected."

Suddenly, being countess of Penhollow didn't appear as appetizing to Eden as it had before. But regardless, she still needed to keep Lord Penhollow entranced.

She slid into the rose muslin and sat down on the vanity bench to do her hair, which she decided to wear simply, pulling it up and tying it in place with a black ribbon. Her gaze met Betsy's in the mirror. "But I can't ride if I don't have a habit to wear, can I?"

"Oh, I'll find a habit," Betsy promised . . . and Eden knew the redheaded maid would do just exactly that.

Nor, in the end, could she avoid Dr. Hargrave. Or his castor oil dosage. Lady Penhollow sent word insisting Eden meet with the good doctor.

Lord Penhollow sent word that he would postpone their lesson until after the doctor's visit.

Eden was trapped.

Fortunately, he got the worst over first—giving her a large tablespoon of castor oil immediately. It didn't taste any better the second time around. "But it cures everything," Dr. Hargrave assured her.

Eden didn't know if she agreed.

Dr. Hargrave's examination was quick and methodical. He spent a great deal of time peering into Eden's eyes and asking her questions about her past. Both he and Eden sat in chairs in front of the French doors to take advantage of the light while Lady Penhollow stood by the corner of the bed, her hands folded in front of her. She had insisted on being present when the doctor made his examination.

He sat back in his chair and pulled pen, ink, and paper from his black case. "I hope you don't mind, Miss Eden, but I would like to take notes of your examination for a letter I am writing to the Royal College of Surgeons. There are many doctors who would be interested in this case. May I have your permission?"

"I'm not certain," Eden answered uncomfortably.

"It's all in the name of science," he urged her.

"I'm sure she won't mind," Lady Penhollow said. "Will you, dear?"

Eden couldn't refuse him, not with Lady Penhollow present. "All right then."

After the exam, Dr. Hargrave scribbled two pages of notes. He finished his writing with a flourish and looked up at her, his spectacles sitting low on his nose. "Lord Penhollow tells me you remember a name from time to time."

"Oh, how interesting," Lady Penhollow drawled. "I hadn't heard this."

Eden winced inwardly at the error she had made the day before. "Yes, that is correct," she said, and held her breath, expecting him to label her a fraud.

Lady Penhollow's smile curled even wider.

Then, to Eden's surprise, the doctor nodded. "Yes, yes, that is how it should be. Memory comes back in stages. A thought here, a reminder of the past there. Eventually, it will add up to the sum of the whole."

"It's how it should be?" Lady Penhollow repeated, her smile disappearing.

"Yes!" Dr. Hargrave confirmed emphatically.

Eden shifted uneasily. "Are there any stories of patients who never regained their memories?"

"Many, many! It's all in the mind, you see, and medicine knows very little about what goes on up here." He tapped his forehead with a finger. "But don't you worry, Miss Eden. You are among friends—"

Eden wondered if he included Lady Penhollow in that number.

"I was thinking to myself last night how disconcerting it must be to not know who you are or how you got to be there," the good doctor continued. "Some amnesia patients have ended up in sanitariums and were forced to stay there for years, even after their memories had returned. But we won't let that happen to you. Hobbles Moor isn't the sort of place to turn its back on a person in need. Is it, Lady Penhollow?"

Lady Penhollow's gaze shifted from the doctor to Eden. She drew a deep breath and then replied with forced pleasantness. "Of course not, Doctor."

He smiled reassuringly at Eden and picked up his bag. "I will see you on the morrow." Lady Penhollow escorted him out and Eden found herself alone.

The minute the door shut behind them, she was assailed with guilt. She was an impostor, a charlatan of the worst sort. She shouldn't keep misleading these people. For a few hours, she'd let herself believe she could live her lie, but now, she wasn't certain.

But then, what choice did she have?

A knock interrupted her worries. Betsy

stuck her head in the room. "Lord Penhollow," she reminded Eden pointedly.

Almost mechanically, Eden followed Betsy down the hall. The windows were open in each of the rooms they passed in spite of the threat of rain. The fog outside had not dissipated but drifted along the ground eerily.

Eden heard Lord Penhollow before she saw him. His voice floated in through one of the windows toward the front of the house.

Her worries evaporated. Instinctively, she moved toward the open front door and the sound of his voice, passing Betsy in the hallway. She would have immediately stepped out on the front step and called to him except he was not alone. Jim and a tall, lean gentleman stood listening to him. A groom held the gentleman's horse.

The gentleman was obviously from London. Eden knew the work of a Bond Street tailor when she saw it and this man patronized the best. Furthermore, his mount was, even to her inexperienced eyes, excellent horseflesh.

Lord Penhollow appeared very handsome this morning, romantically handsome like a figure from a novel. He was hatless and didn't wear a coat although today he wore a vest of dark blue superfine. It contrasted with the snowy white folds of his neckcloth, tight buckskin riding breeches, and shining black topboots.

He sported a single spur. In London, it would have been an affectation and the mark of a dandy. Here, it was the sign of a man.

The London gentleman was arguing with

what Lord Penhollow had said. He waved his arms and punctuated his words in the air with his hands. Frizzy gray hair stuck out on either side of his head beneath his curled-brim hat, giving him an almost comical look. However, the set of Lord Penhollow's mouth as he listened grew increasingly grim.

Eden motioned Betsy away and started to withdraw when she heard the name "Cornish King." She hesitated, and in that instant, Lord Penhollow seemed to sense her presence.

"Miss Eden?"

She had no choice but to step forward into the doorway. "Good morning, Lord Penhollow."

His reaction to her was everything she—and Betsy—could have hoped for. His generous lips curved into a welcoming smile and his dark blue eyes took on a possessive glow. He came up on the step and offered his hand. "Won't you join us?"

She held back, shy in front of the stranger. "I couldn't. In fact, I didn't mean to interrupt. I'm very sorry, my lord."

"Nonsense, we'd be happy for you to join us, wouldn't we, Whitby?" He leaned forward and added in a quick aside, "Otherwise the man will never leave."

At the first sight of her, Lord Whitby had stopped talking in mid-sentence, his hand frozen in the air. Now that same hand swiftly removed his hat. "I'd be charmed."

But Eden immediately regretted coming out the front door. Whitby had just exposed his bald pate and a distinctive raspberry birthmark on it. She recognized it and him at once as a guest at one of Madame Indrani's salons.

And the reason she remembered him clearly was because he had bid on her. Lord Whitby. Why hadn't she recognized the name immediately? Their meeting had been almost two years ago, but she recalled it clearly. He'd wanted to buy her but refused to pay the full price. Madame had said her price was firm. He'd argued, grown unruly, and then been forcibly ushered out of Madame's house by the muscular Firth. He hadn't taken that indignity quietly but had stood on the street shouting at the house. Firth had been forced to see Lord Whitby home.

And now he was here.

Eden drew in her breath, barely hearing the introductions, waiting for Lord Whitby to expose her.

Instead, he bowed. "It is a pleasure to make your acquaintance, Miss Eden."

Eden couldn't answer. Her mouth had gone dry and her throat felt constricted. It took all her courage to smile and make a small curtsy.

He smiled back, no light of recognition in his brown eyes.

She could feel Lord Penhollow staring at her strangely, but Jim and the other groom didn't appear to think anything amiss.

Lord Whitby asked politely, "Are you from Cornwall, Miss Eden, or are you visiting from another part of England?"

Eden couldn't trust herself to issue a coherent answer. Panicked, she wanted to turn and run, but she stood, mute and rooted to the ground.

Then Lord Penhollow came to her rescue. He gave her elbow a small, reassuring squeeze and answered for her. "She is visiting from Devon," he said smoothly.

Caught by surprise again, Eden could only mumble some sort of agreement.

"Well, it's obvious you have an eye for more than good horseflesh, Penhollow," Lord Whitby declared bluntly.

Lord Penhollow's mouth flattened. The light in his eye turned pugnacious, but Whitby seemed oblivious to his insult.

Instead, Whitby boldly pretended to draw Eden aside a step and said in a carrying voice, "In fact, perhaps you can help me here. I wish to purchase Cornish King for my own stud farm but Penhollow stubbornly refuses to sell. No matter what price I offer. I've already gone as high as fifteen thousand pounds."

"Fifteen thousand pounds?" Eden repeated. He'd only offered twelve for her.

"Cornish King is not for sale," Lord Penhollow said in a quiet, firm voice.

"Oh, devil take it, Penhollow, I want that horse. I need him. There's not another like him and there never will be. What do I have to do to get him?"

"He's not for sale."

"Everything's for sale!" Lord Whitby shouted, forgetting Eden's presence entirely. He slapped his hat back on his head and stamped around a moment. "I've come all the way out here for him, and I won't be disappointed!"

"Then we have nothing further to say," Lord Penhollow answered. "He's not for sale. You may arrange stud services but that is all."

Lord Whitby swore a string of curses under his breath and then, remembering Eden's presence, tipped his hat and apologized. "Forgive me, Miss Eden. I'm behaving like an ogre because I'm used to getting my way."

His apology surprised Eden . . . and then she realized this was how men treated women of the upper class. They swore, burped, and worse in front of whores, but they knew how to treat a lady—and everyone at Penhollow Hall considered Eden a lady.

The revelation opened Eden's eyes. No wonder Lord Whitby didn't recognize her. The Eden he knew was not a lady, but a prostitute.

"There is no price I'd accept for Cornish King. Ever," Lord Penhollow was saying. "We've had this conversation before, Whitby."

"Yes, we have," Lord Whitby agreed. "And we'll have it again. I want that horse."

"Well, you'll not have him today."

An angry muscle worked in Lord Whitby's jaw. "I see I'm not going to convince you. May I ask that if you ever decide to sell him, you contact me first?"

"If I ever decide to sell him, you will be the first I notify."

"Then that's the best I can ask," Lord Whitby said, but Eden sensed he wasn't satisfied. He walked to his horse and was about to mount, when he paused.

He glanced in Eden's direction and she saw the question in his eyes. Their gazes held, and she realized he wasn't thinking about Cornish King. Had something in the conversation triggered a memory? She bravely smiled at him.

Lord Whitby shook his head as if deciding he must be wrong about something and, to Eden's relief, climbed into his saddle. He tipped his hat to her. "It was a pleasure meeting you, Miss Eden. Penhollow, don't forget your promise."

"I won't."

"Well, don't wait too long. Cornish King has only five or six good breeding years in him."

"I appreciate your taking the time to visit us at Penhollow Hall, Whitby," Lord Penhollow said with stiff formality.

Lord Whitby's answering smile didn't reach his eyes. He put his spurs to his horse and rode off.

Eden prayed she'd never lay eyes on him again.

"Lord Whitby is not happy," she said in the silence that followed.

Lord Penhollow watched the man ride down his drive until he was out of sight. "He'll be back again next month. He's one of the richest men in England and doesn't understand there are some things that money can't buy. I would never sell Cornish King."

He nodded a dismissal to Jim and the groom and then turned to her with a smile. Eden's stomach went all fluttery and weak. A woman could bask a lifetime in one of his smiles.

"But enough of him," he said. "He'll return again and the answer will be the same and he'll bluster and carry on, but that is what he gets for coming uninvited. However, your interruption was most timely."

Eden wished she'd stayed in her room.

Then all her worries vanished with his next words. "You look lovely this morning. Your dress reminds me of the roses around the fountain."

She hoped Betsy was someplace where she could overhear Lord Penhollow's words.

"But you aren't dressed for our riding lesson," he said.

Now Eden hoped Betsy was far away. "About the lesson, my lord—"

"I have a mount for you. Her name's Velvet and she's the prettiest mare I've ever seen. Well-trained too."

Eden hesitated, not wanting to seem less than perfect in his eyes.

Lady Penhollow's voice from the front step startled her. "She can't go riding with you, Pierce. She doesn't have gloves for this evening and we must go to town for them. After all, she can't appear in front of our friends without the proper gloves."

His disappointment was plain. "We can have our lesson after you return," he suggested to Eden.

Lady Penhollow walked down the steps to them. "Oh, I'm so sorry," she said, her expression anything but one of regret. "But there won't be time. We mustn't overtax Miss Eden's strength. At least, not yet," she added with an overly sweet smile in Eden's direction. "By the way, Miss Eden, we must go all the way to Plympton for gloves. I notice you have not yet breakfasted and I advise you to do so. We probably won't eat until we return later this afternoon."

Something in the gleam in Lady Penhollow's eyes told Eden she was very proud of herself for snuffing out Lord Penhollow's riding lesson. Eden almost wanted to burst her air of superiority by kissing her on both cheeks and shouting "Thank you." She'd been granted a reprieve from the riding lesson.

Then Lord Penhollow said, "We shall go riding tomorrow. Let's say first thing in the morning? We won't be disturbed at that hour by business."

Before Eden could say anything, Lady Penhollow stepped between them and answered smoothly, "Pierce, do you really believe Miss Eden is interested in horses? I mean, she hasn't learned to ride yet, has she? Why push her in a direction for which she is unsuited?"

Eden heard a footfall behind her and glanced up to see Rawlins, Mrs. Meeks, and Betsy in the doorway, listening to the whole conversation, their expressions anxious—and suddenly, she *wanted* to be the woman they thought she was, but not for herself. For them . . . and for the many kindnesses they'd already extended to her. She wanted them to believe in magic and dreams and charms.

She turned to Lord Penhollow and gifted him with one of her most dazzling smiles, one she had practiced and knew quite well its impact. "I do want to learn to ride," she said. "I may be a terrible student, but it is something I wish very much."

"Then you shall be my pupil," he answered and returned her smile with one of his own. Staring up into his smile, her knees went weak and she felt a little giddy.

Lady Penhollow stepped between them. "You don't have the time for riding lessons, Pierce. You have the mine and the stables, not to mention your other duties."

"I'll make time," Lord Penhollow said easily. "You've been telling me for years that I work too hard. I'm beginning to think you're right."

"Well," Lady Penhollow said in a tight voice. She turned to Eden. "Then I guess that is settled." She marched up the steps to the door. Rawlins and the women quickly ducked back into the hallway out of her path.

On the top step, she paused. "We leave in one hour's time, and I should warn you, Miss Eden, that low-cut bodices such as you favor are *de trop* in the country. You will wish to wear a shawl to cover yourself." She slammed the front door behind her.

The joy Eden had felt earlier that day vanished with his mother's angry words. Eden turned to Lord Penhollow. "I didn't mean to upset her."

Lord Penhollow stared at the closed front door a moment before saying, "My mother is not a happy person. She doesn't always know what she wants and searches for it by attempting to control others."

"I don't see why she can't be happy." Eden gestured to the house and the gardens. "Everything a person could want is right here."

"Yes? Well, *I* think so, but I've come to believe that happiness means different things to different people. Each of us decides what makes life meaningful . . . and Mother has never made the right choices." He shook his head, breaking his train of thought. "I'm looking forward to our riding lesson tomorrow."

Eden hedged. "I must warn you, I've never been on the back of a horse."

He laughed. "Miss Eden, you have obviously lived your life in cities. In the country, everyone rides. By the way, have any other memories come back to you?"

She hated deceiving him. "Bits and pieces, but nothing important."

"What of family? Have you had any memory of them?"

Here she could tell the truth. "No."

He took her hand. His fingers closed reassuringly around hers. "Don't worry. Everyone at Penhollow Hall is beside you until the end on this, even Mother."

She read genuine compassion in his eyes. She'd never seen a man show such a thing to a woman. For a moment, she thought of giving him her complete confidence, of telling him the truth—and then she squashed such a idea.

A wise woman trusted no one. Years with Madame Indrani and a hard childhood had taught her that lesson. Even if she was going to rely on Pierce's protection, she must never give him complete power and knowledge over her.

He squeezed her hand gently, bringing her back to reality. With a start, she realized that the pressure of her fingers had tightened around his until he couldn't release himself.

She pulled back her hand, and, murmuring an excuse, turned and headed into the house.

Betsy met her just inside the door. "That was perfect, miss. Perfect! Now we must find you a habit!"

But Eden barely paid attention to what she was saying. Instead her thoughts were on Lord Penhollow. There was something between them. Something that had nothing to do with superstitions and love potions. Something that made her unable to give him up.

Pierce slapped his quirt against his boot, watching his mother and Eden set off on the shopping expedition to Plympton in the landaulet with his coat of arms on the door. His mother's coldness toward Eden irritated him. He wanted the two women to get along, but he feared that was wishful thinking. His mother could be a very selfish woman.

Eden. Even the sound of her name was enough to set his blood boiling. He wanted her with a force he'd never felt with another woman. He'd been tempted to rip Whitby's eyes out of his head for the way he'd ogled her. Whitby wore the veneer of a gentleman but beneath his shell, he was a scoundrel. He'd never sell Cornish King to the man.

But what really bothered him had been

Eden's reaction to Whitby. She knew him. She'd recognized him. Pierce had sensed it in the way her eyes had widened slightly when Whitby had removed his hat and the sudden tension in her body . . . although Whitby had not recognized her.

Thoughtfully, Pierce started walking toward the stables. Amnesia, or was Eden just a good actress?

Chapter 9

It was not a good day for a shopping expedition. Fog still shrouded the countryside while heavy clouds threatened rain all the way to Plympton.

Eden and Lady Penhollow sat beside one another in the narrow confines of the landaulet, hands folded in their laps, faces averted from each. Each pretended to watch the passing scenery. Eden wore a cream-colored Kashmir shawl around her shoulders.

With each sway and bounce of the landaulet, Eden could feel Lady Penhollow tense as if not wanting to lose her balance and inadvertently touch her. Polite comments Eden made to break the tension were met with monosyllabic answers.

The promised rain began coming down at the outskirts of Plympton. The town itself wasn't very large. There was a paved main street of shops, several rows of houses, and, of course, a church.

Eden stared out the coach window in dismay. Lady Penhollow had lent her a straw bonnet and she had no desire to ruin it or the slippers on her feet. Fortunately, their coachman, Leeds, had an umbrella. He held it over their heads as Lady Penhollow marched from one shop in the rain to another, Eden in tow.

After an hour of this, Leeds drove across the street to the shop beneath the sign shaped like a hand with the lettering *Wm. Harrelson, Glover.* The bell on the door tinkled as they entered.

Mr. Harrelson and his wife came out from a back room, their eyebrows raised in surprise that anyone would venture out on a day such as this. Mrs. Harrelson quickly greeted them and offered to brew a cup of tea, "To take the chill out of your bones." Lady Penhollow accepted and sat on a high stool in front of the counter.

"And you, my lady?" the glover's wife asked.

"*Miss* Eden," Lady Penhollow corrected before Eden could reply. "She's a 'Miss.' "

Mrs. Harrelson covered her mouth with her fingers, upset by her blunder.

Eden shook her head to indicate she should not feel bad and gave the woman a reassuring smile. "A cup of tea would be appreciated. Is it possible that I can arrange for a cup for our driver? He has the worst of it since he'll be out in the rain all the way home."

Her words apparently pleased Mrs. Harrelson. "Of course, I can brew a cup for him too, and how nice of you to think of the poor man standing in the rain." She crossed to the door and motioned Leeds inside.

Leeds appeared startled to be summoned. Then when he discovered it was over a cup of tea, he stared at Lady Penhollow as if he could scarce believe his ears. Mrs. Harrelson told him to come to the back room with her.

Lady Penhollow rapped the counter impatiently. "Are we going to have service here or stand around sipping tea all day?"

Mr. Harrelson immediately offered service. "What may I do for you today, my lady?"

"She needs a pair of long kid gloves in oyster or pearl, and perhaps a short pair in York tan," Lady Penhollow informed the shopkeeper.

Her imperious tone set Eden's teeth on edge. She was quickly growing tired of being treated like an unwanted appendage, especially by the woman who had insisted Eden accompany her.

The shopkeeper accurately heard what Lady Penhollow implied without saying—Eden was of no consequence. He reached for a box of lower-priced gloves, their quality, as he laid them out on the counter, definitely reflecting their price.

Lady Penhollow tested a glove by pulling on one of the fingers. She tried them on. "This pair will be perfect for her."

Eden clenched her teeth to hold back her temper. She would not take offense with Lady Penhollow over a pair of gloves.

While the glover wrapped the gloves, she even swallowed her pride and attempted to express gratitude to Lady Penhollow for the purchase. "Thank you. They're lovely—"

"Oh, no, don't thank me," Lady Penhollow said briskly. "If I had my way, you'd be living off the parish where you belong and not under my roof. Your presence here has ruined everything for everyone." She didn't wait for a response but walked to the door. She stopped. "Leeds, I'm ready to leave."

Leeds quickly hurried from the back room to serve his mistress. He opened the door and the umbrella and escorted Lady Penhollow to the landaulet. Eden stood right where Lady Penhollow had left her, shocked by the woman's blatant rudeness.

"Miss?" Mr. Harrelson said timidly.

His voice broke through her shock. She turned to him.

"Here are your gloves," he said, holding out the package. His wife hovered by the back room door. She'd heard Lady Penhollow too.

This time, Eden didn't hold back the anger surging through her. She took the gloves from Mr. Harrelson with a soft "Thank you," and charged out the door to do battle with Lady Penhollow.

Fortunately, the rain had let up a bit and the sky actually looked like it was going to clear, not that Eden cared. She marched up to the coach. Lady Penhollow was already inside. Leeds was in his seat on top of the coach.

"She ordered me up here, miss," he said under his breath.

"Don't worry. My argument isn't with you," Eden answered in a low voice and jerked the door open. She climbed inside. Lady Penhollow sat on her side of the landaulet like a marble statue. Eden drew great satisfaction in slamming the coach door and startling the woman.

Lady Penhollow blinked twice and then knocked on the side of the coach for Leeds to drive on before Eden had taken her seat. Eden smiled. Lady Penhollow might be a player of petty games and nonsense, but Eden had been schooled in that art by masters, the women who lived under Madame Indrani's roof. She herself had never been one to stoop to cattiness. Instead, she'd always confronted the transgressor in a firm, direct manner . . . and she did so with Lady Penhollow now.

"Lady Penhollow, if I have offended you, please accept my apology instead of belittling me in front of shopkeepers. I find that kind of behavior extremely *common*."

Lady Penhollow whipped her head around to face Eden, her eyes blazing with outrage, and Eden felt a measure of triumph. She'd struck the woman's Achilles' heel.

"I don't know what you are talking about," Lady Penhollow said irritably.

"Oh, come now, let us speak plainly, my lady, instead of hiding behind a facade of manners. What exactly have I done to upset you?"

Lady Penhollow drew back into her corner of the coach, the set of her mouth stubborn. They rode in silence this way for several minutes. Eden had almost begun to believe Lady Penhollow wasn't going to answer, but then she spoke.

"I don't like the way my son looks at you.

You're a threat to him and I will protect him at all costs."

"Lord Penhollow has done nothing more than be unfailingly polite."

"Do you really believe that?"

"Yes."

Lady Penhollow smirked. "You lie, girl. You can't possibly be that incredibly green. No woman could look the way you do and be completely oblivious."

"And just exactly what does that mean, my lady?" Eden asked carefully.

Lady Penhollow moved out of her corner. "You *know* what I'm talking about. There is something about you that arouses men and you wield that power effectively. It's a combination of vulnerability combined with an uncommon beauty. But then, you realize that, don't you?"

Eden sat very still. Yes, she did.

"My son is strongly attracted to you. You see, he's a bit of Sir Galahad and Saint George all rolled into one. He enjoys championing lost causes such as farmers' rights and reforms for tin miners. You are his latest cause, Miss Eden."

"And for what reason would he champion me?"

"You? The poor lost waif?" Lady Penhollow mocked. "Come, you wanted honesty and I shall give it to you. You are not good enough for him."

Her words went straight to Eden's heart. "Why are you so certain?"

"Because women sense things about each

other, Miss Eden. There's too much the sensualist about you. A woman of quality doesn't have such an air. Coupled with the vulnerability I discussed earlier, you are a very potent threat to my son's well-being." She leaned toward Eden. "Leave him alone. Leave *all* of us alone."

Eden turned her head toward the window. Purple heather dotted the pastures on either side of the road. Beyond the fields were the moors and the rough beauty of the Cornish countryside.

Lady Penhollow dropped her voice to a conspirator's tone. "I am not ungenerous. If you agree to leave Cornwall, I shall pay your way to wherever it is you wish to go. But you must not let my son know of our agreement."

Eden faced her. "I'm not a blackmailer, my lady. Nor do I pose that great a threat to you."

"You're as bold as they come," she shot back. She shifted to her side of the coach. "But whether you accept my offer or not, understand that I will not let you have him. I will fight you every step of the way."

"Lord Penhollow is not a man to be easily led."

"Every man is easily led when it comes to a pretty face and trim ankles, my son included. But don't put your faith in silly superstitions and rumors. Oh?" Lady Penhollow smiled. "You're surprised I've heard of them, aren't you? It is all the servants have been talking about since the day you appeared, but he won't marry you, Miss Eden. He can't. He has a responsibility to his title. You are a nobody and therefore unsuitable."

Her cruel words pricked Eden's already guilty conscience. She rubbed the gold medallion between her fingers . . . and knew Lady Penhollow was right.

They passed the remainder of the trip in silence. When they reached Penhollow Hall, Eden excused herself and hurried to her room. She opened the French doors and escaped into the garden.

The garden smelled of rain-clean air, blooming plants, and rich earth. How so very different from London and the world she once knew! It was more soothing and comforting than even Mary's little patch had been. How far away her past and Lady Penhollow's words seemed. And how close the smells and the velvety texture of the rose petals on her fingertips.

Standing in the middle of the garden, Eden had a blinding flash of insight. She'd thought she could have no better life than that of a man's mistress or a well-paid prostitute in a brothel like Madame Indrani's. Now she knew differently. Now, she wanted more, *needed* more—and she understood Lady Penhollow's fear.

When had she changed? Had it been her friendship with Mary Westchester? Or did it have to do with her education and love of books?

Or was it her meeting Lord Penhollow?

She turned and faced the wing of the house opposite hers, the wing where his rooms were located. The Widow Haskell was wrong. She didn't belong here. She must leave soon. But for one more night, she'd let herself dream that she could belong. The sun peeped from behind the clouds, sending a ray of light glinting on a window in Lord Penhollow's wing. Perhaps it even belonged to his bedroom.

Staring at the reflection of the sun on the glass, Eden interpreted it as a sign. She could have one more night and then she must leave.

She promised herself she would not waste it.

Lord Penhollow stood in the front drawing room, helping himself to a glass of wine, when Eden made her entrance an hour later. Leeds, the coachman, had told Betsy and the other servants of Lady Penhollow's rudeness. While helping Eden dress, Betsy had worried over the upcoming dinner engagement, since the Penhollow servants wouldn't be present to support Eden.

But Eden had no fear. This was her last night and she would not allow Lady Penhollow and her friends to ruin it.

She'd chosen to wear the dress that had been designed specifically for her first meeting with the Sultan Ibn Sibah. The cream silk was cut daringly low, the very height of fashion, and shimmered with the movement of her body as she walked into the room. Pearls the size of the tip of her small finger had been embroidered in row upon row across the high-waisted bodice.

She wore no jewelry other than her gold medallion, but she didn't need diamonds or other stones to set off this dress. Instead, she'd gathered her hair up in loose curls at the top of her head to let them fall freely down around her shoulders.

Lord Penhollow's reaction to her entrance was everything she'd prayed it would be. He almost overfilled his glass and spilled wine on the floor. He caught himself in time and sat the glass and bottle down before walking across the carpet to greet her.

He wore formal black evening dress, relieved only by the snowy white of his shirt and neckcloth. Aristocratic and elegant, the style suited him. It emphasized the bright blue of his eyes and gave his muscular frame a lithe grace.

Now it was Eden's turn to be dazzled. "You look very handsome this evening, my lord."

He actually blushed, a dull stain that rose from his neck.

He lifted her gloved hand. "And let me say, you look stunning." He kissed the back of her fingers.

Eden's heart was beating so hard against her chest, she was certain he must hear it. This man was the one to whom she wanted to give her virginity. Not for a price, but as a gift, as the one thing she had to give.

They stood there, staring at each other like two fools, until Lady Penhollow's sharp voice interrupted and reminded them of her presence. She rose from a settee by the hearth. "Come! We're already late. We must leave now." She left the room, walking between Eden and her son.

Lord Penhollow offered Eden his arm. "These evenings make Mother nervous."

Eden didn't care. She was with him and that was all that mattered—even if Betsy had warned her to be on her guard since Eden would be away from where the Penhollow servants could protect her.

They took a coach larger than the landaulet, the two women on one side, Lord Penhollow on the other. The sky had cleared and they enjoyed a magnificent sunset as the coach swayed and rolled its way down muddy roads. Whenever the coach hit a rut, Lord Penhollow's knee rubbed against Eden's leg. She pretended not to notice, savoring the contact.

He didn't move or make an apology either until his mother questioned in an overloud voice, "Are we crowding you, Miss Eden?" Lord Penhollow inched his leg aside.

Mr. and Mrs. Willis lived in a lovely three-story brick Georgian less than half an hour from Penhollow Hall. Pulling up in the coach, the Penhollow party was greeted at the door by Mrs. Willis, herself a vision in purple. She wore a purple turban with a big purple plume held in place by a diamond the size of a man's thumb. Her gauzy purple dress flowed behind her as she kissed Lady Penhollow's cheek and then dramatically offered her hand to Lord Penhollow.

"Come in, come in. Everyone is already gathered waiting for you. Oh! And this must be Miss Eden." She covered Eden's hand with her own. The woman's hands were cold. "I am so pleased to make your acquaintance. What an ordeal you have suffered. Dr. Hargrave was just telling us about it. Come let me introduce you to everyone."

Eden followed, feeling a flutter of anxiety. She could find no fault with the woman's words, they sounded very sincere, but the expression in Mrs. Willis's eyes was too calculating for Eden's taste.

In the drawing room, besides Dr. Hargrave, there was also Mr. Willis, a gray-haired gent as lean as his wife was wide, and their daughter Victoria. Victoria's youth surprised Eden. She could barely be seventeen. A tall, narrow woman, she had her father's doleful eyes and her mother's receding chin. The front of her hair was a mass of frizzy curls parted in the middle and then pulled into a bun at the nape of her neck.

Mrs. Willis had barely finished the introductions before she added in a low voice, "And do stand straight, Victoria. A girl does not look her best when she slumps. After all, your intended is here!"

In answer, Victoria seemed to slump even more.

Mrs. Willis rolled her eyes in exasperation and dragged Eden over to another small group of people, Lord and Lady Baines, Lord and Lady Danbury and their houseguest, Mr. Whitacre, a seminary student on his way to London. Mr. Willis cornered Lord Penhollow to discuss recent mining developments.

"Your dress is very attractive, Miss Eden,"

Lady Baines said pleasantly. "Although it is a bit low-cut for country tastes, don't you think?"

Eden didn't dare meet Lady Penhollow's gaze. Instead, she murmured something about it being the latest London fashion, aware that the attention of the men in this small group had shifted to her breasts. She wished she'd brought the Kashmir shawl with her.

"We understand you suffer a loss of memory," Lady Danbury said. "Dr. Hargrave was entertaining us with his opinion on the matter."

"I think it's all nonsense," Lord Baines interjected. "Admit it, girl. Your memory is as good as mine."

He was so blunt, Eden took a step back . . . almost stepping into Lord Penhollow.

Lord Penhollow caught her arm to steady her and, for a moment, their eyes met. She doubted if he'd heard what was said, but his presence created a ring of armor around her where doubts and anxiety could not reach her.

She smiled at Lord Baines. "My memory loss is not something I care to discuss," she said, and silently dared him to challenge her with Lord Penhollow present. He did not.

Pleased, she turned to Mrs. Willis. "Is there a room where I may freshen up before dinner?"

"Victoria, dear," Mrs. Willis called. "Please show Miss Eden to the room we've set aside for the ladies." She then leaned closer and whispered furiously at her daughter, "And do stand straight. You're hunching. You're hunching."

No one else except Eden seemed to think it odd the woman constantly corrected her daughter. They carried on their conversations as if Mrs. Willis had never spoken.

Victoria motioned for Eden to follow her.

They took the stairs to the second floor. A bedroom had been set aside for the use of their female guests.

Eden took a moment to freshen herself and then paused in front of a large wall mirror. She tucked a stray curl behind her ear. "So, is Mr. Whitacre your intended?" she asked Victoria as a way of making conversation.

"No, Lord Penhollow is."

The floor seemed to drop out beneath Eden's feet. She sat down on one of the cushioned chairs beside the bed. Where did Victoria fit into the villagers' determination to marry *her* off to Lord Pennhollow? "He is?" Her voice was barely audible.

Victoria stood by the closed door, her arms crossed against her chest. "You're very pretty."

Eden attempted to smile past the jealousy she felt. "Thank you. You are also."

Victoria almost flinched. "No, I'm not. I'm plain. Mother tells me that's why I won't be having a London season."

"A season?"

Victoria's eyes rounded. "You don't know what a season is?"

Eden shook her head, genuinely puzzled. "I've never heard of such a thing."

"Oh, yes," Victoria reminded herself. "You've lost your memory. Is that true or nonsense like my mother says it is?"

Eden didn't answer.

"A season is when a girl is introduced to Society," Victoria said finally. "After a girl is finished with her education, her parents take her to London to be introduced into Society and there hopefully to contract a good marriage. I was supposed to have mine this year but Papa says it isn't worth the money to take me to London. My parents want me to marry Lord Penhollow."

"And that isn't what you want?" Eden asked.

A small frown formed between Victoria's eyes. "He'll do, I suppose."

"He'll do!" Eden couldn't stop the words from leaving her lips. "He's handsome, wealthy, respectable."

Victoria shrugged. "He's not quite good *ton* and Mother thinks he's far too Cornish."

"Good *ton?*"

"His family background leaves a great deal to be desired. A beautiful girl of breeding could do much better than the countess of Penhollow. Mother says it is why he hasn't married yet. No one wants him. I'm about the best he can expect. Mother says Lord Penhollow needs our family to give his respectability. Of course, we need him to give us looks. Mother says our children would be very handsome, just like their father."

"There's more to a woman than her appearance, Victoria."

"Not according to my mother. She's been in a frightful state all afternoon. She had me spend almost the whole day with her hairdresser and the like. She wants me to make a good impression but I knew the moment you walked in that I am no competition. If anything, I look worse in your presence. Mother knows it too. She just won't admit it. You know she doesn't like you, don't you?"

"I had that feeling," Eden said dryly.

Victoria shrugged. "She fears you will steal Lord Penhollow from me."

Eden was amazed at how just her mere presence in the community had raised so much fuss and excitement. She wondered how they'd all feel when she left tomorrow.

"And what do you think, Victoria?"

"I don't think Lord Penhollow knows I'm alive whether you are here or not," the girl said in her blunt manner. "He's always kind to me but he isn't really my intended—at least, he's not offered for me, no matter what Mother wants to pretend. She insists I must think positive thoughts, but what I really think is that my life is going to be miserable because no man will notice me and my mother will hound me to death."

Tears overflowed from the girl's eyes and Eden, jealousy forgotten, quickly crossed to her and enveloped her in an embrace. She knew the sort of inner strength it took to stay strong and whole in the face of constant criticism and unhappiness.

"You *are* pretty," Eden insisted. "Plus you have intelligence and courage."

"No, I'm a coward. I don't want to marry Lord Penhollow. I want to go to London, but I'm afraid to tell my parents. I want to go to the opera. To meet exciting people and go to plays and museums. Anything but this boring life of being in the country. And I'm not intelligent. If I was, I would be able to say clever things and not disappoint my mother and father."

"Victoria, you are not a disappointment to your parents," Eden said, standing back and taking the girl by her shoulders. "And you *are* pretty."

Victoria loudly sniffed her opinion.

"Victoria, sit here." She indicated the bench in front of the mirror.

"Why?"

"Because I have a talent for dressing hair." She took Victoria's hand and pulled her in front of the mirror. "If you'll let me, I have a style in mind which you will like much better."

"What is it?"

"It's the latest fashion," Eden assured her. "And I'm just from London so I should know." She began pulling out the pins as she spoke. The frizzy curls were not natural but had been done with a curling iron. Using a brush set aside for the guests' use, Eden brushed the curls out and then swept Victoria's hair on top of her head and secured it with a few pins. She trimmed the curls in front with a pair of sewing scissors from a mending kit so that they lightly framed Victoria's face.

Eden studied her handiwork in the mirror.

The extra height of the hairstyle counteracted the receding chin and made Victoria appear a bit more sophisticated.

Victoria stared at herself in the mirror. "Why, I'm almost pretty."

Eden laid her hands on the girl's shoulders. "You have lovely eyes, especially when you smile. Every woman is more alluring when she smiles," she said, reiterating words Madame Indrani said almost daily to her girls.

Victoria's gaze met hers in the mirror. "Why are you helping me? Aren't you after Lord Penhollow for yourself like my mother says?"

"Perhaps your mother is wrong."

Victoria mulled this over thoughtfully, as if she'd never considered the possibility before. "It is what Lady Penhollow told her . . . and you and Lord Penhollow do make a handsome couple."

Eden put the scissors back in the mending kit. "I have no claim on Lord Penhollow, other than he saved my life."

"I think he is old," Victoria confided. "And I think my mother likes him more than I do."

"But he is attractive," Eden reminded her, surprised that Victoria seemed immune to Lord Penhollow's charm.

"So is Mr. Whitacre."

Eden almost laughed at the hint of shyness in the girl's voice.

Victoria blushed, realizing what she'd just given away. "We'd best get back." She took another glimpse of herself in the mirror, preening a bit. "Mother will be angry that my hair is changed, but I don't care. I like it."

She started for the door, but then stopped. "There is something else I must tell you, Miss Eden. Mother and her friends plan to embarrass you this evening in hopes that Lord Penhollow will realize you are an unsuitable match."

"Victoria, I can have no claim on Lord Penhollow."

"Oh, but, Miss Eden, you already do," the girl answered with a wisdom that belied her young years.

"How are you so sure?"

"You remind me of Lord Penhollow himself, in many ways. He's never cared what anyone thinks of him. Mother believes he is far too eccentric." She reached out and gave Eden's hand a squeeze. "But don't worry. I won't let them treat you unkindly." She slipped through the door and Eden followed.

Downstairs, Mrs. Willis greeted them with a loud, "I was beginning to worry about the . . . two . . . of—Victoria, have you done something different to your hair?"

"Yes," Victoria said brightly. "I like it too." Nor did she hunch her shoulders the way she had been earlier.

"I don't think—" Mrs. Willis started, but she was interrupted by Mr. Whitacre.

"I like the style very much, Miss Willis," he said. "Perhaps you will permit me to escort you in to dinner."

Victoria answered "Yes" before her mother could interject an excuse.

"Well," Mrs. Willis said, obviously a bit rattled by this demonstration of independence in her daughter. "Shall we go in to dinner now?"

Dinner was as bad as Victoria had warned her it would be. Eden was placed far down the table away from Lord Penhollow. She had no sooner sat down than Mrs. Willis leaned toward her and said in a loud whisper, "You use this spoon for the soup."

Eden blinked in surprise. "Thank you," she murmured.

Mrs. Willis smiled coldly. "I didn't know if you *remembered* or not."

"Yes, I remember how to eat," Eden answered levelly.

"How nice for you," Mrs. Willis said. She then turned to Mr. Whitacre and silently mouthed, "She was about to use the wrong fork."

Mr. Whitacre did not appear to care about Eden's table manners. However, the two of them began a conversation, snubbing Eden completely.

Several times Victoria or Lord Penhollow attempted to pull Eden into the discussion at the other end of the table but either Lady Baines, Lady Danbury, or even Lady Penhollow managed to interrupt her before she could speak. Not that Eden felt she had anything worth saying.

No, she definitely felt out of place, even without Mrs. Willis's help.

"Miss Eden is from London," Victoria said.

"Ah! She remembers more," Lord Baines said with a touch of sarcasm, spearing a piece of fish with his fork.

Eden glanced at Lord Penhollow. He

seemed more interested in his dinner than the revelation that she was from London.

"Amnesia can happen that way," Dr. Hargrave began, ready to hold forth on the subject when Lady Danbury interrupted him.

"Did you hear that Lord and Lady Valen are leaving for London on Thursday? She's sponsoring her niece's come-out and has already secured vouchers to Almack's."

"How fortunate for her!" Mrs. Willis said. She looked to Eden. "Tell me, Miss Eden, have you ever been to Almack's, or would you be accepted there?"

Before Eden could answer, Lord Penhollow said, "Not everyone gives Almack's such vaulted status, Mrs. Willis. I, for one, have been refused vouchers, as was my father."

Lady Penhollow squirmed uncomfortably, and Eden felt a bit sorry for her now that the woman's plans had once again turned on her. Meanwhile, Mrs. Willis changed the subject of the conversation to something inoffensive, the weather.

Eden glanced in Lord Penhollow's direction. The warm candlelight could not soften the rugged masculinity of his features. He was handsome, very handsome . . . but he was also noble and not afraid to stand for what he believed in. Here was a man she could admire. A worthy man.

He could do so much better than a London prostitute, and this realization accomplished what Mrs. Willis and her petty friends could not. It made Eden recognize that he really was above her touch.

His gaze met hers over the flickering candles. For the space of several heartbeats, it was as if they were the only two people in the room . . . and she knew that if she really cared for him, the best thing she could do would be to remove herself from his life.

The clattering of a fork against china drew Eden's attention. The maid was clearing the table. Mrs. Willis rose. The gentlemen came to their feet.

"I believe it is time to leave the gentlemen to their port and conversation," she said. "Will you ladies join me in the drawing room?"

Eden started to rise but then Lord Penhollow spoke up. "I, for one, would be willing to forgo my port and brandy and join the ladies now. What do the rest of you gentlemen say?"

Mr. Willis frowned. "I like my port."

"But we can have it in the drawing room with the ladies," Lord Penhollow said reasonably.

"I wouldn't mind bypassing it," Mr. Whitacre said. "I prefer feminine company." He glanced at Victoria and she blushed prettily.

"It's not customary," Mrs. Willis said abruptly.

"Nonsense," Lord Penhollow said. "We are all old friends here. What is the joy of friendship if we cannot relax our manners with each other?"

Mr. Whitacre and, to Eden's surprise, Dr. Hargrave agreed with him and against Mrs. Willis's objections, the men adjourned with the women to the drawing room.

Lord Penhollow matched his step with

Eden's. "I believe Mrs. Willis and her friends are being rude. Should I make our excuses and we'll leave now?"

Eden feigned shock. "What? And cry quarter before the evening is done? Never."

He laughed. "There's fire in your eyes when you say those words."

She shook her head. "In truth, they have not been so bad." Certainly, they hadn't treated her worse than what she deserved.

He was quiet a moment and then said, "It's not your fault, you know. Their rudeness has nothing to do with you. Willis wants me to offer for his daughter, but there has never been an agreement or understanding between us."

"I know that."

"You do? I would have thought my mother would have said differently."

Eden smiled. "You mother believes Victoria is the perfect wife for you, but it was Victoria who told me there is no agreement between you. She claims you are too old to be her husband."

He paused in mid-stride. "Old?"

Eden laughed and entered the drawing room. Inside, Mr. Willis was still grumbling about his port while his wife stood before a pianoforte. She clapped her hands for attention. "My daughter Victoria is going to entertain us this evening. She is so *very* accomplished," she said, looking straight at Lord Penhollow.

He nodded and slid a covert glance of annoyance in Eden's direction. Eden covered her mouth with her hand to hide her laughter.

Victoria was a passable player and had a sweet voice. Eden noticed Lord Penhollow's foot kept time to the music and she felt a stab of jealousy. If he enjoyed Victoria's playing, he would admire her own all the more. Then Eden glanced in Mr. Whitacre's direction. The young man watched Victoria with rapt attention.

A moment later, when the last chord was finished and they'd all clapped in appreciation, Mrs. Willis stood and looked to Eden. "Tell, Miss Eden, do you have any *accomplishments* that you would wish to share with us?"

Eden started to say she could play, and then stopped.

This was Victoria's moment. Her chance to shine in front of Mr. Whitacre, to make her parents proud, and to reassert her own sense of self-worth.

Eden was an impostor.

She smiled. "No, Mrs. Willis, I do not. Victoria, your playing was most enjoyable." Her compliment was quickly seconded by Mr. Whitacre and Victoria blossomed under his admiration.

Eden's admittance to a lack of talent pleased Mrs. Willis no end. She appeared ready to gloat except that Lord Penhollow stood and announced that the hour was late and they needed to leave.

Eden had never heard sweeter words.

In the coach, Lady Penhollow carried on a great deal about Victoria—her breeding, her talent, her gentility. "Of course, I am so fortunate to have friends like the Willises and Lord and Lady Baines. Oh, yes, and Lord and Lady Danbury. Good, good friends we are."

Both Eden and Lord Penhollow were quiet. His knee did not brush against her leg in the dark and Eden felt disappointed.

She'd started this day full of wild, impossible dreams. Now it was over . . . and all her dreams had come to naught.

Like Icarus who believed he could fly to the sun and was destroyed by it, she suddenly feared what would happen if she stayed too much longer at Penhollow Hall. She couldn't have Lord Penhollow. Not without telling him the truth about her identity. Nor could she face him once he learned what a pretender she was. Her feelings for him were already too strong.

She was happy when they pulled into the drive leading to Penhollow Hall. At the front door, Eden wished both of them a good night and started to escape to the solitude of her room.

She'd not gone far when she heard him call her name.

She paused. "Yes?" She didn't turn but stood listening to the approach of his footsteps.

"I'm sorry for the actions of my mother and her friends this evening."

"You've already said that, my lord. Furthermore, no apology is needed. They meant only to look after your interests." The lump in her throat surprised her. It hurt to speak.

"Eden." His use of her name without the

formal "Miss" caught her off guard.

For a second, she hovered in indecision. How easy it would be to blow out the candle she held, shroud them in darkness, and beg him to keep her, to take her, right here, this moment.

And if she did, what then?

Would he turn from her in disgust? Or take what she offered without realizing its value?

"It was a wonderful evening," she whispered, and then ran from him without waiting for his response.

Unfortunately, Betsy was waiting in her room.

"Ah, Miss Eden, did Lord Penhollow notice how beautiful you looked? Did he say anything?"

"I don't know."

"Of course he did," Betsy continued as if she hadn't heard Eden speak. She hung the pearl dress in the wardrobe. "He can't help himself. He's balmy over you. Everyone says so."

Dressed in the oversized nightdress, Eden sat down on the bed. She rubbed her temples, feeling the beginning of a headache. She had plans to make. She didn't have time for nonsense. "He can't fall in love with me at all."

Betsy drew back. "He can. He is. The Widow said so."

Eden rolled her eyes heavenward. "Betsy, all of that is just superstition."

The maid's eyebrows snapped together as she drew back in surprise. "You don't believe, do you? The whole village believes, and you don't."

"Because I know it's impossible. Betsy, he's of a different class. I'm a nobody. He's someone special, someone noble and honorable and . . ." *And a man who must someday marry a woman of his own class, not a courtesan.*

Betsy quivered with outrage. "You must believe—deep in your soul you *must*. Every time the two of you are together, the air crackles with tension."

"That isn't magic," Eden replied bluntly. "It's lust."

"It's *love*."

A man like him could never love a woman like me. Eden came to her feet. "Betsy, there is no such thing as love. It's a myth, a fiction."

Betsy glared at her, her hands doubled in fists at her sides. Her voice trembled with the force of pent-up emotion. "You just don't want to believe, that's all that's the matter with you. And if *you* don't believe, it can never happen." She turned on her heel and stormed out of the room, slamming the door behind her.

Eden sat on the bed again. Why had she allowed herself to pick a fight with the maid? Why hadn't she just nodded her head and agreed with all of that nonsense?

Because Betsy had gotten her to believe, to dream that anything was possible—and it wasn't.

Tomorrow, she would approach Lady Penhollow and offer one of her dresses in exchange for coach fare away from Cornwall. Where she went and what she did, didn't matter. What was important was that she leave as quickly as possible.

Her mind made up, Eden lay on the bed. She closed her eyes. She would need her sleep for the morrow, but sleep escaped her.

She couldn't relax. Her mind was too filled with thoughts and plans. For a time, she toyed with the idea of contacting Mary Westchester. Mary would be eager to help but Eden feared Madame Indrani's vengeance against the young couple if she knew they'd been involved with Eden's escape.

Restless, she got up from the bed and left her bedroom with a candle. Perhaps if she could find a book to read in the library, her mind would settle down enough to let her sleep.

As she passed the drawing room door, the sight of moonlight streaming through the window and spilling onto the pianoforte stopped her. She hesitated, and then entered the room, closing the door behind her. She set the candle on the instrument and ran her hands lovingly over the smooth rosewood.

Sitting on the pianoforte bench, she lifted the cover and rested her fingers on the ivory keys. A familiar touch. What would have happened if she'd dared to perform this evening? Closing her eyes, she could picture the look of approval on Lord Penhollow's face. Her fingers began to play.

The music was more soothing than a book. Through it, she could release her soul, leaving worries and fears behind. Time lost meaning while she poured her heart into the notes she knew so well by memory. One song flowed into another until she was done, drained of all emotion.

Only then did she sense she wasn't alone.

The last chord still vibrated in the air as she looked up. Lord Penhollow stood in the open doorway. He'd removed his jacket and vest. His neckcloth hung loose around his neck. For a moment, she believed she'd conjured him from the deep well of her desires. They gazes met.

He was very real. All too real.

"I didn't mean to wake you," she managed to say.

"I was in my study. I couldn't sleep." He waited a beat. "You told us this evening you didn't play."

Eden didn't answer.

He walked toward her, his footsteps silent, until he stood beside her. "You didn't want to take the attention away from Victoria Willis."

Eden found her voice, but had trouble looking at him. He was too handsome, his presence overwhelming. "It seemed best."

He tilted her head up with one finger and whispered, "And you really haven't lost your memory, have you?"

Chapter 10

Eden didn't want to lie, not to him, not anymore. But she couldn't tell him the truth.

Lord Penhollow sat down on the piano bench beside her, his back to the instrument. "Play."

"What shall I play?"

"It doesn't matter."

Her fingers trembled as she touched the ivory keys. She was all too aware of him, of his thigh brushing against hers, of his arm leaning on the wood dividing the keys from the strings, of the intensity in his face.

For a moment, her mind went blank. She could barely remember her name, let alone why she was here. Her fingers stuck a D chord and then began moving almost with a will of their own. Mozart.

The music had been written to be played by moonlight. It wasn't an easy piece. Its mood changed swiftly, flowing from pensive contemplation to almost joyous rapture and back again.

She played for him as she'd played for no other, letting the music speak words that could never, should never be spoken between them.

His expression sober, he leaned his head down on his arm, listening. The light from the single candle encircled them.

Eden didn't feel the burn of tears until the first one trickled down her cheek. She struggled to hold back the others. Her throat ached with the pain of regret.

Still she played, her fingers running over the keys, striking chords. Another tear escaped, this time falling free and striking the back of her hand just as she finished the final chord.

The music vibrated in the air. Neither spoke. Eden couldn't face him. She lowered her head, staring at the contrast of her fingers against the cream-colored keys.

The back of his fingers stroked her cheek. She shivered at his touch, then closed her eyes, pressing her cheek closer, wanting these few moments between them.

Her tears flowed freely now. She tasted them on her lips, and then, tasted him. His fingers brushed her lips softly, before his lips hovered near hers in silent question.

Eden had never kissed before. The women of Madame Indrani's did not kiss. A kiss was too intimate, too personal. A poet had once said that a kiss could claim a woman's soul, and never give it back and Madame had trained her women to believe it.

But now, Eden craved that intimacy. The

blood roaring in her ears, she wet her lips and parted them.

He needed no other invitation. Their lips met.

The kiss was far more gentle than she'd anticipated. His lips were smooth and soft. Kissing him felt as natural as breathing and she relaxed into it with a small sigh.

His arms came around her, pulling her closer. Her hands still rested on the piano keys. She raised them now and placed them awkwardly upon his shoulders.

His lips, pressed against hers, curved into a smile, a heartbeat before his arms tightened and his kiss deepened.

What had started off as simple and innocent flared into passion. Her breasts flattened against the solid strength of his chest. Separated by only the thin layers of cotton material between them, she could feel the quickened pulse of his heart. Her nipples tightened in response.

The tip of his tongue gently stroked her lower lip. It tickled and she gasped in surprise. His tongue sweetly entered her mouth and she really learned how to kiss.

This was *intimate* . . . but very exciting.

Eden drank her fill of him. He'd been sipping brandy. She could taste it in the kiss, mingled with the salt from her tears. His skin smelled of the spice scent of his shaving soap he'd used a few hours earlier.

But it wasn't enough. She wanted to be closer and hooked her arms around his neck.

He chuckled deep in his throat. His hands

on her waist, he lifted her up to sit on his lap.

Eden faced him, her bent legs embracing his body. She kissed him back now. He'd shown her how and she reveled in the feel of his body pressed against hers. Placing her hand against his jaw, she delighted in the texture of his whiskered growth beneath her fingers and the movement of his muscles as he devoured her with his kiss.

Their movements pushed her nightdress up her thighs. Pressed against his black, finely woven breeches, she could feel the long, hard length of him reaching almost to his waistband. Something possessive and proud soared inside her, opening her to him. She pressed closer.

His hand ran up her bare thigh and slipped beneath the nightdress. Their kiss went deeper and deeper as if they could pull the very breath from each other. She tugged at his shirt, wanting clothes removed between them. Her fingers slipped under the waist of his breeches and her fingertips brushed the hard velvety head of his erection.

His hand came round and captured hers, preventing her from exploring further. He broke the kiss and leaned back against the pianoforte, his breathing heavy.

Eden tossed her hair back, a wildness thrumming through her. She leaned her arms on his chest and bit his bottom lip. "Why did you stop? I want to touch you. I need to feel you."

She reached to kiss him again, but he shook his head, taking both her wrists in his hands.

"If we don't stop here, then I'll never stop."

Eden rubbed her breasts against his chest. Her nipples tightened, anticipating his touch. "Then let's not stop."

His eyes glowed in the candlelight. She waited. She felt wanton, she felt powerful . . . she felt honest. This, she was trained for. This, she understood.

Suddenly, he rose, bringing her up with him. Strong arms cradled her shoulders and her legs. He blew out the candle and carried her from the drawing room to the hallway leading to her bedroom.

Eden threw her arms around his shoulders, breathing in the scent of warm man and starched cotton. Tomorrow, she would leave, but she would have tonight.

He pressed her door open with his shoulder. The room was dark save for the moonlight coming in through the panes of the French doors and spreading across the bed. Outside, the fountain splashed and crickets called.

Eden's heartbeat quickened as he didn't waste time but crossed to the bed and laid her down upon the sheets, the bed still indented where she had been resting earlier. She reached for him.

But Lord Penhollow didn't follow her onto the bed. Instead he backed away, moving into the shadows.

Eden came up on one elbow. "Aren't you joining me?"

"No."

Her passion-fuddled mind had difficulty understanding. "No?" She came up on her knees. "But I thought—We were just . . ." Her voice trailed off. She couldn't put into words what they'd been doing in the drawing room. Oh, she knew many descriptions for it, but none of that matched this racing of her heart and the almost desperate need inside her. "Don't you want me?"

He gave a shaky laugh and then whispered, "I burn for you. I want nothing more than to be buried inside you and feel your body around me."

Eden groaned with the aching desire his words inspired. She reached out. "Then come to me."

"I can't."

Eden dropped her hand to the bed, gathering the sheets in a fist clenched in frustration. "Why?"

"Because there is something I want from you more."

"And what is that?"

"I want you to trust me."

Trust. Eden sat back on her heels. She combed her hair back from her face with her hands. "What if I can't give you that?"

"You will," he said fiercely. "Because I always get what I want."

Her heart seemed to stop. "What if what you want . . . is not what you expect?"

"You're an innocent, Eden. I could never believe you guilty of wrongdoing."

"An innocent?" she repeated with disbelief. "What makes you believe that, my lord?"

His teeth flashed white in the darkness. "My sweet Eden, I could tell by your kiss. I'm the first man you've kissed, although you learn quickly."

His absolute conviction frightened her.

"My lord, I'm far from the innocent that you think—"

"No, stop. Aren't we all guilty of something?" he practically growled.

His anger surprised her. She pulled back just as he crossed the room to her. His hands grasped her arms and lifted her to meet his kiss. This kiss was different from the earlier. It was savage, possessive, and branded her completely as his.

He let go and Eden slid to the bed, unable to move.

Her body cried for more.

He stood over the bed. "You're mine," he said. "But I want more than just this, Eden. When I take you, it will be when I can claim all of you. Your heart, your mind . . . your soul." Without another word, he turned and left the room, shutting the door behind him.

It was hours before Eden could fall asleep and when she did, she knew she would not be leaving on the morrow.

"Wake up, Miss Eden! We must get you ready for church. You've already missed your chance at an early morning riding lesson with Lord Penhollow. He said to let you sleep and you can have your lesson tomorrow."

Good, Eden thought, and covered her head with her pillow.

Betsy wasn't going to let her sleep. "Come, Miss Eden. It's time for church. It would please Lady Penhollow no end if you miss church. You'll be the talk of Hobbles Moor."

Eden struggled to open her eyes. She sat up on the bed and pushed her hair out of her face. "Church?" she asked sluggishly. "I don't go to church."

Betsy whirled around. "Don't go to church? You *must* go to church. Everyone in Hobbles Moor goes to church. Why, I've never heard of such a thing. It must be that memory sickness. You've forgotten that you've gone to church."

Eden rubbed her eyes, and stifled a yawn. "You're right, I've forgotten," she muttered and would have fallen back on her pillow again except for Betsy's next words.

"Lord Penhollow is expecting you to be ready within the half hour."

Now Eden was awake. She climbed out of bed. "He's taking me to church?"

"Of course he is. He's taking you and his mother."

Eden began splashing cool water on her face. The last time she'd been in a church was thirteen years ago when she'd slipped inside one to warm up during a freezing winter. The vicar had run her out and she'd not stepped foot in one since.

Remembering the comments about last night's low neckline, Eden suggested, "Why don't you pick something out?"

"I'd be happy to, miss," Betsy answered, and chose the periwinkle blue, Lord Penhollow's favorite color.

Eden eyed the gown's décolletage and

sighed. "You'd best lay out the Kashmir shawl too."

A half hour later, Eden was dressed and ready to go. Lord and Lady Penhollow waited for her in the drawing room.

"I hear you've forgotten what it was like to go to church," Lady Penhollow announced with a skeptical lift of one eyebrow.

Eden wondered how she knew that already. Betsy had only left the bedroom once to get a cup of chocolate. Could the word have traveled so quickly through the servants up to Lady Penhollow?

Eden kept her expression pleasant. "Good morning to you, my lady, my lord. It is true. I don't recall attending a Sunday service." That much *was* true!

Lord Penhollow stepped forward. "It makes no difference, Mother." He changed the subject. "Both of you ladies look lovely this morning. I shall be the envy of the congregation. Are we ready to go?"

Both ladies perked up a bit at his compliment and replied in the affirmative.

The small church was packed by the time they arrived. Betsy was right, everyone in Hobbles Moor was there including Mr. and Mrs. Willis and their friends. Lady Penhollow hurried over to greet them, but Mrs. Willis gave her a cool reception.

"Poor Mother," Lord Penhollow said. "She wants them to like her so very much."

"And don't you care what they think?" Eden asked.

He shot her a heart-stopping smile. "I refuse to worry about what they think."

"Yes, well, it isn't so easy for a woman as it is for a man," she answered honestly.

"Don't let them bother you."

"I won't, but I'm stronger than your mother."

He directed her inside church. A member of the Penhollow family had been attending this church since the day it was built back in 1142. Their pew was located at the front of the church directly beneath the pulpit.

Eden held back, suddenly nervous. "I didn't realize we would be sitting in front of everyone."

"I thought you were made of sterner stuff," he reminded her in a low voice. "There's no reason to be afraid, Eden. I'll be beside you."

She only nodded, not trusting herself to speak. He led her to the pew and they took their places. Lady Penhollow joined them right before the service started.

In the end, Eden's fears had been groundless. Lord Penhollow stood by her side through the church service, whispering cues. "Stand up, head bowed." "Kneel." There was no judgment in his voice. He even turned the pages of the hymnal so that Eden could recite the creeds with the others who knew them by heart and slowly, she relaxed, beginning to feel like a member of this community. She belonged . . . and it was a wonderful feeling.

That afternoon it rained. Instead of going to his study and working on papers, Lord Penhollow stayed with Eden in the drawing room, playing cards and games of chess. He was a terrible chess player but a graceful loser and his teasing comments about her moves brought tears of laughter to her eyes.

Lady Penhollow sat with them, pretending to do needlework. She didn't find anything funny in their lighthearted banter and as the afternoon wore on, her face grew tighter and tighter until it resembled nothing more than a dried apple with a lace cap on top of it. Occasionally she would tell Lord Penhollow she wanted to see him alone, but he deftly ignored her requests and stayed right across the game table from Eden.

After a light dinner of chicken, the three of them returned to the drawing room and Lord Penhollow asked her to play the pianoforte.

Lady Penhollow turned on Eden. "I thought you said last night that you don't play. Is this something else you suddenly *remember?*"

Lord Penhollow answered her. "She said she didn't play because she didn't want anyone to make an unflattering comparison between herself and Miss Willis." He wore a jacket this evening of evergreen superfine over fawn-colored trousers. The jacket color brought out the blue in his eyes.

"An unflattering comparison?" Lady Penhollow raised her eyebrows. "Miss Willis has been trained by the finest music teacher in Cornwall."

Lord Penhollow sighed. "Yes, well, I know it is difficult for Miss Eden to compete against such a fine credential, but I'd like to hear her play this evening all the same."

"Very well," Lady Penhollow said stiffly. "If she is so wonderful, let her play. I for one will not be an easy audience."

"I would never imagine you anything but, Mother." Laughter lurked in his eyes. He turned to Eden. "Will you play?"

For him, she would do anything. As she took her seat at the pianoforte, she wondered what would happen if she did tell him the truth. Would he still accept her?

Her fingers ran over the keys experimentally while her mind drifted to what she and Lord Penhollow had been doing on this same bench last night. She hit a wrong chord and Lady Penhollow snorted in derision.

Determined to win her over, Eden started with a minuet. After the light tune, she moved effortlessly into a sonata. She was halfway through a third piece, a concerto played in allegro, when Lady Penhollow set aside her needlework and gave the music her full attention.

Eden felt a wave of triumph. However, at the end of the small concert, Lady Penhollow stood without a word of praise. "Come, Miss Eden, the hour grows late. We must go to our beds."

"But doesn't she play well, Mother?" Lord Penhollow asked sardonically.

Lady Penhollow's face, so much like her son's, never lost its expression of cool indifference. "She's passable." With that, she walked out of the room.

Lord Penhollow turned to Eden. "I thought your performance superb." He lifted her hand and lightly kissed it.

She closed her fingers around his, not wanting to let him go.

"Trust me," he said quietly, and tucked her hand in the crook of his arm. "She will come around."

Lady Penhollow had apparently gone up to bed. Lord Penhollow walked Eden to her room. "Until tomorrow," he whispered, and pushed a stray curl away from her face.

"I don't want you to leave," she said.

"And I don't want to leave you either, but we're going to do it that way, Eden." His lips brushed hers for the briefest of seconds before he backed away from her.

"Good night," he whispered.

"Good night."

She leaned against the door frame and watched him walk down the hall before turning the handle and entering her room. Betsy waited for her and Eden realized his wisdom in not honoring her request for a private moment alone.

Someone knocked on the door.

Since she was standing close by, Eden opened it. Lady Penhollow stood there.

"You're not going to get him," she said. "I won't let that happen because you don't deserve him." Without waiting for an answer, she left.

Again, Betsy had to wake her the next morning. She swept open the drapes. "It's time to rise, Miss Eden. I've already brought your chocolate and a little surprise, too."

Eden frowned, hugging her pillow closer. "I'm not ready to get up yet."

Betsy leaned down over the bed and said softly, "Ah, but Lord Penhollow is waiting to give you a riding lesson."

That statement popped her eyes open. "Riding lesson?"

"Yes," Betsy continued airily. "He told me he'll meet you in the stable yard. Plus, here is my surprise."

Eden rolled over to look at her. Betsy held up a brown riding habit. It was quite old and the color had faded on the shoulders. At one time, the habit's hat had been stylish with a jaunty plume. Now the hat brim appeared as wilted as the plume.

"It's the best I could do on short notice," Betsy said. "I told Mrs. Ivy, Lady Penhollow's dresser, that you needed a habit to go riding. I made sure she knew I thought you'd make a fool of yourself in front of his lordship, and she provided me with this in no time. Oh, come now, get up. Lord Pierce is expecting you."

Eden didn't want a riding lesson, but she wasn't going to miss an opportunity to spend time with Lord Penhollow, especially without Lady Penhollow. She hopped out of the bed.

Twenty minutes later she was dressed and tripping over the extra-long hem of the habit on her way to the stables. She'd removed the moldy plume but still felt slightly ridiculous under the lopsided brim. No amount of blocking would ever return this hat to any semblance of style.

Lord Penhollow cooled his heels talking to

Jim as he waited for her. He appeared very handsome this morning in buff breeches, boots, and a bottle-green riding jacket. Between the two men stood a bay horse with white stockings.

"This is Velvet," Lord Penhollow said, introducing the horse to Eden. "She's as gentle a mare as ever walked the face of this earth. You'll believe you are sitting in a rocking chair instead of riding a horse."

"I doubt that," she said under her breath, absently petting one of the foxhounds that had charged up to greet her.

"You will," he promised. "Now come and let me help you mount." He led the horse to a mounting block.

Eden didn't move. "I'm still not convinced this is a good idea. I mean, I've managed to make it this far in my life without riding, so it isn't a necessity."

Jim guffawed his response while Lord Penhollow said, "If you are going to live in the country, Miss Eden, you must learn to ride."

If you are going to live in the country—? Now Eden had motivation to learn.

But it wasn't easy.

He might describe Velvet as docile but the animal appeared wild-eyed and shifty to her. Furthermore, she was expected to ride sidesaddle.

Lord Penhollow showed her how himself, ignoring the laughter of the grooms as he sat in Velvet's saddle, one leg hooked over the horn. "See? Nothing simpler."

"Oh, yes, it should make tumbling off much

easier," she replied tartly. "Perhaps if the horse's back was a bit flatter?"

Lord Penhollow laughed. "You'll go on all right once you get your balance." He jumped to the ground. "Now it's your turn." He held out his hand. "Don't worry. If you start to fall, I'll catch you."

Right there was a tempting reason for her to climb onto Velvet's back. Eden came forward. Taking his hand, she stepped up on the block of wood and then gingerly seated herself in the saddle.

Or thought she had.

With a nickered protest, Velvet sidled away. Eden lost her balance and started to slide out of the saddle. Lord Penhollow stepped forward and attempted to catch her in time and push her back up into the saddle.

One hand rested on her thigh, while his other arm looped her waist, but it wasn't enough and she slid down his body to land on her feet on the ground. Once she got over the surprise, Eden decided that, maybe, learning to ride could be great fun.

He spoiled it by saying, "Let's try this again and see if you can stay in the saddle."

Eden answered him with a sigh—but the second time, she did manage to keep her seat. In fact, she rather enjoyed the height of being up on the horse.

"Now you're going to ride her," Lord Penhollow said and he gave Velvet a little pat on the rump.

The horse started moving. Eden tensed.

"Easy, relax," Lord Penhollow said. "Pull

back on the reins gently when you want to stop."

"You are sure of this?" she asked cautiously as the horse ambled forward.

"It's worked for me every time. And smile, so I know you are all right."

Eden was concentrating too hard to smile. She pulled the reins and Velvet stopped. She shot a surprised look in the direction of the watching grooms. "I did it."

"Aye, you sit in the saddle well, Miss Eden," Jim answered.

"Now make the horse go," Lord Penhollow said.

"Go? How?" Eden asked.

"Nudge Velvet with your knee. She's a well trained animal. She'll understand." And Velvet did.

"I think I like this," Eden said as she circled the stable yard a second time.

"Good," Lord Penhollow said. He motioned for one of the grooms to bring Cornish King forward. "Now we can have our ride."

"You mean this isn't it?" Eden asked with a stab of dismay.

He threw back his head and laughed. "You don't want to stay in a stable yard all of your life, do you?"

"What I want to do is stay close to that block of wood so I can get off Velvet when I feel a need to," she answered honestly.

Everyone laughed, only Eden wasn't being funny.

Lord Penhollow climbed into his saddle and led Velvet and Eden toward the main drive.

Eden held the saddle, reins, and a hank of Velvet's mane for good measure.

Cornish King pranced, anxious to charge off over the countryside, but Lord Penhollow kept him firmly in check.

He was completely at ease on a horse. He reminded Eden of a picture she'd seen of an ancient knight and his horse in full armor. If they had lived five hundred years earlier, that was the way he and Cornish King would have been, a formidable team, eager to vanquish all invaders.

Slowly, she began to relax as they walked down the drive. "Ride with the horse," he suggested. "Move with her. You aren't going to become a first-rate horsewoman in one lesson. Right now, I just want you to take pleasure from the ride."

Eden tried his advice and found riding more comfortable. They walked their mounts, in no hurry to go anywhere fast.

Soon she understood what he meant about needing a horse to get around in the country. She became accustomed to the feeling of Velvet beneath her and could enjoy the sights. It had rained last night and the fresh, clean air felt good. A bluebird landed on a hedgerow and took off again, singing.

They rode through the village of Hobbles Moor. Built around a great circular pond and communal pump, the village was a quarter the size of Plympton but far more attractive. Thatched-roof houses lined unpaved streets leading from the pond. Many of the houses had small front yards with flower and vegetable gardens growing in them. Eden wondered which house Betsy lived in.

Even at this early hour, people were out and about. Dane was already at work in his smithy. The air rang with the sound of his hammer striking the anvil. Children ran to the side of the road, waving and calling to Lord Penhollow by name as they passed. A young, blonde girl, little more than ten years of age, stepped forward and offered a small bouquet of daisies to Eden.

Eden reined Velvet to a halt but didn't dare reach down for the bouquet, afraid she would topple off her precarious seat. Lord Penhollow took it from the child and passed it to Eden who made the girl smile when she said, "Daisies are my very favorite."

The child bobbed a curtsy. "We all know that, Miss Eden."

"Make him bow," a chubby lad called to Lord Penhollow. "Make your horse do his tricks."

Lord Penhollow did exactly that. Cornish King bowed to the young girl who curtsied back. All the children laughed.

"I thank heaven Velvet doesn't know any tricks," Eden said fervently, holding her bouquet and reins with both hands. "Or else I would be sent sprawling onto the road."

"Oh, but she can," Lord Penhollow said. "All I have to do is tap her shoulder three times like this—" He reached to do so but Eden caught his hand.

"Don't you dare," she said with a laugh.

He'd leaned over in his saddle and they were now practically nose to nose.

"And what will you do to stop me?" he asked.

It was an invitation for a kiss if ever she'd heard one and she stared at him with incredulity, uncertain if she'd heard him correctly.

"Oh, go ahead and kiss her!" a man's voice shouted. Eden and Lord Penhollow both looked up in surprise to discover they were the center of a ring of villagers. Dane had been the one who shouted. He stood by his fire with his massive arms crossed.

"Why, Dane, I shall do exactly that," Lord Penhollow said, and gave Eden a light smack on the lips. It was the kind of kiss a man gave a sweetheart on a summer's day, affectionate and carefree, but no less potent to Eden.

The villagers shouted their approval, except for Dane who claimed that Lord Penhollow would have to do better than that if he wanted to win a "handsome lass like Miss Eden."

Lord Penhollow laughed and led Velvet through the crowd and down the road. From the corner of her eye, Eden glimpsed the Widow Haskell. The woman stood apart from the others. Her silver hair gleamed in the sunlight.

Their gazes met and held as Eden rode by. And then the Widow Haskell smiled. Eden felt as if she'd received a blessing of some sort.

Outside the village, she followed Lord Penhollow across a field toward an aged oak.

"Where are we going?"

"I want to show you the famous money tree."

"Oh, Betsy told me about it. She says that's why Hobbles Moor is special, because it has its money tree. I didn't imagine such a thing really existed."

"It does, and here it is." He reined in beside Eden.

The oak's branches spread out almost ten feet from the solid trunk. It was the type of tree children could climb easily to play in its boughs. Adults would use it as a landmark.

"But can you believe it's magic?" Eden stared up into the leafy ceiling over her head.

"Yes," he said.

She looked at him. "You're not joking."

"I'd never joke about magic."

"I've never known magic," she admitted soberly. "And I don't know if I believe in money trees. Everything I've ever been given has in some way or another had conditions attached to it."

"Just because you haven't seen something, doesn't mean it doesn't exist."

Eden searched the tree's heavy limbs. "I don't see money hidden among the leaves."

"And what about love?"

She jerked her head to stare at him. *Love?*

He reined Cornish King closer to Velvet. His leg brushed against Eden's. He looked down into her eyes.

For a second, Eden felt he was going to kiss her again. Her heart stepped up its beat in anticipation.

But instead he said, "I'm going to teach you

about magic." He reached into the pocket of his coat and pulled out a handful of copper pennies. He offered some to her.

They felt heavy in her hand. "What do I do with these?"

"You throw them, Eden. Up in the sky as high as you can." He demonstrated, tossing his handful of coins up into the air. She heard them hit the leaves of the tree and then fall to the earth like hard raindrops.

"It's your turn," he said. "Throw your pennies. We haven't much time."

Eden did as he asked. Her pennies didn't go as high or as far. Velvet moved as one hit her. Lord Penhollow reached out and steadied the horse. He kept his hands on the reins as he pulled her round.

"Come." He started Cornish King and Velvet in the direction of a large clump of bushes by a stream. They rode around to the back of the bushes where they could not be seen from the road.

"What are we waiting for?" Eden asked, and a second later had her answer. She heard the sound of voices, children's voices.

"Peek around and watch," he told her.

She did and a second later saw the village children come running down the road. There must have been two dozen of them.

"Is there money under the tree today?" one of the older children asked rhetorically and the younger children made a mad dash for the tree.

"There's money! There's money!" the youngest shouted and began scooping up pennies from the ground.

"Here now, make sure we all get a share," a girl called, hurrying to join them. "The tree doesn't like it when we're greedy."

Eden watched the children laughingly gather the pennies. It was a magic moment. She knew what those pennies meant to a child. There'd been a time when she would have sold her soul for even a halfpenny to buy a loaf of bread.

"Do you do this often?" she asked without taking her eyes from the scene.

"About once a week or so. I started it when Cornish King won his first race. That was over sixteen years ago. Another favorite place to throw pennies is down by Hermit's Cove. The fishing is good there and the children go often." He tapped her shoulder. "Come, we must go now."

Reluctantly, Eden reined Velvet around to follow him. He took them home in a different direction, through the forest on the other side of the stream so the children wouldn't see them.

"Do you think the children know you are behind their money tree?"

"The older ones do, but they keep it a secret for as long as they can from the little ones."

Eden looked down at the daisies she held in her gloved hand. "Why would they do that?"

He looked puzzled. "Do what?"

"Keep a secret like that. Why should they care if the little ones believe the tree is magic or not? Why wouldn't they want all the pennies for themselves?"

Lord Penhollow pulled Cornish King to a halt. Velvet stopped too. "Because it wouldn't be any fun if they kept all the pennies themselves. It's the sharing that creates the magic."

Eden considered this new concept, this idea of everyone sharing, no, *giving* so that others would be happy.

He brushed her cheek with his gloved hand. "Eden, everyone needs to believe that life holds a little magic. If we didn't, it wouldn't be worth living."

"And the children protect that belief because they care for each other."

"Of course," he said, and urged Cornish King on.

Eden rode in silence beside him for a moment, digesting these new ideas. "And is Hermit's Cove considered magic too?" she asked.

"Yes," he answered. "After all, it's where I found you."

His words shot straight to her heart and, for a moment, she was dazzled by the most incredible magic of all. It swept through her like a clean, bracing wind, and changed something within her.

Now she saw Lord Penhollow with new eyes. Life was suddenly richer and more valuable—especially in his presence.

Because Eden had discovered the unthinkable, the unbelievable.

She had discovered love.

Chapter 11

That afternoon, Pierce had two visitors, Lord Danbury and Captain Harry Dutton. He'd been sitting at his desk in the study thinking of Miss Eden and their ride that morning. His thoughts were so distracting that after an hour's work, he'd only made three new notations in the open ledger on his desk before him. He closed the ledger and greeted the men warmly, inviting them to sit down in the chairs in front of his desk. He rang for wine.

Ten minutes later, he almost threw them out of his house.

"We're concerned for you," Harry said quickly, realizing his suggestion to turn Miss Eden's care and welfare over to the parish was the cause of Pierce's fury. "That's the only reason we're here."

"Besides, it's your mother who asked us to talk to you," Lord Danbury added. "People are speculating. They say you kissed her right in the middle of Hobbles Moor. Really, Penhollow, you must think of your station in life."

His criticism hit its mark. Pierce knew he shouldn't have kissed Eden in public. He'd been caught up in the joy of the moment. However, he should have been more protective of her. "Miss Eden is none of your affair. Nor will I allow any man to cast a shadow across her name."

"It's not us gossiping," Lord Danbury hotly denied. "It's others. *We* are your friends. But be cautious. After all, no one knows Miss Eden or her family. She appeared out of nowhere."

"Yes, Penhollow, you must be careful," Harry agreed. He scooted to the edge of his seat to add in a confiding tone, "After all, a man of your wealth is a prime target for all sorts of scoundrels, male and female."

Pierce sat back in his chair and stared at him in disbelief. "Let me see if I understand this correctly. You're saying that without benefit of compass or map, Miss Eden maneuvered the boat toward a tiny cove that I haven't visited in—How long has it been, Harry? Two years? Just so she can snare herself an earl? And, of course, she had to be sure to arrive at the right time. After all, two hours later and she would have missed us." He paused. "Do you really believe that is possible?"

Harry shifted uncomfortably. Lord Danbury studied the floor.

Pierce brought his hands down on the desk. "Your suspicions are ridiculous."

"Perhaps so. But it still doesn't preclude the possibility that she turned mercenary once she saw how much she had to gain," Harry said, defending himself. "And she's succeeding. I watched you in church with her yesterday. I saw the way you looked at her and how close you stood next to her. Today, you were out riding with her most of the morning. I've never known you to waste a morning on anything resembling pleasure, Penhollow. Work has always come first. It's obvious she's charmed you, and all we are asking is that you be cautious."

Pierce felt dangerously close to losing his hold on his temper. "Do you think me stupid?"

Lord Danbury cleared his throat and shook his head. "No, no, it was your mother's idea. *She* asked us to speak to you—"

Harry interrupted, coming to his feet and leaning across the desk. "No, I don't think you've lost your head, not yet completely. But she's a lovely piece, Penhollow. The sort that sets a man's blood racing. Be careful."

Pierce studied him a moment before saying softly, "No, *you* should be careful. If you value my goodwill and friendship, you will not speak a word of this matter again to anyone. I will call out the man who slanders Miss Eden's reputation."

Harry straightened and rubbed his palms nervously against his leg. "I mean no insult, Penhollow. My words are motivated by our long-standing friendship. I'm concerned for your position and your reputation. You've worked hard to build both. I know what they mean to you."

"And you hope I don't throw them both

away?" Pierce finished, the anger boiling inside him.

Lord Danbury and Harry wisely kept silent.

Pierce smiled grimly. "I believe this interview is at an end. You will understand if I don't show you to the door."

Harry opened his mouth as if he were about to say something else and then changed his mind. "Very well, Penhollow." He headed for the door.

Lord Danbury hesitated. "Penhollow, you understand I'm only doing this because your mother asked me to. I mean, you won't forget that you promised to work with my agent and help drain that field with that new method you've fashioned?"

"I will help, Danbury," Pierce said coldly. "But I advise you to stay out of my affairs."

"Penhollow, I was caught between two women, your mother and my wife. What would you have me do?"

"I've already told you what I want from you."

"Yes, yes, that you did," Danbury said, bowing his way out of the room. A second later, he was gone and Pierce went in search of his mother.

He found her in the Garden Room doing needlework. Mrs. Ivy sat with her. "Leave us," he ordered the dresser.

Startled, Mrs. Ivy looked to his mother. At her nod of assent, the dresser hurried from the room. Pierce shut the door behind her.

"You didn't have to ask her to leave," his

mother said without looking up from her embroidery hoop. "You can say anything in front of Mrs. Ivy that you wish to say to me."

He didn't answer her immediately. Instead, his attention was on the scene out in the garden. Eden was there, following the gardener as he clipped dead rose heads. Pierce couldn't hear her words but he knew she was asking questions. A second later, the gardener handed her the snips and she began clipping the roses while he supervised.

Eden's concentration was completely on her task. She didn't wear a bonnet and the sunlight highlighted the auburn in her dark hair.

Desire, lust . . . and another emotion he didn't dare put a name to yet, flared inside him. He took a step toward the window.

His mother's voice intruded on his thoughts. "She's a complete hoyden." She lifted her nose disdainfully. "She'll freckle if she isn't careful."

"I had two callers this afternoon," he said without preamble. "Lord Danbury and Captain Dutton."

"Did you?" Lady Penhollow asked with interest.

He faced her. "You know I did. You probably knew the minute they stepped into this house and you also know why they came."

She set the needlework aside. "They are worried for you. All your friends are worried."

"*You* asked them to speak to me. You're the one who is worried."

For a moment, he thought she would deny

it and then the set of her jaw turned stubborn. "I am. This woman isn't good for you. We don't know who she is or who her family is."

"That doesn't matter, Mother—"

"Yes, it does! It's important not just to you, but also to me." She rose from the chair to emphasize her point.

Outside, Eden laughed at something the gardener said before trying her new skills on another rosebush.

Since Eden had come into his life, his whole house seemed full of laughter; the servants acted happier. He heard their voices often and caught them smiling at each other. He hadn't realized before how silent and lonely Penhollow Hall had been when there was only his mother and himself.

"It's important what other people think of us," his mother said, coming to stand by his side. "If you aren't careful, you will lose your chance at a match with Victoria Willis."

"Mother, I have told you numerous times, I have no intention of offering for Miss Willis."

"But it would be a good marriage," she protested, deliberately blocking his view of Eden with her body. "You would be respected by all of our friends, and Miss Willis has a nice dowry. It's everything I could wish for you."

"What about what I wish?" he snapped. "As for friends, are you completely blind? The Willises and the Danburys and the others aren't our friends. Where were they when father was gambling away everything we owned? Or when he became too ill to walk? Did Mrs. Willis come knocking at your door then? Or were you invited to tea by Lady Danbury or Lady Baines?"

Her complexion paled and her blue eyes, so much like his own, burned with fury. "Your father shamed us. As long as he was under our roof, they couldn't risk their reputations and be seen with us."

"What nonsense!" he exploded. "They turned their backs on us, *on you*—because they didn't think you were good enough for them. Perhaps you want to forget what happened, but I will not. I remember the day you went to church and they snubbed you, right there in the Lord's house—how old was I? Eight? And you were so hurt you wouldn't step a foot into the church again until five years ago when I forced you to go."

She shook her head, denying his words. "That was a long time ago. Our circumstances have changed."

"They tolerate us, Mother, because they want something from us. Danbury needs my advice and Baines wants the income from colts sired by Cornish King. They know that if they treat you the way they did in the past, I would cut off all support."

"No," she answered in a petulant voice. "They're my friends. They accept me. They've forgotten who I am."

Pierce swore under his breath. She was a fragile shell of a woman really, who'd never been able to stand against the injustices in her life. It made her dislike of Eden all that much more incomprehensible to him.

He took her hand and led her back to the

chair. He sat in a chair opposite hers. "The time has come for us to talk, Mother."

She folded her hands in her lap. "We *are* talking. And I think you should send Miss Eden away. I think you should marry Miss Willis."

"The devil take Miss Willis—"

"Pierce, you can't talk about her that way!"

"I don't want to talk about her at all! I'm talking about you and Father, and the day they snubbed you in church. I want to talk about your taking to your room and not coming out until after Father died." He paused, remembering. "Mother, my father was a complete blackguard, but nothing he ever did frightened me the way your rejection of me did."

"Reject you—?" She shook her head. Tears welled in her eyes. "No, it was him I rejected. Not you. Never you. Tell me you believe that." She reached for his hand. "I must hear you say you believe me. I love you and only want what is best for you."

"Mother, what is best for me is not Victoria Willis. I have no desire to marry a woman I don't love. I saw what such a marriage did to you and I don't want it in my life. You and Father had nothing. I want everything."

The tears spilled over. She pressed the back of her hand against her cheeks to stop their flow, before saying, "It wasn't like that, Pierce. Not completely."

"Then how was it? You never talk about it. There isn't a person in this house brave enough to mention Father's name in your presence."

She sat back in her chair, her shoulders slumped. "I had no fewer than five offers for my hand in marriage when I met Garret Penhollow. I fell in love with him, Pierce, from the moment I first saw him. Passionately." She smiled at the memory, then her smile flattened into a bitter frown. "But he was the wrong person. I wasted myself on him. It turned out that all he wanted was my money and an heir. Once I'd given him these things, he left me."

She looked up at her son. "I'm not completely heartless. But I've made the mistake of falling in love with a person I didn't truly know and I don't want to see you do the same." She nodded toward Eden. "Beware of this woman. Be careful of her. She's too lovely, too stirring, and far too available."

"I'm not a fool, Mother."

"Really, my son? Are you going to deny that you almost live to see her smile? Or that she's the last thing you think of as you drift off to sleep? Or that if you had your way, she'd be lying beside you?"

Now it was Pierce's turn to feel uncomfortable. He came to his feet. Eden and the gardener had moved on to another part of the garden.

"You are still searching for information on her, aren't you?" she asked.

"I have dispatched messengers to London searching for news of a missing girl," he answered.

The lines of his mother's mouth tightened

cynically. "Promise me you'll wait until they return and we have information verifying Miss Eden's background before you do anything rash."

"Anything like what?"

"Like offering marriage."

Pierce shook his head. "I've never mentioned marriage."

"Oh, it's there in your eyes every time you look at her. You're the kind of man, my son, who champions those who are weak and in need. You like protecting damsels in distress. I pray you are not protecting the wrong woman."

"We'll just have to see, won't we?" He left the room without giving his promise.

Not far from Portsmouth, Nasim and Gadi were being chased off a local squire's property.

"You bloody foreigners! Stay off my land or I'll bloody shoot you," the squire shouted, brandishing an aged blunderbuss in Nasim and Gadi's direction.

The two Arabs rode off until they were out of sight. This was their third brush today with angry Englishmen. Yesterday, they'd almost been escorted to the parish jail when the house they had approached to ask questions in their search for the virgin turned out to be owned by a magistrate.

Their flowing robes, dark skin, and accents made them immediately unwelcome in a countryside far away from the sophistication of London. Then when they mentioned they were looking for an English girl, the yokels' mistrust turned to violence.

"This is not working," Gadi said.

"We must find the scent of her trail. That's all," Nasim said.

"We have no trail," Gadi answered grimly. "England is a big country. It could take us years to find her."

"It could," Nasim agreed. "There must be another way."

They rode back to the inn. The innkeeper's wife met them at the door. "We've had complaints about you," she said rudely. "The whole countryside's talking about your hunt for a girl. An English girl. You can get out now. You'll not be staying under our roof."

Gadi started to growl at her, but Nasim placed a warning hand on his arm. He bowed to the innkeeper's wife. "We understand and appreciate your hospitality for as long as it has lasted."

She snorted at that. "Get out. Now."

The two men went up to the room to gather their belongings. "Why must we let her talk to us that way?" Gadi demanded behind a closed door.

"Because we are strangers. But worse, we are missing something here, Gadi, something important," Nasim said thoughtfully.

"Do you believe they could be hiding the virgin from us?"

"They know nothing of her. No, my thoughts are spurred by your comment that England is a big country. You are right, my friend, we can't continue to go from house to house. It is a waste of our time."

"Then what shall we do? We cannot return to Ibn Sibah empty-handed."

"Think! The virgin has no money, no family, no friends except one person."

Gadi frowned. "I do not know who that person is."

Nasim leaned across the table. "Madame Indrani."

"Ah, yes," Gadi said, starting to see the direction of Nasim's thoughts.

"Why should we attempt to search this plague-ridden country when the girl has no choice and must return to Madame Indrani eventually?"

"But what if she doesn't? What do you think Madame will say when the virgin shows up on her doorstep? She will turn her out or slit her throat so that no one can trace the girl back to her. Madame Indrani knows the wrath of Ibn Sibah!"

"Perhaps the girl makes up a story. One Madame Indrani will believe."

Gadi considered that for a moment. "I don't know."

"I do. The key to the girl's whereabouts will be with Madame Indrani. I feel it here." Nasim touched his heart. "And here," he added, touching his temple. "Besides, if we do not find the girl, Madame Indrani should pay back her price. Do you not agree?"

Gadi's lips curved into a genuine smile. "If we have the money, then Ibn Sibah will be disappointed but not angry. I agree most heartily, my friend. Perhaps it was even a plan between them from the first?"

"That thought crossed my mind also, except how would Madame Indrani know about the storm? Let us ride to London. There we will find the answers to at least some of our questions, no?" Their decision made, they packed their few belongings and left the inn.

Chapter 12

The next week was the very best in Eden's life, in spite of Dr. Hargrave's daily examinations filled with questions for the paper he was writing and his doses of castor oil.

She was in love. She no longer worried about the future, but lived for the moment and the chance of being with *him*.

Betsy didn't have to wake her in the mornings. Usually, Eden was up and dressed in the worn brown habit well before Betsy knocked on her door. She loved her morning rides with Lord Penhollow because it was the two of them, alone. Otherwise, Lady Penhollow hounded their every opportunity to be together. Even if they met by accident in the hall, Lady Penhollow often appeared.

Eden spent her afternoons doing parish work or working in the garden. In a matter of days, she knew almost every villager in Hobbles Moor and felt a welcome part of this small community.

After dinner, Lady Penhollow chaperoned Eden and Lord Penhollow while they played cards or read aloud to each other. One night, Eden gave a small concert for the servants. Lucy, the cook, had been moved to tears.

At night, in bed, Eden would relive the whole day in her mind. What he'd said, how he'd looked, how he'd reacted to what she'd said . . . She felt keyed-up and restless, waiting for the morning to come and another opportunity to be with him again.

When sleep did come, it was filled with intense, erotic dreams that left her aching and hungry for more.

But there were no more stolen kisses. She knew he wanted her. She could read his hunger in his eyes and feel it in the way his body tensed whenever she'd "accidentally" brush against him. In the mornings, he didn't appear to have slept any better than she had.

So why did he hold back? Was he still waiting for her to tell him the truth? Or was there something else?

In those wee hours in the morning when she'd wake, her body feverish and hot, she knew nothing would assuage it but his touch. She toyed with the idea of telling him the complete truth and offering to be his mistress. But there was something selfish inside Eden, something that wanted to believe in the power of the Widow Haskell's charms.

God help her, she wanted to be this man's wife.

This morning, she was helping Mrs. Meeks, Lucy, and the kitchen maids pack hampers of food for the charity cases in Hobbles Moor. At Penhollow Hall, charity was given freely to all.

This attitude was just one more reason why she loved Pierce Kirrier, the lord of Penhollow.

Pierce. Even his name was strong and masculine.

Lucy interrupted her daydreams. "I never thought I would miss rain. You know, we haven't had any for a week or so. 'Course, it's a perfect day for a picnic."

"A picnic?" Eden asked.

"Yes, a picnic," Mrs. Meeks said. "You know, where you eat out of doors under a shady tree. Oh, when Mr. Meeks was alive, we celebrated every sunny day we could with a picnic. There's a nice breeze out there today too." She placed a smoked ham in the basket. "It's too bad you and Lord Penhollow can't have a little one yourselves. We have so much food, and an extra basket. Of course, *someone* could ask him to go on a picnic if she wished. I believe he is in his study."

Eden frowned. "Do you think he would? He's very busy right now."

"Oh, I think he'd make time for you," Lucy answered with a broad wink at Mrs. Meeks. The kitchen maids giggled.

Eden was tempted. A visitor from Devon had arrived early this morning to talk about stud arrangements and their ride had been cut short. The Devon man had left an hour ago. "Perhaps I could ask him."

"Oh, yes, do ask him," Mrs. Meeks said. "He works too hard. And while you're about that, I'll find a nice blanket for you to take on your picnic."

"A blanket?" Eden asked, startled.

"To lay on the ground while you eat," Mrs. Meeks answered. "What did you think I meant?"

Eden blushed, and Lucy and the maids guffawed loudly.

"Wait, I can't go," Eden said to Mrs. Meeks. "I promised you I'd deliver these baskets."

"The baskets will wait," Mrs. Meeks said. "There's only two of them to deliver and you can do that when you come back."

Lucy hurried Eden out the door into the hall. "Go on now, and ask our Lord Pierce to a picnic. Oh, but wait." She addressed one of the kitchen maids. "Liz, you go find Mrs. Ivy and keep her busy." She winked at Eden. "Mrs. Ivy is the one that tips off Lady Penhollow whenever you and Lord Pierce get together alone."

"But what do I say to her?" Liz asked.

"Ask her how to wash wool or some such nonsense," Mrs. Meeks said. "She'll spout off for hours about what she *thinks* she knows."

Liz nodded and hurried ahead of Eden. A few minutes later, Lucy and Mrs. Meeks gave Eden the sign that it was safe for her to go to Lord Penhollow's study. They sent her off with whispered instructions and a basket of food in her hand.

Eden took a moment to smooth her rose muslin dress and knocked on his door. He called for her to enter.

Lord Penhollow sat behind his great desk. A stack of papers was piled in front of him. He'd removed the jacket he'd worn to greet his visitor and his neckcloth was now slightly askew.

"Are you terribly busy?" she asked.

He laid his pen down. "I always have time for you. Why?"

"I wanted to invite you on a picnic lunch with me." She held up her basket.

He grinned. "I'd be delighted." He rose from the desk and started to reach for his jacket. "Did you have any place special in mind?"

"I thought we could walk to the duck pond. I must be back by three to deliver the charity baskets."

He took the basket from her, testing its weight. "One of Lucy's hampers, is it?" He pulled out a bottle of wine and winked at Eden. "Lucy always packs a good hamper."

They started toward the back door leading to the garden when Mrs. Meeks darted in their path, a blanket over one arm.

"You don't want to use *that* door," she said pointedly to Eden who understood Lady Penhollow must be in the garden. "Here, take the blanket and go out the front," Mrs. Meeks suggested.

"But this is quicker," Lord Penhollow started, but Eden had already turned on her heel and headed in the opposite direction.

He caught up with her. His eyes narrowed with speculation. "Avoiding Mother, are we?"

Eden hummed her answer and slipped out the door Rawlins held open. "Enjoy your afternoon, my lord," the butler said as Lord Penhollow followed her.

"The servants are matchmaking," he said, surprising her.

"You know it?"

"Do *you* know it?"

She wasn't prepared to answer that question. Instead, she said, "Do you know what they call you when they talk amongst themselves? Lord Pierce. And they say it with such pride. I've never known anyone who commanded the respect you do."

"Oh, yes, they respect me," he said easily. "Until I do something they don't like. Then I have burnt meals for a week and a disordered household."

Eden laughed. "I could see Mrs. Meeks making her views known through such methods. I wouldn't dare cross her."

"It's best you remember that," he rejoined.

The stable yard was empty as they walked through it. On the other side of the stable, by the pond, the ducks came swimming to greet them, quacking greedily at the sight of Eden. She'd taken to feeding them on a daily basis. Even the goose welcomed her. She threw out bread crumbs, while Lord Penhollow spread the blanket out on the ground.

Throwing the last of the bread into the pond, which sent the ducks hurrying to gobble it, she returned to the blanket and started to unpack the hamper. "I was sorry our ride was cut short this morning," she confessed.

He stretched out on the blanket beside her, one knee bent, and pulled a peach and a knife from the hamper. "I am too." His fingers deftly started peeling the peach.

Eden hesitated. A robin's cheerful call sounded from somewhere beyond the pond. If ever there was a time for confidences, this was it. But did she dare tell him the truth?

He offered her a slice of peach. The juice ran down over his fingers. She had the urge to lick it from his hands.

Suddenly restless and tense, she popped the whole peach slice in her mouth to stop from acting on her impulse.

"Something is bothering you," he said.

She swallowed the peach. His gaze held hers.

"What is the matter?" he asked.

Eden told him part of the truth. "I want to taste the juice from the peach on your fingers."

He froze and she sensed his body tightening in response to her words. He came up on one hand. "You what?"

Eden shook her head. She wouldn't repeat her words. She already feared they were a mistake.

He got up off the blanket and looked down at her. "Sometimes I think you are the most naive woman I've ever met and the next moment you're offering to lick my body. It's like you're a creature of contradictions, teasing and flirting with me and yet wholly innocent."

"I shouldn't have said what I did."

He knelt beside her and, with one finger, lifted her chin to meet his gaze. "Eden, your passion pleases me. But I told you once that I want more than just that from you." His eyes searched hers. "I keep waiting for you to tell me your story, but you won't share it, will you?"

She found it difficult to meet his gaze and turned to look away—

"Eden, tell me about Madame Indrani."

He held her attention now. Madame's presence seemed to loom around them at the mere mention of her name.

"Tell me," he ordered.

She opened her mouth. *Yes, she could tell him* . . . But the words caught in her throat. She shook her head. "I can't." She would have pulled away but he took hold of her shoulder and held her fast.

"Or is it that you won't? Eden, remove this barrier between us. Don't you understand? *I'm* waiting for you, but you must trust me. You must tell me what you fear."

Still she couldn't speak.

He gave her shoulder a squeeze. "Eden, I must know more."

When she spoke, the words came out haltingly. "She was a . . . teacher to me. Someone who . . . was very instrumental in my being on a ship." It was all she was brave enough to say.

"There's more," he said.

I'm a courtesan, a harlot, a whore.

She could never speak those words. Their worlds were too different. If she told him the truth, a chasm would split them apart.

"Does my past mean so much to you?" Her voice was barely a whisper.

"Your honesty means everything."

He made it so tempting to set her doubts aside . . .

His hand brushed a curling tendril from her face. "Eden, why do you hide from me? What is it you don't want me to know?"

. . . But she did not want to see him turn from her in disgust.

Bittersweet regret washed through her, but she'd made her decision. He must never know her past. He would not understand.

She turned away from him and he let her go.

"I must return to the house now. I promised Mrs. Meeks I would deliver the parish baskets."

She reached down to repack the hamper, but he caught her arm and pulled her around. "Eden. Eden, look at me."

She forced herself to face up at him. A muscle worked in his jaw and she realized he was angry with her.

Lovingly, she pushed back the lock of his hair that fell over his brow. "If I could give you my soul, I would do so."

He jerked away as if her touch scalded him and walked down to the edge of the pond. There he stood, hands on hips, his back to her. Helplessly, she wished it could be different . . . but then, perhaps this was for the best.

She loved him too much to disgrace him.

His voice cut through the stillness. "Well." He turned back to her. The set of his mouth was tense. His gaze didn't met hers. "We should, ah, clean up the picnic. I have work to do."

Eden nodded dumbly and put the cheese and fruit back in the hamper. All the joy had left the day. Even the robin no longer sang happily.

They walked back to the house. At the edge of the front drive, Eden stopped.

"I think it would be best if I left tomorrow."

He didn't look at her. "You might be right." He took a few steps toward the house and turned. "Tell me what you want to do and when and I shall make the arrangements."

He left her then. Eden stood rooted to the earth. The decision had been made. It was done. She would leave.

She drew a deep, steadying breath, and slowly followed him into the house, repeating over and over in her mind, *It's for the best.*

Eden decided to let Lord Penhollow break the news that she was leaving. She would rather slip out of the house and deliver the charity baskets, pretending for just a few more hours that everything was going to be fine.

Since he had a single tree that needed to be repaired by Dane, Jim drove her to Hobbles Moor in the trap. He was in a talkative mood and all that was required of her were single-syllable responses. He didn't even notice she was unusually quiet.

He drove Eden to the other side of Hobbles Moor where row after row of small thatched-roof cottages were neatly laid out. Lord Penhollow had built these cottages for the miners. They were one- or two-room houses with a small yard in front for vegetables and flowers.

Behind several of the cottages were chicken coops and even a milk cow tethered here and there.

"Living like kings, they are, since Lord Penhollow built these fine cottages," Jim said with pride.

"What were their lives like before?" Eden asked, her heart heavy over the prospect of leaving.

"They lived where they could. Hand to mouth they were. One family lived in a cave by the sea. Lord Penhollow heard about them and insisted they move to Hobbles Moor and taught the man a trade. Aye, there's many a family here that wouldn't have a roof over their heads without the help of our Lord Pierce." He watched Eden out of the corner of his eye as he added, "A woman couldn't do any better than his lordship. He's a rum one, he is."

Eden managed to keep her face expressionless and changed the subject. "How far is the tin mine from here?"

"Two miles over yonder field." Jim nodded toward the north. "That's another thing Lord Penhollow did. Everyone thought the mine was dried up until he took over. He's even worked it himself. He pays a fair wage because he's wielded the pick himself and knows how hard the work is. The track and carts he's designed are really going to change how the men work."

"He's designed tracks?" They drove around the circular pond in the middle of Hobbles Moor.

"Aye, the track will make it easier to get the ore out of the pit. Tinning's backbreaking work. The tinners are anxious for any help they can get. Lord Pierce also has plans to build a foundry right there close to the mine. He's hired an engineer and all. The man will show up in a month or so to start the work."

Jim reined the trap to a halt in front of a cottage with a crying toddler sitting in the front yard. He set the brake and hopped out over the side to open the back door for Eden. He handed one of the baskets to her.

"Thank you, Jim, and let me have both baskets. You can go to Dane's while I'm here."

"I don't think so, Miss Eden," he replied. "It's probably best I wait for you."

"Then we won't return home for hours." And she had packing to do. "You go ahead and I will visit with Mrs. Tucker and Mrs. Furman. I'll be fine and Mrs. Furman could use the company. Her son was down with the fever the other day and I want to check on him."

For a second, the loneliness of no longer being a part of this community hurt almost as much as giving up Lord Penhollow. Eden blinked back the tears, ducking her head lest Jim see them.

"I don't think Lord Penhollow would like for me to leave you, Miss Eden."

"Lord Penhollow will be grateful if you get me back to Penhollow Hall at a decent hour."

Jim relented. "I'll only be an hour or so, miss," he promised.

"That's fine. I'll be here," Eden said. Of course, Jim waited until she'd walked into the

Tuckers' yard before he snapped the reins and turned the trap around toward the smithy.

Eden knelt down to the crying toddler's eye level. "Harry, what has you upset?" she asked softly. Aside from Lord Penhollow, she would miss the children the most.

Large brown eyes stared at her before he began howling even louder than before. There came the answering sound of another child crying from inside the cottage. Mrs. Tucker appeared in the doorway. She was the mother of six children, the last two being the twins, Sarah and Willie. She balanced Sarah on one hip. She was a hardworking woman who'd been sickly since the twins were born a year and a half ago. Lord Penhollow—through the parish—had been providing extra support for the family.

"I have a basket for you today, Mrs. Tucker." Eden set the basket down and held out her arms for Sarah. "Here, let me hold this one, while you take the basket inside."

"I don't know if she'll go to you, Miss Eden. She's been fussy today with a tooth coming in." But Sarah was already reaching for Eden.

Eden took the babe in her arms and hugged her close. She was very affectionate with all the children and never missed a hug. Mary Westchester would be proud of her if she could see Eden now.

"Where's Willie?" Eden asked, looking around the yard for one of her favorite boys.

"Asleep, where this one should be," Mrs. Tucker answered. She and Eden were roughly the same age, but childbirth and hard work made her appear much older, except for the good humor in her eyes. She smiled at Eden. "Come inside, won't you, and we'll have a spot of tea. I see Mrs. Meeks packed some in the hamper."

"Oh, I'd love to come in for a moment, but no tea today. I have this other basket for the Furmans' and Jim is only letting me have an hour today. Have you heard how their son is doing?" Sarah had taken one of Eden's curls in her chubby fist and put it in her mouth.

Mrs. Tucker stepped forward, pulled Sarah's hand away from Eden's hair, and then kissed the baby's fingers. "I haven't heard. Let me put me babies down for their nap and I'll go over with you."

"I'd like that."

"Come then, Harry. It's time for your nap," his mother said. Harry howled louder, but his mother was relentless.

Eden trailed after her, laughing at Sarah's obvious enjoyment of her curls.

Inside, in spite of the constant smoke and soot from the peat fire, the sparsely furnished cottage was spotless. A bed large enough to sleep two adults was pushed up against the wall. Stored neatly beneath the bed were the straw-filled pallets the children used to sleep upon the floor. His thumb in his mouth, tow-headed Willie slept in the center of the bed.

"We saw you riding with Lord Penhollow yesterday morning," Mrs. Tucker said. She set the hamper on the table and pulled out a loaf of bread. Slicing off a thin piece, she handed it to Harry, who immediately stopped crying.

"If'n you don't mind my saying, the two of you are a fine couple."

Eden smiled her thank you, deciding the less said the better. She laid Sarah on the bed next to her brother. Mrs. Tucker handed Sarah a piece of crust and the child settled down, holding the crust with one hand and sucking the thumb of the other.

"How are you feeling?" Eden asked.

"Better and better," Mrs. Tucker said absently, more interested in getting the children down for a nap. She laid Harry on one of the straw pallets.

He immediately started to roll off. Mrs. Tucker snapped her fingers and pointed back to the pallet. For a second, Harry eyed his mother in indecision.

"Harry," she warned. He laid back down on the pallet.

Eden had moved to the doorway and now Mrs. Tucker joined her.

Mrs. Tucker smiled. "Thomas said it rained at the mine all yesterday, but we didn't get a drop here. Cornwall's strange, isn't it? Almost as if God teases us with the weather." She glanced over her shoulder. Harry was staring up at the rafter ceiling.

"Where are the older children?" Eden asked.

"Tommy is sheepherding with old Milo. One of my girls is over helping card wool." She nodded in the direction up the road leading to the weaver's cottage. "And my other is helping Mrs. Furman keep her babies quiet. Ah, there she is now." She waved at a pretty brown-haired girl with eyes like her own who was leading two dark-headed children down the road.

Mrs. Tucker went out into the yard. Eden followed. "Where are you off to, Clara?"

"I'm taking them on a walk to the pond, Mum."

"Aye, that's a good girl. Watch them now, and don't let them get too near the water," Mrs. Tucker said with satisfaction and waved the child on. She tiptoed back to the open cottage door. "They're asleep," she said to Eden. "Quick, let's run over to Mrs. Furman's."

Eden picked up the other hamper she'd left in the Tucker yard. Leaving the cottage door open, they crossed the dirt road and walked one cottage down to the Furmans'. Mrs. Furman sat in a chair by the front door, her pregnant stomach resting on her lap. She looked very uncomfortable in the summer heat. This would be her fifth child. "Miss Eden, we bid you welcome."

"Thank you, Mrs. Furman. Mrs. Meeks and Lucy have packed another one of their hampers for you. How's your son? Is he feeling better?"

Mrs. Furman got up from the chair with effort and took the hamper from Eden. "Aye, he is now. The Widow Haskell came in to see him this morning and she pronounced him almost cured."

"What about Dr. Hargrave? Has he come by?"

Mrs. Furman shook her head. "What need have we of Dr. Hargrave if the Widow Haskell has already seen him? And she doesn't expect payment for her services." She turned to Mrs. Tucker. "Your Clara is a good girl, Mary. Thank you for sending her over."

"Mrs. Meeks packed tea in the basket," Mrs. Tucker hinted.

"Ah, that's a blessing," Mrs. Furman answered. "Would you stay for a cup of tea, Miss Eden?"

Eden looked down the road. There was no sign of Jim and the trap, so she agreed.

Mrs. Furman, like almost all the wives in the village, kept an iron kettle heating by the fire. She measured out the tea into two cups. One cup was badly chipped and Eden realized the family had no more than two. She also knew that tea was a rare luxury to these women and their generosity touched her. Their poverty was not the poverty of spirit she had suffered as a child. These people had little, yet they were neat and proud.

Daniel Furman slept in his parents' bed. Eden could tell by his color that he was doing much better than he had been when she'd seen him two days ago.

Mrs. Furman let the tea steep a few minutes. She'd just handed Eden her cup of tea when they heard shouting.

"I wonder what the racket is?" Mrs. Furman said, going to the door.

Mrs. Tucker set her cup down. "They'd better not wake my babies."

At that moment, someone outside distinctly shouted, "Fire!"

All three women ran out into the yard. A

man charged down the street toward the pond with a bucket. A few other women came out into their front yards, their expressions curious.

Eden sniffed the air. She could smell smoke but couldn't tell where it was coming from until Mrs. Tucker cried out next to her. The back of the roof of the cottage across the street was on fire.

The bell in the church began ringing, its clang loud and urgent, calling men from the fields to fight the fire. Its sound would be heard for miles around. People started gathering out in the road. Several already carried pails of water.

The two village women beside Eden didn't waste a moment. Mrs. Furman picked up a bucket inside her front door. It was the slop bucket but she hurried across the road to throw it on the flames that in seconds seemed to have engulfed the dry thatch. Mrs. Tucker ran for her own bucket. Eden came out in the street, ready to join the others in fighting the fire.

The owner of the cottage, an old woman, sat on the roadside weeping loudly as the women and what men there were in the village at this time of the day formed a line from the commons pond to pass water to douse the flames.

The church bell kept ringing, a desperate plea for help. The acrid smell of smoke was stronger now, stinging Eden's nostrils. The first bucket of water from the pond came her way and she passed it on to the next in line. Then another bucket and another. Young boys ran the empty buckets back to the pond.

They were working as fast as they could, but it wasn't fast enough. Flames devoured the whole cottage. Still, they worked to put the fire out. When her chip bonnet got in her way, Eden ripped it off her head and tossed it aside without missing a bucket. Her arms and back began to ache, but she worked alongside Mrs. Furman and Mrs. Tucker.

Then, what they feared most happened. The thatched-roof cottage on the far side of the burning one caught fire.

Reaching mechanically for the next pail, Eden discovered Jim beside her. "It'll burn the whole village down if we don't catch it now," he shouted in her ear.

She nodded and passed the pail down to the next person. It wasn't an efficient system but it was the only one they had.

The owners of the newly burning cottage could be heard shouting. Drawn by the ringing of the bell, men finally came running from the fields, their curses and orders adding to the confusion. The smoke was heavier now. The whole village seemed to be working, racing against the spreading fire. The flames easily consumed the second cottage. The wind shifted. Burning embers floated through the sky and the thatched roofs were like dry kindling.

Her hands busy, Eden wiped the sweat from her forehead on the puffed sleeve of the rose muslin. That's when she noticed the roof of Mrs. Tucker's cottage was on fire.

She broke out of the line and took two steps

forward. Behind her, she heard Mrs. Tucker scream, "My babies! My babies!"

Eden's feet were already moving toward the burning building. In what seemed like seconds the fire consumed the entire roof.

A man's hand came out to grab her arm. "It's too late," he said. "That roof will collapse at any moment."

Mrs. Tucker screamed, but Eden acted. With a quick twist of her arm, she broke free of the man's hold and ran into the burning cottage.

Chapter 13

Pierce rode Cornish King into Hobbles Moor at a gallop. He'd heard the clanging of the bell and had seen the ominous black smoke even from Penhollow Hall.

He arrived in time to see Eden dash into a burning cottage.

Mrs. Tucker, one of the village women, chased after Eden, screaming for her babies, but a flaming rafter fell in front of the doorway, knocking the woman to the ground.

Pierce put his heels to the great stallion, jumping him over small hedge fences, driving the horse toward the cottage he'd seen Eden enter. He was out of the saddle before Cornish King had stopped, pausing just long enough to ensure the others had Mrs. Tucker safely away from the fire before he leaped over the burning rafter and went after Eden.

Inside, the cottage looked like the bowels of hell. Smoke filled the air. Small fires burned on the ground and up the walls. The roof cracked and snapped.

Eden stood next to a bed. She was weaving

slightly as she struggled with a toddler and squalling baby in her arms. She stared at him as if she couldn't believe her eyes.

Pierce grabbed hold of her, ready to drag her out of the cottage. But Eden arched her back, turning from him.

"Ba—" she started, before smoke filled her lungs and set her coughing. "Baby," she managed to get out, pushing against him toward the bed.

Pierce tossed a quick look over his shoulder; another baby, the size of the one in Eden's arms, lay on the bed. Small flames lapped their way toward the baby's head. He wasn't even sure it was still alive.

"Go!" he shouted, and pushed her toward the door. Villagers waited outside to help her over the burning rafter and into fresh air.

Pierce turned back and snatched the baby up in his arms just as the roof began to cave. Protecting the child with his body, he threw himself out the front door. He landed on one shoulder and rolled, the baby cradled in his arms. Over and over they rolled until they hit the hedge border of the yard.

Pierce lay there a second until a hand reached down and slapped the places where his shirt was on fire. His skin tingled with burns, but he was alive.

Where was Eden?

Dane offered his hand and Pierce took it, coming to his feet. The baby was still tucked into the crook of his arm. "Where's Eden?" he demanded . . . and then saw her. She stood coughing, supported by Mrs. Furman. Two other women had taken the toddler and the baby from her. Both children were crying. The toddler reached for his mother who still lay unconscious.

Pierce moved toward Eden. Her face was smudged with smoke, her hair a tangled mess. There were holes burned into her dress and one sleeve was ripped clean to the bodice. She'd never looked so beautiful to him.

She looked up at him. "How is Sarah?" she whispered, her voice hoarse from the smoke she'd inhaled.

Around them the villagers still fought the fire that had spread to two more cottages. Men with long hooked poles rapidly pulled down the burning thatch.

"Sarah?"

"The baby you've saved. Her name is Sarah."

He'd been so thankful to see Eden alive and well, he'd almost forgotten the babe in his arms. He looked down. The child appeared to be asleep in his arms, her soft downy hair curled around her face, her thumb resting between rosebud lips. A black line of soot marred her forehead. She lay still in Pierce's arm, too still.

Eden gave a small cry of alarm. Pierce lifted the baby. She had to be alive. She *must* be alive. He and Eden couldn't have failed her.

He pressed his fingers against her small chest but he could feel no heartbeat. He lowered his head, praying he would hear her breath, but there was too much noise and excitement around them.

Mrs. Furman gave a sob and turned her back. Eden's eyes filled with tears. "Not Sarah. Please, not Sarah."

Pierce turned the child over on her stomach. He could hold her easily with one hand.

Nothing.

Eden's hand was on his sleeve now, her fingers gripping the singed cotton material. "My lord, what shall I tell her mother?"

Pierce had never felt so helpless in his life. He placed his other hand on the baby's back and pressed. The child's thumb disengaged from her mouth. Her arm fell to dangle in the air.

Then . . . there was a cough, a gentle, ethereal sound. And another, and then another. Pierce could almost imagine he saw puffs of smoke come from the child's mouth as he turned her over. Large brown eyes sleepily opened to stare at him. "Asleep," Pierce said in disbelief, and then louder and with a hint of amazed laughter, he repeated, "The babe was asleep."

Eden began laughing and crying at the same time. Dane hugged Mrs. Furman. Jim shouted to the villagers that the baby was alive.

Eden took Sarah from Pierce and looked up at him with shining eyes. "You saved her. I wasn't going to make it. The smoke was too much for me. I've never been more thankful than when I saw you come through that door."

In that moment, he felt omnipotent.

In that moment, he knew he was in love.

Love. There'd been times in his youth when

he'd thought he'd been in love, but this was stronger, brighter, deeper.

Suddenly, he felt whole, complete, secure. It was the most incredible realization . . . and he knew that tomorrow his love for her would be stronger than it was today, and the next day after, stronger still.

He'd found what he'd been searching for. She'd been delivered into his arms for his safe-keeping. He saw that now, and it filled him with wonder.

The baby's mother came to her senses. She took Sarah from Eden and noisily kissed and hugged all her children.

Eden returned to Pierce's side and he put his arm around her and hugged her close as the precious gift she was. He could feel her heart beating against his chest. Amid the destruction of the village, he found a reason to celebrate. Of course, he would rebuild, but he knew that nothing he did would have meaning without this woman by his side.

She was beautiful, even with her soot-streaked face and tangled hair. He buried his nose in her rich tresses, inhaling the scent of smoke and sweat. In that moment, he realized she was everything he could want in a wife.

A cry went up that the fires were finally out. They were lucky. They'd only lost five cottages. Buckets fell to the ground and several people dropped right where they were from exhaustion.

Pulling Eden with him, Pierce went out on the road. The villagers gathered around him.

Hands came out to slap his back. He was hailed a hero.

Pierce held up his hand for silence. "Today we were most fortunate the whole village didn't burn down. To those of you who have lost your homes, you have my pledge to see these cottages rebuilt. Each of you shall receive a pig, a bed, and a table to replace what you have lost. I ask the rest of you to open your homes to those who have suffered a loss until their cottages are replaced."

Weary heads nodded. He was doing the right thing and they approved. He knew these people well. They were his family. There was the mighty Dane and Kyle, the poacher he could not and would not catch. Jim stood with crossed arms. Clustered behind him were the other grooms from his stable, along with Mrs. Meeks, Betsy, and Rawlins, who had come running to help the moment the church bells had sounded. Vicar Thomas hovered anxiously beside Mrs. Tucker and on the other side of the yard was the Widow Haskell leaning on her gnarled walking stick.

Pierce's chest swelled with pride and gratitude. His life was rich because of these people. It was only right they share in his happiness now.

"I have another announcement to make," he said. The crowd quieted. "I am going to marry the woman by my side as soon as I can procure a special license. Penhollow Hall and the village of Hobbles Moor are to have a new countess."

A swell of approval swept through the

crowd around them. Children joined hands and ran in a circle, laughing over the prospect of a wedding feast. The adults offered congratulations, while Dane shouted, "It's about bloody time!" Everyone laughed.

Pierce looked down at Eden. "Is it all right?" he asked in a low voice. "Will you marry me?"

For a moment, her eyes shone with unparalleled joy which swiftly died. She shook her head. "No, my lord, you can't. I must not let you—"

He silenced her with a kiss.

She responded, against her better judgment he knew, because he could feel her hesitation. He crushed her closer, demanding that she open herself to him, that she accept him—and she did.

He didn't pay attention to the "Woooooo" of the villagers witnessing this kiss. It had taken on a life of its own. Eden was his and he would bind her to him for eternity.

He broke off the kiss and Dane cried, "Three cheers! Three cheers for the earl and countess of Penhollow!" The villagers shouted in unison.

A village boy led Cornish King to them. The stallion stamped his feet impatiently. Pierce lifted Eden up into the saddle and then swung up behind her. With a press of Pierce's heels, Cornish King proudly pranced his way through Hobbles Moor.

Neither of them spoke until they were free of the village and alone on the road. As they turned into the drive in front of Penhollow

Hall, Eden spoke. "You know I can't marry you."

"Look me in the eye and say that," Pierce said to her bowed head.

She did. Defiance, and, yes, regret, flashed in her green eyes as she repeated her words.

He laughed, loving her courage, her strength of will. "It won't work, Eden. I no longer care where you came from or why you are here. It doesn't matter. I love you. I've waited a long time to fall in love and now that it's happened, I'll have no other woman but you for my wife."

She stared at him, her lower lip trembling.

He nudged her playfully. "I believe this is where you say, 'I love you too, Pierce.' I'm not certain, but I think you should right about now."

For a second, he thought she wouldn't say it. And then she whispered, "I love you."

"Pierce," he prompted.

"Pierce." Her lips curved into a smile. "I love you, Pierce. I've loved you since the day you threw pennies into the air and maybe before. I love your kindness, your strength, your compassion. I even love the dimple that shows up right here—" She pointed to the corner of his mouth. "—whenever you tease me." She pressed her hand against his face. "I shall always love you."

He had to be the most fortunate man in the world. "You could say it with more enthusiasm," he pouted, a hint of laughter in his voice.

She laughed now too, her eyes sparkling. "I

love you, Pierce Kirrier!" she shouted. Her words echoed against the stone front of Penhollow Hall and she threw her arms around his neck, almost toppling them off the horse.

They kissed again and again and again. Pierce didn't think he'd ever tire of kissing her, and he could barely wait to make love to her, to make her fully and completely his.

"We shall be married before the end of another week."

She brushed his lips with her fingers. "You are certain? You love me?"

"With all my heart."

"You will never regret this, my lord—"

"Pierce," he corrected her.

"Pierce," she repeated dutifully and then promised, "I shall be the perfect wife."

He kissed her again to seal her promise.

Pierce bounded up the stairs leading to his mother's floor. He'd already checked the Garden Room. She wasn't there.

He knocked on the door to her sitting room. Mrs. Ivy opened it. His mother stood, her back to him, beside the window overlooking the front of the house.

He wondered how long she had been standing there.

"Do you have a moment for me?" he asked.

His mother turned then. She didn't smile in greeting. "Of course. Mrs. Ivy, will you leave us?"

The dresser bowed out.

Pierce waited until the door closed behind her. He walked over to the window. "Hobbles

Moor had a fire this afternoon. Five of the cottagers were burned out."

Her eyebrows raised in surprise. "Oh. What a pity." Empathy was not one of her strengths.

She turned to him, her expression serious. "Actually, Pierce, I'm glad you came to see me. I was about to go in search for you."

"Really? Whatever for?"

She hesitated, drawing a deep breath as if uncertain how to continue. "Pierce, darling, I don't like to criticize but I witnessed something today that has given me some concern."

Pierce grew impatient. "You saw me kissing Eden."

"Yes, I did. Right there on the drive where anyone could have seen you."

"I had good reason."

"To kiss her in public? I doubt that! Of course, I'm scarcely surprised she let you. Behavior like that is what I am coming to expect from her—"

"Mother—"

"She's common, Pierce. As common as they come, I fear. I must demand that you send her to the parish or wherever immediately—"

"I've asked her to be my wife."

His mother's mouth closed with a snap. Her hand came up to cover her heart and she reached for a chair in which to sit down.

Pierce stared out the window, embarrassed by her dramatics. The grooms were coming up the drive from Hobbles Moor, their work done, their voices raised in song. They'd no doubt stopped at the pub on their way home for a quick pint. He clasped his hands behind his back, impatient to get back to Eden. They had so many plans to make.

She groaned, closing her eyes. "Oh, Pierce."

"Come now, Mother," he practically growled. "Five families losing their homes is a tragedy. My announcement of marriage is not."

Her lids fluttered open. "How can you say it's not? Oh, I knew it, I knew it! From the moment I laid eyes upon that girl, I knew she was here for one purpose and one purpose only."

"Oh, Mother—"

"Don't patronize me," she said shooting up from the chair. "That woman set her sights on you from the moment you met her. There is something very suspicious about her story. What have you heard from London?"

"Nothing." It was the one thing that dampened his happiness.

"You promised me you would do nothing rash until you knew who she is."

"I don't consider marrying the woman I love a rash action."

"You said you would wait."

"No, I didn't. You wanted me to wait. I made no promise."

She made an angry sound of frustration. "I can't believe you are doing this because of a few kisses."

"It's more than that," Pierce said. "I've been half in love with her since I saw her in that boat. And then today, I almost lost her. She ran into a burning cottage to save those children. I'll never find another woman with her courage, her depth of character. And I can't live without her."

"Pierce, you are so blind. I warned you once the woman was too . . . too . . ." She waved her hands as if words failed her. "Perfect!"

"You're convinced she's a scheming harpy through and through, aren't you?" he said bitterly.

"No, what I'm saying is that you don't know her!"

"I *do* know her!" he shot back. "I know what it is like to sit across a table from her and talk for hours on end and not be bored. I like her lack of pretension. I enjoy seeing her dig in the garden and hearing her laugh and talking easily with the servants. Since she's come to Penhollow Hall, there has been more happiness than I've ever known. I *love* her, Mother."

His mother's mouth flattened. "I never thought I would hear my son speak like a mewling calf about a woman. If you want her, take her! You don't have to marry her. I saw the way she was kissing you. She has no class. She's not a Willis or a Danbury or a Baines. She's nothing."

"She is the woman who is going to be my wife," he said, his voice steady and firm. "And you will respect her. If you cannot do that, then I won't have her live in the same house with your contempt. I will move you to the dowager's cottage."

The color drained from her face. She sagged back into her chair. "You would send me away over her?"

"I will not let you openly disapprove of my wife."

"I think only of your happiness, my son."

"Then you will attend my wedding and wish my bride well."

Her jaw tightened. "I don't know if I can do that. My friends will not like that."

He snorted. "Your friends!" He crossed to the door. "The choice is yours, Mother. We'll be married by special license in one week's time. You will either be there or you repair to the dowager's cottage."

Her back went ramrod-straight. The features of her face could have been carved in stone. "I will begin packing," she said.

He let himself out of her room.

Eden waited for Pierce at the bottom of the stairs. Doubts had already started to set in. How could she be doing this? She wasn't any more fit to be a countess than Mrs. Meeks!

And yet, when she saw him come down the stairs toward her, her protests died without being spoken.

Pierce paused on the last step.

"What did your mother say?" Eden asked anxiously.

"She's happy for us," he replied, but his smile of assurance didn't quite reach his eyes.

She reached up to lay her hand against the side of his face. "Pierce—" she began, but he caught her hand and stepped beside her.

"Everything is all right, Eden. Everything."

She wanted to believe him.

He pressed his lips against the tips of her

fingers. "We shall have the finest wedding ever known to Cornwall." A muscle tightened in his jaw and his eyes blazed with fierce pride. "And it will be done before the members of the gentry. Every one of them. I plan on marrying you with all pomp and ceremony due the Lord of Penhollow. You will be my countess, Eden, and I shall love you till the end of my life."

"I don't deserve you," she whispered.

His hold on her hand tightened. "Never say that, Eden. Never."

Humbled by his unconditional declaration of love, she was tempted to tell the truth. To confess all.

The moment was broken by the entrance of Mrs. Meeks and Rawlins, both of them laughing at some private jest. Seeing Eden and their lord standing closely together, they came to an abrupt halt.

"Beg pardon, my lord, miss," Mrs. Meeks mumbled and would have retreated with Rawlins except that Lord Penhollow called her forward.

"Mrs. Meeks, you and Rawlins are exactly the people we need to see. After all, we have a wedding to plan."

"Oh and happy we all are for you, my lord," Mrs. Meeks chirped.

"Thank you, Mrs. Meeks. I'm expecting you to help Miss Eden with the wedding arrangements."

"But of course, my lord! I would consider it an honor. But what of Lady Penhollow—"

"Rawlins, you will help too," Lord Penhollow interjected smoothly. "I want all our neighbors invited. The Willises, Lord and Lady Danbury, Lord and Lady Baines, Captain and Mrs. Dutton. I don't want any name left off the list," he insisted firmly. "Miss Eden and Mrs. Meeks will prepare the invitations and, Rawlins, you will see they are delivered."

"Yes, my lord," Rawkins responded. "And may I add my own congratulations, sir?"

"Yes. Thank you," Lord Penhollow said, and then flashed Eden a smile. "There you have it. Rawlins, Mrs. Meeks, and the staff is at your disposal. It will be a busy week. Can you manage it?"

"I—" She hesitated. *What did she know about planning a wedding?*

Her answer wasn't necessary. Lord Penhollow continued on, in full charge of plans, "Come, Mrs. Meeks, Rawlins. I have paper in my study which will be perfect for the invitations." Without a backward glance, he started down the hall.

Both servants trailed behind him, Mrs. Meeks chattering happily. "This is so exciting, my lord. We had almost given up all hope of your marrying."

Lord Penhollow didn't answer her. Rawlins elbowed her as a sign that she should watch herself but nothing could contain Mrs. Meek's excitement.

Eden watched them go with a sense of disquietude. She raised her gaze up the stairs toward Lady Penhollow's room. *What had his conversation with his mother really been like?* She couldn't imagine Lady Penhollow accepting the news gracefully.

And there was something about Lord Penhollow's insistence to invite all the gentry that was not quite right. It was almost as if he was daring them to refuse his invitation. Yes, that was it. He was challenging them.

Eden took two steps up the stairs and then paused. What would happen if she followed her impulse and spoke to Lady Penhollow directly?

She knew the answer. The woman would only confirm what Eden's intuition had already told her. Lady Penhollow did not want Eden to marry her son. His friends would not wish it.

And they all would be right.

Eden stood in indecision. She should tell Lord Penhollow the truth, now, before the idea of this wedding went further . . . and yet, if she did, what did she stand to lose?

The love of the man who had in a very short period of time become the center of her universe.

Eden had spent her life taking advantage of what opportunities had presented themselves. If she told Lord Penhollow the truth now, especially after he'd made a public declaration, it could cost her his love.

The price for the truth was too high.

She came down the steps and walked, slowly at first and then with increasing determination, toward the study. With each step her fears receded and her excitement grew. She had a wedding to plan.

* * *

Two days later, Mrs. Willis was astounded to receive an invitation to Lord Penhollow's wedding. She marched into the sitting room where her husband read the papers while her daughter sewed a new ribbon on a hat.

"This is infamous! Shocking!" she announced, and threw the invitation on the floor in front of her husband.

"What is shocking, Dovie?" he asked.

"*That* is an invitation to Lord Penhollow's wedding. He's going to marry that baggage next Wednesday morning. In the church, no less."

"He's marrying Miss Eden?" Victoria asked. She laughed. "How happy I am for her!"

"You're happy for her?" Mrs. Willis spun around to face her daughter. "Don't you understand? This has ruined your hopes of landing Lord Penhollow. Oh, when I think of the time I wasted on Lady Penhollow, and she didn't even send me a warning to expect the worst. She'd even assured me that her son *wouldn't* marry that creature."

"I like Miss Eden," Victoria declared mutinously.

"Of course you do, dear," her mother answered. "Because you are young and the young always counter whatever their parents say." She sat in a chair beside her husband, the wheels of her mind working. "Well, there's nothing to be done for it. Of course, *we* will not attend the wedding."

"But that would be an insult to Lord Penhollow!"

"That's right, Dovie," Mr. Willis said, lowering his paper. "We don't want to tweak Penhollow's nose."

"We have a prior engagement."

"We do? What's that?" he asked.

"We're . . ." Mrs. Willis paused. "We're going to see your sister in Bristol. She's been hounding us to visit. I shall write and tell her we are coming. Then I will send our regrets to Penhollow Hall."

"Is that wise, Dovie?"

"The Penhollows are not good *ton,* " she told her husband. "To be seen there would be a disaster socially. I'm quite sure Lady Baines and Lady Danbury will do the same. Besides, you can't disappoint your sister, can you? I'll tell her to expect us Monday. It's short notice, but she will manage." Her mind made up, she rose from the chair. "However, I shall never forgive Lady Penhollow. Ever."

She started from the room, when Victoria's voice called her back. "Does this mean I will have a season in London, Mama?"

"We really have no choice now, do we?" She shook her head. "I had so wanted Lord Penhollow for you."

Victoria could barely hide her excitement. "I understand Mr. Whitacre is in London. The next time you see Lady Danbury, will you ask? He promised to call on me should I come to the city."

"Mr. Whitacre, hmmm?" Mrs. Willis said with new interest. "Good family. Bit of money there. Yes, he might do. He might do very well. Perhaps we can manage a trip to London next month. But I will tell you this and mark my words well, I will never set foot in Penhollow Hall again! And if I see Lady Penhollow or her son, I shall give them the cut direct—and will recommend my friends do so also!"

Chapter 14

The day before their wedding, Eden searched out Pierce in his study. The door was slightly open but she hesitated. This was not an interview she looked forward to with anticipation.

Through the crack in the door, she could see him sitting at his desk. A lock of his dark hair fell over his brow as he studied the papers before him. He picked up a pen, dipped it in the inkwell, and began writing.

The nib scratched its way across the paper. The clock over the mantel ticked the passing time. She was tempted to steal away quietly, when he looked up.

"Eden?"

She couldn't run now. She pushed the door open with her fingertips. "I didn't mean to disturb you."

"You could never disturb me." He flashed her a smile so welcoming, she could almost convince herself that her doubts were groundless. "Come in," he urged.

She entered, shutting the door behind her. "I need a moment of your time."

He tossed the pen down and rose, coming around the desk to her. "You can have all my time you wish." He indicated for her to sit in a chair in front of the desk. He took the chair opposite. "What is it, Eden?"

She rubbed her hands together nervously. The muscles in her back felt tight and strained. She didn't know where to begin.

He began for her. "It's the wedding."

She studied him a moment and then nodded. "I don't think it's a wise idea."

"Because of Mother?" Lady Penhollow had taken to her rooms after the Hobbles Moor fire and had not come out even for meals. Mrs. Ivy was making a great production of the packing process and everyone knew Lady Penhollow was moving out.

"That is one of my concerns."

Pierce leaned forward. "Mother is her own worst enemy. You can't let her interfere with our happiness. I learned that lesson early in life. She's done this before."

Eden attempted to smile and meet his gaze. "Yes, well, Mrs. Meeks has told me the same thing."

He sat back. "There. You see?"

"But it isn't just your mother. Pierce, I know the vicar has counseled you against this marriage."

He sat still for a moment. "How do you know this?"

"There are no secrets in Hobbles Moor."

"I did not ask the vicar's opinion, Eden."

"I know that. He was put up to it by Captain Dutton and some of your mother's friends. Pierce, all of your neighbors, including Captain Dutton, have sent their regrets. Even Dr. Hargrave is not coming."

Pierce's face was an inscrutable mask. "We are marrying on short notice. It's to be expected."

Eden wouldn't accept the excuse. "They are not coming because of me."

"What they think is of no concern to me. What is important is that the vicar has agreed to perform the ceremony."

Eden gripped her hands tightly in her lap. "Well, perhaps that has something to do with your owning his benefice."

"Perhaps," came his answer.

"Pierce, we can't marry."

He was on his feet in an instant. His hands came down on her arms and he pulled her up to meet him. "Is this what you want?"

She started to speak, but he interrupted her. "No, don't give me some nonsense about doing what's best for me. That excuse is weak." His blue eyes bored into her as if he could read her very soul. "I love you. I can barely wait until tomorrow. I want you, Eden, as I've never wanted another woman before. So knowing that, what is your answer?"

"You don't know who I am."

"Then tell me all your secrets and be done with it."

For a second, she wavered in indecision . . . but the risk was so great.

He pulled her into his arms. "I don't care.

Can't you understand? I would marry you if you were a milkmaid."

Resting in the haven of his embrace, Eden whispered, "They'd probably accept a milk-maid."

"Do you believe that?"

"No."

He released his hold, and brushed her hair gently away from her face. "What they think, what anyone thinks, doesn't matter anymore. Don't you understand?"

And then he kissed her. There was desire and need in his kiss and she answered it in the only way she knew—by opening herself to him. She slipped her arms up around his neck.

He fitted her against him until she could feel his hardness. This was wrong, she told herself. It was selfish . . . but, heaven help her, she could not turn away from everything she'd ever wanted.

Not if he wanted her.

He broke the kiss off, his breathing heavy. "You'd best leave now, Eden. If you stay, I'll sweep my desk clean, lay you on top of it, and claim you there. I'm no longer a patient man. I want you."

His bold words thrilled her. "Then don't wait. Pierce, take me, please. Right here. Now. I want you."

"Eden, I can't—"

"Yes, you can. It's mine to give. Please." *Take what I offer. Don't marry me!*

The ticking of the clock on the mantel measured the passage of time. They stared into each other's eyes. Eden could feel his desire pressed against her. Her body trembled with hunger for him, a hunger she knew he also felt.

Very deliberately, he stepped back from her. "No, Eden, we won't do it this way."

"Pierce—"

"You don't understand, do you? You don't believe, even yet."

"Believe what?"

"That I love you." He moved away from her, stabbing his fingers through his hair, before turning. "Eden, I want you for more than just my bed. I want you to be the mother of my children and to raise them with your gift of laughter and music. When you are out in the garden, wearing that threadbare maid's outfit that you wormed out of Mrs. Meeks, I don't think I've ever seen a more lovely woman. I watch you digging in the soil and taking delight in the bloom of a flower, and I feel I am the richest man on earth. I need you in my life, Eden. I need what you can give to me because otherwise, I shall grow more and more alone."

She bowed her head, crossing her arms against her stomach and wishing she were not so weak. "There could be someone else for you," she insisted.

"But will that person love me as much as you do?" he asked in his deep baritone.

Eden's gaze flashed up to his face. "No! Never as much as I do!" she answered fiercely, and ran into his arms.

He twirled her around as if they danced together. Eden laid her head against his chest, safe in his embrace. He was rock solid, a pillar of strength. "I hope you'll never be sorry, Pierce. I promise you. I will try to be everything a good wife should be and more."

"I only ask that you be yourself, Eden, because it is that person I've fallen in love with."

She buried her face in the clean folds of his shirt. *Be yourself.* His words dampened some of her joy, but she forced the dark thoughts away. *She would be a good wife!*

She slipped out from his hold. "I must see Mrs. Meeks about some of the wedding plans."

"Did the kegs of ale arrive?" he asked.

"They are in the barn and waiting for the wedding feast," she told him with a weak smile.

"Eden, we shall have a grand party to celebrate our marriage and I don't give a damn if Dutton and Danbury and the others are there or not. We'll have all of Hobbles Moor and only those who would wish us happy." He kissed the back of her hands.

She parted from him reluctantly. If she'd had a choice, she'd stay and watch him work . . . but she had much to do before the wedding and one thing in particular she must do if they were going to be completely happy.

Outside in the hallway she ran into Mrs. Meeks who earlier that morning had chastised her for not being more involved in the wedding plans. The smell of baking bread wafted through the house.

"Mrs. Meeks, I want the church filled with flowers."

"Flowers, miss? That's somewhat irregular. Do you think the vicar will allow it?"

"I will talk to him myself. He'll either let me do it or I shall be married in the garden."

Mrs. Meeks shook her head. "Oh, he won't let you do that."

"I know. Come, you must help me find every vase in the house. Tomorrow morning, I want you to supervise the footmen and have them cut the best blooms in the garden. I want the church full of color. And what are our plans for afterward?"

"Well, we were planning a formal wedding breakfast although it will be sparsely attended—"

"No, not anymore. We are inviting everyone in the village."

Mrs. Meeks's mouth opened in surprise. "But I thought they were going to have a party of their own by the stables? Lord Penhollow is having an ox roasted to celebrate the event."

"Yes, and he shall still do that. But we shall serve everything out in the garden and everyone is welcome. Those who come to my wedding will feast all day. And music?" she asked suddenly. "What music have we planned?"

"There is a band from the village, but you haven't said anything about music for the breakfast."

"They must play for the breakfast too," Eden declared.

Mrs. Meeks clapped her hands together. "Oh, this is going to be a grand wedding!"

Eden smiled, feeling stronger and stronger with each decision. "And Mrs. Meeks, I don't want anyone staying behind during the wedding ceremony itself. I want you and Lucy and Rawlins and everyone to join us."

Tears formed in Mrs. Meeks eyes. "Oh, miss, I'm so happy you are out of the blue devils that were bothering you. You are exactly what our Lord Pierce needs."

"I pray that you are right." Eden moved to the stairs leading to the second floor. "Is Lady Penhollow still up in her rooms?" She started up the stairs.

Mrs. Meeks trailed after her. "What are you going to do, Miss Eden?"

"I wish to talk with my future mother-in-law."

"Oh, I don't know," Mrs. Meeks said, worried. "She's a very difficult woman and she isn't in the best of moods today."

"Yes. I understand that," Eden said, continuing to climb.

"I don't think *you* should bother her." Mrs. Meeks lowered her voice. "She says she wants nothing to do with you."

"Well, she must tell me that in person," Eden answered, leaving Mrs. Meeks standing on the landing, worry lines marring her forehead.

Eden hadn't considered what she was going to say, but feared if she waited, she would lose her nerve. She knocked on Lady Penhollow's door. Footsteps walked toward the door from the other side. It opened. Mrs. Ivy stood there.

Eden now knew that Mrs. Ivy had accompanied Lady Penhollow as a bride from London and none of the other servants trusted her.

The thin woman was over fifty with high cheekbones and a sullen expression. The thought crossed Eden's mind that this woman couldn't be a cheerful influence on Lady Penhollow.

Lady Penhollow herself sat in the window seat, concentrating on her needlework. She didn't look up, but her back stiffened.

"I wish to speak to Lady Penhollow," Eden told the dresser.

"I will see if my mistress is available," Mrs. Ivy said in a disinterested voice and started to shut the door.

Eden put out her hand and pushed on the door, refusing to let it close.

"You must wait a moment, miss," Miss Ivy said indignantly.

"I'll wait with the door open," Eden answered.

Mrs. Ivy raised her eyebrows slightly, but stepped back. "Lady Penhollow, Miss Eden wishes an audience with you."

Eden didn't wait for her response but slipped around Mrs. Ivy into the room.

Mrs. Ivy hissed in anger, but Lady Penhollow silenced her with a raised hand. Her chin lifted to a proud angle, she said, "I have nothing to say to you, Miss Eden. Please remove yourself from my rooms."

"No," Eden answered. "Not until I've said what I've come to say."

Lady Penhollow's eyes blazed bright blue. She was not accustomed to being defied. "If you have come to order me to vacate these rooms for your use, then know that we have already started packing. However, you are not the countess yet and I will not leave until *after* the ceremony."

Eden looked around the sitting room. Two huge trunks sat open, half packed with clothing and knickknacks.

"I have not come to ask you to leave."

"You haven't?" Lady Penhollow said, surprised. She frowned. "Well then, say what you wish and be done with it." She turned her attention back to her needlework.

Eden glanced at Mrs. Ivy whose presence was like a black sentinel in the room. "What I have to say must be said to you alone."

Lady Penhollow's head jerked up. "Miss Ivy will stay."

"No, my lady."

She frowned her displeasure. Eden's gaze didn't waver.

At last, Lady Penhollow gave Mrs. Ivy a curt nod of dismissal. Mrs. Ivy protested with a sniff, but left the room.

Lady Penhollow lowered her needlework to her lap. "What is it you wish to say?"

Eden's heart was pounding in her chest. What did she want to say? And what if her words only alienated the woman all the more?

"I want you at my wedding."

Lady Penhollow's chin lifted, her eyes narrowing.

Eden knew immediately she'd said the wrong thing, but she couldn't stop. Not now. If the woman rejected her, then so be it—but Eden wasn't giving up without a fight.

"I don't have a family," she admitted. "I've

always been alone, even when I've been surrounded by other people."

Lady Penhollow stared directly at Eden now.

She forged on. "You will be the closest thing I've ever had to a parent. I realize that I am not your first choice for a daughter-in-law, and that I may have cost you friends that you've held dear. But Lady Penhollow, I love him . . . and try as I might, I can't seem to do what is noble and leave him. Of course, I don't know what kind of countess I will be. But I do know I will need your help."

Eden walked over and knelt in front of her. "But most of all, I want us to be friends. Perhaps we can't be close. Maybe we are too different or I'm too much of a disappointment to you; however, we have one thing in common—we both love Pierce. Can't we, out of our love for him, at least attempt friendship? If that is too difficult, then I understand, but I'm willing to set aside my pride and beg you to come to the wedding tomorrow. It will mean a great deal to your son."

Lady Penhollow's expression didn't change. Eden shifted her weight back, feeling awkward and stupid.

Slowly, deliberately, Lady Penhollow turned and looked out the window. It was a dismissal.

Eden had failed. She walked to the door and placed her hand on the handle. But she wasn't done yet. "Either way, I don't want you to leave Penhollow Hall," Eden said. "I hope to give Pierce children. I want them to know their grandmother. Please consider staying here in these rooms for as long as you wish."

The woman sitting in the window seat remained silent.

Turning the handle, Eden left the room, shutting the door behind her.

That evening, she and Pierce sat on the bench in the garden and talked until the stars were high in the sky. Their conversation mingled with the sound of the fountain and the night sounds of crickets and frogs. He held her in his arms while she told him about her conversation with his mother.

"It's her way," he said curtly, and would say no more.

Frustrated, Eden said, "I've dreamed of having a family, of belonging somewhere. Now I learn it is possible to have a family and still be alone."

He raised her hand to his lips. "After tomorrow, you will never be alone."

The next morning was overcast and gray. The footmen were out in the garden cutting flowers.

Betsy practically danced into Eden's room. "It's a great day to be married," she sang. "Everyone is excited about your idea of filling the church with flowers." She poured Eden's chocolate from the pot on the bedside tray and threw open the wardrobe doors.

Carefully, she removed the cream silk dress with its overdress of gold lace. "This is the most beautiful gown I've ever seen." She hung the dress on an ornate hook in the wall. "You shall be the most lovely bride Penhollow Hall has ever seen. Lord Pierce should have your portrait painted in this dress and hung in the gallery."

"I wish I could give more than just beauty."

"What else would you give?"

"Oh, a dowry or family lines. The usual things that nobility marry for."

"Miss Eden, why do you insist on always looking at the negative?" Betsy asked stoutly. "You give him happiness. A man can't ask for more."

Eden sat up in bed, thinking of Lady Penhollow. "But what is happiness, Betsy?"

Betsy smiled. "It's the way he whistles and the sense of purpose in his steps, Miss Eden. I've heard that he plans on expanding the stables. He made a comment to Jim that he wants his sons to have a thriving business when they come of age. His sons. You are going to give him that. The Widow Haskell said so." She dropped her voice. "She says you'll give him a daughter too. We're all so very happy you have come, my lady. You're our gift to his lordship."

Eden desperately wanted to believe her words. She wanted her past, Madame Indrani, and the sultan to become distant memories.

Anxious to get started with the day, she bounded out of bed and put on her gardening outfit. She spent the next hour helping Mrs. Meeks arrange flowers in vases before Betsy forced her to return to her room.

No one had seen or heard from Lady Penhollow or Mrs. Ivy.

The ceremony was scheduled for eleven. By ten-thirty, Eden was bathed and almost dressed. Lord Penhollow had already gone on to the church. Betsy told her he looked "dashing" in his wedding finery astride Cornish King. "He's wearing a jacket cut out of a blue superfine that's so dark it almost looks black. His pants are made of the same material and he has on a white waistcoat in figured silk." She pretended to be overheated and fanned herself. "There isn't another man in all of Cornwall more handsome."

Mrs. Meeks came to the door, asking, "Is it time to put on the dress?"

"Yes," Eden said, happy for the additional help. Her hair was done. She and Betsy had piled it high on her head and she'd taken rosebuds and pinned them among the curls. She wore Mary Westchester's chain and medallion around her neck.

It was an ordeal to lower the gold lace overdress over her head. "We're going to be late," Mrs. Meeks chastised, helping Betsy button the row of buttons up Eden's back. Finished, she opened the door. "Hurry, hurry. It's not wise to be late to your own wedding. The groom will think you've gotten cold feet."

Eden grabbed the elbow-length gloves and pulled them on as she walked up the hall to the front foyer. Betsy and Mrs. Meeks trailed behind, both dressed in their Sunday best.

Eden had taken two steps into the foyer before she came to an abrupt halt.

Lady Penhollow stood waiting for them. She

wore a frock of peacock blue and a lace and silk bonnet.

For several seconds, the two women stared at each other and then Lady Penhollow lifted her chin, and asked softly, "Am I too late to join the wedding party?"

For a second, Eden couldn't speak. She took a step forward. "We would be honored by your presence."

Lady Penhollow reached for a box sitting on a table along the wall. "This is for you."

"For me?" Eden took it from her, somewhat dazed.

"Open it," Lady Penhollow urged.

Eden lifted the cover of the box. Inside lay a lace veil. Carefully, she pulled it from the box and spread it open.

"It was my wedding veil. My father gave it to me," Lady Penhollow said. "Pierce was very close to his grandfather. He was an earthy man. Except for wanting to see his daughter marry well, he was not grand and given to airs. I seem to have forgotten that."

"No, you haven't," Eden countered. "And I shall treasure this gift all my life. Someday, I shall pass it on to the next countess."

Her words found their mark. The stiffness left Lady Penhollow's face. She pulled a handkerchief from her reticule. "Oh, dear, the wedding hasn't started and already I'm turning sentimental."

Eden felt the sting of tears too. She'd never realized before that a person could cry out of happiness as well as sorrow. "Come, my lady," she said, holding her hand out to Lady

Penhollow. "Let us ride together to the wedding. Pierce will be overjoyed to see you."

And so they did, riding in the coach with Betsy and Mrs. Meeks. Jim drove the coach himself.

The church was full to overflowing with villagers as they pulled up in front of it. They'd taken Eden's idea a step further and held flowers in their hands, which they waved as the coach approached, shouting out, "Penhollow!"

The sun came out just as Jim reined in the horses by the lichen-covered posts of the church's front walk and all the world seemed blessed.

Pierce waited for her in front of the altar. She'd never seen him so handsome, or so intensely serious.

For a moment, she stood rooted in place. Then Lady Penhollow gave her hand a squeeze. "This is not the time for second-thoughts," she warned, and Eden knew she was right.

She loved Pierce Kirrier. She would be a good wife to him. Mrs. Meeks gave her a small push and Eden went forward to meet the man who was to be her husband. Her satin slippers barely made a sound on the cold stone floor.

If the vicar had any doubts previous to the ceremony, they appeared to be gone now. The words were new to Eden, who had never attended a wedding, and therefore more sacred. She promised to love, honor, and obey this man. But she made a silent, extra vow of her own. She promised God she would do whatever necessary to keep her marriage happy.

At last, Pierce slid his ring down the ring finger of her left hand. It was a band of solid gold, etched with the crest of the earl of Penhollow. This ring had been worn by a century and a half of Penhollow brides.

Taking her arm, he walked her through the church and out the open doors to face their life together. Almost immediately, they were crowded by well-wishers who pelted them with flower petals and sometimes the whole flower!

Lady Penhollow rode with them in the coach back to Penhollow Hall. Pierce kissed his mother's cheek. "Thank you."

Her eyes sparkling with tears, Lady Penhollow whispered to Eden, "You were right."

The wedding breakfast was everything it should be. Lucy had outdone herself. There were muffins and breads of all shapes and sizes. She'd roasted a lamb and three geese. The kitchen staff must have worked through the night to create all the creams and puddings on the sideboard and, of course, there was the ox that had been roasting in a pit since the day before.

The day was not uncomfortably warm and everyone stayed outside. The music from the fiddler and his companions harmonized with the sound of the fountain and the buzz of bees. No one missed the local gentry.

Pierce remained at Eden's side and he touched her often, as she did him. His hand would rest on her waist possessively and she found herself anxiously awaiting the moment when they would be alone.

By six that evening, the villagers began to make their way home. The servants started cleaning up.

Eden felt suddenly nervous. She picked up several plates and would have taken them to the kitchen except Pierce stopped her. He took the plates from her, handed them to Mrs. Meeks, and said, "Come."

Her heart seemed to leap to her throat. Her hand trembled slightly in his. His smile was reassuring. Lacing his fingers with hers, he drew her into the house.

Their feet echoed on the marble in the foyer as he led her to his wing of the house. They climbed the steps, and then walked down the carpeted hallway to his set of rooms.

He opened the door and stepped back for her to enter. Eden hesitated. Once she crossed this threshold, she would be in his life permanently.

"Eden?"

Her stomach felt nervous and fluttery. She drew a deep breath and stepped into the sitting room. It was filled with heavy, masculine furniture. Paintings of horses hung on the wall, including a print of Cornish King over the desk.

She walked across the thick India carpet for a closer look, conscious that Pierce had shut the door and watched her.

"This picture is good. It has completely captured Cornish King."

"Yes, it has," he said, and she thought she

heard a hint of laughter in his voice. A second later, he added, "Eden, I'm not going to attack you."

"Oh, I know," she said nervously. "It's just . . ." She ran her hand along the desk's cool, polished wood, and noticed the open door leading into the bedroom. The first thing that caught her attention was a huge, canopied bed. The bed curtains and spread were of a marine blue. The walls were beige and the whole room seemed to shimmer with light.

Eden forgot her self-consciousness and moved through the doorway adjoining the two rooms. His bedroom was located at the end of the wing and the bedroom walls featured one window after another on three sides so that the room was filled with late afternoon sunlight.

She stood in the center of the room by the bed. To her left, the windows overlooked the stables and the pasture, to her right was the garden. Off in the distance, she could see the thin line of the sea.

"It's like being on top of the world," she said softly.

Pierce leaned against the door. "I knew you would like it."

He pushed away from the door and approached her. Eden waited. She knew what was about to happen between them. She'd been trained for this moment . . . and yet, she sensed this was something completely different than what Madame Indrani had planned for her.

He removed the lace veil she wore as a

shawl from around her shoulders and tossed it aside. His eyes were on her lips.

Anticipation shivered through her. "I want to make you happy."

His lips curved into a slow, sure smile. "Oh, you do, Eden. You make me very happy." And he lowered his lips to hers.

Chapter 15

Pierce warned himself to go slow with her. He'd hungered for her from the moment they'd met, yet she was an innocent. He had no doubt of it.

But she was eager as he was now, pressing her body close to his in just the right way . . .

He swung her up in his arms and carried her over to the bed. On the bedside table was a jar of scented goose grease that Mrs. Meeks had offered him. But he could already feel the heat rising from her and knew he wouldn't need it.

"Eden, I want this to be so good for you," he said, lying on the bed. He kicked off his shoes.

Then she grabbed his lapels, pulled him to her, and kissed him so fully and completely, Pierce could barely remember his own name.

He forgot about going slow as she impatiently began tugging his jacket off. He searched for the line of buttons down the back of her dress. The two sets, one for the underdress and another lace-covered set for the overdress, were tiny and his fingers had trouble unfastening them—especially since his bride was anything but shy.

He left the frustrating buttons to help her yank his jacket off, and reached again for her. She didn't wait but began working the knot in his neckcloth loose. Her fingers were nimbler than his and she soon pulled the neckcloth from around his neck. Then she set to work at removing his vest.

Meanwhile, Pierce went back to the lace-covered buttons. He couldn't get the damn things undone!

She'd have him naked in no time while he'd still be struggling with her clothes. With a low, impatient growl, he rolled over on his back, pulling her on top of him.

"Pierce—?"

He gently bit her lower lip. The pins from her hair came loose and rained down upon him with the rosebuds. He didn't give a tinker's damn. Her kisses were as heady as the most potent wine and twice as intoxicating . . . which, of course, didn't help him when he returned his attention to those damned lace-covered buttons. He'd gotten one undone when her silky hair tangled with his fingers and the second button.

He groaned out loud, breaking the kiss and she burst out laughing.

"This isn't funny," he declared, laughing himself. "I'm ready to rip this dress off of you."

"Let me help you," she said softly. Before

he could protest, she sat up, straddling him, her skirts spread out around him. He realized then that although she wore a corset, she didn't wear pantaloons or a petticoat—and the very female part of her rested almost on top of him.

He stopped laughing. His wife was full of surprises. His body strained the buttons of his breeches, wanting her, *needing* her.

"Eden." He placed his hands on her thighs and pushed her skirts higher, untying the ribbons holding her stockings in place.

She reached back to undo the buttons. Her actions thrust her breasts forward and Pierce boldly cupped them in his hands. Her nipples hardened into tight buds beneath his palms.

"You're beautiful," he whispered.

She unbuttoned the last button and placed her hands over his. Her legs pressed against his body and she moved experimentally against him. Pierce closed his eyes and rolled his head back. What exquisite torture.

"Do you know what you have given me today, my lord?" she said, her voice low and husky. "Something I've never had before, a last name. Today, I became Eden Kirrier. Today, I am a complete person."

"Together, *we* will become complete," he corrected her, and slipped her dress down over her shoulders. Her nipples, hard and brownish-red, peeked out over the edge of her corset.

He suddenly was impatient to be done with clothing between them. He sat up with her in his lap and stripped off his shirt and waistcoat. He began unlacing her corset, lowering his head down to taste those tempting nipples.

She gasped in surprise . . . and then pleasure as his lips closed over her. She buried her fingers in his hair and pressed him closer to her.

His wife was a lusty woman. A woman made for loving and who enjoyed it as much as he did. He couldn't thank his Maker enough for such a wife.

He lowered her to the bed and slipped the dress down past her legs, his lips not leaving her breasts.

Her fingers moved down and began unfastening his breeches. He shoved her dress completely down and onto the floor. One stocking, then another followed it until he had her almost naked. With deft fingers, he began unlacing her corset.

She'd released him from his breeches and her fingers closed around him. She began stroking him with such expertise, Pierce lay down at her side, paralyzed by the sheer pleasure of it.

Dear sweet Lord, she would take the life right out of him if he let her go on . . . but it felt so good—too good.

He covered her hand with his own. "Would you unman me here and now?"

She froze, her dark green eyes surprised. "Am I doing something wrong? Oh, Pierce, tell me if you do not like what I do."

"I like it too much," he admitted in a ragged voice. He raised her hand and kissed the back of her fingers. "The time has come, my love." He pressed her back onto the pillows.

"What do you want me to do?"

He smiled. "I want you to relax and enjoy."

She nodded, her eyes wide in apprehension. He got up and removed his breeches.

The room was bathed in the fading light of the day, that magical hour right before twilight. Her skin was white against the dark blue spread, except for the circles of her nipples and the dark hair between her thighs. The sound of birds and the fountain drifted in through the open windows.

"You're perfect," he whispered.

"No, 'tis you who is perfect." She offered her hand to him and Pierce let her pull him down beside her. He kissed her now, one full of promise, while he caressed her breast and then swept lower, along the outside of her thigh, inward, and then up.

She was moist and ready for him. Her skin smelled of the flowers she loved so much. He buried his face in her hair and intimately stroked her, testing.

She arched beneath his hand, welcoming him and Pierce knew he didn't have to wait any longer. The time had come. But he needed to exercise great control. He wanted this first time to be remembered as the best.

He settled himself between her legs, fitting them together. At his first probing touch, she tensed.

"I'll try not to hurt you," he promised, knowing that it might be a physical impossibility, especially since he wanted her so much.

She traced the line of his lower lip. "I'm not afraid, Pierce. Please, there are so many feelings inside of me. I love you . . . and now I know that love makes all the difference. I'd never realized that before." She smiled up at him bravely.

Dear Lord, he didn't want to hurt her, but she was his, his for all time. He lowered his lips to hers and kissed her deeply, fully, possessively, and slid into her with one smooth motion.

He felt the fragile barrier, and with a ruthless selfishness born of necessity, broke through it.

She stiffened, her knees coming up as if to buck him but only serving to bury him deeper inside. She turned her head away from him, and he held himself still, letting her grow accustomed to the feel of him. She was tight.

He kissed her ear and began telling her how good she felt and how this was what was meant to be. They were one now and no one could take them away from each other.

Her arms around his neck hugged him closer and he interpreted that as permission to continue. Slowly, deliberately, he began moving inside her, watching the changing expressions on her face. He'd stop if she requested it—that is, if he *could* stop.

Then nature took over and the demands of his own body overrode his intentions. Her breathing was heavier now and she began moving to meet his strokes. It almost proved his undoing. He slid his hands under her buttocks and lifted her to better guide her toward greater pleasure for them both.

The sound of the fountain and the call of the birds faded. The room around them ceased to exist. Even the bed was no longer material. There was only the two of them joined together as one.

Eden urged him on with soft cries, the expression in her eyes one of mindless wonder. A wonder he himself felt. Love was the secret, the answer, the cure . . .

And with that last thought, he felt her contract around him, pulling the life from his body and accepting it into hers.

Only then did he allow himself release, and none had been sweeter or more fulfilling.

How long they lay with their arms around each other, Pierce didn't know.

At last he felt her shift beneath him and realized he must be heavy. He rolled over to the side and gathered her close in his arms. Reaching for the edge of the spread, he slipped the cover over their nakedness, protecting them from the slight chill in the evening air. He pushed her hair from her face and then ran the back of his fingers lightly over her soft cheek.

She broke the silence. "I didn't know it could be like that. No one had ever said . . ."

"It isn't always. It's never been like that before for me."

He didn't realize what he'd said until she tilted her head up at him, her eyes alight with humor. "There will be no others," he promised, kissing the top of her forehead. "We're one now. Forever."

She nuzzled his chest. "There will never be another man in my life but you. Only you," she promised, her gaze coming up to meet his.

"I never expected anything but," he answered with a smile.

He rose then and, naked, crossed over to the washbasin and pitcher. Pouring a little water into the basin, he walked back to the bed with it and a cloth.

Her lips were swollen from his kisses, her hair in tangles around her—and she'd never looked more lovely.

"What's that for?" she asked.

"For you." He sat on the edge of the bed, the basin in his lap, and dipped the cloth in it. Wringing it out, he gently began washing between her thighs. There wasn't a great deal of blood, but she would be sore.

"I had a bath prepared. It is behind that screen," he said, nodding to the corner of the room. Beside the screen was a table set with cold foods and several bottles of wine. "I told Mrs. Meeks to make the water boiling hot, so it should be tepid by now." He rested his hand on her thigh. "Of course, I'll have to act as your lady's maid."

"And can I serve as your valet?" she countered, her eyes intent with promise.

He grinned. "I could want no other."

Eden took the first bath, tying her hair atop her head. The tub was a good-sized copper one that a man of Pierce's size could stretch out in. He lathered her with lavender-scented soap and fed her bites of chicken in between sips of champagne.

Eden had never had champagne before and the bubbles tickled her nose and made her laugh. She was giddy after only one glass and he was as hard as an iron pike from running his soaped hands over his wife's delectable body.

She leaned forward in the tub, her fingers lightly brushing his erection. "Do you want me to get back in bed?"

He marveled at her eagerness, but shook his head. "No, it's too soon for you. You're tender right now and I could hurt you."

Eden leaned her head on her arm against the edge of the bath, her green eyes wide with wonder. "You would think of me first?"

He dabbed her nose with a soap-lathered finger. "Always. You're my wife." He didn't hide the pride he felt. "Now out of the tub, wench."

She laughed and rose out of the water. Pierce dried her off and then took his turn in the bath.

Wearing nothing but a towel, she wandered over to the table. "I like this room. The furniture is masculine without being too heavy."

"I'm glad to hear you say that. It's our room now."

Her lips parted. "Do you mean we won't have separate rooms?"

"Does that bother you?"

She shook her head. "I thought you were the one who would want that. Mrs. Meeks said your parents and most of the gentry had separate rooms."

"Absolutely not. Especially after watching my parents with their separate rooms in separate wings. I warned you I would not settle for a loveless marriage like theirs and that means we sleep together, every night, no matter what. If there is a disagreement between us, then we shall be forced to stay up all night, if necessary, to resolve it."

She knelt beside the tub. "I can't believe my good fortune in being with you. You are my life, my savior, my king."

She clearly meant those words and they embarrassed him. One shouldn't be idolized for doing nothing more than honoring the love they both shared. "All I really want is my back scrubbed," he hinted, dryly.

She laughed, popped a grape in her mouth, and picked up the violet soap. "With this?"

"No," he answered with mock sternness.

She picked up his spice-scented soap and sniffed it. "I could recognize you with my eyes closed just by the scent of your soap."

Kneeling, she washed his back. She'd learned a lesson or two from him and demonstrated a creative flair of her own. When she leaned over, her breasts were not far from his mouth and he held his breath, waiting, no, praying, for the damn towel to drop.

What did drop was the soap. Eden frowned with mock alarm. "Oh, dear, I shall have to find the soap." She put her hands in the water to search.

Her hands ran across his abdomen, down

along his legs, and caressed the inside of his thighs. He sprang to life again. "I don't think it's there," he whispered hoarsely.

She ran the tip of her nail up the length of him. "Are you certain?"

Pierce groaned and sank deeper in the water.

She slowly traced a circle around its head.

Where had she learned this boldness? Pierce leaned his head back against the tub and tried to think of anything other than sex. "We must wait until tomorrow."

"And will we make love tomorrow?"

"At dawn, at noon, at four, and all the next night," he promised.

"But what about now?" She slid him a look of invitation as old as time.

She was a siren, tempting him—and he almost succumbed. But she was still too tender. When she reached for him again, he climbed out of the tub, water dripping off of him.

Burying his fingers in her glossy hair, he brought her up to kiss him. Their kiss was one of longing and regret, and once he knew she was pliant, he swiped her towel from her.

She laughed, completely unembarrassed by her nudity. He wrapped her towel around his waist and walked to the bed with as much dignity as he could muster in light of the fact that he was still very aroused.

Eden poured him a glass of champagne. "Here," she purred, walking toward him. "This will help you relax."

She'd taken the ribbon from her hair and it hung past her shoulders and curled around her breasts. It was going to be a long night if he had to lie next to her without touching her.

She sat on the bed next to him. "It's difficult seeing you so . . . ummm, uncomfortable."

There was a hint of mischief in her eyes.

She leaned forward, placing a hand on either side of his hips. The tips of her breasts brushed his abdomen right above the line of the towel.

Pierce drained the glass.

Her hand moved to the towel. Her fingers slid under it. She wet her lips until they were shiny and inviting. Her eyes watching him, she undid the towel from around his waist.

"Eden—?"

She shook her head, silencing him. "I don't want you to be so rigid," she said, her voice slightly breathless . . . and then took his breath away by lowering her head and taking him into her mouth.

Pierce dropped the champagne glass to the floor, part in surprise, part in ecstasy. He leaned back against the pillows, closed his eyes, and discovered paradise.

Much later, as Pierce slept, his head lying on the pillow beside hers, his arms holding her close, Eden lay wide awake.

She reached out and ran her hand along his muscled thigh, taking pleasure in touching him. She had not expected him to put her needs before his, or for him to be such a gentle and caring lover. Making love to him was a pleasure and she would treasure him in the only way she knew how . . . by seeing to his every need. This she could do for him, and, closing her eyes, she fell asleep.

They didn't leave their room the next day or the next or the next. No one bothered them except to deliver meals or pick up empty trays.

Pierce didn't care what the servants thought or what business lay waiting. He and Eden were perfectly matched, two sensual creatures who enjoyed each other to the fullest. They didn't wear clothes. They had no need for them.

Nor were they ever bored. They read aloud to each other or spent hours talking about nothing or everything. And they made love.

She teased him for not having a valet early one morning while they lay in bed waiting for the rest of the house to wake. "Your mother says you should have one."

"My mother says many things." He kissed the hollow where her shoulder met her neck.

Eden gently drew away and held his face in her hands. "I have something to tell you that I didn't tell you before."

He waited.

"I told your mother that she would not have to move. I don't want her to feel displaced and I'd like for her to live with us."

He nodded. "I appreciate your feelings as long as you are happy. But if she grows difficult, do not humor her, Eden. I will not tolerate her behaving badly toward you."

Her hand stroked the muscles of his chest and slid lower. An invitation. He hardened.

"I don't think she will," Eden whispered in

his ear. "I know she doesn't like me, but she loves you very much."

"Then she will honor my wife." He covered her hand with his, brought it to his lips, and kissed it. The passion between them rose in full bloom and they made love.

They fell asleep afterward, Eden curled up next to him like a contented kitten, but in the early hours of the morning Pierce woke and lay restless, unable to get back to sleep.

Absently he stroked her hair, searching his mind for why he felt so unsettled.

Eden was everything he could wish for in a wife. She was intelligent, beautiful, kind, and thoughtful in so many ways . . . and in bed, well, he was a very lucky man.

Almost too lucky.

Over the past few days, she'd taught him a thing or two and, while he was no Lothario, he hadn't been a monk before his marriage either. How could such an innocent young woman be so inventive?

It was almost as if she performed for him.

He didn't doubt that she loved him, but he wondered if she believed he loved her. Why else would she be so completely generous and unselfish? Eden always gave more than she received and seemed satisfied with him, but since their first time, she hadn't reached that sought-after pinnacle of release.

Being a man, he'd done as a man will—he'd taken. But it hadn't been all his fault. She was very good at pleasuring him.

Pierce grinned. He could be good too.

He shifted, moving his arm out from under

her head. Skimming his hand along her soft, pliant body, he turned her on her back. The first rays of dawn were coming in through the windows, bathing her body in rosy light.

Eden made a sleepy mew of protest. He smiled. She could hug the pillow for hours after he was up—but not this morning.

He was going to wake her up, and this time she'd be the one to do the taking. He slid down to the end of the bed and gently opened her thighs.

Her skin was as smooth as satin. He blew on the inside of her thigh, first on one, then on the other. She attempted to kick him away.

Then Pierce pressed his lips to the soft down between her legs.

Eden jerked in her sleep and he pursued her further, tasting her with his lips, refusing to let her go.

Her eyes came open, and she gave a sharp cry of surprise and that turned into a low moan of pleasure as his movements became more purposeful.

As he'd anticipated, she tried to pull away, to stroke and touch him, but he kept out of her reach. This was for her alone. He wanted to feel her come against him, to give without expecting anything in return.

"Pierce, let me touch you. Let me love you."

He ignored her, lifting her to better indulge his appetite. Eden's breathing grew more rapid. She was whimpering now. He could feel the tension vibrating through her body.

"Pierce . . . darling. I don't know what to do. Please, *please!*"

Her legs pressed against his head. Her flesh quivered beneath his lips and she cried out in completion, arching up to him.

Now he lifted up and kissed her on the lips. She clung to him, her body sated. "I should be the one pleasing you," she whispered. "I must please you."

"You do please me. *We please each other*. Do you understand, Eden? You're my wife, not some concubine."

He brought her to a sitting position, turning her in the direction of the full-length mirror only five feet from the bed. Sitting behind her, he placed his hands on her shoulders and whispered, "Look at us. See? Husband and wife."

She nodded, her eyes dark and glazed with passion.

His arms around her, he covered her breasts with his hands. Then, deliberately, he brought one hand down to the triangle between her legs and stroked her. She started, still sensitive.

"We are one, Eden, and not a slave to the other's wishes." He rolled a nipple between his fingers, feeling it tighten. He was hard and ready for her. "I don't always want to take from you. I want to give. I rejoice in pleasing you."

He ran his teeth along the tender line of her neck. She closed her eyes and tilted her head, giving him access to the delicate skin beneath her earlobe.

Pierce came up on his knees, bringing her up with him. "Open your eyes, Eden," he said, his voice low in her ear. "I want to see them as I enter you."

Her lashes lifted in surprise and he slid into her from behind in one fluid movement, his fingers still stroking and teasing her.

"Watch us, Eden. Look in the mirror."

He thrust deep and she arched against him. She was his now. He could feel it as she began moving, pressing her body down on him, taking what she needed, what she had to have.

It was a wild and wicked ride. Neither one of them could take their gaze off their reflection in the mirror. Once she tried to turn in his arms, to take over the control in their lovemaking, but he wouldn't let her. This was for her. She allowed herself to participate then. Her cries filled the air. She called his name over and over begging for more, while he whispered promises of what he could do for her, what he was going to do to her.

Her hair fell down over her shoulders as she leaned forward to better receive him. They both forgot about the mirror or control. Instead, they gave in to their need for each other.

And then he felt it. The quickening inside her. The release. She'd reached the pinnacle of desire.

He lost himself with her then, his own release explosive.

They fell on the bed together, his arms still around her, and listened to their racing heartbeats.

It was Eden who finally broke the silence. "I don't believe I'll be able to move for days."

Pierce laughed. It started as a deep chuckle

and rose steadily until it filled the room. She joined him and they lay entwined together, laughing with the joy of living . . . and loving.

Pierce had taken everything Eden had believed about men and shattered it.

Being a wife was wonderful. She loved every moment of it, even after they left the haven they'd created and rejoined the rest of the world.

She threw herself into the workings of Penhollow Hall and being a full partner. At night, when their work was done, the two of them would lie fitted like spoons, dreamily discussing their plans for the future.

She now believed that nothing was out of her reach. She would have children. Why, she might already be pregnant for that matter, and she thanked this God whom she'd newly discovered for her many blessings. Even her mother-in-law, Lady Penhollow, seemed content.

Eden told Pierce she wanted their children to have blue eyes just like his, with a dimple at the corner of their tiny mouths. He laughed and said he would ask for green-eyed babes blessed with their mother's many talents.

Eden didn't believe she could ever be happier. The past was a dim memory.

Two weeks passed. Two weeks of pleasure, work, and contentment.

On the Tuesday of the third week, Eden drove into Hobbles Moor to view the building of the new cottages. When she returned, there was a hired coach parked in their drive. She hadn't expected company. She went into the house.

"Rawlins, who is here for a visit?" she asked, handing the butler her hat and gloves. She half expected him to say it was someone to talk about horses.

Instead, he said, "I don't know their names. They refused to give them but his lordship asked them into his study anyway. It's three men and a woman. Two of the men are dressed strangely in loose-fitting robes. They say they've come all the way from London. Do you believe they will be staying for luncheon, my lady?"

Three men and a lady from London. Eden nodded absently, not caring what answer she gave. Her feet moved with a will of their own toward Pierce's study. She could hear low voices.

At that moment, the door to her husband's study opened. He stepped out. "Eden, I'm glad you're back." His voice sounded strangely flat, as if he were tired. "Will you please come in here and join us?"

His question wasn't a request, but an order.

"Of course, Pierce." She couldn't make out his expression because the light was behind him but as she drew closer, she wished she'd stayed away. She'd never seen him look so grim.

He stared searchingly at her for a moment, and then without another word, turned and walked into his study.

Cautiously, Eden followed. The first person she saw was Firth, Madame Indrani's giant manservant. At his side stood Gadi, with his beard and long, flowing white robes.

Nasim sat in a chair in front of Pierce's desk. He turned at her entrance, his eyes glittering with triumph.

Then Madame Indrani captured her complete attention as she rose from the chair next to Nasim's. She wore a silk and brocade gown. The gold bangles on her wrist clinked together as she offered Eden her hand.

"Eden, *cher,* it is so good to see you again."

Chapter 16

"This woman says she knows you well," Pierce said. He stood in front of his desk, his fingertips touching the polished wood. He waited for her to confirm or deny the statement.

Ignoring Madame's hand, Eden admitted, "That is correct."

Pierce pulled back slightly, his expression impenetrable.

Eden turned to Madame Indrani. "How did you know I was here?"

Madame smiled. "Lord Penhollow came searching for me. He'd hired a man to seek me out."

She turned to her husband with surprise. "Is that true, my lord?"

"You mentioned her name, remember?" he said brusquely. "I sent a man in search of her."

Eden shook her head. "I'd forgotten that. It seems so long ago."

Pierce said, "Eden, you told me that this

woman is your teacher. Why were you hiding from her?"

"Yes, *cher*, why were you hiding from me?" Madame echoed in a mocking voice. "And did you tell him *what* I taught you?" She was enjoying herself.

Trapped, Eden spoke to Pierce. "Please, let me have a moment in private with her. We have some business to discuss and then everything will be right again."

Pierce's brows came together in concern. "Business?" He looked at Madame Indrani. "What business do you have with my wife?"

Madame stared at him a moment as if she didn't believe her ears, and then burst out into peals of laughter.

Nasim didn't laugh. He came to his feet. "You are a married woman?" He practically spit the words out at Eden.

Without waiting for her answer, he turned to Gadi and spewed out a torrent of Arabic. Gadi's face reflected surprise, and then undisguised anger as his gaze fell on Eden. He took a menacing step toward her.

Pierce placed himself between Eden and the Arab, blocking his way while Firth, in answer to a sharp command from Madame Indrani, placed a restraining hand on Gadi's sword arm.

Nasim said something to Gadi in Arabic that made him relax. He then confronted Madame Indrani. "So, the girl is no longer a virgin?"

"What the bloody—?" Pierce started but Eden placed her hand on his arm. He turned to her and she silently pleaded for patience.

Madame sent a speculative glance in Pierce's direction. The heat of a blush rose on Eden's cheeks. She removed her hand from Pierce's arm.

"No, I think not," Madame said in answer to Nasim's question.

"Then you will understand, Madame Indrani," Nasim said, "that Ibn Sibah is no longer interested in her. We will take back his money. He paid for a virgin."

"And he shall receive it," Madame said. She was not laughing now. "You must return with me to London. I do not have the money here."

"If I must," Nasim said with a curl of his lip. He spoke a few words to Gadi who nodded. "We will wait for you in the coach." Without another glance at Eden, he left the room. Gadi followed.

When the door closed, Madame broke the silence. "It appears we now have a problem." She leaned forward, looking directly at Eden. "I wonder how we shall resolve it?"

Eden didn't speak, but no answer was necessary.

"A countess," Madame said softly. "It's truly astounding, but no less than what I had anticipated from you, *cher*. I knew it the moment we met, you were destined for finer things." Her mood changed, growing harder. "But what am I going to do about disappointing Ibn Sibah, hmmm?"

She slowly assessed Pierce from his shiny black riding boots up to his dark hair and blue eyes blazing with anger. Rubbing her lower lip with one finger, she added thoughtfully, "You have done *very* well for yourself, *cher*."

Eden stepped forward. "I don't care about Ibn Sibah. You can tell him whatever you wish. He's not part of my life now."

Anger flared in Madame Indrani's dark eyes and then was quickly hidden behind a mask of cool indifference. "You have created a problem for me, Eden, and you will help me solve it."

"Eden, tell me what is going on here," Pierce said quietly.

Eden turned to him, but she didn't know what to say or how to explain.

"*Cher*, you cannot avoid the truth," Madame said, a hint of sadness in her voice. "Any more than you can give yourself to another man after one has already purchased you."

Pierce tensed. "Purchased?"

This was going to be worse than Eden had ever imagined it. She wished she had something to say to make it more palatable.

Sensing her indecision, Madame Indrani whispered, "The truth, *cher*. It is the only way."

The truth. She would have to tell Pierce everything. The idea made her weak. The air in the room suddenly seemed stifling. She opened her mouth, but was unable to speak.

Madame Indrani answered Pierce. "I run a discreet brothel, my lord, catering to the tastes of very wealthy men. I provide them with companionship and, for a very fine price, a mistress trained by me personally. Your wife is one of those girls I trained."

Pierce stared at Madame as if he hadn't comprehended a word she'd said. "My wife was another man's mistress?"

Eden felt incapable of doing anything more than staring straight past Madame, waiting for this nightmare to end.

"No, not yet," Madame corrected. She smiled. "She had been trained, but she is a very special woman. She has that rare combination of beauty and intelligence. There was nothing my Eden didn't learn easily whether it was poetry, music, science, or—" She paused a moment before finishing. "—or love." She savored the last word. "I'm certain you have found her quite satisfactory, haven't you, my lord?"

"I will have you thrown out," he answered levelly.

"Oh, no, you won't," she countered. She sat back in the chair. "We now have a secret, the three of us. A secret, I'm certain, you don't want anyone else to know outside these four walls. Your wife had been purchased by the Sultan Ibn Sibah to serve as a concubine in his harem. He paid a princely price for her. Unfortunately, Eden escaped and apparently ran into your arms. It must be quite an exciting story, *cher*."

Eden turned. "Please, Madame. He is not part of this. Leave him out of it."

"I can't, Eden. Ibn Sibah paid a great deal of money for you. You heard Nasim. I must now repay the money. It is only right that your husband pay me for my loss. That's good business."

"But he is not involved in it. He knew nothing about me. I pretended to lose my memory. I didn't want to live in a harem."

"You pretended to lose your memory?" Madame said. "I've never heard of such a thing. And you believed this, Lord Penhollow?" She shook her head, dismissing the thought.

Eden was afraid to meet Pierce's eyes.

"*Tiens!* The choice has already been made," Madame said, her voice hardening. "You knew what the terms were, *cher*. I didn't take you in from that filthy gutter and feed and clothe you all these years out of the goodness of my heart. Besides, Lord Penhollow is receiving a good value. You are a beautiful woman. You will give him many happy years. All I want is the money due me for your virginity. Whether the man who purchases you makes you his wife or his mistress is of no difference to me." Her eyes gleamed with ruthlessness as a new thought struck her. "Then again, I suppose I could take you back and work it out of you . . . but it would take many years. What do you say, Lord Penhollow? Perhaps you will be happy to have her off your hands now that you know the truth?"

Eden found her tongue, half-afraid that Madame might be right about Pierce. "You have no heart, Madame. Furthermore, you can't force me to return with you or pay you!"

Madame Indrani stared at Eden in wide-eyed surprise. "*Cher*, you're changing. You would never have dared to question me before. You were always so thankful."

"I'm still thankful, Madame. I would have died if you hadn't taken me in that night." She looked at Pierce. "I was a child when I went with her. I was starving and frightened. I'd seen a man murdered and feared I would be next. I begged her to take me. She was my only hope."

"And we had an agreement, didn't we?" Madame said. "You may have been young, *cher*, but you were shrewd and you knew what my business was. Now the time has come to pay up."

"You know I don't have money. If I had it, I would give it all to you."

"I will not be cheated out of what is rightfully mine." Madame pointed to Pierce. "He must pay me."

"*He* didn't cheat you. It was me. He knew nothing about it. I pretended to lose my memory—"

"Yes, you and your pretending! Did you also pretend to love this man so that he would protect you?"

The air left Eden in a rush. "What are you saying? What are you trying to do?" She took a step toward Madame and then whirled to face her husband. "Pierce, don't believe her. Please, darling, don't believe her."

"Please, darling, don't believe her," Madame mimicked, pulling on her gloves. "I was merely pointing out the obvious, *cher*," she said without pity.

Eden could have lunged at her with nails

bared. She wanted to wipe the smirk off the woman's face.

Pierce's voice interrupted them. "How much does she owe you?"

"No!" Eden cried, but they both ignored her.

Madame smiled. "Twenty-five thousand pounds."

Pierce's mouth dropped open. "Twenty-five thousand pounds," he repeated in disbelief. "That's a fortune."

"And she has been worth every penny, hasn't she?" Madame replied.

A telltale heat rose in Eden's cheeks, but her husband's eyes flashed with anger.

He moved to his desk and opened a drawer. "You will accept my bank draft?"

"But of course, my lord," Madame replied smoothly.

Eden watched in horror as his pen scratched its way across the bank draft. "Pierce, no."

He ignored her.

She reached across the desk and slammed her hand down on the page. "No!"

He was forced to look up at her then . . . and she did not like what she saw in his eyes. Gone was the softness of a tender lover and in its place was the cool resolution of a stranger. "There is no other way."

"There must be!" Her voice was barely a whisper. "This isn't right. It's not fair."

The set of his mouth turned grim. "I only do what is necessary."

"Necessary for what?" Eden demanded.

He didn't answer, but began writing again.

She stepped back, uncertain.

He blew on the ink and then sanded it dry. Rising from the desk, he walked around to Madame Indrani. He didn't hand the draft to her immediately. "And what do I receive for my money, or am I going to see you on my doorstep next month?"

Madame lifted her chin. "I'm a businesswoman, my lord, not a blackmailer. You have purchased my silence with this money. I will reimburse my Arab friends, and we are quit of each other. I will have what I earned and you will have what you want. You need never see me again."

He held the draft up between two fingers and Madame took it. Folding it in half, she tucked it inside her bodice. "It was a pleasure doing business with you, Lord Penhollow. Come, Firth."

They left the room.

Eden and Pierce were alone.

Neither spoke a word.

Eden listened for the sound of the front door shutting. Madame Indrani was out of her life. It almost didn't seem possible. She sank down in the chair in front of Pierce's desk. It was still warm from the heat of Madame's body.

Pierce walked back around his desk and closed the bank ledger. He placed it in the drawer.

What now?

"Pierce, I'm sorry," Eden said. She stared at the intricate pattern of the India carpet.

He didn't answer.

She raised her gaze and discovered him facing away from her, staring out the window. The afternoon sun highlighted the strength in his jaw and the planes and lines of the face of this man she loved so much.

Love. Sitting in this quiet room with him, the air charged with unsaid words, Eden realized the depth of her love for him.

She'd thought she'd loved him before their marriage but over the past couple of weeks, it was as if that love had been replaced by a new and stronger emotion. She had not expected this growing and deepening of emotion between them.

His voice broke the silence. "Did you marry me for my money?"

"No!" The word shot out of her. She stood. "Pierce, you must know better than that, especially after everything that has passed between us these last weeks."

He looked up at her, his clear blue eyes like two pieces of stained glass. "I'm not certain I know you at all."

His words cut right through her.

"Why didn't you tell me, Eden?"

"I was afraid to."

He made an impatient gesture with his hands. "I could understand your fear in the beginning, but later . . . Eden, why didn't you say *something?*"

Her heart began pounding. She had no answer. Instead, she asked, "What would you have had me say?"

His eyes glittered dangerously. "The truth."

Eden lowered her head, unable to bear his scrutiny. "I wanted to. In the beginning, I was afraid Nasim and Gadi would find me and drag me back with them."

"Did you really think I would let them?"

She forced herself to face him. "I didn't know. Not at first." A lump had formed in her throat. It was hard to talk.

"But what about later, Eden, later when it wasn't so hard to tell me things? We've talked about everything! I've opened my soul to you and not once, not by any word or action, have you led me to suspect this."

"You told me once, you would love me even if I was a milkmaid."

"There's a bit of a difference between milkmaid and a prost—" He paused before finishing, "Concubine."

Eden flinched at his choice of words. "I didn't mean for matters to go this far. I'd intended to leave, but then . . ." She paused, uncertain what to say. Now all the servants' talk and her meeting with the Widow Haskell in the woods seemed silly.

"Then what?"

She forced herself to look at him. "That night . . . at the piano, it changed things. I didn't want to leave. I knew I should, but I couldn't. Then there was the fire and you asked me to marry you and . . . I wanted to be the person you thought I was."

He turned his head, staring out the window, his expression bleak.

"Pierce, would you have married me if I had told the truth in the beginning? Would we be what we are now?"

He turned abruptly and crossed over to the liquor cabinet.

She wet dry lips. "Pierce?"

He took out the whiskey bottle and poured himself a generous draught in a glass.

"Pierce, please forgive me."

Putting the glass stopper in the bottle, he turned to her. "It's not that simple. Nothing is simple anymore. You see, I'm the one who erred. I wanted to believe in the love I thought we shared."

"You should! I do love you. I would do anything for you."

"Except tell me the truth."

Eden bowed her head, realizing he was right. "Yes." She took a step and then added, "But only because I feared the truth would tear us apart."

"It's more than that," he said softly. "I'm ruined." With a small mocking toast, he downed the contents of the glass.

"Ruined?" Eden repeated dumbly. "What do you mean?"

He didn't answer her directly, but tapped his fingers lightly against the glass as if lost in thought. She had to echo her question again before he seemed to realize she was still in the room.

"After Madame presents the bank draft to my banker, I won't have the money to cover the payment I promised for the new mine equipment," he said succinctly. "It's due in three weeks."

Eden felt herself flush cold, then hot, with apprehension.

He smiled, his expression harsh. "All those people who warned and counseled me to not trust my instincts about you . . . begging me to wait just a while longer . . ."

He poured himself another drink. "I thought I knew better. I trusted you. By the way," he said, a trace of bitterness in his voice, "twenty-five thousand pounds is actually a very fair price for you." He picked up the whiskey. "You are an exquisite creature and certainly worth every shilling—"

"Don't," she interrupted. "Please don't talk about us that way."

"There is no *us*, Eden. There has only been you and your secrets."

"You said you loved me."

"That's before I found out what a lying little whore you were." He said the words in cold anger. Then he set the glass down. "I'm sorry. I shouldn't have said that. It's what I think, but I shouldn't have said it. You have ruined me, Eden, and everything I've worked to build."

She crossed her arms protectively against her chest, not liking this resentful stranger her husband had become. "Can't we sell off some of the land? Or something in the house?"

"My estate is entailed, Eden. I can't sell off the lands even if I should wish to do so. I've already committed my ready cash to the mining operation, and then there was the fire in Hobbles Moor and the cottages that I'm rebuilding. I'm at least ten thousand pounds short of covering everything."

It took several moments for Eden's stunned

mind to think. There had to be a way to salvage the situation. She would do anything. "Pierce, I'll go to Madame Indrani. I'll get the draft back from her—"

He moved like lightning, his hands grabbed her arms, his face contorted with anger. "You'll do no such thing. You're my bloody wife."

"I only want to help. I'm responsible for this. I love you, Pierce. I don't want this to come between us. Please." The tears she'd struggled hard to hold back now ran freely down her face. "Perhaps we can borrow the money?"

He shook his head angrily. "I won't go to the moneylenders and I won't borrow from my friends. The whole reason I paid that bloody money to Madame Indrani is to protect you and Mother. If word gets out of what you were and what it has cost me, it will ruin both of you. I have no desire to see you treated the way she's been treated over the years by the other women. Eventually, you'd give up and withdraw the way she did and our children would forever hear the whispers of the gossips."

Just as he had as a child. "But what about you?"

The anger died in his eyes. He crossed over to the cabinet and picked up the whiskey. "I'll survive. I've been there before. I can work my way out of it again."

"Pierce." Her voice shook. "I'm sorry."

He closed his eyes and drew a deep steadying breath.

It was going to be all right, she told herself. He was upset, but it would be all right.

As if to confirm her words, Pierce set the whiskey back on the cabinet. "Eden . . ." He didn't continue.

"Please say we're going to be all right, Pierce. I need to hear you say it." *I need to hear you say you love me.*

He faced her, his expression devoid of all emotion. "We'll be fine."

They stood facing each other, Eden feeling foolish as tears that would not stop rolled down her face. She was conscious of the everyday things, like the servants' voices echoing in the hall outside the room, the masculine smells of leather and her husband's shaving soap—

The knock on the door sounded like a cannon shot. Eden jumped and then quickly crossed to the other side of the room, wiping her face with her hands.

Pierce stepped in front of her. "Come in."

The door opened. It was Lady Penhollow. "Pierce, I saw a rather strange woman leave the house a bit ago. Did she have business here with you?"

"Yes."

"Heavens," Lady Penhollow said. "I hope it wasn't serious. You appear as if you've just received news that a good friend has died."

"No, it isn't anything like that," he said, noncommittally.

"Eden? Are you all right?"

"I'm fine, thank you," Eden managed, hiding her tearstained face behind her husband's back.

Lady Penhollow waited as if expecting one of them to say more. No one spoke and the silence became awkward. Seeing they weren't going to say anything, she started to leave. "Well, I'm glad to hear there isn't a problem. Rawlins told me the woman came from London with some very dangerous-looking characters in Arab robes. You don't think Rawlins has been tippling, do you?"

She said the words half in jest, even as her gaze rested on the glass of whiskey on the liquor cabinet. "Pierce, you're drinking. What is going on?"

"Nothing," he said calmly, and smiled. His smile didn't reach his eyes.

"But you never drink during the day."

He crossed the room to take her arm. "I was having a nip with those lads from London."

"What did they want?" Lady Penhollow demanded quietly.

"Nothing, Mother." He skillfully guided her to the door. "We'll see you at supper."

Lady Penhollow had no choice but to leave. She cast Eden a curious glance and went out the door. Pierce shut it behind her. "Have you pulled yourself together now?"

Eden nodded. "I shouldn't have cried. I'd forgotten that it never solves anything." She drew a deep breath and faced him. "Do we need to tell her the truth?"

"I think that is up to you," he said, and crossed around to sit at his desk. It was a dismissal, plain and simple, but Eden refused to give up.

"Pierce, I love you."

For the past several weeks, every time she'd said those words, he'd been quick to answer, "No, *I* love you." It had become a game between them. Silly, foolish, fun.

Now he didn't answer.

"Pierce?"

"Eden, I need some time to think, to sort this all out. It's sudden, and I don't know what I'm going to do."

"Can you cancel the shipment of equipment?" she asked, eager to help.

He stared at her as if seeing her for the first time. "You are so beautiful." Then he spoke to himself. "Have I really been that blind?"

His words almost broke her heart. "Pierce, being a countess means nothing to me. Not even the money matters. But being your wife is *everything* I ever wanted. I'd hoped I made you happy."

He sat still.

She waited.

"You did make me happy," he said at last. "I just fear the price is going to be too much."

"Pierce—"

His fist came down on his desk. "Damn you, leave me! I've spent years rebuilding my family's reputation. In less than an hour, you have destroyed me. Now go!"

Eden didn't wait for him to tell her twice. She took one step backward, then turned and ran. The sound of the door slamming behind her resounded through the hallway.

She hid in their room, thankful the too-observant Betsy wasn't there. Pierce needed time. She'd wait until after dinner and then they would talk. They always talked after dinner.

Except for tonight.

Rawlins conveyed the message to them that Lord Penhollow was detained by business matters and would not be able to join the women for dinner. He sent his regrets.

"That's odd," Lady Penhollow said. "I didn't think that now he was married, Pierce would work late into the night."

Eden shrugged her response and pushed her food around on her plate, pretending to eat.

After dinner, she waited for Pierce in the Garden Room. He didn't come and, at last, she decided to brave going to him.

There was no light under his study door. The rest of the house was quiet since Lady Penhollow had gone to bed.

Holding a candle in one hand, Eden tentatively knocked.

No answer.

She knocked again and then opened the door.

The only light in the room came from the lamp burning on his desk. Its light reflected off the stacks of open ledgers and papers in front of him. His neckcloth hung loose around his neck, his shirt collar open. A glass of whiskey sat close to his hand.

"Yes," he asked abruptly. His eyes were very sober.

"I wondered if you were ready to come to bed?" Could he see her knees shaking?

"Not yet." He said the words distinct and separate.

"Shall I sit with you until you're done?" she forced herself to ask.

He laughed, silently at first and then with more force.

"What's so funny?" Eden asked when he paused for a breath.

"I'm trying to figure a way to save us from financial ruin, and you're worried about if I'm ready for bed."

Eden's lips parted with surprise. "No, Pierce, I mean, I just . . . I just want to help. It's my fault. Blame me."

"Oh, I do," he said almost sadly. "But I also blame my own damnable pride and the lust I felt for you."

His words hurt. "I thought it was love, not lust."

He closed his eyes and then opened them. "Right now, I don't even know what I'm saying, Eden. Go to bed. Everything will be better in the morning."

"Pierce—?"

"I said go!"

She hurried away like a startled doe, pulling the door closed behind her. Behind her, she heard a smashing sound and realized he'd thrown the whiskey glass at the door.

Betsy had looked at her queerly when she came up alone for the night. "His lordship has pressing matters to attend to," Eden told her.

"Does it have anything to do with that strange woman who was here this afternoon?"

"I don't know," she lied, silently praying Betsy knew nothing else.

She undressed and climbed into the lonely canopy bed, certain she would never be able to fall asleep without Pierce by her side. However, she must have slept because she woke several hours later when the opposite side of the bed shifted. "Pierce?"

He didn't answer, but stretched out beside her. She moved toward him, eager to make amends in the only way she knew how, in the way she was trained.

His hands came down and captured her wrists. "Pierce, please," she whispered, wanting this finished between them. "I'm sorry." How many times could she say it?

He didn't answer, but rolled over on top of her. She knew the weight and feel of his body as if it were her own. He shifted, placing himself between her legs. He smelled of whiskey, but that was fine with her.

He didn't speak but entered her quickly and without warning. Eden accepted the small discomfort as a penance. Her body promptly warmed and accommodated him. He moved inside her.

Previous to this, their couplings had been joyful, playful even, full of soft laughter and whispered words of love.

Tonight, there was no laughter, no endearments, no joy.

He took her without ceremony. She lay beneath him unmoving, allowing him to slake his need, giving him what he wanted. As she listened to his harsh breathing and felt him thrusting inside her, she realized that there were many sides to this act of making love. She'd been raised to believe there was no feeling in it, that it was merely a commodity sold in exchange for money.

Pierce had taught her that it was the closest a man and a woman could be. It was becoming one. The miracle of life and love. The most beautiful moments between a man and a woman.

Now he taught her it could also be the loneliest moment between two people.

She felt him release, the life force emptying into her. She ached to hold him close, but instinctively realized that would be a mistake.

Pierce collapsed upon her, completely spent.

He'd promised that everything would be fine in the morning, she reminded herself and, with a child's need for reassurance, she put her faith in that pledge.

Pierce moved off of her and rolled over on his back. "What have I done?" he whispered to the ceiling.

She didn't speak, afraid of what his words meant. Just when she'd mustered her courage to reach for him, he rose from the bed and dressed in the dark. His boots were almost silent on the carpet as he crossed the room. She heard the door shut behind him.

Eden sat up, wondering where he'd gone. She expected him to come back, but he didn't. Fifteen minutes later, she heard the sound of hooves on the drive. She ran to the window and looked out over the moonlit yard between the stables.

Pierce was riding out across the yard in the direction of the moors. He rode without a saddle, his fingers buried in Cornish King's mane. The stallion's coat gleamed like silver in the night. She watched them until they were out of sight.

They didn't come back until the wee hours of the morning. Eden knew because she sat waiting. For four hours she'd waited, praying that Pierce hadn't lost his way in the moors or run afoul of the dangers lurking there.

She saw them come in from a distance, man and beast moving as one. They knew each other so well. She leaned her head against the window frame, jealous of a horse.

Pierce didn't come back to their bedroom but, apparently, spent what was left of the night in the stables.

Eden finally fell asleep in the window seat.

She didn't see Pierce until breakfast. She was dining with Lady Penhollow who chattered about the weather. It was a dreary day, the sort that threatened rain but rarely delivered. Eden listened with half an ear.

"Are you feeling fine?" Lady Penhollow asked abruptly, interrupting her own monologue. "You are looking peaked."

"I didn't sleep well," Eden confessed. She'd decided never to lie again.

"A sleepless night. I hate those. That's why I always enjoy a cup of warm milk before bedtime. You should ask Betsy to bring you one this evening."

"Yes, that's a good idea," Eden said, barely heeding the advice—then her world spun to a stop. Pierce stood in the breakfast room doorway.

He'd been to their bedroom, for he'd shaved and dressed for riding. His eyes were heavy-lidded, the only sign of his restless night. Her body, remembering his demanding possession of her last night, reacted immediately to his presence.

Their gazes met. *I'm sorry,* she wanted to whisper. *Please forgive me.*

Pierce walked into the room. "Good morning, Mother. Eden." He dutifully pecked his mother's cheek and sat next to Eden. His hand rested on the back of her chair but his thumb didn't brush her neck as it often did.

"Breakfast, my lord?" Rawlins asked.

Pierce nodded. "Give me anything and a cup of strong tea."

"Yes, my lord."

"Well, it is good to see your appetite has returned," Lady Penhollow said in a motherly fashion. "I was quite worried when I discovered you hadn't asked for even a tray delivered to your study last night."

"I was fine," he answered her. Rawlins sat a plate of sausages and eggs before him while Gordon poured tea.

"You work too hard, Pierce," Lady Penhollow chastised. "You appear this morning as if you worked the night through."

"In a way, I did," Pierce said. He made a pretense of eating.

Eden felt her cheeks color as she realized a double meaning in his words.

Lady Penhollow didn't notice. She put jam

on a piece of toast and asked conversationally, "So, what do you have planned for this morning?"

"I'm arranging the sale of Cornish King," Pierce answered.

Chapter 17

Eden sat paralyzed, staring at him. She couldn't have heard him correctly. She glanced over at Lady Penhollow, who'd reacted in the same way, a piece of toasted bread halfway to her lips. Even Rawlins and the footman appeared to have been struck dumb.

Pierce, evidently discovering his appetite, began to eat as if nothing was amiss.

"You can't," Eden said when she found her voice.

He didn't look at her, but wiped his hands on his napkin and set it beside his plate. "I have already," he answered almost absently. "I'm leaving for London in the next hour or so to arrange the sale."

"When will you be back?" Lady Penhollow asked.

"By the end of the week. I'll sell him to Whitby. I'd take him with me now but Lambert's mare is here and will be for the next week or so. Well, if you'll excuse me," he said, changing the subject abruptly, "I must go down to the stables." He pushed back from the table and left the room.

There was a beat of silence before Lady Penhollow said, "I've always believed he cared more for that horse than he did for anything else in this world." Her sharp gaze honed in on Eden. "How long are the two of you going to keep pretending to me that nothing is wrong?"

Eden barely heard what she was saying. Her attention was still on the door where Pierce had just made his exit. "Excuse me," she murmured, placing her napkin beside her plate. Before Lady Penhollow could answer, she was out the door after Pierce.

In the foyer, a small portmanteau sat ready by the front door. It had to be Pierce's.

She caught up with him on the path to the stable. He was close enough that he should have heard her call his name, but he continued walking.

Lifting her skirts, Eden ran until she was by his side. "We need to talk."

He didn't slow his pace and she had to practically skip to keep up with his long strides. "It won't be right now," he said. "I'm busy."

Eden grabbed hold of his arm and pulled with all her strength, digging her heels into the soft earth. Pierce had no choice but to stop.

He faced her with ill-disguised impatience.

"You can't sell that horse," she insisted stubbornly. "Cornish King is a part of you. He means more to you than this land or the tin mine." *Or me.*

"Right now, I have twenty mine families living in Hobbles Moor. Twenty families, Eden, who are depending upon that new equipment to keep their loved ones safe. What do I tell them? 'I'm sorry, I had to pay a ransom for my wife. Turns out she's a harlot and to protect my family name, you can sacrifice your husband'?"

Eden felt sick, deep in the pit of her stomach. "Is that what last night was about? Were you taking what you paid for?"

Pierce looked away, a haunted expression in his eyes. "I wasn't myself last night. The man in the bed wasn't me . . . I can barely remember being there."

"Pierce, I've never played the whore. I lived with Madame, and yes, I would have if I'd been sold, but you know yourself I was a virgin."

"A virgin with incredible talents."

Eden didn't flinch. "I've seen a good number of things in my life, the sort of things a person doesn't talk about."

He walked away from her a few steps before stopping. His back to her, his hands on his hips, he studied the ground for a long silent moment.

"You should never have married me," Eden said.

He straightened his shoulders and turned to her. The pain in his eyes tore through her. "Eden, let us leave this alone for now. Everything inside of me is jumbled and confused. I'll be gone a week. We'll talk when I return."

He didn't wait for her answer but continued toward the stables.

Suddenly, Eden knew she must confess all. She took a step after him. "Lord Whitby could recognize me."

Pierce stopped in mid-stride and came round to face her. "Whitby?"

She nodded. "He didn't remember me the day he was here, but I recognized him."

He was by her side immediately. He took hold of her arm, his fingers pressing into her flesh. "How would he know you?"

There was something frightening about the expression in his eyes—the fire of possessiveness, the anger of betrayal, and, yes, the fear of discovery.

"Madame Indrani had me play the piano once for a party of men. It was a private sale. She had about five girls she was auctioning."

"But you remember Whitby?"

She nodded. "No one could forget the birthmark on his head. He'd been deep in his cups that night and started an argument." She would not tell him it was over her. "I don't believe he remembers me."

Pierce was silent a moment. "Are there others who will recognize you, Eden?"

"There may be a few . . . in London. I doubt if anyone here would. Madame Indrani had known for years that she would sell me to the sultan. If it hadn't been for the war and some political intrigues in Kurdufan, I would have been sent to him several years ago. She occasionally had me perform and I suppose if one of the men had been willing to pay her price, I would have been sold."

"Did it ever bother you to be sold like a brood mare?"

The same question Mary Westchester had asked. "Pierce, my life with Madame was so much better than the fate I had escaped, I considered myself the most fortunate of souls." She said the words as a statement of fact. "But I never knew what love was until I met you—and it makes all the difference."

"You still don't know what love is," he answered sadly. "Eden, love is more than an animal attraction. It's honesty and good faith. It's understanding how your actions impact others."

"When you said you loved me, you meant all of those things?"

"I did," he admitted simply.

"Then I pray you find it in your heart to love me again. But I ask you to not sell Cornish King. There must be another way."

They stood no less than a few feet from each other, but there might as well have been an ocean between them for all the good her pleading did.

His eyes turned distant. "Eden, one thing I've learned in my life is that you can't go back. It will never be the same between us."

"How will it change?"

"I don't know." He turned and, without a backward glance, headed for the stables.

Frightened, Eden let him go. He mustn't sell Cornish King. If he did, he would never forgive her.

Lady Penhollow had been wrong earlier about the weather. The rain wasn't an idle threat for it began to drizzle, but Eden didn't heed the weather. Suddenly, she knew someone who could help her—the Widow Haskell.

She didn't even return to the house for a shawl but started in the direction of Hobbles Moor. Her legs had grown accustomed to exercise and she managed the distance to the village in less than fifteen minutes.

She skirted the edge of Hobbles Moor, afraid to run into anyone who would question the countess of Penhollow walking around in a wet dress, but she had to act fast before Pierce left.

She was almost soaked to the bone by the time she arrived at the Widow's cottage. The small house sat on the far side of a pasture, nestled between several old willow trees that guarded the path leading to the moors beyond Hobbles Moor. A candle burned in the window. Smoke came from the chimney that was sheltered from the rain by the overhanging tree branches. She could smell the peat fire in the air.

The long grass and thistles of the pasture pulled at Eden's dress as she made her way across. The ground felt soggy beneath her feet. Her kid slippers were ruined and her hair hung in a bedraggled mess down her back. Eden didn't care.

She marched to the cottage door, but before she could knock, the door opened. The Widow Haskell glared at her with dark, shiny eyes. Her silver hair hung loose around her shoulders. "I've been waiting for you. Come in."

Eden entered the smoky cottage. The door

was so low, she had to stoop to go through it.

Leaning heavily on her walking stick, the Widow hobbled over to a small rocker in front of the smoky fire. Eden stood just inside the door.

She pushed wet strands of her hair back from her face and took stock of the Widow's home. The walls were lined with shelves. Boxes and small jars holding herbs and various items were stacked on the shelves. One jar held chicken's feet, preserved in what appeared to be oil. Another was filled with bird beaks, still others contained items Eden preferred not to question.

The air smelled of peat, tobacco, and the savory contents of whatever was cooking in a black pot close to the fire. The Widow pulled out her pipe and tamped the tobacco before lighting it. It was then that Eden noticed the young rooster sitting on the back of the Widow's chair. He appeared very at home.

"Is that chicken a pet?" Eden asked.

"He's my Gorgeous," the Widow said, rewarding Eden with her gap-toothed smile. "Say hello to the countess, Gorgeous."

The bird did nothing but eye Eden in that peculiar manner common to all chickens.

"Sit down, Countess." The Widow Haskell indicated a chair across from her.

Eden didn't sit. Instead, she asked the question that had burned inside of her all the way to Hobbles Moor. "Why is he leaving me?"

The Widow Haskell puffed on her pipe before answering. "You have come to me because you fear Lord Penhollow no longer cares for you."

"Tell me, does he care?"

"From the moment he laid eyes on you."

"But what about now?" Eden asked, fearing the answer. "Why must he lose Cornish King for me?"

The Widow Haskell leaned forward. "Lady Penhollow, I am no witch or magician. I work with the forces of nature, not against them. If you want the answer to that question, you must ask your husband."

"I can't," Eden admitted. "He is leaving for London. He feels I've betrayed him and I fear for my marriage. Please, I want it to be the way it was between us."

"Nothing can ever stay the same, my lady. The world changes day by day, hour by hour."

"But not love," Eden answered. "Love is a constant."

"Love changes like everything else." The Widow sat back in her rocker. Gorgeous ruffled his wings a bit to keep his balance as the rocker moved back and forth. "Yes, love must change most of all. If it doesn't, it withers and dies."

Eden sank down onto the hard dirt floor at the Widow's feet. "I am not who everyone thought I was," she confessed. "I don't believe I can keep his love, not after what I have done."

"Did you lie to him?"

Eden shook her head. "Yes. I didn't trust him, and I still am not sure that I didn't do the right thing by not telling him." She touched the worn hem of the woman's faded dress. "Please, you must help me."

"And what do you think I should do?"

"I don't know. But you're the one whom everyone said brought me here. And if you knew I was a fraud, you should have told Lord Penhollow, but you didn't."

The Widow's eyes narrowed. "What makes you think I knew?"

"I sensed it, from the moment we first met in the stable yard."

The Widow reached out and placed her hand on Eden's head. "I didn't bring you here, child. You brought yourself and you could have chosen to tell him the truth at any time."

"But then he would not have looked at me the way he did. He would not have married me. And now he may set me aside." Eden reached out, grasping her hand. "Please, you must help me."

The Widow removed the pipe from her lips. "This may be a hard lesson, Countess, and my heart goes out to you—but I will not help."

Eden came to her feet. "Why not?" she demanded.

"There is nothing I can do," the Widow said gently. "Even if I did deal in sorcery, there is still only one way to save a marriage. You must fight for it."

"But what about Cornish King? Pierce will never give me a chance if he loses that horse."

"Then you must see that he doesn't."

"How can I? I have no money. I have nothing except for the clothes on my back and Pierce has already used all his money helping the people of Hobbles Moor and the miners. I offered to go back to London with Madame, but he wouldn't let me. He became furious at the suggestion."

"A marriage is work. And it doesn't grow stronger when others help you deal with your problems. You must solve them yourself."

"What if he doesn't want me?"

The Widow Haskell pulled Gorgeous down into her arms and started petting the rooster. "Then you will fail, for a marriage is a union of two souls. If one begs release, there is no hope for the other."

"I'm doomed," Eden said softly. This wise woman was her last hope and all she offered were platitudes. "I have no way to keep him. Don't you hear me? My marriage is over!"

The Widow rocked back and forth, closing her eyes, a ring of smoke around her head. "It will be as you say."

Eden covered her mouth with her hand, suddenly afraid. What had she done? Had she cursed herself?

The Widow heaved a deep sigh. "Go now. I am tired and want to be alone." With those words, she rested her chin on her chest, the pipe still clamped between her teeth. A moment later, Eden heard her gently snoring.

Numb, Eden walked out of the cottage. It rained heavily now.

Home. She had nowhere else to go but home.

She started across the pasture when a voice called her name. It was Leeds, the coachman. He stood with the pony trap in the shelter of the trees.

"Lord Penhollow sent me, my lady. He told me to follow you and bring you home."

"He sent you?" she asked, hope surging inside of her. "Then he isn't going to London?"

"No, my lady, he's on his way if he hasn't left already," Leeds said regretfully.

Eden stood in the rain, rooted to the ground.

"My lady, shouldn't we be going? You appear very wet and cold."

"No, Leeds, I don't feel a thing," she said sadly, and walked over to the trap.

Lady Penhollow waited by the front door. She'd been wrong about the rain.

Her son rode up from the stables.

Fearful that an umbrella would frighten the horse, she pulled a shawl over her head and stepped outside. Rawlins hovered anxiously. "I go alone," she told him briskly, and he stepped back.

Descending the front steps, Lady Penhollow planted herself firmly in her son's path. He reined in.

"What is going on between you and Eden?" she demanded. She placed her hand on the reins so that he could not get away from her easily.

"Nothing."

She shook her head. "There is something and you are running away from it."

"What do you mean by that?" he asked testily.

"You don't need to go to London to sell Cornish King. You hate London and only go when you must."

"I need to speak with Whitby."

"Nonsense. You could write the man a letter from here. Furthermore, the weather is terrible for a journey. You're running away, Pierce, just like your father used to."

"I don't know what you mean."

She made an impatient sound. "Whenever your father wanted to avoid something unpleasant, he left for London. What are you leaving to avoid?"

Pierce, his beaver-rim hat low on his head and dripping rain, shifted uneasily. "I'll be home in a week."

"And then what?"

"Then things will be as usual."

She could tell he was lying to her. It was one of the things only a mother could sense. "Pierce, I have never seen two people so in love as you and Eden. Watching you these past several weeks has made me realize how much I've missed in life. Don't be foolish like I was. Don't throw it away."

He stared at her, an angry muscle working in the side of his jaw. He was like her in so many ways, she could almost tell what he was thinking.

"I'll be back in a week," he said tersely, and she let go of the reins.

"Then Godspeed, my son. But think about what I said. You see, love can die if it isn't treasured. Remember that."

He didn't say anything, and she expected him to ride off. At the last moment, he surprised her by bending and kissing her cheek. Then, putting his heels to his horse, he left.

Lady Penhollow raised her fingers to the place he'd kissed, watching him go. In her heart, she knew he was very unhappy. She'd never seen him like this.

Rawlins ran out with an umbrella. "Shouldn't you come in, my lady?"

Absently, she nodded and let him lead her back inside. He shook off the umbrella and asked, "I know I may be speaking out of turn, my lady, but has something happened to Penhollow Hall to cause his lordship to sell his horse? I mean, Cornish King has been a bit of a talisman for all of us."

"I don't know why he has made this decision," Lady Penhollow answered truthfully. She handed him her damp shawl. "Please tell me when my daughter-in-law returns."

She then went in search of Betsy, only to be disappointed. For once, the nosy maid didn't know anything other than what they all knew about the visitors from yesterday afternoon. There was a sound in the front yard. Lady Penhollow crossed to a window and watched Eden, soaking wet, step down from the trap.

"Draw a bath for your mistress," she ordered Betsy and went downstairs to greet her daughter-in-law.

But Eden was not in the foyer when Lady Penhollow arrived there. "Where is she?" she asked Rawlins.

"I suggested she go to her room to dry off but instead she went to Lord Penhollow's study."

"Thank you." Lady Penhollow walked down the hall. The study was shadowy dark.

She paused in the doorway. "Eden?"

No answer. She walked in. Moving to a side table, she struck a lucifer. It flared, the sulfur stinging her nostrils, and she lit a candle.

Eden was sitting in Pierce's chair behind his desk. Her arms were crossed and she was shivering. Her eyes were swollen from crying.

"Eden, what are you doing sitting here in the gloom?"

Eden blinked as if just realizing Lady Penhollow was in the room. She didn't answer but shook her head and turned her thoughts back to their dark contemplation. The girl appeared to be drained of her spirit and vitality.

Lady Penhollow walked over to the desk chair. "Eden, listen to me. You must go upstairs and change into dry clothes."

She frowned. "Not yet. I've got something to tell you. I don't expect you will like it but I won't pretend any longer. The past has caught up with me."

"Whatever do you mean?" Lady Penhollow asked, and Eden told her the whole story, her voice a monotone.

"So you see, you and your friends were right about me," she finished. "I'm not the sort of person who belongs here. I've done the unforgivable . . . and discovered the price is so high—Oh, what have I done?" Eden broke down into heartfelt sobs.

Putting her arms around her daughter-in-law, Lady Penhollow said, "You will make yourself sick if you carry on this way. Now, come to your senses or I shall send for my hartshorn and you won't like that one bit."

When that didn't work, Lady Penhollow said bluntly, "Well, when you are through wallowing in your self-pity, we shall talk."

Eden lifted her head in surprise. "Self-pity? Didn't you hear what I said?"

"I don't know what I think about your tale," Lady Penhollow said. "But I do know my son is madly in love with you."

"Not anymore. He's disgusted with me."

"Oh, what silliness. He's disappointed but not disgusted. Of course, I have no doubt that you are completely miserable, both of you. The Kirriers are a hardheaded lot and can make a person feel very guilty. I should know, since I taught him those tricks."

"It's more than that—"

Lady Penhollow gave an angry wave of her hand, cutting her off. "Pierce is not made of fluff and nonsense. He is a man with heart and the courage to follow it. Why, there have been times I've had my house full of the neighbors swearing at Pierce and declaring that he was about to ruin the whole family. He was only nineteen when he reopened the mines. Everyone told him he would fail, but he stood his ground then. He knew his own mind, and he knows it now."

"Yes, well, he can change his mind too. The Widow Haskell said there is nothing I can do." The thought almost threw her back into tears again.

Lady Penhollow took Eden's hands in hers. "Oh, Eden, I've never believed that silliness about her charms being the reason you and my son made a match. And it wasn't just your beauty that attracted him, although I imagine he is saying that now."

"He calls it lust."

"He's had plenty of that these last few weeks," his mother observed dryly. "But what is between you is more than that, Eden. He loves the person inside you." She pushed a lock of wet hair away from Eden's face. "My son is smarter than I am. He always said he would marry for love and that is exactly what he did. Nor is he a man to love lightly. If he chooses to sell Cornish King, it is because it's the best decision he can make to protect those he loves."

"But he also loves that horse."

"Yes," his mother agreed. "But Cornish King is only an animal. You are going to be the mother of his children. Pierce is very confused, and yes, a bit angry right now. Still, I have faith that he will make the right decision."

Eden tilted her head doubtfully. "I want to believe you, but he's so proud . . . nor do I want to hurt him further."

"Oh, poo," Lady Penhollow said with exasperation. "You are no worse than myself, the daughter of a butcher. In Millie Willis's book, we are both equally to be avoided. I'll warn you, it won't be easy putting up with the snubs and stares of women like her, but perhaps you will be wiser than I was. Oh, Eden, I allowed myself to go into a terrible dark period. I felt like you do now, that I wasn't worthy of anything, not even my own son . . . and

Pierce was the one who suffered for it. I just realized that recently."

She gave Eden's hands a squeeze. "I don't think I've ever seen him as happy as he's been since you came into his life. But now it is time to test the mettle the two of you are made from. The question is, are you going to give Pierce up, mewling that you don't deserve him? Or are you going to fight for him?"

"That's the question the Widow Haskell asked me. I don't want to ruin his life."

"Answer us then! *Do you love my son enough to fight for him?*"

"Yes!" Eden said, coming to her feet. "Yes, I do, but it may be too late."

"Eden, it is never too late. But you must teach him not to run away from a problem between the two of you again."

"How am I going to do that?"

"First, you are going to take the hot bath I've had Betsy prepare for you and get yourself in dry clothes. After that, we are going to put together a plan."

"A plan?" Eden asked, following her as she started to leave the study.

Lady Penhollow paused to blow out the candle before saying, "We're going to attempt a little sorcery of our own." She took Eden's hand and led her out of the study.

Chapter 18

Pierce spent his first two days in London wandering. He told himself he was busy.

He wasn't.

Since he so seldom came to the city, he had a great deal of business to keep him occupied and many acquaintances to see. Some had been friends of his father's. Pierce didn't enjoy spending very much time with them and one visit to the club his father used to favor was more than enough.

The one thing he couldn't motivate himself to do was contact Whitby about Cornish King. The word was that Whitby was not in town and could be reached at his stables in Sawston. Pierce could ride up to meet with him, but something held him back. He couldn't even make himself write a letter to Whitby.

Cornish King had helped to make Pierce a man. When he hadn't a friend in the world, the horse had been there. He knew his feelings were sentimental, yet there they were. Cornish King would always be more than just a horse. He was a major part of Pierce's life.

With that in mind, Pierce had even gone so far as to visit the moneylenders. They were not an avenue for him. They wanted Cornish King as collateral and the interest rates were so exorbitant, Pierce feared he would lose the horse anyway.

Meanwhile, his mind was constantly on Eden. He was very angry with her. She'd used him, betrayed him . . . and still he missed her.

He'd wake in the middle of the night unable to return to sleep. He wondered what she was doing and whether she missed him.

And there were darker questions too. Jealousy almost made him insane when he thought of how knowing she was in the ways of men and how she might have learned those lessons.

Finally, on the third day, against all reason, he paid a call at the Abbey, the brothel owned by Madame Indrani. It was located in a discreet neighborhood not far from the Bank of England. The homes lining the streets belonged to tradesmen and shopkeepers. Madame's house was the largest on her block. It sat next to a small vicarage and was surrounded by a high wall for privacy. Iron gates opened to a drive leading to the front door.

Pierce hesitated at the gates and then, almost drawn against his will, he approached the front step and rang the bell. Firth answered it immediately, his large frame filling the doorway.

"I'm here to see Madame Indrani."

"Do you have an appointment with Madame?" There wasn't a flicker of recognition on his solemn face.

Pierce handed him his card. The giant flicked a glance at it and then, without question, escorted Pierce to a library. "I will present your card to Madame."

In the library, as well as the rest of the house, incense perfumed the air. Large vases of flowers set on every table and the whole decor was one of obvious elegance and extreme wealth. The furniture showed a definite woman's touch. The desk and chairs were carved with birds and flowers. Huge pillows were stacked on the floor and on the long divan which took up almost one wall of the room. A painting of a lush, naked Turkish woman hung over the divan.

It took Pierce a moment to recognize the woman in the painting as a much younger Madame Indrani.

The library door opened. "Lord Penhollow, what a surprise," Madame Indrani said in her accented English. She glided toward him, the bangles on her wrist making a soft musical noise with her movements. She wore a red and gold brocade gown and a turban of matching fabric. The light streaming in from the floor-to-ceiling windows caught the gold in her dress and made it shimmer.

"I understood that you rarely visited London," she said, before adding bluntly, "Why are you here now?"

Why was he here? Pierce wondered that himself. He stood awkward and stiff in the middle of the room.

Madame draped herself dramatically on the divan. "Obviously you are here about Eden," she answered herself. "Am I right?"

"In a way."

"I pray nothing is the matter with her?"

"She's fine."

"That is good. Please, sit down." She waved her hand toward the other side of the divan and reached for a carved wooden box on a table in front of her. Inside the box were long, thin cheroots. "Would you care for a smoke?"

Pierce sat uneasily on the plush cushions and shook his head. "No, thank you."

"Then you don't mind if I do?" She didn't wait for an answer but placed one of the cheroots between her lips, lit it off a candle burning on the table, and inhaled deeply. She leaned back on the couch, relaxed. "You have come because you have questions, whether you wish to admit it or not," she said, smiling.

When he didn't reply, she continued, "You wonder where she came from? What type of life did she lead? It is giving you problems, this idea of accepting the woman you thought she was with the woman she is."

"You are very perceptive, Madame."

She shrugged. "It is a good talent to have in my business. Tell me, my lord, how did you find the location of my house?"

"Does it matter?"

"I am always curious."

"I asked several friends. One of them is a patron of yours."

"And did you speculate whether or not he knew your wife?"

"Yes, damn you," Pierce said, the words concise.

Madame laughed quietly. "He wouldn't, you know. Eden was like a beautiful rare jewel kept only for certain people. I knew Ibn Sibah would buy her, but she is so gifted musically. There were times when I had to have her play for special guests. Have you heard Eden play yet?"

"Yes." He now knew one of the reasons he'd come—jealous curiosity. It burned inside of him.

Madame stubbed out the cheroot. "Come," she ordered, rising.

"Where are we going?"

"To show you what you think you want to see."

Pierce had no choice but to follow her. She led him across the main hallway to a large parlor tastefully decorated in green and rose. It was the sort of place his mother and her friends would enjoy using for a cozy chat. Then Pierce noticed the smell of stale tobacco and alcohol lingering in the air in spite of the windows being open and the burning incense. A large bar was hidden on the opposite side of the room behind a set of screens.

"Here is where my gentlemen guests meet my ladies," she said with a sweep of her hand. She nodded to the pianoforte. "This is the instrument on which Eden learned to play. I believe it is important for every woman to know something of music. It calms the savage soul, and men too," she added as a small jest.

She did not wait for comment but took

Pierce up the wide, sweeping curve of stairs. On their way up, they met two women dressed for shopping coming down. If Pierce were to have met these women on the street, he would have thought them ladies of breeding, not ladies of the night. From under their eyelashes, they watched him pass with more than just idle curiosity. They had Eden's openness about them and appraised him with the eye of experience.

"Do they know who I am?"

"I imagine so," Madame answered. "In a house full of women, there are few secrets. In spite of her beauty, Eden was very popular. They were all concerned about her fate when we learned she had disappeared."

She paused on the second floor. There was a line of doorways. Several other women appeared in the hallway. They lingered, watching him.

"This is where we entertain," Madame said, nodding toward the doorways. "Do you wish to see one of the rooms?"

Pierce shook his head no.

She smiled slightly and started to climb the stairs leading to the third floor.

Pierce was beginning to feel uncomfortable in the presence of so many women, especially since many were in various states of undress. They were all attractive but most of them lacked his wife's fresh innocence and lightheartedness.

On the third floor, Madame stopped. "This is the floor where the girls live." She opened the door to a room holding nothing but chairs.

"This is my classroom. It is where I teach my girls about deportment and the matters a lady should know."

"You do your job well."

"I do, but then Eden was a good pupil. She wanted to better herself. I've never had a girl work as hard as she did. Please follow me."

She took him up another flight of steps to the fourth and final floor. Madame went to a door and unlocked it, using a ring of keys hanging from her waist.

The small room behind the door fit beneath the gables of the house. "Eden's room," she said.

Pierce went in. The ceiling was so low he had to bow his head. There was a simple cot in the room and a small chest. It appeared more the abode of a monk than a prostitute. He went to the room's single window. It had a small balcony and overlooked a lovely garden on the other side of the wall.

"She lived here thirteen years," Madame Indrani said without sentimentality. "The other girls would have complained or demanded the opportunity to move to the more comfortable rooms but Eden was very happy here."

Pierce ran his fingers over the smooth wood of the chest.

"This is what you wanted to see, isn't it?" Madame Indrani asked. "What you wanted to know?"

"Yes, I wanted to know." And this was a far cry from the sort of place he'd lain awake nights imagining.

Madame Indrani pursed her lips together,

studying him with a critical eye. "I think there is something else I should also show you."

Pierce felt numb. "I believe I've seen enough."

"No, you must make one more visit with me." She turned and walked out of the room.

Again Pierce could only follow.

Downstairs, she issued an order for Firth to prepare her carriage. It was at her door in a matter of minutes, the late afternoon sun shining off the brass trappings.

Pierce didn't want to go anywhere with her. Visiting this house had not laid his questions to rest.

He stepped out the door, ignoring the open carriage waiting for them. "I'm certain I've seen enough. I will not take more of your time, Madame."

He tipped his hat and would have walked off but Madame captured his arm. "You will not leave, not yet. You came because of something more than your curiosity. You are an unusual man, Lord Penhollow, one of great passion. I recognized that quality about you the moment we met. Eden weighs on your mind, doesn't she? You are angry with her. I can see it in your eyes, but still you care about her and that is what bothers you most of all."

"I don't think this is your business."

"Oh, yes, it is. I have been mother, teacher, and sister to that child. I am the only one to defend her and I will not let you pass judgment until you've seen it all. Until you understand why she made the choices she did." Her eyes flashed with challenge. "The question is, are you strong enough to seek the truth?"

She dropped her hand and Firth opened the carriage door for her to climb in. "Come, my lord. Let us go for a ride."

Pierce got in the carriage. Firth climbed up beside the driver.

It was a lovely day by London standards. The air was relatively clear and he could smell the coming of autumn in the air.

From the vicarage, a young woman came out the front door carrying a flaxen-haired toddler. The woman watched them drive down the street before crossing to an adjacent park.

"Where are we going?" Pierce asked.

"You'll see."

They quickly left the quiet respectable neighborhood behind and plunged into the heavy traffic of Threadneedle Street. Evening was fast approaching. Long shadows stretched across the streets.

The driver made a turn and then another. Soon, Pierce didn't recognize any landmarks. The streets grew narrower and more crowded. The number of gin shops multiplied with each block. The stench of refuse grew stronger and more offensive, while the traffic in the streets grew more crowded. The expressions of the people grew more pinched and vacant. Driving by, Pierce noticed a man get his pocket picked by a yellow-haired prostitute pretending to solicit him.

Here the whole world seemed shrouded in shadow.

These were the streets of London's poor, the

home to those doomed to poverty. Bustling, angry, dangerous . . . cruel. A man could get his throat slit without a passerby even batting an eye or he could disappear without being seen again.

"Where are we?" Pierce asked quietly.

"It's called the Rookery. It is the most vile spot on earth," Madame answered. She rode with her turbanned head held high, at home with her surroundings in spite of the richness of her dress.

At last, she tapped the driver's shoulder with an ivory-inlaid walking stick. Dutifully, he pulled the carriage over.

Madame waved the walking stick in the direction of a dark alley. "Over there is where I found her, digging through a pile of garbage along with several other children. They were searching for something to eat."

She turned to Pierce. "Many people assume that I lifted Eden from this hellhole because of her beauty. I assure you, my lord, there was nothing beautiful about her the first time I saw her. What struck me, though, was her bearing. While the others scurried like little rats, Eden stood up and stared back at me without flinching. It was almost as if she sensed that here was her chance out of the Rookery."

"She's good at seizing opportunities," he said, unable to keep the bitterness from his voice.

"We all are," Madame said blithely. "Besides, beauty is such a fleeting thing, but *spirit* . . . spirit is with one forever, and I saw it in that child. I crooked my finger, that's all, just a little movement, and quick as a wink she climbed into my coach. I asked her, Do you know who I am? She said everyone knew me. I was the whores' mistress who took girls and gave them work. She said it just that bluntly too. The whores' mistress."

Madame Indrani closed her eyes at the memory and then opened them, her focus on Pierce. "You don't approve of me, Lord Penhollow, and that is fine. You can't understand that for some women the only hope they have is to sell themselves. Our bodies are a commodity, a lucrative one. I've saved many women from a life of poverty."

"And given them a life of enforced slavery such as the harem you'd marked Eden for."

She laughed. "What do you call marriage?"

"I call it a bond, a vow between two people."

"Then what are you doing here, my lord?" she asked, leaning back in the seat and putting a hand on her hip. "Why the questions? Are you discovering that 'till death do you part' may be a very, *very* long time?"

Pierce had an urge to wipe the smug smile off her face. Firth turned at that moment and gave him a warning glance. In answer, Pierce climbed out of the carriage.

He tipped his hat. "Thank you for the tour, Madame Indrani, but I'll find my own way back to my lodgings from here."

She offered him her hand as if his had been a social call. "It was a pleasure to meet again, my lord."

He made a curt bow over her hand, turned on his heel, and started walking. The carriage began moving.

Her voice drifted back to him. "Be careful, Lord Penhollow. These are dangerous streets."

Pierce walked on. He wasn't concerned about being waylaid. He'd welcome the opportunity to bash a few heads. Perhaps it was just what he needed to release this anger pent up inside him.

Eden had used him. She was accustomed to grabbing opportunities when they came her way, and he, like some lovesick fool, had played right into her hands. He'd come to Madame Indrani searching for answers, but he didn't like what he'd found.

Pierce stopped for a moment to gather his bearings. He'd been walking without direction and now wondered if he had started off in the wrong way. Two sailors, their arms wrapped around a girl between them, stumbled out of a gin shop and almost ran into him. The girl's dress was down around her waist.

"'Ere, out of the way, mate," one of the sailors shouted at him while the other gave him a rude shove. The trio drunkenly lurched their way down the street. No one on the street seemed to notice anything unusual about a half-dressed young woman.

As it grew darker, the streets became less and less crowded. Pierce wasn't fool enough to linger longer. He started walking west toward his hotel. He estimated he was only a fifteen-minute, maybe half-hour, brisk walk away. He kept his head down, not making eye contact with anyone passing him.

A shout came from over his head. Someone started to empty a slop bucket right on the street. Pierce just managed to escape it. As he stepped back, a woman bumped into him clumsily. He felt a hand slide into his pocket. He clamped his hand down on her thin wrist. "What the bloody—"

Any other words died in his throat. His pickpocket wasn't a woman, but a girl. She couldn't be older than twelve. She had haunted dark eyes and cheeks gaunt from hunger.

"Sorry, guv, I st-stumbled," the child stammered out. "You can release me hand now."

But Pierce didn't let go of her. Instead he stared, picturing another girl in her place, a girl with large green eyes and tumbling dark hair. A girl named Eden.

Had Eden learned to pick a man's pocket so she could eat? Had she worn a dress cut far too old, and too low, for her? And if she'd stayed longer, would her face be scabbed by the pox?

Realizing where he was staring, the girl self-consciously rubbed her face with her free hand.

"You tried to pick my pocket," he said.

Her brows came together and her expression softened. "I did not. I was only lookin' for a bit of sport." She pressed her body closer to him. "You'd like a bit of sport, wouldn't you, guv? We could go down this alley and 'ave a good time for twenty shillings. That's not much, is it, guv?"

"How old are you?" he demanded.

Her loose neckline hung over one shoulder. She shifted so that it exposed the soft nipple of one breast. "Old enough to know wot pleases you."

He released his hold, took his purse, and opened it. There was ten pounds in it. "Here, take this. It's all I have."

A smile lit the girl's thin features. "Why, guv, I can keep you happy all night for this." She rubbed up against him again. "And yer a 'andsome one too."

Pierce placed his hand on her shoulder and gently pushed her back. "That's not what I want. Take the money and get out of this place. Leave London. Save yourself!"

"Why would I want to go when I 'ave all this money 'ere? Are you queer?" She didn't wait for an answer but turned and disappeared into the darkness of the side alley from whence she'd come.

Pierce stood a moment, reflecting. He'd given her a chance and she'd done nothing with it. In fact, she'd judged him weak for his charity.

He began walking again, his pace slower, more thoughtful. In the middle of the greatest civilized city known to man there was a jungle where women had little or no value . . . and his wife had managed to escape it.

Once in his room at the hotel, he took out paper and pen and wrote the letter to Whitby offering to sell Cornish King.

He sat up for a long time after he'd written the letter. It had been hard, but he had reached his decision. He no longer questioned whether Eden loved him or not . . . in fact, he was certain she did.

The question was, could he forgive her?

He thought he could. Either way, he was willing to take a chance on his marriage.

The next morning, he left for Cornwall.

Pierce entered Penhollow Hall. After two days of riding, he was hot and tired. His first thought was of a bath and a shave. He'd been so anxious to come home, he hadn't even bothered to stay at an inn last night but had caught a few hours' sleep on the ground.

He couldn't wait to see Eden and tell her he had forgiven her. He remembered how distraught she'd been when he'd left. She'd be overjoyed to see him and eternally grateful for his forgiveness.

Rawlins greeted him at the door. Pierce handed him his hat, riding gloves, and the portmanteau.

"Where is my wife?" he asked without preamble. He searched the foyer with his eyes, expecting to see Eden at any second.

"The Countess?" Rawlins questioned with a touch of uneasiness.

Pierce brought his attention back to the butler. "Of course, the Countess. What else would you call my wife?"

"I . . ." Rawlins drew the word out in indecision. "I suppose I'd call her the Countess, my lord."

"Good. Now where is she?"

"Where is whom?"

Pierce stared at Rawlins, wondering if he'd gone daft. When he spoke, there was a definite edge to his voice. "I want my wife. I want her now. Where is she?"

Rawlins's face paled and his mouth opened and shut like a hungry fish gobbling bubbles. He didn't answer.

Instead, his mother's calm, collected voice said from the hall behind him, "She isn't here."

Pierce stepped around Rawlins. He noticed Mrs. Meeks peering at him from the dining room, while Betsy and Gordon watched him wide-eyed from the doorway of his study. All three immediately drew back as if afraid of catching his attention.

Leaning over, he gave his mother a kiss on the cheek. She carried a vase of flowers freshly picked from the garden. "Is Eden delivering charity baskets in Hobbles Moor?"

"No," Lady Penhollow said, unconcerned. "I do so like that midnight-blue riding jacket on you, Pierce. Very handsome." She started walking toward the Garden Room.

Pierce had no choice but to follow. "Is she taking a ride?"

Lady Penhollow shook her head. "No."

"Well, when will she be back from wherever she is?" This wasn't how he'd pictured his homecoming.

His mother paused. "Oh, she's not coming back, Pierce."

"Not coming back?" he repeated, uncertain he'd heard correctly.

"Well, you left, didn't you?" she asked, matter-of-factly. "What did you expect Eden to do? Wait for your return?"

That was exactly what he had expected—but he still couldn't believe that she'd left him.

He turned on his heel and, bounding up the stairs two at a time, headed for his bedroom and slammed open the door.

Everything was as he left it . . . or so he thought.

Eden hadn't taken up much room actually. She had no knickknacks or other folderols enjoyed by women. She hadn't even had jewelry other than her wedding band and the gold chain she always wore around her neck.

Where her presence was noticeably missing was in the dressing room. The silver comb and brush he'd given her no longer set on the vanity. He threw open the wardrobe. Her dresses were missing.

Eden was gone.

He charged down to the Garden Room where his mother was fooling with the flowers in the vase. "Where is she?" he demanded.

His mother smiled. "She's gone, Pierce. She isn't a foolish girl like I was. She learned from my story what happens when a woman lingers where she is not wanted. She said she couldn't accept a half marriage and has moved out."

"Moved out?" His voice thundered through the room. "Where'd she move to?"

"She's living with the Widow Haskell,"

Lady Penhollow said calmly, repositioning a daisy in her arrangement.

Pierce was gone before she'd even finished speaking.

After the front door slammed behind Pierce, Mrs. Meeks, Betsy, Rawlins, and even Mrs. Ivy anxiously entered the Garden Room.

"Do you think the plan's going to work, my lady?" Mrs. Meeks asked, speaking for all of them.

At that moment, Pierce's voice could be heard all the way from the stables shouting for a fresh mount.

Lady Penhollow smiled serenely. "I think it's going to work very well."

Chapter 19

Pierce stormed down to the stables, calling for Jim to saddle Cornish King. Cornish King stuck his head out of his box and nickered a greeting. Pierce paused long enough to rub the horse's muzzle as Jim and another groom threw a saddle on the stallion's back.

"I'm going to miss you, old boy," Pierce said quietly. "But I can't live without her, even if she is going to drive me to madness."

Cornish King pushed him with his nose as if encouraging Pierce to go find Eden.

In a matter of minutes, they were off. The ground flew beneath them as they ate up the distance to Hobbles Moor.

Dane stepped out from behind his smithy as Pierce rode past. "It's about bleeding time you showed your face, Lord Pierce!"

Villagers looked up from their work at the sound of his name and children ran to the roadside to watch him ride by. They were a blur of color as he rode through the town on his way to the tiny cottage on the edge of the moors.

Arriving at the Widow Haskell's cottage, Pierce jumped out of the saddle.

The Widow sat on her rocker in the front of her house petting her rooster, Gorgeous. She didn't act surprised to see Pierce.

"Where's Eden?"

"The lass is at Hermit's Cove."

"Hermit's Cove? What the devil is she doing there?"

"Aye, it's where it all began, isn't it?" she asked with her gap-toothed smile. "She wanted to stretch her legs and had a yearning to see that spot. But ye better hurry, your lordship. It'll be sundown soon."

She spoke to the wind. Pierce was already on his way.

As he rode back through Hobbles Moor, more of the villagers were outside their houses lining the street, waiting for him. They shouted words of advice about marriage and love.

He wondered if anything was a secret in Cornwall!

Cornish King made good time reaching the rocky path leading to Hermit's Cove. Throwing the reins over a scraggly shrub, Pierce followed the path leading to the beach. He could hear the sound of the water rushing into the narrow gorge of the small cove from the open sea.

He moved with the sure-footedness of one who knew these rocks well. He hopped up to the top ledge of natural stone steps leading down to the small beach . . . and there was Eden.

She was wading along the edge of the water. Her shoes and stockings lay in a small heap on the rocky beach. The waves washed over her bare feet and she lifted her skirts a little higher and laughed.

Dear God, she was beautiful.

Her dark hair was loosely gathered at the nape of her neck and she wore his favorite periwinkle-blue dress. But it was something more than just her looks that drew him to her. A sense of peace and well-being flooded him the moment he saw her. A feeling that he was now united with a half of himself that had been missing. He felt whole again just being in her presence.

His wife. His love. His life.

She turned back to shore, her eyes sparkling with the enjoyment of life—until they settled on him. She gave a small scream of surprise and took a step back before recognizing him. "Pierce?"

He nodded, happy for this reunion.

Her brows snapped together in a frown. "What are you doing here?"

Not exactly the response he had anticipated. "I've come to take you home."

Her shoulders straightened and a martial gleam appeared in her eye. "I don't have a home with you, don't you remember? You left me."

He walked down to the beach closer to her. When she started to move back into the water away from him, he stopped. "I won't ever leave you again," he said magnanimously. "I've forgiven you."

"*Forgiven* me?"

"Yes. It's what you wanted, isn't it?"

He took another step toward her and she backed deeper into the water. The bottom half of her skirt was soaked. She lifted her chin to an obstinate angle. "Well, I haven't forgiven you."

Pierce hesitated. "Forgiven me for what?"

"For leaving me."

He rolled his eyes heavenward. "Eden, I didn't leave you, nor were you pushed aside like my mother was. I went to London. On business."

"But you didn't know if you were going to come back, did you?"

She had him there. He'd been so angry when he'd left, he had foolishly toyed with that idea. "I was upset—"

"So was I, Pierce."

The truth of her words hit him squarely. "You're right. I shouldn't have left you in anger. But I'm back now, Eden, and we're together."

"No, we are not." She crossed her arms against her chest. "I rather like living with the Widow Haskell. I don't have to answer to anyone or justify who I am. If I return to you, it will always linger in your mind what I was and how you believe I tricked you."

"No, it won't," he said with a touch of exasperation.

"Yes, it will."

"No! It won't."

"Yes! It will."

For a long second, he stared at her. Then he marched forward. "When did you turn so damned stubborn?"

Her eyes widened and she took a few more steps backward. The waves swelled up to her waist. "When did you become so autocratic?"

He couldn't help smiling. He stood at the edge of the water. "Eden, you have more pride than a duchess—and I wouldn't have you any other way. Come," he said, holding out his hand. "Let us put this aside and go home."

"Home to bed?" she asked archly.

He couldn't help grinning. "Now *that's* a good suggestion. I've an overwhelming desire to kiss my wife." He took another step toward her, the water lapping at the toes of his riding boots.

"Well, she doesn't want to kiss you."

For a second, Pierce couldn't believe he'd heard her correctly. He felt a flash of temper. "Eden, I'm tired. I have ridden like a hussar to come home to you. I've had my fill of your foolishness. Now come out of the water and let's go home."

"No." Her green eyes glittered with defiance, and Pierce's temper went up a degree or two higher.

"I'm not playing a game, Eden. Get out of the water."

"I'm not playing a game either, Pierce. I'll get out once you leave."

Pierce put a touch of steel in his voice. "Well, I'm not going to leave without you. You're my wife and I'm taking you home."

She had the audacity to answer, "Then we shall both be here staring at each other for a long time."

Pierce quietly analyzed the situation. He wasn't about to ride back to Penhollow Hall without his wife, and if she wasn't going to come willingly . . . He started walking into the water toward her. His boots be damned.

"Pierce, what are you doing?" she yelled.

He kept coming.

She started backing up further. The water was up to her breasts. He knew she didn't know how to swim. She couldn't go much deeper. He continued toward her.

"Pierce, stop. Think of your jacket."

That gave him pause. He shrugged off his jacket and threw it on the beach before marching toward her.

Her eyes were bright with alarm and something else too . . . a hint of anticipation? She started moving sideways in the water away from him.

He discovered the going was a bit slow once his boots filled with water. He yanked off one, then another, tossing each on the beach beyond his jacket.

"Now what are you doing?" she asked. The water was up to her shoulders, her hair floating around her. She looked like a desirable mermaid and Pierce knew he couldn't let her reject him.

"I'm not going home without you." He didn't wait for her response but drew a deep breath and plunged into the water after her.

He heard Eden give a whoop of surprise,

but he didn't give her time to flee. Swimming toward her thrashing legs, he pulled her under and then brought her up in his arms.

Eden was sputtering angrily. "You know I can't swim! Why did you do that?"

He grinned, unrepentant. "Do what? This?" he asked and pretended to drop her.

Eden gave a small desperate scream and threw her arms around his neck.

"Now this is exactly where I want you," Pierce said, tightening his hold.

She glared at him, but her ire no longer provoked him. Instead he tightened his hold and turned serious. "I love you, Eden Kirrier. I was wrong to have left you in anger. I'll never do it again."

Tears welled in her eyes. "I'm so sorry, Pierce."

He leaned his head against hers. "Oh, darling, I don't want you to cry and I don't want you to be sorry. I was wrong. I saw where you grew up, and I don't blame you for using any means possible to escape. I'm just thankful fate brought you into my arms. Give our children a measure of that resiliency that kept you alive against almost impossible odds and I shall be happy."

She did cry then, and the only way he could think to stop the flow of tears was to kiss her. But one kiss wasn't enough, especially when she kissed him back with sweet promise.

Pierce started walking toward the shore. Her skirt was up around her thighs in the water. He slipped his hand beneath it. Her skin was smooth as the finest silk.

"I've been anxious to do this ever since I left," he said, nibbling the line of her neck.

Her legs hooked around his waist and he took a step back, not certain if he wanted to go to shore just yet.

"I've missed you too," she whispered. She kissed him.

He broke the kiss, struck by a random thought. "Eden, when we make love, you don't do it because you feel you must, do you?"

Her eyes widened for a moment and then she laughed, a light, happy sound. "No, Pierce. Making love to you is a bond between us."

The honesty of her love and her devotion for him was plain in the depths of her startlingly green eyes and he felt humbled. "I am blessed."

Eden pushed a lock of his wet hair away from his forehead. "As am I."

He kissed her again, and his kiss reflected this new understanding between them.

Her body slid against his in the water. Her legs tightened and the embrace took on new purpose.

Pierce walked out onto the beach and lowered her down on top of his jacket. Their lips didn't part. He unlaced the back of her dress while she fumbled with the buttons on his breeches.

Her laces were wet and didn't cooperate. She was far more effective at the buttons and when her fingers touched him, he lost his patience with her lacings. Drawing her skirt up, he searched for the slit in her pantaloons.

Then she winced.

"What's wrong?" he asked.

"There's a rock beneath me."

"Here," Pierce said, and easily rolled them both over so that she was on top, her legs straddling him. "Is that better?"

"Yes, but what about you?"

"Ah, Eden, I'm beyond feeling pain right now," he answered truthfully.

Her lips twitched and she stroked the length of him.

Pierce sighed. "There's a lot to be said for marrying such a *knowing* young woman," he said happily.

She laughed and proceeded to show him *everything* she knew. Pierce was in heaven.

He'd loosened her dress enough for her bodice to sag so he could reach her breasts. Her nipples puckered in the cool evening air and he warmed them with his lips.

She moved, positioning herself over him, and then slowly sank down on top of him. They both practically purred in satisfaction. She began moving.

He let her set the pace, his thumbs teasing her sensitive nipples while he watched the expression on her face. It was so good between them. It would always be good, but then this wasn't the most important part of their marriage.

"Eden, I love you."

Her eyes opened, their expression slightly dazed by bliss. "I love you, Pierce. I will always love you."

In that moment she tightened around him with a small gasp of satisfaction. He followed her then, thrusting until he was spent and happy.

Eden collapsed against his chest. They lay entwined for several minutes before either could speak. He shifted.

Her head came up. "Is something wrong?"

"I found that rock," he said, and they both laughed.

A while later, Pierce led her through the narrow passage where Cornish King awaited. He mounted and then offered his hand to help her up in the saddle before him.

He was about to take them both home, when Eden stopped him. "Pierce, do you have any pennies?"

"A few." He pulled out the purse he used to collect his pennies. There were only fifteen or so and he poured those in Eden's outstretched hand. She leaned forward and threw the shiny copper pennies up in the air around the entrance to Hermit's Cove.

Eden gave a soft sound of disappointment.

"What's the matter?" he asked.

"Not all the pennies landed on the path. They will be hard for the children to find."

He laughed and cuddled her close. "It's all right, Eden. Someday they will all be found and when they are, the person who finds them will know this is a magical place."

She leaned back in his arms and together they rode home to Penhollow Hall.

They were riding up the drive when Eden

said, "I wish you didn't have to sell him, Pierce."

He gave her a squeeze. "It'll be all right. It's what is meant to be. We must both believe that."

If his mother was surprised to see them arrive home soaked to the skin, she didn't make a comment . . . although Pierce thought Rawlins hid a smile.

They went to their room, bathed, and made love the rest of the night.

The next morning, Eden sent Betsy to the Widow Haskell's for her dresses. Pierce found Eden later putting the clothes away herself in the wardrobe.

"Where's Betsy?" he asked.

"She wasn't feeling well so I sent her home." She hung the green lace dress in the wardrobe. "You know, the dress I was wearing yesterday is hopelessly ruined from the saltwater. Neither Mrs. Meeks or Mrs. Ivy working together could save it a second time and they both let me know it."

"Don't tell me those two are starting to get along?" Pierce asked, sitting down on the bed by the stack of clothes.

"Isn't it amazing? Your mother is especially surprised. She said the two of them have been rivals since the first day she came here as a bride." She picked up the gold lace dress and straightened it on the hanger before moving toward the wardrobe. "Pierce, Annabelle and I—"

"What ho, you and Mother are on first names?"

"Yes, I think she likes me."

"Eden, she loves you. You are one of the family now."

"That may be true." She smiled at the thought. "Anyway, we saw Mrs. Willis and her friends at church last Sunday. They scurried in and out as if they were afraid Annabelle would speak to them. I suggested she go to them and deliberately say hello, daring them to snub her, but she said to do such a thing would only make matters worse. Such are the rules in society. I wonder if I wasn't better off not knowing them . . . but I'm sorry that my presence has brought her discomfort."

"Did you tell her that?"

"I did. She told me those women had never been her friends and she much preferred having a daughter-in-law." She hung the dress in the wardrobe.

"I'll have to take you shopping," Pierce said. "You could use a few more articles in your wardrobe. Perhaps we should go to London."

Eden shuddered. "I don't care if I ever see that city again. I prefer it here. From the moment I first saw your garden, I couldn't believe there was a more perfect spot on earth."

"It is perfect—now," Pierce told her with a smile and she laughed and gave him a quick kiss on the forehead as she reached for the last dress lying on the bed, the cream silk with the pearl bodice.

Watching her, Pierce said, "It's unfortunate those pearls aren't real."

"But they are," Eden said. She held the bodice up for his inspection.

Pierce thought his heart would stop. He came to his feet. "They can't be. Pearls aren't this large or this perfect."

"These are. The sultan is very wealthy. Madame Indrani said that his family vaults are filled with pearls such as these. She was upset that this was all he sent me because he considered pearls the most inferior of his treasures. Plus, she felt these were rather small even if they are the largest I've ever seen."

Pierce took the dress from her hands and ran his thumbs over the creamy pearls sewn like beads across the bodice. They glowed with a life of their own and were each perfectly matched. He could scarcely believe his eyes. He tilted back his head and laughed with the full force of his being.

"What is so funny, Pierce?"

He held out the dress for her to see the pearls shimmer in the light from the window. "Eden, do you not realize what these are worth? My darling, we can keep Cornish King!"

Her lips parted in dawning awareness. Her arms came around his neck and they danced together around the room until they were both giddy with good fortune, happiness, and love.

Pierce didn't waste any time in sending the pearls off to London for evaluation. There were four hundred and thirty-six perfect pearls. The same day, he also wrote a letter of apology to Whitby explaining that Cornish King was no longer for sale.

He and Eden didn't have to wait long for a response concerning the pearls. The London jeweler had an immediate buyer. The duchess of Langsley purchased them for twenty-three thousand pounds for her new Court dress which she hoped would outshine the duchess of Bedford's Court dress.

The Penhollow coffers were once again full.

Mrs. Willis burst into her husband's boudoir without knocking. She wore her nightclothes and slippers. He was still fast asleep under the covers, snoring heavily.

With both hands, she gave his shoulder a rude shake, almost rolling him out of the bed. "Wake up, Mr. Willis, wake up! Disaster has struck!"

Mr. Willis recovered his balance and sleepily stared at his wife. "Disaster?"

His wife threw herself dramatically into the chair opposite his bed. "Yes, disaster. My dresser has heard from the upstairs maid who learned from the cook who lives with her sister in Hobbles Moor that Lord Penhollow's new bride is an heiress! A fabulously wealthy one!"

Mr. Willis swung his legs over the side of the bed. "An heiress? Why, I thought Lord Penhollow's mother said the girl was a nobody."

"She did, or at least that's what I thought she said. And then there was all that nonsense about the girl losing her memory . . ." She paused, raising her hand to her lips "You don't believe that could be true, do you?"

Mr. Willis pulled off his nightcap and scratched his head. "Tell me exactly what the servants are saying."

His wife drew a long-suffering breath. "My dresser said the word is that Lord Penhollow's wife has recovered her memory and he's discovered she is a great heiress."

"If she's recovered her memory, who's her family?"

"I don't know. My dresser doesn't know and she says even the new Lady Penhollow's own maid doesn't know. Do you think she could be from the merchant class?" Mrs. Willis asked hopefully, thinking that would justify her snubbing the wedding invitation.

"I don't know," her husband said gravely. He rose from the bed and began pacing furiously, the tail of his nightshirt flapping behind him. "Dovie, we have made an error," he said at last.

"An error? Oh, I'd feared you would say that. But what if she *is* some shopkeeper's daughter?"

"It doesn't matter. Penhollow is the force to be reckoned with in Cornwall and now he is richer than ever. Besides, his wife is a countess now. You will pay a call on her and express our sincere regrets for being unable to attend the wedding. Invite them to dinner too. Yes, that will make a good impression. Oh, did we send a gift?"

"No," Mrs. Willis said miserably. This was not how she'd wanted matters to go. What if the new countess snubbed her after her behavior last Sunday in church?

"Then we'd better," Mr. Willis said, sitting at his writing desk. He pulled out paper and dipped his pen in the inkwell. "Deliver it to her personally today."

Mrs. Willis came to her feet, hovering anxiously around his desk. "But I have nothing to give them on such short notice."

Her husband frowned thoughtfully. "What of that silver centerpiece downstairs on our dining room table?"

"Why, that's been in my family for several generations!"

"Then we are bloody tired of it, aren't we? Wrap it up and present it to the new countess."

"But Mr. Willis—"

"Dovie, do you ever want to return to London again?"

"And escape the *ennui* of being buried alive in Cornwall? I'd do anything! Besides, Victoria is planning on a London season now."

"Then you won't quibble when I tell you to package up your silver geegaw and toddle over to pay your respects to the new countess. Lord Penhollow has power, Dovie, and if we ever wish to see our fortunes reversed, we need his influence. Now off with you while I draft a note to Danbury and Baines to tell them of this new turn of events." He turned his attention back to his writing and his wife had no choice but to do as he'd ordered.

In spite of Pierce's letter withdrawing the offer, Lord Whitby arrived at Penhollow Hall demanding that Pierce sell him Cornish King.

Eden hid in their bedroom to avoid more contact with Lord Whitby. Pierce hurried Lord Whitby down to the stables to have their discussion there rather than in his study.

Unfortunately, Lady Danbury, Lady Baines, Mrs. Willis, and Victoria Willis all decided to call. Eden felt she had no choice but to receive them, especially since their presence made Lady Penhollow very happy. They brought some lovely wedding gifts including a very expensive silver centerpiece from Mrs. Willis.

"Mrs. Willis, the workmanship on this piece is exquisite," Eden said, examining the design of merhorses rising out of the waves around Neptune. "It's so heavy. It must be quite old."

"One hundred and thirty-seven years to be exact," the older woman said with a smile that appeared more like a grimace. Eden invited them all into the Garden Room, reasoning that Lord Whitby would not see her if she stayed in the back of the house.

Overjoyed at seeing her friends and being included in their number again, Lady Penhollow quickly accepted their excuses for not attending the wedding. Even the servants were pleased. At a moment's notice, Lucy sent up a tray of cakes that made Lady Danbury very happy. Rawlins seemed to stand taller with his chest puffed out, while Mrs. Meeks bustled around importantly.

"Where is Lord Penhollow?" Lady Baines asked conversationally.

"He has a visitor," Eden answered, trying not to convey the anxiety she felt.

"Oh," Lady Baines said with mild interest.

"My husband was wondering if he could call later and discuss a mining question with Lord Penhollow."

Eden and Lady Penhollow's gazes met momentarily and she saw a twinkle of laughter in her mother-in-law's eyes.

"I'm certain that will be fine," Eden replied, tranquil and relaxed. Everything would be all right now, she told herself. Life could not be better.

She was offering another cake to Lady Baines when a man's angry voice drifted in from the open windows. The women all turned in the direction of the sound.

Lord Whitby was stomping up from the stables and coming through the garden. Pierce followed him at a more leisurely place. Whitby's face was red with anger, his hat down low over his eyes. He shouted at Pierce, calling him vile names.

Eden realized with a start that Pierce assumed she was still upstairs. She prayed Lord Whitby didn't come into the house and struggled to keep her composure in front of their guests.

"Who is that rude man?" Mrs. Willis asked.

"Lord Whitby wishes to purchase Cornish King and can't seem to understand Pierce refuses to sell," Eden offered in explanation. "I am so sorry for the interruption."

"Lord Whitby?" Lady Danbury searched her memory and then frowned. "I remember him. He's known for having a disagreeable temper."

"Eden, perhaps you should play the pianoforte for us?" Lady Penhollow asked. "To cover up the sound of his voice?"

"I didn't know you played," Mrs. Willis said, and Eden couldn't help smiling.

"A bit. However, the pianoforte is in the other room."

"Well, let us go," Mrs. Willis said. The other women quickly seconded her opinion.

Eden had no choice but to lead them to the drawing room. Fortunately, she could see out the window that Lord Whitby was mounting his horse and would soon be leaving.

She sat on the bench, placed her fingers on the keys, and began playing a concerto that had been adapted from harpsichord for the pianoforte.

As always, she lost herself in the music. The women listened with rapt attention and the sound of Lord Whitby's voice seemed to fade away—

"I know you!"

Startled, Eden looked up. Lord Whitby stood in the doorway. His eyes burned with righteous anger.

He stepped into the room, ignoring the other ladies. "We've met before," he announced. "At a whorehouse in London."

For a moment, Eden was paralyzed. She could do nothing but stare at him.

Her guests were all too stunned to speak. Then Lady Baines said, "Have you gone quite daft, Whitby? This is the countess of Penhollow you are talking to!"

Lady Danbury leaned toward Lady Penhollow, Victoria, and Mrs. Willis. "Bad *ton*, bad *ton*," she whispered as an indictment against Whitby. "He's scandalous."

Whitby realized he had an unintended audience. He turned to the women. "It's she, I tell you. No one else could be so beautiful and also have her talent at the pianoforte."

"Whitby, have you been drinking?" Lady Danbury drawled.

At that moment, Pierce came up behind Whitby and said in a deadly voice, "You shall meet me, sir, for that slur against my wife."

Whitby paled. He backed into the room, away from Pierce. "It's her. I remember her."

Pierce's hand shot out and grabbed him by the neckcloth. "You would stake your life on it?"

Whitby's Adam's apple bobbed up and down. He looked nervously toward Eden and then back at Pierce. "I had been drinking quite a bit that night," he managed to squeak out around Pierce's choke hold.

"Then I suggest you apologize to my lady wife."

"Accept my apology?" was all he croaked out.

Eden bowed her head, too overwhelmed for a second by the close call to answer immediately. She got up from the bench and walked over to him. "I accept your apology and ask you, my lord," she said to Pierce, "to not take this matter further."

"I won't take it further, if Whitby doesn't," Pierce said pleasantly.

"I . . . won't." Whitby almost choked on the words.

"Very well, then." Pierce released his hold and Whitby drew a great shuddering breath of relief.

Pierce appeared totally unconcerned. "For your impertinence, Whitby, no horse from my stable will ever be sold to you. Nor is Cornish King available to you for breeding purposes."

Whitby could only nod.

"And," Pierce continued, "if I ever see your face at Penhollow Hall again, I will call you out."

"Yes, I understand," Whitby said, backing toward the door. His voice sounded strained. "I'm so sorry for the interruption, ladies, and for the misunderstanding, my lady." He nodded to Eden. "Good day to you all."

The second his heel touched the foyer, he whirled about and was gone. They all waited until they heard his horse riding off in the distance.

"Well," Lady Penhollow said. "That was rather fun. He is such an unpleasant man."

The other women giggled their agreement. Then Mrs. Willis changed the subject by saying the Penhollows must come to dine soon.

"But you will come to my house first," Lady Danbury said, as if unwilling to be outdone.

"No, mine," Lady Baines chimed in.

"I said something first," Mrs. Willis snapped, and the three began to argue.

Lady Penhollow sat watching them with a small, contented smile on her face. Eden knew then that everything was going to be all right.

Pierce lifted her hand and kissed the tips of her fingers. "Forever," he promised.

"Yes, forever," she whispered.

Epilogue

Penhollow Hall, 1824

"Mama, Mama!" four-year-old Julian cried out excitedly as he ran through the garden to where Eden sat on the bench next to the fountain. His brothers, eight-year-old Giles and six-year-old Matthew, followed at a more sedate, worldly pace, while Pierce carried two-year-old Brock, the baby of the family. Asleep, Brock rested his head on his father's shoulder.

Pierce doted on each of his sons. They'd all been blessed with his dark good looks—although two of the boys had Eden's green eyes—and were all excellent riders.

"What is it, Julian?" Eden asked, setting her book aside. She was over nine months' pregnant and definitely feeling the strains of these last few weeks of waiting.

Julian skidded to a stop in front of his mother. "Father showed me the money tree!" He opened his fist and there was a copper penny. "We went with all the children in Hobbles Moor and I found this all by myself."

"Well, aren't you clever?" Eden said, ruffling his dark hair.

Julian grinned with pride.

"I helped him," Giles interjected. "He wouldn't have found anything without me."

Julian was ready to object, but Eden valued peace in her home. "I'm certain that both you boys worked together," she said soothingly.

Giles snorted his opinion.

Pierce handed Brock to Betsy who had come running at the first sound of the boys' voices. She now served as the boys' nursemaid and dearly loved them. "I'll just take this one and tuck him in. Come, Master Julian, it is time for your nap too."

Julian wasn't happy about that until he remembered his penny. "Look, Betsy, I found a penny under the money tree."

"Oh, did you now? You know, magic things happen to those who have found pennies."

Now she had all three boys' attention. Julian slipped his hand in hers and even Giles and Matthew trailed after her. They all loved Betsy's stories, especially the one about the day their father had rescued a beautiful mermaid from the sea. "Well, there's supposed to be a powerful charm in each and every penny you find under that tree . . ." Betsy began as she led the boys inside.

Pierce sat down on the bench beside Eden, placing his arm around her. "How are you feeling?"

"My back aches, Pierce. I can't wait for this to be over."

"You say that with every child."

"Yes? Well, you'd think that after four, I'd get it right. I'm not a good pregnant woman," she admitted.

"You are a beautiful pregnant woman."

His words brought her close to tears. Mary Westchester and her husband had come to visit a few months ago as they did every year and Mary had pointed out that Pierce's love for Eden had never dimmed over the years. Eden fingered the gold medallion she still wore around her neck and realized once again how blessed she was.

Still . . . "I love my boys, but I pray this one will be a girl," she said wistfully.

"It has to be. The Widow Haskell has predicted it," he said lightly.

She made an impatient sound. "She said the last two would be girls and she was wrong!" She smiled up at her husband, struck by a sudden thought. "She isn't really much of a sorceress, is she?"

His eyes softened. "Eden, she brought you to me and that is all the sorcery I ever wanted from her."

"I love you, Pierce."

"I love you, Eden."

Life had never been so rich and fulfilling. Cornish King had been retired as a stud and put to pasture this last year, but his offspring filled the Penhollow stables. Lady Penhollow still lived with them and loved being a grandmother, doting on everything her high-spirited grandsons did—even when they climbed on the table and cracked one of the merhorses on the silver centerpiece. She confided to Eden that she felt she was making up for the time she had missed during Pierce's childhood.

Pierce stood up and offered his hand. "Come, let me take you upstairs and I'll rub your back."

"That sounds delightful," she said, letting him pull her to her swollen feet. She knew all these symptoms were temporary. As soon as the baby was born, the aches and pains would disappear and she would have her figure back again.

"I shouldn't complain," she said as they walked toward the house. "You know I love my babies."

He chuckled. "If I was the one who had to bear the children, people would be heartily tired of my moaning and groaning."

Eden laughed because it would be true. "If you could get pregnant, my lord, we would have had only one child!"

"I'm not certain about that," he countered with mock seriousness. "After all, I enjoy the activity that brings about that state too much to abandon it."

"And I enjoy it too," she said softly. "Besides, the birthing isn't the hard part. It's the waiting that makes me half mad with anxiety."

At that moment, as if her words had been a signal, Eden's water broke. She stopped, at first confused, and then surprised as she always was when the moment arrived. "Oh. Pierce."

His eyes were bright with anticipation. "Is it time, Eden?"

Eden took a moment to evaluate the different sensations inside herself and slowly nodded her head.

The whole house went into an uproar. The midwife was sent for and arrived just in time.

The baby came quickly. After an easy three hours of labor, Eden gave birth to a lovely baby girl whom they named Annabelle after her grandmother. She was perfect in every way, and already loved before she'd drawn her first breath.

Meanwhile, on the other side of Hobbles Moor, in her cottage by the edge of the moors, the Widow Haskell woke from her light nap with a start. She paused, sensing something momentous had just happened . . . and then she knew what it was.

"The countess has had her baby, Gorgeous," she whispered to her pet. The rooster eyed her with interest.

Reaching beneath her, under the cushion of her rocking chair, she pulled out the charm bag that Lady Penhollow had asked her to make for her daughter-in-law's fifth pregnancy. The small muslin full of herbs and secret scents had done its job.

She threw the bag into the fire where it sparked and flamed. "And it was a girl," she added to Gorgeous before tilting back her head and laughing.

Dear Reader,

If you loved the book you've just finished, then make sure you look for more terrific love stories coming next month from Avon Books. First, there's Connie Mason's TO TAME A RENEGADE. In this sassy, sexy love story a tender-hearted bad boy returns to a Wyoming town, and his life is turned upside down when he meets a falsely disreputable single mother.

There's nothing quite like a sexy hero in a kilt, so don't miss the latest in Lois Greiman's *Highland Brides* series, HIGHLAND SCOUNDREL. Pretty, pert Shonna has vowed to never marry, but her parents have other ideas. They invite all the handsome highlanders from miles around to court her. But only one—Dugald—catches her eye…

Rachelle Morgan creates western romances filled with love and laughter, and in WILD CAT CAIT you'll meet an unforgettable heroine who learns to love again when a sexy mountainman rescues her from danger.

ABSOLUTE TROUBLE, September's contemporary romance, is an exciting debut from Michelle Jerott. Stunning sensuality and taut romantic tension are hallmarks of Michelle's writing, and in this sultry love story a strong-yet-vulnerable heroine meets a dynamic man bent on revenge. Can she show him that the best choice in life…is love?

Until next month, happy reading!

Lucia Macro

Lucia Macro

Senior Editor

AEL 0898

http://www.AvonBooks.com

Vote for your favorite hero in "He's the One."

Take a romance trivia quiz, or just "Get a Little Love."

Look up today's date in romantic history in "Datebook."

Subscribe to our monthly e-mail newsletter for all the buzz on upcoming romances.

Browse through our list of new and upcoming titles and read chapter excerpts.

RWS 0898